*One scandalous night
is <u>never</u> enough . . .*

GRIFFIN

DUD 12/1/4
CSD 10/1/14

*He could feel
her astonishment
when his mouth
touched hers.*

She stiffened, and her hands went up to his chest to push him away. That was right. A little push and he'd come to his senses.

But she didn't push at him. She went all soft instead, and her hands crept up to his shoulders.

She kissed him back.

And there it was, the taste he remembered. It was like biting into a ripe cherry, a taste that made one forget all other tastes in that first ambrosial moment, and made one think it must have been a cherry that Eve gave Adam, because what other fruit seemed quite so sinful?

That was Olivia, all the sweetness and sinfulness mixed up in one strange girl unlike any other in all the world. And he couldn't resist her any better than he'd ever done before.

No, he was worse at it now.

By Loretta Chase

LORETTA CHASE

Last Night's Scandal

AVON
An Imprint of HarperCollinsPublishers

This is a work of fiction. Names, characters, places, and incidents are products of the author's imagination or are used fictitiously and are not to be construed as real. Any resemblance to actual events, locales, organizations, or persons, living or dead, is entirely coincidental.

AVON BOOKS
An Imprint of HarperCollins*Publishers*
10 East 53rd Street
New York, New York 10022-5299

Copyright © 2010 by Loretta Chekani
Excerpt from *The Duke's Captive* copyright © 2010 by Adele Budnick
ISBN 978-0-06-163267-9
www.avonromance.com

First Avon Books paperback printing: August 2010

Avon Trademark Reg. U.S. Pat. Off. and in Other Countries, Marca Registrada, Hecho en U.S.A.
HarperCollins® is a registered trademark of HarperCollins Publishers.

Printed in the U.S.A.

10 9 8 7 6 5 4 3 2 1

Acknowledgments

Thanks to:

Eric and Nick, for impeccable service, inspiration, and comic genius;

The interpreters of Colonial Williamsburg, who patiently shared their formidable knowledge, endured the endless picture-taking, and inspired me more than they can know—with special thanks to Mark Schneider and Susan Cochrane for unlocking the mysteries of horses and carriages in olden times;

Sherrie Holmes, for helping to keep chaos at bay—and for explaining equine nuances;

Walter, for everything, and especially the part where he galloped in on his white charger and saved me again;

Nancy, Susan, and Cynthia, who already know why.

Prologue

London
5 October 1822

My Lord,

You _must_ Burn this Letter after reading it. Should it fall into the Wrong Hands, I shall be once again Exiled to the COUNTRY, to one of my Carsington step-uncles' Domiciles, where I shall _most certainly_ be placed in ISOLATION. I don't mind Ruralizing in _Small Doses_, but to be LOCKED IN and forbidden any Social Intercourse of any Kind (for fear of my forming Unsuitable Acquaintances or Leading Innocents Astray) is _intolerable_, and _will surely_ lead me to Desperate Acts.

I am Watched _constantly_. The only way to send you a proper, Unexpurgated and Uncensored Letter is to write in my Secret Place and arrange with Certain Persons—who must remain Nameless, the Undertaking being _uncommonly dangerous_—to put this Epistle among the Diplomatic Dispatches.

I should not undertake this Perilous Enterprise merely to note that it is <u>Exactly One Year</u> since we set out upon our <u>Most Interesting</u> Journey to Bristol. Nor should I endanger my Freedom merely to Convey the Usual Harmless News a Young Lady is permitted to communicate to a young Gentleman of her acquaintance—even if he is practically her <u>Brother</u> or at least a Cousin of sorts. I am driven to Subterfuge because it is my DUTY to Inform you of a <u>further change in your Circumstances</u>. We Children are supposed to <u>know nothing</u> of these Matters, but I am not Blind, and the fact is, your Mama is <u>expecting</u> again.

Yes, it is shocking, at her age, and the more so as it's scarcely a year since your first brother was born. Little David, by the way, is turning out amazingly like you, outwardly at least. Babies are chameleon-like in the Early Stages, but his Looks seem to have settled. His Hair is growing in fair like yours and his Eye color seems to have resolved itself to the same <u>unusual</u> shade of grey. But I digress.

I was always Mystified by your Mama's sudden FERTILITY after <u>thirteen barren years</u>. But Great-Grandmama Hargate says that your parents' <u>lengthy visits</u> in Recent Years to what she calls their <u>Cottage Love Nest In Scotland</u>, explain everything. Great-Grandmama says the Haggis & the Scottish Whiskey <u>Did the Trick</u>. She said the combination always had a <u>prodigious</u> effect on Great-Grandpapa. ~~I know what she meant by "prodigious" because I happened to come upon her Secret Collection of Engrav~~

I must make short work of this, if it is to get safely

into the Dispatch Bag. The Ordeal will require my slipping out of a Certain Relative's House <u>Unnoticed</u> and finding a Hackney. Luckily I have Allies. If I am caught, IMPRISONMENT IN THE COUNTRY awaits me—but as you know, I regard my own Safety and Happiness as of <u>No Consequence</u> in the Pursuit of a Noble Cause.

Yours sincerely,
Olivia Wingate-Carsington

Thebes, Egypt
10 November 1822

Dear Olivia,

I received your letter some days ago and should have answered sooner, but my studies and our work consume all my time. Today, though, Uncle Rupert is away ejecting a party of Frenchmen from one of our excavations—for the third time. The scoundrels wait for our servants to clear all the sand away—weeks and weeks of work. Then the devious Gauls produce a firman from a nonexistent kashef or such, which they claim gives them sole rights to the site.

I can break heads as well as the next fellow, and would have gone, but Aunt Daphne tied me to a rail of the dahabeeya (a type of Nile boat, quite commodious) and told me to write to my family. If I write to my parents, it will only remind them I exist, and incite the usual irrational urge to have me home to watch their histrionics until they forget why they wanted me and send me away to yet another dismal school.

Since, as Lord Rathbourne's stepdaughter, you qualify as family, no one can logically object to my writing to you instead. I find myself torn regarding your news. On the one hand, I am very sorry to learn that yet another innocent child will be thrown into the parental tempest. On the other, I'm selfishly glad to have siblings at last, and pleased that David is thriving.

I don't see why anybody should mind your apprising me of my mother's pregnancy, but then I've never understood the strictures placed on females. It's worse here for women, if that's any consolation. In any case, I hope you suffer no imprisonment for enlightening me. Your temperament is not suited to rules, let alone captivity. This I learned firsthand during the adventure you refer to.

Of course I recall vividly the day on which I suddenly and unexpectedly—two words I shall always associate with you—departed London with you.

Every moment of our journey to Bristol is as deeply incised in my brain as the Greek and Egyptian inscriptions on the Rosetta Stone, and bound to endure as long. If someone, centuries hence, happens to dig up my corpse and anatomize my brain, he will find, etched there in unmistakable characters: Olivia. Suddenly. Unexpectedly.

You know I leave sentiment to my parents. My thinking must be guided by facts. The fact is, my life took a remarkable turn after our journey. Had I not gone with you, I should have been sent to one of the many schools in Scotland run on Spartan principles—though to be fair, the Spartans were soft by comparison. I should have had to put up with the same sort of infuriating narrow-mindedness prevailing at other schools, but under even more sadistic conditions, such as impenetrable Scottish accents and hideous weather. And the bagpipes.

In thanks, I enclose a small token. According to Aunt Daphne, the scarab beetle sign is said as "kheper"—with the "kh" pronounced like the German "ach." The hieroglyphic signs have several meanings and uses. The scarab signifies rebirth. I look upon this journey to Egypt as a rebirth.

It's turned out more exciting than I'd dared to hope. Over the centuries the sand has swallowed whole worlds, which we've scarcely begun to uncover. The people fascinate me, and my days are mentally and physically stimulating, as they never were at home. I'm not sure when we'll return to England. I hope it isn't for a very long time.

I must end here. Uncle Rupert has returned—all in one piece, we're pleased to note—and I cannot wait to hear about his encounter with those worthless slugs.

> Yours sincerely,
> Lisle

P.S. I wish you would not address me as My Lord. I can hear you say it with that provoking hint of mockery in your voice, and I can see you making an exces-

sive sort of curtsey—or perhaps, given your confusion regarding what girls may and may not do—a bow.

L

P.P.S. What ~~Engrav~~?

Four years later .

London
12 February 1826

My dear L,

Felicitations on your EIGHTEENTH BIRTHDAY!

I must be Quick with this, because I'm about to go into Exile again, to Cheshire with Uncle Darius this time. That will <u>teach</u> me to take a Little TATTLE-TALE like Sophy Hubble to a Gaming Hell.

How I wish your recent Visit home had been longer. Then we might have Celebrated this <u>Momentous Day together</u>. But you are <u>far better off</u> in Egypt, I know.

Too, had you lingered here, you might not have been permitted to return to Egypt at all.

Not long after your Departure, we had a CRISIS with your Parents. As you know, I've always <u>protected</u> Adults from the Truth. I gave Lord and Lady Atherton to understand that Plague in Egypt was <u>not</u> the GHASTLY & FATAL CONTAGION one associates with Medieval Times, but merely one of the minor Ailments travelers *often* experience. But mere <u>Weeks</u> after your ship set sail, some Busybody Told Them the Truth! They became HYSTERICAL, going so far as to DEMAND the Ship be <u>recalled</u>! I told them it would kill you to turn back, but they said I was <u>over-dramatizing</u>. I! Can you credit it? ~~Talk of the pot calling the kett~~ But I must stop. The boy is here.

No time to Tell It All. Enough to say that Step-Papa has Dealt with the Matter, and you are SAFE <u>for now</u>.

Adieu, my Friend. I wonder if I shall ever <u>see you</u> again, and— Oh, drat. Must go.

Yours sincerely,
Olivia Carsington

P.S. Yes, I've dropped "Wingate," and you won't wonder why when I tell you what my Paternal Uncle said about Mama. If Papa were alive, he'd disown them, and you know—Curse the boy! He will not wait.

O

In a village ten miles from Edinburgh, Scotland
May 1826

No one had lived in Gorewood Castle for two years. Old Mr. Dalmay, whose health was failing, had had to move out a few years before that, into a modern, warmer and drier house in Edinburgh. His agent hadn't yet found a tenant, and the caretaker, who'd had an accident last spring, still wasn't back. That was why the restoration and repair work, which had been going on for as long as anybody could remember—which was to say, for all the time Mr. Dalmay had lived in the castle—had gradually slackened.

That was why, on this spring evening, Jock and Roy Rankin had the castle to themselves.

They were scavenging, as usual. They'd learned the hard way that the splendid stones on the battlements didn't survive the more-than-one-hundred-foot drop to the ground below. The castle basement, being filled with rubble, offered easier pickings. Someone had already tried to steal a piece of the stairway. Their employer would pay well for the remaining stone blocks.

As they were digging out a sizable fragment of a stair from a bed of crumbled mortar and rubble, the lantern light shone on a round object that didn't look like a bit of mortar or stone fragment.

Jock picked it up and squinted at it. "Look at this," he said.

That isn't exactly what he said. He and Roy spoke a Scottish version of English that the average English speaker might easily mistake for Sanskrit or Albanian.

If they had spoken recognizable English, it would have sounded like this:

"What have you got there?"

"Dunno. Brass button?"

"Let me see."

After scraping off dirt, Roy said, "A medal, maybe." He peered at the object.

"Old medal?" said Jock. "Some of them fetch a good price."

"Could be." Roy scraped some more and peered some more. Then he spelled out painfully, "R-E-X. Then a mark, not a letter. Then C-A-R-O-L-V-S."

Jock, whose reading skills extended to recognizing a tavern sign, said, "What is it?"

Roy looked at him. "Money," he said.

They returned to digging with renewed energy.

Chapter One

London
3 October 1831

*P*eregrine Dalmay, Earl of Lisle, looked from one parent to the other. "Scotland? I most certainly won't."

The Marquess and Marchioness of Atherton exchanged glances. Lisle didn't try to guess what it meant. His parents lived in their own world.

"But we were *relying* upon you," his mother said.

"Why?" he said. "I made it clear in my last letter that I'd stay only a short time before returning to Egypt."

They'd waited until now—moments before they were due to leave for Hargate House—to tell him about the crisis at one of the Dalmay family's Scottish properties.

Tonight the Earl and Countess of Hargate were giving a ball in honor of the ninety-fifth birthday of Eugenia, Dowager Countess of Hargate, matriarch of the Carsington family. Lisle had returned from Egypt to attend, and not simply because it might be his last chance to see the wicked old lady alive.

Though a grown man of nearly four and twenty, no longer in Rupert and Daphne Carsington's care, Lisle still regarded the Carsingtons as his family. They were the only proper family he'd ever known. He wouldn't dream of missing the celebration.

He looked forward to seeing them all, especially Olivia. He hadn't seen her in five years, since his last visit home. When he arrived in London a fortnight ago, she'd been in Derbyshire. She'd returned only yesterday.

She'd gone to her parents' country house early in September, mere days after the coronation, on account of a broken engagement. It was her third or fourth or tenth—she'd reported them all in her letters but he'd lost track—and reputed to have beat all her previous records for brevity. Not two hours had passed between her accepting Lord Gradfield's ring and sending it back to him with one of her heavily underlined and capitalized letters. His lordship had taken his rejection hard, and provoked an innocent bystander into a duel, during which the men had wounded each other, though not mortally.

The usual excitement with Olivia, in other words.

Lisle certainly hadn't come home on his parents' account. They were ridiculous. They had children, but it wasn't a family. They were entirely wrapped up in each other and their endless dramas.

This was typical: a great scene in the drawing room, about a topic normal people would have reserved for a rational discussion at a suitable time—not minutes before setting out for a ball.

Gorewood Castle, it seemed, had been falling down

for the last three or four hundred years and sporadically undergoing repairs in the course of those centuries. For some reason they'd suddenly decided it must be restored to its former glory, and he must go there to oversee the work because of some trouble with . . . ghosts?

"But you *must* go," his mother said. "Somebody must go. Somebody must do *something*."

"That somebody ought to be your land agent," Lisle said. "It's absurd that Mains can find no workers in all of Midlothian. I thought the Scots were desperate for work."

He moved to the fire to warm his hands.

The few weeks since his return from Egypt weren't enough to acclimate him. This English autumn felt like dead winter to him. Scotland would be intolerable. The weather there was vile enough in midsummer: grey, windy, and rainy, when it wasn't snowing or sleeting.

He didn't mind harsh conditions. Strictly speaking, Egypt was a more brutal environment. But Egypt offered worlds for him to uncover. Scotland offered nothing to discover, no ancient mysteries to solve.

"Mains has tried everything, even bribery," Father said. "What we need is the presence of a male family member. You know how clannish the Scots are. They want the laird of the castle to take charge. I cannot go. I cannot leave your mother when her health is so fragile."

She was pregnant again, in other words.

"It seems you must abandon me, my love," said Mother, lifting a limp hand to her head. "Peregrine has never cared about anything but his Greek and Latin and Toxic."

"Coptic," Lisle said. "The ancient language of—"

"It's always Egypt," Mother said with an ominous little sob. "Always your pyramids and mummies and scrolls, and never us. Your brothers don't even know who you are!"

"They know me well enough," Lisle said. "I'm the one who sends them all the jolly things from foreign parts."

To them he was the dashing and mysterious older brother who had exciting adventures in a wild and dangerous land. And he did send them the kinds of gifts that delighted boys: bird and cat mummies, snakeskins, crocodile teeth, and beautifully preserved scorpions. He wrote to the lads, too, regularly.

Yet he couldn't altogether quiet the inner voice telling him he'd abandoned his brothers. It was no good answering that he could do nothing for them here, except share their misery.

Only Lord Rathbourne—known throughout Society as Lord Perfect—had ever been able to manage his parents. He'd saved Lisle from them. But Rathbourne had a family of his own now.

Lisle knew he needed to do something for his brothers. But this castle business was nonsense. He'd have to postpone his return to Egypt for how long? And for what?

"I don't see what good my shivering in a dank, crumbling old castle does my brothers," he said. "I can think of no more ridiculous errand than traveling four hundred miles to save a lot of superstitious laborers from hobgoblins. Not that I understand what your villagers are afraid of. Every castle in Scotland is haunted. Every *place* is haunted. Battlefields. Trees. Rocks. They love their ghosts."

"It's more than ghosts," his father said. "There have been shocking accidents, bloodcurdling screams in the dead of night."

"They say a long-dormant curse was reawakened when your cousin Frederick Dalmay accidentally trod on the grave of Malcom MacFetridge's great-great-grandmother," his mother said with a shudder. "Frederick's health began to fail immediately thereafter. In three years, he was *dead*!"

Lisle looked about him, wishing—not for the first time—there was someone he could turn to and say, "Do you believe this?"

Though his parents were no more capable of seeing reason than Lisle was of seeing unicorns, his own sanity demanded that he introduce facts into the conversation.

"Frederick Dalmay was ninety-four years old," he said. "He died in his sleep. In a house in Edinburgh ten miles from the supposedly cursed castle."

"That isn't the point," said his father. "The point is, Gorewood Castle is Dalmay property and it's falling to pieces!"

And you never cared about it until now, Lisle thought. Cousin Frederick had left the castle years ago, and they'd let it be neglected.

Why, suddenly, had it become so important?

Why else? He was home and couldn't ignore them the way he ignored their letters. It was a ploy to keep him in England. Not because they needed him or wanted him. Merely because they thought this was where he ought to be.

"What does he care?" his mother cried. "When has Peregrine ever cared about us?" She flung herself out of her chair and toward one of the windows, as though she would hurl herself out of it in despair.

Lisle was not alarmed. His mother never threw herself out of windows or dashed her brains out against the chimneypiece. She only acted as though she'd do it.

Drama was what his parents did instead of thinking.

"What monstrous crime did we commit, Jasper, to be punished with this stonyhearted child?" she wailed.

"Oh, Lisle, oh, Lisle." Lord Atherton put his hand to his head and assumed his favorite King Lear pose. "Who can a man turn to if not to his eldest son and heir?"

Before he could launch into the usual speech about ingratitude and marble-hearted fiends and thankless children, Mother took up the cause. "This is our payment for indulging you," she said, her eyes filling. "This is our reward for putting you into the care of Rupert Carsington, the most irresponsible man in England."

"Only the Carsingtons matter to you," Father said. "How many letters have you written to us, in all the years you've spent in Egypt? I can count them on one hand."

"But why should he write, when he never thinks of us?" said Mother.

"I make a simple request, and he answers with mockery!" Father stormed to the fire, and struck his fist upon the mantelpiece. "By God, how am I to bear it? With worry and care, you'll drive me to an early grave, Lisle, I vow."

"Oh, my dearest love, don't say so!" Mother shrieked.

"I could never go on without you. I should swiftly follow you, and the poor boys will be orphaned." She hurtled away from the window to sink into a chair, and commenced sobbing hysterically.

His father flung out his hand, indicating his distraught spouse. "Now look what you've done to your mother!"

"She always does that," said Lisle.

Father let his hand fall, and turned from him in a huff. He drew out his handkerchief and pressed it into Mother's hand—in the nick of time, too, because her own would soon need wringing out. She was the most prodigious weeper.

"For the boy's sake, we must pray that dreadful day never comes," Father said, patting her shoulder. His eyes filled, too. "Lisle, naturally, will be off on his jaunts among the heathens, leaving his brothers to uncaring strangers."

His brothers already lived among uncaring strangers, Lisle thought. If orphaned, they'd go to one of his father's sisters. Though Lord Atherton had lost one—Lord Rathbourne's first wife—some years ago, the other six were in fine fettle, and wouldn't notice a few more added to their own large broods. It wasn't as though any of them actually cared for their children directly. Servants, tutors, and governesses reared one's offspring. Parents had little to do but put their noses in when not wanted and find ways to annoy everybody and devise ridiculous and inconvenient schemes to waste one's time.

He wouldn't allow them to manipulate him. If he let himself be drawn into the emotional whirlpool, he'd never get out.

The way to keep on solid ground was to keep to the facts.

"The boys have scores of relatives to look after them, and more than sufficient money to live on," he said. "They won't end up abused and starved in an orphanage. And I will not go to Scotland on a fool's errand."

"How can you be so heartless?" his mother cried. "A family treasure faces extinction!" She sank back in the chair, letting her husband's handkerchief drop from her trembling fingers as she prepared to swoon.

The butler entered. He pretended, as he always did, that an emotional extravaganza was not in progress.

The carriage, he told them, was waiting.

The drama didn't end with their departure, but continued throughout the drive to Hargate House. Thanks to the late start and the press of traffic, they were among the last to arrive.

Lisle's parents resumed their reproaches before and after greeting their hosts and the assorted Carsington husbands and wives, and in the interval before they made their way through the crowd to the guest of honor.

The birthday girl, the Dowager Countess of Hargate, appeared unchanged. Lisle knew, thanks to Olivia's letters, that the old lady still gossiped, drank, and played whist with her friends—known among the Carsingtons as the Harpies—and still found ample time and energy to terrorize her family.

At present, garbed in the latest and most expensive mode, a drink in her hand, she sat on a sort of throne, the Harpies clustered about her like ladies in waiting to a queen. Or perhaps like vultures about the queen vulture, depending on one's point of view.

"You're looking sadly peakish, Penelope," she told Mother. "Some bloom when they're breeding and some don't. A pity you're not one of the blooming ones— except for your nose. That's red enough, and your eyes, too. I shouldn't weep so much, was I your age, nor dropping brats, either. If you'd asked me, I'd have advised you to stick with the birthing business when once you'd started, instead of stopping and leaving it until all your looks went and your muscles stretched past mending."

Leaving Mother temporarily speechless and red in the face, her ancient ladyship nodded at Lisle. "Ah, the wanderer returns, brown as a berry, as usual. It'll be a shock to you, I daresay, seeing girls fully clothed, but you'll have to bear it."

Her friends caught the pun and laughed loudly.

"Bare it, indeed," said Lady Cooper, one of the younger ones. She was only about seventy. "What will you wager, Eugenia, that the girls wonder if he's as brown everywhere as his face?"

Beside him, Mother gave a faint moan.

The dowager leaned toward him. "Always was a missish little prune," she said in a stage whisper. "Never mind her. It's my party, and I want the young people to have their fun. We're awash in pretty girls, and they're all panting to meet our great adventurer. Run along now, Lisle. If you find Olivia getting engaged to anybody, tell her not to be ridiculous."

She waved him away, and reverted to torturing his parents. Lisle abandoned them without the slightest twinge of conscience, and let himself become lost in the throng.

The ballroom, as the dowager had promised, was overrun with beautiful girls, and Lisle was by no means immune to the species, fully clothed or not. He certainly wasn't averse to dancing. He found partners easily, and danced happily.

All the while, though, his gaze roamed the crowd, seeking one head of violently red hair.

If Olivia wasn't dancing, she must be playing cards— and fleecing whoever was dim-witted enough to play with her. Or maybe she was in a dark corner, getting engaged again, as the dowager suspected. Olivia's many broken engagements, which would have ruined a girl of lesser fortune and less powerful family, wouldn't discourage suitors. They wouldn't mind her not being a beauty, either. Olivia Carsington was a catch.

Her late father, Jack Wingate, had been the feckless younger son of the recently deceased Earl of Fosbury, who'd left her a fortune. Her stepfather and Lisle's uncle, the Viscount Rathbourne, had pots of money, too, and he was heir to the Earl of Hargate, who had even more.

Between and during dances, she was a frequent topic of conversation: the daring gown she'd worn to the coronation last month, her carriage race with Lady Davenport, the duel she'd challenged Lord Bentwhistle to—because he'd whipped a footboy—and so on and so on.

She'd been "out" in Society for four years, she still wasn't married, and she was still the talk of London.

This didn't surprise him in the least.

Her mother, Bathsheba, came from the rotten branch of the DeLucey family: a famous lot of swindlers, imposters, and bigamists. Before Bathsheba Wingate married Lord Rathbourne, Olivia had shown clear signs of following in the ancestral footsteps. Since then, an aristocratic education had hidden the signs, but Olivia's character, clearly, had changed not at all.

Lisle remembered some lines from a letter she'd written to him in Egypt, shortly after his first brother was born.

I look forward to the day when I become a Bachelor. I should like to live an <u>*unsettled life.*</u>

Judging by the talk, she'd succeeded.

He was about to start actively searching for her when he noticed the men preening and jockeying for position in one corner of the room—competing for the current reigning beauty, no doubt.

He went that way.

The crowd was so thick that at first all he could see was the fashionably absurd coiffure rising above the men's heads. Two birds of paradise seemed to have their beaks stuck into a great loop of . . . red hair. Very red hair.

Only one girl in all the world had that hair.

Well, then, no surprise to find Olivia at the center of a crowd of men. She had rank and a thumping great dowry. That would more than make up for. . .

The crowd parted then, giving him a full view. She turned his way and he stopped short.

He'd forgotten.

Those great blue eyes.

For a moment he stood, lost in a blue as deep as an Egyptian evening sky.

Then he blinked, and took in the rest, from the ridiculous birds hanging over the stiff loops of red hair to the pointed slippers peeping out from under the ruffles and furbelows at the hem of her pale green gown.

Then his gaze went up again, and his brain slowed to a crawl.

Between coiffure and shoes appeared a graceful arc of neck and smooth shoulders and a creamy bosom more than amply on display . . . and lower down, an armful of waist curving out gracefully into womanly hips. . .

No, that had to be wrong. Olivia was many things. *Beautiful* wasn't one of them. Striking, yes: the fatally blue eyes and the vivid hair. Those were hers and no one else's. And yes, that was her face under the absurd coiffure . . . but no, it wasn't.

He stared, his gaze going up then down, again and again. The room's heat was suddenly beyond oppressive and his heart was beating strangely and his mind was a thick haze of memories where he was searching to make sense of what his eyes told him.

He was dimly aware that he was supposed to say something, but he had no idea what. His manners had never been quite so instinctive as they ought to be. He was used to another world, another clime, other kinds of men and women. Though he'd learned to fit in this one, fitting in didn't come naturally to him. He'd never learned to say what he didn't mean, and now he didn't know what he meant to say.

At the moment, everything anybody had ever done to civilize him was lost. He beheld a vision that stripped away all the rules and meaningless phrases and proper ways to look and move and shredded them to bits and blew them away.

"Lord Lisle," she said, with a graceful dip of her head that made the birds' plumes flutter. "There's a wager on, as to whether you'd turn up for Great-Grandmama's party."

At the sound of her voice, so familiar, Reason began to slog its way through the muck of confusion.

This was Olivia, Reason said. Here were the facts: her voice, her eyes, her hair, her face. Yes, her face was different because it had softened into womanliness. Her cheeks were softer, rounder. Her mouth was fuller. . .

He was aware of people talking, of this one asking that one who he was, and another answering. But all of that seemed to be in another world, irrelevant. He couldn't see or hear or think anything but Olivia.

Then he discerned the glint of laughter in her eyes and the slight upturn of her mouth.

He came back to earth with a *thunk* that should have been audible on the other side of the great ballroom.

"I wouldn't miss it for the world," he said.

"I'm glad to see you," she said, "and not merely because I've won the wager." She gave him one slow, assessing look that slid over his skin like fingertips and sent heat arrowing straight to his groin.

Ye gods, she was more dangerous than ever.

He wondered whose benefit that look was for. Was she simply exercising her power or was she trying to provoke all her admirers simultaneously by pretending he was the only man in the room?

Excellent work, either way.

All the same, enough was enough.

She wasn't a little girl anymore—if she'd ever been a little girl—and he wasn't a little boy. He knew how to play this game. He let his gaze drift down again to her breasts. "You've grown," he said.

"I knew you'd mock my hair," she said.

She knew he wasn't referring to her hair. One thing Olivia had never been was naïve.

But he took the hint and dutifully regarded the coiffure. Though it towered over many other men, he was tall enough to look the birds in the eye. Other women wore equally fantastical hair arrangements, he was aware. While men's fashions had grown increasingly sober in recent decades, women's had grown increasingly deranged.

"Some birds have landed on your head," he said. "And died there."

"They must think they've gone to heaven," said a male voice nearby.

"Looks like rigor mortis," Lisle said.

Olivia sent him a fleeting smile. Something curious happened inside his chest. Something else happened lower down, not at all curious and all too familiar.

He willed the feelings into oblivion.

She couldn't help it, he told himself. She was born that way, a Dreadful DeLucey through and through. He mustn't take it personally. She was his friend and ally, practically his sister. He made himself picture her as she'd been on the day when he first met her: a skinny twelve-year-old who'd tried to brain him with his sketchbook. A provoking, dangerously fascinating girl.

"I dressed for *you*," she said. "In honor of your Noble

Quest in Egypt. I ordered the silk for my gown to match the green of the Nile in your watercolors. We had to use birds of paradise because we couldn't find ibises."

Voice dropping to a conspiratorial tone, she leaned toward him, offering a nearer and fuller view of alabaster flesh, curved precisely to fit a man's hands. At these close quarters he was acutely aware of the faint sheen of moisture the ballroom's heat had brought to her skin. He was aware, too, of the scent of a woman arising therefrom: a dangerous blend of humid flesh and a light, flowery fragrance.

She should have warned him, drat her.

Think about the skinny twelve-year-old, he counseled himself.

"I wanted to dress like one of the ladies in the copies of the tomb paintings you sent," she went on, "but that was *forbidden.*"

The scent and the stress on *forbidden* were softening his brain.

Facts, he told himself. *Stick to facts, like. . .*

Where were her freckles?

Perhaps the room's gentle candlelight made them less obvious. Or maybe she'd powdered her breasts. Or had she bleached them with lemon juice?

Stop thinking about her breasts. That way madness lies. What's she saying? Something about tomb paintings.

He filled his mind with images of flat figures on stone walls.

"The ladies in the tomb paintings are not, technically speaking, dressed," he said. "When alive, they seem to be tightly wrapped in an extremely thin piece of linen."

The costume left nothing to the imagination, which was probably why even he—who preferred to stick to facts and leave the realm of imagination to his parents— had no trouble at all picturing Olivia's curvaceous new body wrapped in a thin piece of linen.

"Then, when they're dead," he went on, "they're overdressed, tightly wrapped in layers of linen from head to foot. Neither form of attire seems practical for an English ball."

"You never change," she said, drawing back. "Always so *literal*."

"Leave it to Lisle to throw away a golden opportunity," said another male voice. "Instead of complimenting the lady—as any man with eyes must do—and trying to win her favor, he must wander into a boring lecture about pagan customs."

Yes, because it's safe there.

"My attention has not wandered, I assure you, Miss Carsington," Lisle said. "At present it could not be more firmly fixed."

He'd like to fix his hands on the throat of the fiend who'd given her this face and body—as though she needed any more weapons. It must have been the devil. A trade of some kind, sometime in the five years since Lisle had last seen her. Naturally Satan, like anyone else, would have had the worst of any bargain with her.

In a corner of his mind, the voice that warned him of snakes, scorpions, and cutthroats lurking in the darkness said, *Watch out.*

But he already knew that, because he knew Olivia.

She was dangerous. Beautiful or striking, with or without breasts, she exerted a fatal fascination. She easily captivated otherwise intelligent men, most of whom had already seen her destroy the peace of other equally intelligent men.

He knew that. Her letters had been filled with her numerous "romantic disappointments," among other things. He'd heard other stories since entering this ballroom. He knew what she was like.

He was merely temporarily unhinged because he was a man. It was a purely physical reaction, completely natural when one encountered a beautiful woman. He had such reactions all the time. This was disturbing only because he was reacting to *Olivia*.

Who was his friend and ally, practically his sister.

He'd always thought of her that way.

And that was the way he'd continue to think of her, he told himself.

He'd had a bit of a shock, that was all. He was a man who encountered shocks nearly every day of his life, and thrived on them.

"Having fixed my attention for the moment," he said, "perhaps the lady would be so kind as to grant the next dance."

"That's mine," said one of the men hovering at her shoulder. "Miss Carsington promised."

Olivia snapped her fan shut. "You may have another, Lord Belder," she said. "I haven't seen Lord Lisle this age, and he'll soon be gone again. He's the most elusive man in the world. If I don't take this dance, who knows when I should have another? He could be drowned in a shipwreck. He could be eaten by crocodiles or bitten by a viper or a scorpion. He could succumb to plague. He's never happy, you know, except when risking his life to advance our knowledge of an ancient civilization. I can dance with *you* anytime."

Belder looked murder at Lisle, but he smiled at Olivia and yielded his claim.

As Lisle led her away, he finally understood why so many men kept shooting each other on her account.

They all wanted her and they couldn't help it; she knew it and she didn't care.

Chapter Two

The gloved hand Olivia had taken was warm, and stronger and firmer than she remembered. When it clasped hers, she grew warm everywhere, which startled her—and that was by no means her first shock this evening.

Had she ever taken Lisle's hand before? She couldn't remember. But it had been instinctive to do so, to go with him, though he wasn't the young man she used to know.

For one thing, he was much larger, and not simply physically, though that change was impressive enough.

When he first drew near, moments ago, he blocked her view of the rest of the room. He'd always been taller than she. But he wasn't a lanky youth anymore. He was a man, exuding virility to a dizzying degree.

She wasn't the only one he made dizzy. Among the hordes of men about her were a few women friends. She'd seen the way they looked at Lisle when he entered her circle. Now, as he and she passed into the crowd proper, on their way to the dancing area, she saw heads turn—and for once it wasn't only men, and they weren't all staring at her.

She'd stared, too, when she'd first spotted him, though she knew him so well. He captured one's attention because he wasn't like anybody else.

She studied him surreptitiously, sizing him up as she sized up everybody, as any Dreadful DeLucey would do.

The Egyptian sun had darkened his skin to bronze and lightened his hair to pale gold, but that wasn't the only way he was different.

The black coat hugged his broad shoulders and lean torso, and the trousers outlined his long, muscled legs. His linen was immaculately white, his evening slippers glossy black. Though he wore the same impeccable evening attire as other men, he seemed not fully clothed somehow, perhaps because no other gentleman made one so forcefully aware of the powerful body underneath the elegant attire.

She saw other women taking him in, pausing in their conversations to study him or try to catch his eye.

They saw only the outside. That, she admitted, was exciting enough.

She knew he was different in other, less obvious ways. His wasn't the usual gentleman's education. Daphne Carsington had taught him all and more than he would have learned at public school and university. Rupert Carsington had taught him survival skills few gentlemen had need for: how to handle a knife, for instance, and how to throw a man out of a window.

All this she knew. What she hadn't been prepared for was the change in his voice: the tantalizing hint of a non-English lilt in the aristocratic accents, and the way the sound conjured images of tents and turbans and half-naked women languishing on Turkey carpets.

He didn't carry himself in the way he used to do, either. For nearly ten years he'd lived in a complicated and dangerous world, where he'd learned to move as quietly and smoothly as a cat or a cobra.

The deep gold skin and golden hair made one think of tigers, but that didn't quite capture his otherness. He moved like . . . water. As he threaded his way through the crowd, he sent ripples through it. Watching him pass, women fainted mentally and men contemplated killing him.

As one who'd learned to be acutely aware of his surroundings, he'd sense this, she was sure, though his face gave nothing away.

But she, who'd known him for so long, was aware that he wasn't as coolly contained and detached as he seemed. The logical, pedantic surface hid a fierce, obstinate nature. That, she suspected, hadn't changed. Too, he had a temper—which, the set of his mouth told her, had been sorely tried recently.

She tugged his hand. He looked down at her, his grey eyes glinting silver in the candlelight.

"This way," she said.

She led him past a cluster of servants bearing trays, dropped his hand to take two glasses of champagne from one of the trays, then passed out of the ballroom into the corridor and thence into an antechamber. After the briefest hesitation, he followed her in.

"Close the door," she said.

"Olivia," he said.

"Oh, please," she said. "As though I've any reputation to lose."

He closed the door. "As a matter of fact, you do, though I'm sure you ought to have been ruined ages ago."

"There isn't much that money and rank can't buy, including reputation," she said. "Here, take one of these, and let me welcome you home properly." He took one of the glasses she offered, his gloved fingertips brushing hers.

She felt the spark of contact under her glove, under her skin. Her heart sparked, too, and its beating grew hurried.

She stepped back half a pace, and clinked her glass against his.

"Welcome home, my dear friend," she said. "I was never so glad to see anybody as I was to see you."

She'd wanted to launch herself at him and throw her arms about his neck. She would have done it, too, whatever Propriety said, but the look in his silvery eyes when he first caught sight of her stopped her in her tracks.

He was her friend, yes, and only Great-Grandmama knew her better than he did. But he was a man now, not the boy she used to know.

"I was bored senseless," she went on, "but the look on your face when you discovered my bosoms was priceless. It was all I could do to keep a straight face."

He looked there now, and the heat started where he looked, and spread outward and deepened. In an instant she was in a sweat again, the way she'd been a little while ago, when he first looked at her. That was

all the warning she needed: This was one fire she'd
better not play with.

He studied her bosom critically, the way he might
have examined a line of hieroglyphic writing. "You
didn't have them the last time I saw you," he said. "I
was completely flummoxed. Where did you get them?"

"Where did I *get* them?" Gad, that was so like him,
puzzling over her breasts as though they were a bit of
ancient pottery. "They simply grew. Everything grew.
Very slowly. Isn't that odd? I was precocious in every
other way." She drank. "But never mind my bosoms,
Lisle."

"Easy for you to say. You're not a man. And I haven't
got used to them yet."

And she hadn't got used to what happened when he
looked at her in that way. She laughed. "Well, look,
then, if you must. Great-Grandmama told me the time
will come all too soon when men won't be interested in
looking there, and I ought to enjoy it while I can."

"She hasn't changed at all."

"She's frailer, and tires more quickly than she used
to do, though she still gets about. I don't know what I'll
do when she's gone."

Great-Grandmama was her confidante, the only one
who knew all of Olivia's secrets. She couldn't possibly
tell Mama or Step-Papa everything. They'd done their
very best for her. The truth would only distress them.
She had to protect them from it.

"I don't know what I should have done tonight without her," Lisle said. "She took my parents prisoner and
let me escape." He dragged his hand through his hair,
turning it into a wild tousle that would make women

swoon. "I oughtn't to let them trouble me, but I can't seem to master the art of ignoring them."

"What can't you ignore this time?" she said.

He shrugged. "The usual madness. I needn't bore you with the details."

His parents, she knew, were the cross he had to bear. All their world revolved around them. All others, including their children, were merely supporting players in the great drama of their life.

Great-Grandmama was the only one who could cut them down to size effortlessly, because she said and did exactly as she pleased. Everyone else was either at a loss or too polite or kind or didn't think it worth the trouble. Even Step-Papa could do no more than manage them, and that was so trying to his temper that he did so only in extreme circumstances.

"You must tell me all," she said. "I dote on Lord and Lady Atherton's madnesses. They make me feel utterly sober and logical and rather sweetly dull by comparison."

He smiled a little, a crooked upturn of the right side of his mouth.

Her heart gave a sharp lurch.

She moved away and threw herself carelessly into a thickly cushioned chair by the fire. "Come, get warm," she said. "The ballroom was as hot as Hades, but not to you, I know. Away from that crush of warm bodies, you must think you're in an ice house." She waved a hand at the chair opposite. "Tell me what your parents want from you now."

He came to the fire but he didn't take the chair. He looked at the fire for a long time, then at her, but briefly, before reverting to the fascinating flames.

"It's to do with a crumbling wreck of a castle we own, about ten miles from Edinburgh," he said.

"How very strange," Olivia said after Lisle had summarized the scene with his parents. He knew she could fill in the histrionic details herself. In the last nine years, she'd spent more time with Father and Mother than he had.

"I wish it were strange," he said. "But it isn't in the least odd for them."

"I meant the ghosts," she said. "How strange that workers keep away on account of ghosts. Only think of how many haunt the Tower of London. There's the executioner chasing the Countess of Salisbury round the chopping block."

"Anne Boleyn carrying her head."

"The young princes," she said. "That's only a few—and it's only one building. We've ghosts everywhere, and nobody seems to mind. How odd that Scottish laborers should be afraid. I thought they liked to be haunted."

"I made the same point to my parents, but logic is a language they refuse to understand," he said. "Not that this has anything to do with ghosts or castles, really. It's all about keeping me at home."

"But you'd go mad here," she said.

She'd always understood, from the day they'd met and he'd told her of his determination to go to Egypt. She'd called it a Noble Quest.

"I shouldn't mind so much," he said, "if they truly needed me here. My brothers need me—they need somebody—but I'm at a loss what to do. I doubt my parents would miss them if I took them to Egypt. But they're too young. Children from northern climes don't thrive there."

She put her head back a little to gaze up at him. When those great blue eyes turned upward to his face, things happened inside him, complicated things, involving not merely animal instincts and his reproductive organs. The things jumped about in his chest, and there was a kind of pain, like little stabs, when they did it.

He looked away, into the fire again.

"What will you do?" she said.

"I haven't decided," he said. "The so-called crisis broke minutes before we were to set out this evening. I haven't had time to consider what to do. Not that I mean to do anything about the castle nonsense. It's my brothers I need to think about. I shall have to spend more time with them, and decide then."

"You're right," she said. "The castle isn't worth your troubling about. A great waste of your time. If you—"

She broke off because the door flew open and Lady Rathbourne entered. Dark haired, her eyes not quite the same blue as her daughter's, she was a great beauty in her own right.

Lisle could regard her with equanimity, though, and with affection, and without bewildering feelings.

"For heaven's sake, Olivia, Belder's been looking everywhere for you," she said. "You were supposed to be dancing. Lisle, you ought to know better than to let Olivia lure you into a tête-à-tête."

"Mama, we haven't seen each other in five years!"

"Lisle can call on you tomorrow, if he doesn't mind fighting his way through the hordes of besotted gentlemen," said her ladyship. "At present, the other young ladies are clamoring to dance with him. He is not your property, and your prolonged absence is making Belder agitated. Come, Lisle, I'm sure you don't want to end the party by fighting one of Olivia's jealous swains, poor fools. It's too ridiculous for words."

They left the antechamber, and Lisle and Olivia soon parted ways, she to Lord Belder and her other admirers, and he to the scores of young ladies who could not have been less like her had they belonged to another species.

It wasn't until later, when he was dancing with one of them, that he remembered what he'd seen, in the instant before Lady Rathbourne interrupted the conversation: the gleam in Olivia's too-blue eyes before their expression turned inward in the way he'd learned to recognize so many years ago.

Thinking. She'd been thinking.

And that, as her mother could have told anybody, was always dangerous.

Somerset House, London
Wednesday 5 October

It was not an official meeting of the Society of Antiquaries. For one thing, they usually met on Thursday. For another, their meetings did not begin until November.

But the Earl of Lisle did not return to London every day, and he would likely be gone again by November. Any scholar interested in Egyptian antiquities wanted to hear what he had to say, and the event, though arranged on short notice, was well attended.

The last time he'd returned, though merely eighteen years old, he had presented a significant paper dealing with the names of the Egyptian pharaohs. Technically speaking, the decipherment of hieroglyphs was Daphne Carsington's specialty. Everyone knew this. Everyone knew she was a genius. The trouble was, she was a woman. A male had to represent her, or her discoveries and theories would be mercilessly attacked and mocked by the large and noisy element who feared and hated women who had any intelligence, let alone more than they.

Her brother, who most usually represented her, was abroad. Her husband, Rupert Carsington, though not nearly as stupid as everyone believed him to be, would never be able to read a scholarly paper with a straight face—if, that is, he didn't fall asleep while reading it.

Since Lisle and Daphne had collaborated for years, and since he had the highest regard for her abilities, he was more than happy to stand in her place and present her latest paper with the seriousness it deserved.

But one person in the audience thought the whole thing a great joke.

Lord Belder sat in the front row next to Olivia, and he was mocking every word Lisle uttered.

If he was trying to impress Olivia with that technique, he was barking up the wrong tree.

More likely, though, Belder merely wanted to provoke Lisle. He'd made sure to be in the way yesterday, when Lisle had called on her. But half the world was

at her parents' house, and Lisle hadn't a chance to exchange more than a few words with her. He'd told her
about the paper he was presenting, and she'd said she
would attend, and Belder had said he'd escort her: He
wouldn't dream of missing Lord Lisle's "little lecture,"
he said.

Lisle's temper was easily ignited at the best of times.
At present he was seething on Daphne's account: Belder
was mocking *her* hard work. Still, the idiot wouldn't
be let to continue for much longer, Lisle told himself.
Belder wasn't at Almack's or a ball, and the present
audience had little patience with this sort of behavior.

Sure enough, Lisle had scarcely thought it when one
of the scholars spoke up. "Sir," the gentleman said
coldly, "perhaps you would be good enough to reserve
your wit for a more suitable milieu: I suggest your
club—or a coffee house or tavern. We came to hear the
gentleman at the lectern, not you."

Lisle pretended to brush a speck of dust from his
notes. Without looking up, he said, "Wit? Was that
what it was? I beg your pardon, Lord Belder, for
not responding to your remarks. I mistook you for
a saint."

"A saint?" said Belder with a laugh—for Olivia's
benefit, no doubt, to show how little he cared about
being reprimanded publicly like a boorish schoolboy.

"Certainly," Lisle said. "In Egypt, you see, those
of slow understanding or no understanding are called
saints, and their peculiarities of appearance, speech,
and behavior are regarded as signs of divine blessing."

The audience roared. The scholars took a moment
to exact their revenge, making Belder the butt of their

jokes. He obliged them by turning redder than Olivia's hair.

Having administered the setdown Belder had been begging for, Lisle delivered the rest of Daphne's paper in peace.

When he'd finished answering questions and the audience began to disperse, he broke through the wall of men surrounding Olivia—dim-witted fowl clustered about a dozing crocodile, as he saw it—and offered to take her home. Turning away from Belder, she bestowed a smile on Lisle so dazzling that he couldn't see straight for a moment. Then she took his arm. They walked to her carriage, her maid, Bailey, trailing after them.

The footman had put down the step and Olivia was moving toward it when a boy flew along the pavement straight at them. He was running at top speed, dodging the groups of scholarly gentlemen arguing about pharaohs as they walked along the Strand.

He dodged Lisle as well, but then he made the mistake of glancing Olivia's way, and the blaze of beauty blinded and unbalanced him. His step faltered and his focus went astray, even while his legs kept moving.

At this same moment, Lord Belder was hurrying toward Olivia's carriage. The boy ran straight into him, and they both stumbled. The boy landed on the pavement and Belder in the gutter.

The lad scrambled to his feet, threw Belder a horrified look, and set off.

"Stop, thief!" Belder roared. A couple of his friends caught the boy as he tried to run past them.

His lordship rose from the gutter. Passing acquaintances treated him to the usual lumbering wit: "Just waking up, Belder?" or "Is that the latest in beauty baths, Belder?" and so on.

Brown and black substances of unsavory origin splotched his fawn trousers and blue coat, his elaborately tied neckcloth, his waistcoat, and his gloves. He looked down at his clothes, then at the boy. The look made the boy squirm and yell, "It was an accident, your worship! I didn't take nothing!"

"It's true," Olivia called over the noise. "I saw what happened. If he'd been stealing, he would—"

"Wait in the carriage, and let me deal with it," Lisle cut in before she could explain how petty theft was properly done. She was, after all, an expert.

"Don't be silly," she said. "I can settle this."

He tried to lead her away, but she shook him off and marched to the men holding the boy.

"Let him go," she said. "It was an *accident.*"

To Lisle, the warning signs were obvious: the flush rising from her neck to her cheeks and the *You blockheads* implied in her stress on "accident."

Since he couldn't drag her away bodily, he would have to drown her out. But Belder spoke first.

"You don't know what these wretched creatures get up to, Miss Carsington," he said. "They bump into people on purpose, to pick our pockets."

Lisle said, "That may be so but—"

"Not this one," Olivia said. "A proper thief would have been so quick and efficient, you'd hardly notice him. He'd take care not to knock you down or draw attention to himself, and he wouldn't pause, but get away instantly. Furthermore, they usually work in pairs."

She was absolutely right, and any rational man would recognize this.

But Belder was in a temper, he had scores to settle, and the boy was the easiest target. He only gave her a patronizing smile and turned to the bystanders. "Someone fetch a constable," he called.

"No!" the boy shouted. "I didn't take nothing!"

He pulled and kicked, trying to get free.

Lord Belder cuffed his head.

"You great *bully*!" Olivia cried. Up went her furled umbrella, and down, sharply, on his shoulder.

"Ow!"

"Release that child!" She swung the umbrella at the men holding the boy.

Belder grabbed her arm to stop her beating his friends.

Lisle saw the dirty, gloved hand wrapped about Olivia's arm. Then he saw red.

He advanced, took Belder roughly by the arm, and yanked him away. "Don't touch her," he said in a low, hard voice. "Don't ever touch her."

Chapter Three

Two minutes later

O h, miss," said Bailey. "They're going to kill each other."

Lisle had flung Belder away almost as soon as he'd grabbed him, but Belder wasn't about to let it end there. He pushed Lisle, and Lisle pushed back harder, knocking Belder against the fence. Belder bounced up, tore off his gloves, threw down his hat, and put up his fists. Lisle did the same.

Don't touch her, he'd said, in a low, deadly voice that made her shiver.

How silly. She was no schoolroom miss—yet her heart raced as it had never done before, though men fought over her all the time, and though she knew it meant nothing special to Lisle. He acted instinctively, protective by nature. Belligerent, too.

But she hadn't seen him fight in years.

She hadn't seen any fights in years, she reminded herself. Men usually met at dawn, well out of the public eye, because dueling was illegal.

Fisticuffs, however, were not. Still, they were hardly common among gentlemen, in broad day, on a major London thoroughfare.

No wonder she was excited.

"They will *try* to kill each other," she told Bailey. "But all they'll do is pummel each other, and that's preferable to pistols at twenty paces. Belder's spoiling for a fight, and Lisle will enjoy accommodating him."

A glance at her maid told her that Bailey, too, was not unmoved. A petite, pretty brunette, Bailey was not as delicate as she looked. She would not have survived her employment with Olivia otherwise.

"You've never seen Lisle fight," Olivia said. "He looks so angelic, I know, with his fair hair and those cool grey eyes of his, but he's a ferocious pugilist. I once saw him make mincemeat of a great ox of a boy, easily twice his size."

It had happened on the day she'd started on her Noble Quest to Bristol. Lisle hadn't approved of Nat Diggerby as a traveling companion for her.

Truth to tell, she hadn't been overly fond of Diggerby, either. Though she'd pretended not to care, she'd been vastly relieved when Lisle took his place.

She turned her attention to the fight, wishing she could see more of it. She could hear the grunts and the thuds of fists connecting with body parts, but a great crowd of men blocked her view. They were shouting encouragement in between betting on the outcome.

Even she knew better than to try to break into that

circle. A lady did not get mixed up in throngs of blood-thirsty males. A lady waited at a safe distance from the fray.

If she could have climbed onto the footmen's perch at the back of the carriage she could have a better view, but she mustn't do that, either.

She could only wait, listening and making do with glimpses, and hoping Lisle would come out of it in one piece. He was used to fighting, she told herself. People were always trying to kill him in Egypt. Still, Belder was for some reason madly jealous of him, and Lisle had humiliated the man in front of an audience of important men.

After what seemed hours but could only have been minutes, there was a shout, then quiet. Then the wall of men began to give way. She saw Belder lying on the ground, and some of his friends going to him.

She pushed forward, using her elbows and her umbrella to make way through the thinning crowd.

She grabbed Lisle's arm and tugged. "Come away," she said.

He looked at her blankly. His hair was tangled and filthy and his lip was bleeding. Blood spattered his neckcloth, which was torn. A sleeve of his coat had been partly ripped away from the shoulder seam.

"Come away," she said. "He can't fight anymore."

Lisle looked at the man on the ground, then turned back to her. "Are you not going to comfort him?"

"No."

He took out his handkerchief and started to wipe his lip, and winced.

She took the handkerchief from him and dabbed at

his lip. "You'll have a prime black eye by tomorrow, and you'll be eating soft foods for the next few days," she said.

"You have a knack for attracting idiots," he said.

She stopped dabbing. "Your lip is going to swell," she said. "With any luck, you won't be able to talk." She shook her head, turned away, and started for her carriage.

He followed. "You oughtn't to encourage them when you don't want them," he said.

"I don't have to encourage them," she said. "DeLucey women attract men. And men, by and large, are idiots. That includes you. You were looking for an excuse to fight, just as he was."

"Perhaps I was," Lisle said. "I can't remember when last I had so much fun thrashing somebody."

He offered his bruised and dirty hand to help her keep her balance on the narrow carriage step. She looked down at his hand and raised an eyebrow.

"Squeamish?" he said.

"Not likely," she said. "I was thinking that's going to hurt later."

"It was worth it," he said.

Men, she thought.

She took his hand, climbed into the carriage, and settled onto her seat. Bailey followed and took the seat opposite.

"I'm not sure the fun of beating Belder will be worth the price," she said.

"I'm used to black eyes and sore jaws," he said.

"That isn't what I meant," she said. "Your parents won't be pleased when they hear about it."

He shrugged.

"You'd better let me drive you home," she said.

He shook his head. "It's out of your way. Nichols will be along in a minute, as soon as he recovers my hat."

The slim valet hurried toward them at that moment, brushing at Lisle's hat with his handkerchief.

Bailey gave Lisle's handsome manservant a sharp glance, and sniffed disdainfully. "We'd better go straight home, miss," she said.

"She's right," Lisle said. "It won't be long before all of London hears how you beat Belder with your umbrella. You'll want to be at home before the news arrives, so you can shape the tale to suit you."

It wouldn't matter what version of the story Olivia gave her parents. They were growing tired of the scandals. Grandmama and Grandpapa Hargate would have something to say, too, and that wouldn't be pleasant. They thought it was long past time she was married. She needed a husband and children to settle her, they believed. They'd settled all their children satisfactorily. But their offspring were all men, and they weren't in the least like her. No one was like her, except other Dreadful DeLuceys: restless, untrustworthy creatures.

If she married, her life would narrow down to wifehood and motherhood, and she'd spend the years slowly suffocating. She'd never do anything truly interesting, ever again. Certainly, she'd never have the great adventures she'd always dreamed of.

Not that she had much hope of any at present, in a society bound by increasingly strict rules.

But so long as she was nobody's wife—and so long as

Great-Grandmama was alive, to stand up to the others for her—Olivia had a measure of freedom, at least.

She wouldn't give that up until she had absolutely no other choice.

"Join us for dinner," she told Lisle. "We can talk then."

"I reckon I'd better wash first," he said.

He grinned at her, looking for a moment like a grubby schoolboy, and reminding her of the schoolboy who'd pummeled Nat Diggerby and played the part of her loyal squire en route to Bristol.

The grin, combined with the recollection, set things fluttering inside her. "I reckon you'd better," she said.

He closed the carriage door.

She sat back in her seat, so that she wouldn't be tempted to look out of the window and watch him walk away.

She felt the carriage bounce slightly as the footmen leapt up to their places. One of them rapped on the carriage roof, and the vehicle lurched into motion.

After a minute or two, Bailey said, "Miss, you've still got his lordship's handkerchief."

Olivia looked down at it. She'd have it laundered, then add it to her collection. The glove of her right hand concealed the scarab he'd sent her long ago. She'd had it made into a ring, which she wore constantly. There were his letters as well, too few of them: one for every half dozen of hers.

She had his friendship and every one of his letters. She had the trinkets he'd sent her and odd, rubbishy remembrances she'd collected. That, she knew, was as much as anyone would ever get from him. He'd given

himself—heart and mind and soul—to Egypt a long
time ago.

"He won't miss it," she said.

Atherton House
The same evening

"Oh, Peregrine, how could you?" Lady Atherton
wailed. "Brawling! Like a common ruffian! In the
Strand, of all places, for all the world to see!"

She turned to her husband. "You see, Jasper? This is
what comes of leaving Rupert Carsington in charge of
him for all these years."

That was completely illogical. Lisle had been getting
into fights for as long as he could remember. He hadn't
needed any guidance from Uncle Rupert in that department. He'd never in his life run from a fight, no matter
who the adversary or how big or how many. Never had,
never would.

"You've turned into a savage!" his father raged. "You
cannot even present a paper to the Society of Antiquaries without instigating a riot."

"Hardly a riot," Lisle said. "More like a scuffle. The
papers have more interesting matters to report."

"The newspapers like nothing better than lurid stories about men fighting over Olivia Carsington," Mama
said. "I cannot believe you let her make a fool of you,
too. I am *mortified*. How shall I face my friends after
this? How shall I hold my head up?" She sank onto the
chaise longue and burst into tears.

"This is what comes of indulging your Egyptian

nonsense," said Father. "Well, I'm putting a stop to it, once and for all. Until I see a glimmer of filial duty, a semblance of gentlemanly behavior, you shall not get another farthing from me."

Lisle stared at him for a moment. He'd expected a scene, naturally. He would have been shocked if his parents had not ranted and raved.

But this was new. He wasn't sure he'd heard aright. Like other noblemen's sons, Lisle was utterly dependent on his father financially. Money was all he got from his parents. They'd never given him affection or understanding. Those the Carsingtons gave him, abundantly. But he couldn't go to the Carsingtons for money.

"You're cutting me off?" he said.

"You've mocked us, ignored us, used us, and abused our generosity," Father said. "We've borne it all patiently, but this time you've gone too far. You've *embarrassed* your mother."

On cue, his mother fainted.

"This is mad," Lisle said. "How am I to live?"

His father hurried to his mother's side to administer smelling salts. "If you want money, you'll do as other gentlemen do," he said as he tenderly lifted Mother's head from the pillow onto which it had conveniently fallen. "You'll respect your parents' wishes. You'll go to Scotland as we ask, and you'll assume responsibility for once in your life. You'll go to Egypt again over my dead body!"

Lisle didn't come to dinner, after all. Late in the afternoon, Olivia received a note from him:

If I come to dinner, I'll have to kill somebody. Best to keep away. You're probably in enough trouble.

                                        L

She wrote back:

It isn't <u>safe</u> to Write. Meet me at Hyde Park Corner. Tomorrow. Ten o'clock in the Morning. DO NOT FAIL ME.

                                        O

Hyde Park
The following morning

Only a few years ago, London's most fashionable gentlemen could be counted on to take a stroll in Hyde Park every morning, then return at the fashionable hour, between five and seven o'clock in the afternoon.

These days a stroll in the forenoon was not merely unfashionable but *vulgar*.

Morning was, therefore, the perfect time for a Clandestine Rendezvous, as Olivia would have written in one of her missives.

She was late, naturally, and Lisle had never been good at waiting. But he forgot his impatience when she came into view, a great pale blue plume waving from the top of her hat like a banner carried into battle. She wore a riding dress of military cut, of a deep blue that matched her eyes.

The low slant of morning sun caught the curly hair escaping the confines of her hat and pins, and made it shimmer like garnets.

When she came alongside him, he still hadn't caught his breath.

"You've no idea the difficulty I had getting away from Bailey," she said. "You'd think she'd be glad to be excused, as she hates riding in Town, but no, she was determined to come with me. I had the devil's own time persuading her to stay and *allay suspicion.* As it was, I was obliged to take a groom." She tipped her beplumed head in the direction of a young male in livery trailing at a tactful distance behind her. "Not that you and I have anything to hide, but all the family are vexed with me for getting you into the fight with Belder."

"I got myself into it," he said.

"Your eye is very bad," she said, leaning forward a little to peer at it.

"It looks worse than it is," he said. "Nichols knows how to treat these things." If he hadn't known, that eye would be swollen shut at present. "It'll turn a few ugly colors over the next few days, and then it'll fade. My mouth, as you have no doubt observed with regret, is not so much damaged as you thought."

"You are not as pretty as you were at the ball," she said. "Mama had a lively description of the fight and your injuries from somebody, and she's furious. She says I ought to keep away from you. She says you have enough difficulties without my getting you into trouble."

"Nonsense," he said. "Who will I talk to if you keep away? Come along. It's too noisy here."

Though the park itself was deserted—by the haut

ton, at any rate—Hyde Park Corner bustled. Peddlers, milkmaids, soldiers, and loiterers of all sorts crowded the pavement. On the Knightsbridge Road, the Royal Mail and the stagecoaches vied for space with lowly farm wagons, elegant private carriages, riders, and pedestrians. Stray children, cats, and dogs darted among the vehicles and horses.

It was here, at Hyde Park Corner, that their first adventure together had begun. The memory came back vividly: Olivia, standing with a surly ox of a boy . . . Lisle having to beat the boy out of the way . . . then climbing onto a farm wagon after her. . .

Every time he awaited her, he expected the skinny girl he used to know, with her striking hair and eyes. Every time, seeing her as she was now threw him off balance. He still wasn't used to the beauty she'd become. It almost hurt to look at her face, and the soft curves of her body—which the snug tailoring of her riding dress emphasized—made a muddle of feelings inside.

Wrong feelings. They were the kind any attractive woman could inspire in a man. Any number of loose women could tend to them.

What he needed at this moment was a friend and ally.

Yet even when they entered the park, he found he wasn't quite ready to talk. He needed to clear the jumbled feelings from his head or his heart—he wasn't sure where they were, exactly.

"Race?" he said.

Her eyes lit.

Their horses were fresh, happy to gallop westward along the deserted Rotten Row. Her mare was as powerful as his, and she rode with the same skill and daring she applied to everything in her life. He won, but not by much, and at the end, they were laughing—at themselves, and at the sheer pleasure of a gallop on a fine autumn morning.

They eased to a trot, then headed further into the park.

When they reached a stand of trees, well out of sight of the more traveled pathways, they slowed their mounts to a walk.

Then he told her what had happened.

"They've cut you off?" she said incredulously. "But they can't! You'll go mad here. You must return to Egypt."

"I told you they were determined to keep me home," he said. "I didn't realize how determined. I thought they might settle down after a while, or forget, as they usually do. But they're even more adamant today than they were yesterday about that dratted castle. Father will only extend funds for me to undertake their restoration fantasy."

"I can imagine what he's thinking," she said. "He thinks you'll become involved in the project, and transfer your passion to it."

His heart raced guiltily. "My passion?" he said.

"Your parents are jealous of Egypt," she said. "They don't understand the difference between an old castle and ancient monuments. It's all 'old' to them."

He wouldn't have called Egypt a passion, but Olivia would, and perhaps, after all, what he felt for the place and his work there was a sort of passion.

She understood so well, sometimes better than he

did. But then, she was a DeLucey, and they'd survived for so many generations because they were adept at reading people and manipulating them.

"I suppose I should be grateful they didn't think of using the purse strings before," he said.

"If they had, Lord Rathbourne would have paid your way," she said.

"Your stepfather's done more than enough for me," Lisle said. "He has you and your sisters and brothers to think of now."

"I would give you my money," she said. "You know I would."

"That would be monstrous improper," he said. "I'm glad it's not possible." Her funds, he knew, had been very carefully tied up, to protect her not only from fortune hunters but from herself. She was a strange mixture of contradictions: her mind calculating and her heart generous. Her leaping to the ragamuffin's defense yesterday was typical.

She drew nearer and put out her gloved hand to touch his. "I won't let you be trapped here," she said. "We'll think of something."

There it was, the gleam in her great blue eyes.

"No, we won't," he said firmly.

She was his friend and ally and confidante, but her impulsiveness, ethical blind spots, and fervent nature sometimes made his hair stand on end—he, who dealt daily with snakes, scorpions, crocodiles, thieves, cutthroats, and—worst of all—officials.

To say her judgment was dubious at best was putting it very mildly, indeed.

Nine years ago she'd lured him into a journey to Bristol on a hunt for a pirate's treasure, of all things. That was one of her Ideas, with a capital I. It could have ended very badly for him—in a sadistic Scottish school, for instance—had Lord Rathbourne not intervened.

Lisle knew very well that his journeying to Egypt instead was entirely thanks to Rathbourne. Lisle knew, too, that one couldn't rely on miracles. Furthermore, he was a man now, not a boy. He couldn't expect and didn't want friends and relatives to get him out of every difficulty.

"No, Lisle, you must listen," she said eagerly. "I have the most wonderful Idea."

Olivia with an Idea.

A prospect to strike terror into the heart of any man with a modicum of intelligence and any sense of self-preservation.

"No Ideas," he said. "Not on any account."

"Let's go to Scotland," she said. "Together."

Her heart pounded so hard it must be audible at Kensington Palace. She'd been thinking about the castle in Scotland since Saturday.

"Have you lost your mind?" he said.

"I knew you'd say that," she said.

"I'm not going to Scotland."

"But we'll go *together*," she said. "It'll be fun. An adventure."

"Don't be ridiculous," he said. "We're not children anymore. Even you can't get away with going to

Scotland with a man. Your parents will never approve."

"They don't have to know."

His grey eyes widened. "Olivia."

"Tomorrow morning they're leaving for Derbyshire," she said. "I'm staying in London with Great-Grandmama."

He looked away. "This grows worse by the minute."

"I've thought it through," she said.

"Since when?" he said, his too-keen gaze coming back to her. "I told you only a moment ago what's happened."

"I've been thinking about the castle," she said. That was absolutely true. It was better to stick as close to the truth as possible with Lisle. He was not only viciously logical and straightforward to a fault, but she thought he could read her mind a little. "I was trying to devise a plan to save you from it."

"You are not rescuing me," he said. "You are not my knight in shining armor or whatever you think you are. I'm nearly four and twenty years old, and perfectly capable of taking care of myself."

"Please don't turn all proud male on me," she said. "If you would only listen, you'll understand how practical my Idea is."

"Nine years ago you had the practical Idea of saving your mother from penury by running away to Bristol to dig up a pirate's treasure in the Earl of Mandeville's garden!"

"Yes, and it was fun, wasn't it?" she said. "It was an adventure. You have adventures all the time. I—" She waved one gloved hand in the air. "I break engagements and hit men with my umbrella."

He shot her a glance she couldn't read. Then he nudged his horse into motion.

* * *

He needed distance.

He didn't want to be thinking about this, about the girl she used to be, who wanted to be a knight and undertake Noble Quests.

She followed him. "Don't close your mind," she said. "You're a scholar, and a scholar keeps an open mind."

"Not to insanity," he said. "You can't simply jaunt off to Scotland because you're bored with breaking engagements and hitting men with your umbrella. I'm sorry you have to abide by silly rules for women, but I can't change them. And even I know you can't pop into a carriage and travel four hundred miles on your own without stirring up a terrific scandal."

"I always stir up scandal," she said. "I'm known for it. Whatever I do or say at this dinner or that party makes the rounds of the ton the following morning. Olivia Carsington, Last Night's Scandal, that's me. I should have it engraved on my visiting cards."

He looked about him. The park was quiet this morning, activity in the surrounding streets sounding so faintly that one heard clearly the leaves rustling in the trees, the *clip-clop* of their horses' hooves, and the call of a pair of birds, one to the other.

He could hear his heart pounding, too. He was tempted, horribly tempted.

But she always tempted him. She'd been doing it since she was twelve years old. If he hadn't spent most of the last ten years in Egypt, she would have made a shambles of his life.

"I should not have to tell you this," he said. "But since you've lost your mind, I reckon I must: You may think of me as a brother but I'm not. You can't travel with me unchaperoned."

"Of course I must be chaperoned," she said. "But you can leave all the arrangements to me. All you have to do—"

"I'm not doing anything," he said. "Of all the hare-brained schemes—" He broke off, shaking his head. "I can't believe this. My father has cut off my money, I have nowhere to go and nothing to live on—and you want me to take you four hundred miles to a moldering old castle. In October, no less! Do you know what Scotland's like in October?"

"It's dark and wet and cold and gloomy and terribly romantic," she said.

"I'm not going!" he said. "I can't believe I'm even arguing with you about this."

"It'll be fun," she said. "An adventure."

An adventure. He had them all the time. But not with Olivia. Not in years.

But this wasn't the same Olivia. He'd been able to manage that one. To a point. But then he'd been a thirteen-year-old boy, oblivious when not actively hostile to females.

"It's my one and only, my very last chance for an adventure," she said. "The family is sick to death of my carryings on, and Grandmama and Grandpapa Hargate are insisting I marry. When *they* start insisting, one might as well give up fighting. You know how they like to have everybody wed and settled. I shall have to settle on somebody and settle down and be a wife and mother. Settle, settle, settle. I shall never have a chance to do anything interesting, ever again."

He remembered how fearless she'd been, setting out on her own . . . climbing into wagons . . . luring a pair of grooms into a card game. He thought about her life now, one party after another, where the mildest departure from propriety set the scandalmongers whispering behind their fans.

"Dammit, don't do this to me, Olivia," he said.

"You know it's true," she said. "Women lead narrow lives. We're somebody's daughters, then somebody's wives and somebody's mothers. We never *do* anything, not as men do."

He shook his head. "No," he said. "I will not let my parents coerce me."

"You don't have a choice," she said. "You've always been able to ignore them or get around them, but they've finally realized they have one powerful hold over you."

"And you're playing into their hands," he said. "Have you any idea what's involved in rebuilding an old castle?"

"I have an excellent idea," she said.

"It could take years. *Years!* In *Scotland.* With the *bagpipes!*"

She smiled. "It won't take years if I help you," she said. "And it won't hurt to let your parents think they've won one battle. If we play this game properly, you'll be back in Egypt in—oh, by spring, very likely."

The smile was enough to make him yield. But the guardian voice that had kept him alive all these years said *Wait. Think.*

It was very hard to think when the full power of those blue eyes was turned upon him, and things were stabbing at his heart.

Yet he wasn't altogether bewitched. He was still the stubborn boy who'd known her long ago, as well as the scholar, the detached observer who'd watched her in action recently. He knew she could make people, especially men, believe anything.

"No," he said as gently as he could. "If I let them control me this way, they'll use it again and again. If I give in to this demand, they'll make more."

Her smile didn't falter. "Ah, well, if you won't agree, you won't," she said cheerfully.

"I knew you'd understand."

"Oh, I *do*. Absolutely."

"Good, because—"

"You needn't explain," she said. "I understand *completely*. But I can't stay. I've a great deal to do today."

She touched her crop to the brim of her hat and galloped away.

Chapter Four

*L*isle should have realized.

He should have been prepared.

But of course that was out of the question in anything involving Olivia.

Olivia. Suddenly. Unexpectedly.

The three words engraved in his mind.

He came down to breakfast, and there she was.

Not only Olivia, either. She'd brought along the dowager Lady Hargate and two of the Harpies, Lady Cooper and Lady Withcote.

Lisle hadn't slept well. In the quiet of his club he'd come up with any number of schemes for dealing with his parents, but each proved fatally flawed. Then Lord Winterton turned up. Their paths had crossed in Egypt more than once, and they had a great deal to talk about. Winterton invited Lisle to his house to examine a fine set of papyri he'd brought back from his latest trip. The papyri were a welcome distraction from Lisle's parents and Olivia, and the cool-headed Winterton made an agreeable antidote to all the emotional turmoil. Lisle accepted an invitation to dine, and time slipped away.

As a result, he had no more idea this morning how to deal with his parents than he'd had yesterday when Olivia galloped away.

Everyone beamed at him as he entered the breakfast room.

Lisle prided himself on having no imagination. He didn't believe in a sense of impending doom.

Until now.

He went to the sideboard and filled his plate. He walked to the table and sat down next to Lady Withcote and opposite Olivia.

"Olivia has been telling us of your plan," said Mother.

Lisle's insides went cold. "My plan," he repeated. He looked at Olivia.

"To take me to Scotland to help you with the castle," she said.

"*What?*"

"I thought you would have told them already," she said. "I'm sorry I spoiled the surprise."

"Everyone understands, child, I'm sure," said the dowager. "You were carried away with excitement and couldn't wait."

"*What?*"

"It was a surprise, indeed," said Mother. "And I will confess I was not altogether enthusiastic at first."

"But—"

"She thought it wasn't the thing," the dowager told Lisle. "A pair of young people setting out for Scotland together. Not at all suitable for a young lady, she said. As though we didn't know that and hadn't already worked it out."

"Worked out—"

"Lady Cooper and Lady Withcote have kindly agreed to act as chaperons," Olivia said. "We'll each take our lady's maids. Great-Grandmama has agreed to lend us some housemaids and footmen until we can hire permanent ones. And I shall borrow Mama's cook and butler, since they won't be needed while the family is in Derbyshire."

Lisle looked about him at the cheerful faces. She'd done it. She'd gone ahead and done it after he'd told her in no uncertain terms. . .

No, this was a nightmare. He wasn't awake.

Were his parents blind? Was he the only one who noticed how suspiciously well the dowager was behaving? Did no one else see the evil gleam in her eye? No, they saw nothing, because Olivia had completely bamboozled everybody.

It was mad, mad.

Cooper and Withcote as chaperons! Like all of the dowager's friends, they lived to gossip, drink, gamble, and ogle young men. There couldn't exist more unsuitable chaperons outside of a brothel.

This was absurd. He would have to bring everybody to their senses.

"Olivia, I thought I made it clear—"

"But you *did*," she said, all wide-eyed innocence. "I

understand *completely*. If I had a calling, as you do, only a matter of life and death could distract me from it. Your calling is ancient Egypt. A Scottish castle does not seize your imagination."

"I have no imagination," he said. "I see what's there and not what isn't."

"Yes, I know, and that would make it *excruciating* for you to try to discover the beauty in a ruined castle," she said. "What you need is an expert eye, and an imagination. I shall supply them, while you supply the practical side of things."

"I'm so sorry I didn't understand the difficulties, my dear," said Mother. "As Olivia said, sending you alone would be like sending a soldier into battle with a rifle but no ammunition."

He looked at his father, who smiled indulgently back at him. Indulgent! Father!

And why not? Olivia had merely done to his parents what she did to everybody: She'd made them *believe*.

"It's a brilliant solution," his lordship said. "You'll be there to protect the ladies from any dreadful things that may be lurking about the place, and to get to the bottom of whatever has set off the unfortunate series of events."

"And Olivia will be there to protect you from decorating," Mother said. She laughed. They all laughed.

"Ha-ha," said Lisle. "I find I'm too excited to eat my breakfast. I think I'll take a turn in the garden. Olivia, would you care to join me?"

"I should like nothing better," she said, all glowing guilelessness.

In the garden
Ten minutes later

Lisle loomed over Olivia, his grey eyes as hard as flint.

"Have you lost your mind?" he said. "Weren't you listening to me yesterday? Are you becoming like my parents, hearing only the voices in your head?"

To be compared to his insane parents was infuriating. Nonetheless, Olivia maintained her cheerfully innocent expression, and didn't kick him in the shins.

"Of course I was listening," she said. "That's how I realized you were completely irrational about the subject, and I would have to take desperate measures to save you from yourself."

"I?" he said. "I'm not the one who needs saving. I know exactly what I'm doing and why. I told you we couldn't give in to them."

"You don't have a choice," she said.

"There are always choices," he said. "I only need time to ascertain what they are. You didn't even give me time to think about it!"

"You don't have time," she said. "If you don't take control of the situation now, they'll raise the stakes. You don't understand them. You don't know how they think. I do." That was what DeLuceys did and that was how they survived. They looked into others' hearts and minds and used what they found there. "For once, you need to trust my judgment."

"You have no judgment," he said. "You don't know what you want. You're feeling stifled here, and my parents have offered an opportunity for excitement. That's all you're thinking about. I saw the gleam in your eye when I first told you about our haunted castle. I could practically hear what you were thinking. Ghosts. A mystery. Danger. To you it's an adventure. You told me so. But it's no adventure to me."

"Because it isn't Egypt," she said. "Because nothing but Egypt can be interesting or important."

"That isn't—"

"And because you're obstinate," she said. "Because you won't open your mind to the possibilities. Because you want to fight, as usual, instead of finding a way to make the best of the opportunity. You're not an opportunist, I know. That's my specialty. Why can't you see that the cleverest thing to do is to pool our resources?"

"I don't care about being clever!" he said. "This isn't a game to me."

"Is that what you think? That it's a game to me?"

"Everything is," he said. "I spoke to you yesterday in confidence. I thought you understood. But it's merely sport to you, playing people as though they were cards."

"I did it for your sake, you thickheaded man!"

But he was too busy being all hurt and indignant to listen to anything she said.

He went on as though she hadn't spoken, "You've played well, I'll admit. You've shown me you can manage even my parents and make them fall in with your ridiculous schemes. But I'm not them. I know you. I know your tricks. And I won't have my life upended because you're bored with yours!"

"That is one of the most detestable, hurtful, will-fully obtuse things you've ever said to me," she said. "You're acting like a complete idiot, and idiots bore me. Go to the devil." She gave him a hard shove.

He wasn't expecting it. He stumbled and lost his balance and fell backward into the shrubbery.

"Moron," she said, and stormed away.

White's Club
Shortly after midnight

Lisle had spent the day trying to wear out his rage by boxing, fencing, riding hard, and, in desperation, firing at targets in a shooting gallery.

He still wanted to kill somebody.

He was sitting in the card room, eyeing the occupants over the rim of his glass and debating which one was worth picking a fight with, when a deferential voice at his shoulder said, "I apologize for disturbing your lordship, but a message has come."

Lisle looked around. The servant placed a silver tray on the table at his elbow.

The folded and sealed notepaper bore his name. Although, thanks to a bottle or two, he was not as clear-headed as he'd been when he arrived, he had no trouble identifying the penmanship.

Moreover, it wanted no special mental gifts to ascertain that a message from Olivia after midnight could not contain news he'd enjoy.

He tore open the note.

Ormont House
Friday 7 October

My Lord,

Having waited <u>In Vain</u> all day for an APOLOGY, I can wait <u>no longer</u>. I shall leave it to <u>you</u> to Explain to Lord and Lady Atherton your <u>Absurd Refusal</u> to do what will make <u>EVERYBODY happy</u>. My Arrangements are <u>made</u>. My Bags are <u>packed</u>. The servants are ready for the Great Expedition. The Dear Ladies who have so <u>kindly</u> agreed to leave the Comforts of their Domiciles in order to accompany ~us~ me on this Noble Quest are Ready and <u>impatient</u> to set out.

If you deem yourself Abandoned, you have <u>only yourself</u> and your <u>base ingratitude</u> to thank for it. My Conscience is <u>Clear</u>. You have left me NO CHOICE.

By the time you read this, I shall be Gone.

Yours sincerely,
Olivia Carsington

"No," he said. "Not again."

On the Old North Road
An hour later

"I vow, it's been an age since I was in a traveling carriage," said Lady Withcote as the carriage stopped to pay the Kingsland Turnpike toll. "I'd altogether forgotten what a hard ride it is, especially over the paving stones."

"A hard ride, indeed," said Lady Cooper. "Put me in mind of my wedding night. What a jarring exercise that turned out to be. Almost put me off the business permanent."

"Always the way with the first husband," said Lady Withcote. "It's due to a girl being young and knowing no more than what goes where."

"And maybe she doesn't know even that," said Lady Cooper.

"As a consequence, she doesn't know how to train him," said Lady Withcote.

"And by the time she does know, he's past learning." Lady Cooper sighed.

Lady Withcote leaned toward Olivia, who shared the opposite seat with Bailey. "Still, it wasn't as bad as you'd think. Our parents chose the first one, and he'd be twice our age or more. But then it was good odds we'd be young widows. Being older and wiser, we knew better how to get what we liked the second time."

"Some of us did try the second husband first, before consenting to marry," said Lady Cooper.

"And there were those who never troubled with marrying a second time," said Lady Withcote.

Olivia knew they referred to Great-Grandmama. She'd been scrupulously faithful to her spouse. After he died, she wasn't faithful to anybody.

"Well, we're done with the paving stones for the present," she said cheerfully as the carriage jolted into motion again.

Even a luxurious, well-sprung traveling carriage like this was built for enduring rough roads and long journeys. It was not, as the town carriages were, built strictly for comfort. The wheels rattling over the stones made for a noisy as well as jarring ride.

For the last hour, the ladies had shouted over the noise of the carriage wheels on paving stones, and bounced in their seats. Olivia had shouted and bounced along with them. Her bottom was sore and her back was aching, though Shoreditch Church, from which the distance from London was measured, was only a mile and a quarter behind them.

But now the houses had thinned, and the road was smoother. The coach moved a degree faster, and the next mile passed more swiftly than the last. They passed through the Stamford Tollgate and climbed Stamford Hill. From the top, one was supposed to be able to see St. Paul's.

Olivia stood to put down the window panel. She leaned out and looked back, but the night was dark. She could see only the occasional faint glow of streetlamps and a bit more of a glow in the great houses where balls would continue for hours yet. The moon would not rise until after dawn, when it would be of no use at all, even if it hadn't been only a degree past new, the thinnest of sickles.

She raised the panel again, hooked it into place, and sank into her seat.

"Any sign of him?" said Lady Cooper.

"Oh, no, it's far too soon," Olivia said. "We'll be well upon our way by the time he catches up. Too far to turn back."

"It would be dreadful to have to turn back," said Lady Withcote.

"This is the most exciting thing we've done in ages."

"So dull, these modern times."

"Not like the old days."

"Oh, that was a time, my dear," said Lady Cooper. "I wish you could have known what it was like."

"The men dressed so beautifully," said Lady Withcote.

"Peacocks, they were, truly."

"But for all their fine silks and lace, they were wilder and rougher than the present generation."

Lisle excepted, Olivia thought. But then, he'd grown up among the Carsington men, and they weren't tame, even the civilized ones.

"Remember when Eugenia quarreled with Lord Drayhew?" said Lady Cooper.

Lady Withcote nodded. "How could I forget? I was a newlywed then, and she was the most dashing of widows. He'd become too dictatorial, she said, and she wouldn't tolerate it. She bolted."

"He *hunted her down*," said Lady Cooper. "She'd gone to Lord Morden in Dorset. What a row there was when Drayhew found them!"

"The men fought a duel. It went on for an age."

"It was swords in those days."

"*Real* fighting. None of this twenty paces and shooting off a pistol. All that wants is aim."

"But a sword, now: That wants skill."

"The trouble was, the two gentlemen were equally deadly with the blades. They scratched each other well, but neither could finish the other and neither would yield."

"They finally collapsed, the two of them. Couldn't fight to the death but they fought to exhaustion."

"Those were the days." Lady Withcote let out a nostalgic sigh.

"Oh, they were, my dear. Men were men." Lady Cooper sighed, too.

Men would always be men, Olivia thought. The outer trappings changed, but their brains didn't.

"Never fear," she said. "We don't need men for excitement. With or without them, I know we'll have a great adventure."

Meanwhile in London

Lisle arrived at Ormont House as a carriage heaped with luggage and servants was making its way up the street.

With any luck, that would be the advance carriage, not the last one.

He didn't count on having any luck.

He paid the hackney driver, ran up the steps, and slammed the door knocker.

The dowager's butler, Dudley, opened the door. As his gaze took in Lisle, his blank expression soured into annoyance. Undoubtedly he was on the brink of summoning a footman to throw the intruder into the street.

Though the Earl of Lisle's other scrapes and bruises were fading quickly, his black eye had grown more colorful: green and red and purple and yellow. In his wild haste, he'd left his hat and gloves at the club. Nichols would never have let him out of the house in this condition, but Nichols had not been about to tend to him.

Wise and experienced butlers, however, did not leap to hasty conclusions. Dudley took a moment to better scrutinize the deranged male standing on the doorstep at an hour when drunkards, vagabonds, and house-breakers began their rounds.

The butler's face smoothed into the usual blank, and he said, "Good evening, Lord Lisle."

"Here already, is he?" came a cracked but clearly audible voice from behind the servant. "Send him in, send him in."

The butler bowed and stepped to one side. Lisle strode into the vestibule. He heard the door close behind him as he continued to the great entrance hall.

There stood the Dowager Countess of Hargate, leaning on her cane. She was dressed in an elaborately ruffled and laced silken robe of a style already long out of fashion when the Parisian mob stormed the Bastille.

She eyed him up and she eyed him down. "Looks like someone ruffled your feathers," she said.

She might be a thousand years old, and everyone in the family, including him, might be afraid of her, but the art of saying what he didn't mean didn't come naturally to him. At the moment, he had no patience with mannerly niceties.

"You've let her go," he said. "You must be completely besotted with that awful girl to let her do this."

She cackled, the wicked witch.

"When did she leave?" he said.

"At the stroke of midnight," she said. "You know Olivia. Loves her dramatic entrances and exits."

Midnight had struck more than an hour ago.

"This is mad," he said. "I cannot believe you let her

set out for Scotland on her own. In the dead of night, no less."

"Hardly the dead of night," said her ladyship. "The parties are only starting. And she's hardly on her own. She's got Agatha and Millicent with her, not to mention a brace of servants. I'll admit that the butler is a featherweight, but her cook weighs sixteen stone. She's taken half a dozen sturdy housemaids and another half dozen footmen with her as well, and you know I like big, good-looking fellows about me. Not that I can do much these days but admire the view."

Lisle's mind started down the path of wondering what she'd done to or with footmen before old age got the better of her. He hauled it back to Olivia. "A motley assortment of servants," he said. "Two eccentric old ladies. I know you dote on her and indulge her in everything, but this is beyond outrageous."

"Olivia can take care of herself," said her ladyship. "Everyone underestimates her, especially men."

"I don't."

"Don't you?"

He refused to let the unwavering hazel gaze disconcert him. "She's the wickedest girl who ever lived," he said. "She did this on purpose."

She knew he'd feel guilty and responsible, even though she was clearly in the wrong. She knew he couldn't tell his parents she'd gone to Gorewood without him, and he was staying home.

Staying home.

Possibly forever.

Home. Without Olivia to make it bearable, though she could be unbearable herself at times.

Curse her!

"I can't believe that there isn't one person in this family who can control her," he said. "Now I must turn my life upside down, drop everything, and race after her—in the middle of the night, no less—"

"No hurry," said the dowager. "Remember, she's got those two beldams with her. She'll be lucky to reach Hertfordshire before dawn."

Meanwhile on the Old North Road

Olivia had known that, traveling with an entourage, one couldn't match the speed of the Royal Mail. Still, when the dowager had said it would take a fortnight to reach Edinburgh, Olivia had thought she was joking, or referring to the last century.

She was revising her thinking.

She'd known they'd stop to change horses about every ten miles, and at shorter intervals during uphill stretches. While the best hostlers could change a team in two minutes, to accommodate the strict schedules of mail and stage, that didn't apply to her and her retinue.

Now it dawned on her that elderly ladies would require longer pauses at the posting inns. They'd disembark more often than mail or stagecoach travelers were allowed to do and spend more time, visiting the privy or walking about to stretch their legs or fortifying themselves with food and drink. Especially drink.

The ladies had made short work of the large basket Cook had prepared. Now empty, it rested on the carriage floor at Bailey's feet.

Looking on the bright side, though, one couldn't ask for more entertaining company for a long journey.

They traveled on, the two older women telling hair-raising stories about their younger days until, at last, at Waltham Cross, they reached Hertfordshire.

Given the easy pace, the same team probably could have taken them another ten miles, to Ware. But the coachman would stop here, at the Falcon Inn, to change horses. The Carsington family made the same stops, at the same posting inns, every time, the selection based on many years' traveling experience. On Olivia's copy of *Paterson's Roads*, the dowager had marked the stops and written down the names of favored inns.

"At last," said Lady Withcote as the carriage entered the courtyard.

"I'm perishing for a cup of tea," said Lady Cooper. She knocked on the roof with her umbrella. "I know we mustn't dawdle, dear. We won't be but a minute."

Olivia doubted that. She'd have to hurry them along. "I'll go with you," she said. "It's dead dark, the yard's poorly lit, and it's raining." She could hear it now, a patter on the carriage roof.

"Lud, child, we don't need a nursemaid to walk a few steps," Lady Cooper said indignantly. "I hope I'm not so decrepit as that."

"Certainly not," Olivia said. "But—"

"If we've been here once we've been here a thousand times," said Lady Withcote.

"I could find my way blindfolded and drunk," said Lady Cooper.

"You've done that," said Lady Withcote. "Coming home from one of Lady Jersey's breakfasts, as I recollect."

During this exchange, a servant opened the carriage door and put down the step. Unsteadily, the ladies descended.

"That was a *party*," said Lady Cooper. "Nothing like it nowadays. Only one paltry, dull affair after another."

"Nobody ever gets killed anymore."

The coach door closed, cutting off their voices. Watching from the window, Olivia soon lost sight of them. The rain turned them into a pair of dark shapes, Lady Cooper a trifle shorter and plumper than her friend, before the gloom absorbed them completely.

Olivia sank back into her seat.

Though, according to Mr. Paterson, they'd traveled only eleven and a half miles, it had taken nearly three hours. The bustle and excitement of their hasty departure was long behind them. With that distraction gone, the storm of anger and hurt returned.

That stupid, obstinate, ungrateful man.

She wished she'd pushed him harder. She wished she'd had her umbrella with her. She'd have enjoyed knocking it against his thick skull.

Well, she'd teach him to try those high-handed tactics with her. She'd thought he understood her—but no, he'd turned into a man, and he behaved the way they all did.

Minutes passed. Rain drummed on the roof and on the cobblestones, dulling the clatter of wheels and the clop of hooves. Even in the small hours of morning, on a dark, wet night, travelers came and went. Coaching inns never slept.

In spite of her temper—or perhaps worn out by it—she must have dozed, because her head jerked upright at the sound of voices outside the carriage.

The door opened. There stood the coachman and several other men, including two of her great-grand-mother's footmen, all holding umbrellas.

"If you please, miss," said the coachman. "A bad storm blowing in."

"It's very bad, miss," said the other man—the inn-keeper, apparently. "And getting worse by the minute. I urged the other ladies to wait until it blows over. I judge it won't be more than an hour or two."

A gust of wind wailed through the courtyard, trying to take the umbrellas with it. The drumming had swelled to a thunderous pounding.

Olivia was impatient to be off again. It was better to be far from London by the time Lisle caught up. All the same, whatever he thought of her judgment, she wasn't a reckless fool who'd risk the servants or the horses.

She and Bailey climbed down from the carriage and hurried into the inn.

Though the dowager seemed to think he'd easily catch up with Olivia, and though he'd spent a wearying day, Lisle did not go to bed and take a few hours to rest, like the sensible gentleman he was.

Instead, as soon as he returned home, he speedily bathed, changed his clothes, and ordered his valet to pack. Nichols being accustomed to hasty departures, they were able to set out from London by half-past two o'clock in the morning.

A carriage followed, bearing trunks and valises and whatever household goods Nichols thought they'd need and could be collected on short notice.

That was how Lisle and his manservant came to be riding on the Old North Road, ten miles from London, when the wind gusted up, tearing over the countryside, and the great black clouds massing over his head gave way, and the rain went from drizzle to downpour to deluge in three and a half minutes.

Chapter Five

Olivia found her traveling companions already comfortably settled at a large table in a corner of the public dining room, food and drink before them. Other stranded travelers had gathered here as well. Some were drying off in front of the fire, others were at table, and still others were using the respite for a shave or boot cleaning.

She'd always liked stopping for a meal at a coaching inn. There one encountered so many different kinds of people, of all classes, unlike the beau monde, where they were all the same, and most of them were related.

Since her usual stops were never long enough, she would have happily joined the company here, if the short nap in the carriage had not made her aware of how deeply tired she was.

It usually wanted a week or more to prepare for a long journey like this one. She'd organized everything—for herself as well as the two ladies—in less than forty-eight hours. That left almost no time for sleep.

That was why, instead of joining the company, she

hired what the innkeeper claimed was the best bed-chamber in the house. She sank into the large, comfortable armchair placed before the fire.

Despite the warmth and quiet, her mind wouldn't still. It was a long time before the whirl of thoughts and feelings began to blur and she sank into forgetfulness. A moment later, it seemed, she felt the light touch of a hand on her arm, and jolted awake.

"I'm sorry to startle you, miss," said Bailey.

Her mind still thick, Olivia looked up. A crease had appeared between Bailey's sleek eyebrows. Not a good sign. Bailey didn't worry easily.

"The ladies," said Olivia. She stood up so abruptly that her head spun.

"Yes, miss. A row about a card game. I'm sorry to trouble you, but they've upset the local squire's son. He's making an ugly scene and calling for constables and magistrates, and nobody's putting him in his place. The innkeeper's afraid of him, it looks like. I thought you'd wish to take the ladies safe away."

While she spoke, Bailey was tidying Olivia's hair and shaking the wrinkles out of her skirts and otherwise concealing evidence of her mistress having slept in her clothes.

Aware they'd probably need to make a speedy exit from the inn, she contrived to get Olivia into most of her outer garments while they hurried along the corridor. At the top of the stairs, the raised voices were plainly audible. Olivia raced down and into the public dining room.

That was when she realized she'd spent more time with her unquiet mind than she'd supposed. Not only had the rain stopped but grey daylight illuminated the scene outside of the windows. The dining room was a-bustle. The rain must have delayed a number of travelers, and they were all hungry. Those eager to be on their way hastily swallowed their food and departed. Even so, the room was more crowded than it had been a few hours earlier. Busy servants rushed in and out, carrying trays.

Meanwhile, one male voice continued shouting, and the mood of the room was growing ugly. The innkeeper having failed to take charge, a fracas was brewing.

Normally Olivia wouldn't have minded. A melee could be exciting. The trouble was, it usually led to authorities being summoned. That would mean a long delay, which she preferred to avoid.

All this went through her mind while she sized up the source of the disturbance.

A stout sandy-haired young man, who must have been drinking all night, was pounding on the table where Olivia had last left the ladies. By the looks of the table, they'd emptied mine host's wine cellar as well as his larder and his guests' pockets.

"You cheated!" the drunkard shouted. "I saw you do it!"

Lady Cooper rose from her chair. "If there's anything I can't abide," she said, "it's a sore loser. Cheating, indeed."

"Now, now, Mr. Flood, sir," said the innkeeper. "It's only a little game—"

"Little game! This pair robbed me of fifty pounds!"

"Robbed you, indeed," said Lady Withcote. "It's not our fault you can't hold your liquor."

"And can't see straight," said Lady Cooper. "And can't tell a knave from a king."

"Not our doing," said Lady Withcote, "if your mind's too muddled to remember the cards in your own hand."

"I saw well enough to see you cheat, you thieving old hags!"

"Hags?" shrieked Lady Withcote.

"I'll hag you, you sotted moron," said Lady Cooper. "Why, was I a man—"

"Was you a man, I'd knock you down!" the young man shouted.

Olivia pushed her way through the crowd.

"Ladies, come away," she said. "The man is obviously out of his senses, else he wouldn't behave in this ungentlemanly manner, threatening harmless women."

Face red, the young drunkard whirled round toward her. He opened his mouth but nothing came out.

Olivia often had this effect on men seeing her for the first time. He was very drunk but not blind.

Taking advantage of his momentary distraction, she tried to herd the ladies out of the room.

To her annoyance, he recovered quickly.

"Oh, no, you don't!" he shouted. "They got me drunk and took advantage and robbed me, and they won't get away with it! I'm taking them to magistrate and I'll see them carted and flogged for it!" He picked up a chair and threw it at a wall. "I want my money!"

The threat did not alarm her. Any Dreadful DeLucey could make a magistrate putty in her hands. But Olivia was in no mood to beguile magistrates or waste time calming obstinate, obnoxious men.

She'd spent the last two days in a frenzy of preparation—all for the sake of a stubborn, rude, idiot male. She'd scarcely fallen asleep before being wakened on account of yet another obstinate, rude, idiot male.

She was tired and hungry and the man she'd considered her best friend had turned out to be exactly like every other thickheaded man.

"You, sir," she said, in the cold, clipped accents her stepfather used to crush upstarts and ignoramuses. "You have insulted these ladies. You will apologize."

He paused in the act of picking up another chair. He set it down and stared at her. "*What?*"

The onlookers' grumbling and muttering subsided.

"Apologize," she said.

He laughed. "To them battle-axes?" He jerked a dirty thumb at her companions. "Are you daft?"

"Then choose your weapon," she said.

"*What?*"

"Choose," she said. "Pistols or swords."

He looked about the room. "Is this a joke? Because I won't be made a fool of."

She stripped off her gloves, walked up to him, and slapped him with one of them. "Coward," she said.

A collective gasp.

She stepped back a pace while surreptitiously taking note of her surroundings: escape routes, obstacles, and possible weapons.

"Your behavior is despicable," she said. "You are contemptible."

"Why you—"

He lunged at her. She grabbed a coffeepot from the table at her right and swung it against his head.

Then matters grew lively, indeed.

*   *   *

While the storm raged, Lisle had had to take shelter at an inn in Enfield, more than a mile down the road.

By the time he rode into the courtyard of the Falcon Inn, the sun was well up. He expected the inn yard to be bustling with stranded travelers eager to be on their way. What he found was a lot of people milling about near the door to the dining room, all of them straining, apparently, to see what was going on inside.

He dismounted, leaving Nichols to deal with the horses, and started toward the door.

"What is it?" he heard somebody say.

"Squire's son, drunk again, and raging about something," someone answered.

"Nothing new in that."

"This time a redheaded female's raking him over the coals."

Lisle hurried into the dining room in time to hear Olivia insult somebody. He thrust through the crowd, but he wasn't quick enough. He saw—and heard—her slap an obviously drunk young man with her glove.

Thanks to a gawking onlooker getting in the way, Lisle hadn't time to tackle the drunkard before the man went for her. Olivia hit him with a coffeepot, and he went down. A servant carrying a tray tripped over him and knocked over a guest in the process. Some people ran to the doors, and a few climbed onto chairs and tables, but the majority crowded close to the center of the fray.

While Lisle was clearing a path to Olivia, he caught sight of Bailey. Unlike everyone else, the maid kept her head, calmly gathering the two old ladies and shooing them toward the courtyard.

Olivia's voice called his attention back.

"You are a disgrace to your entire benighted sex," he heard her say in the icy tones she must have learned from Rathbourne.

The dazed drunkard lay where he'd fallen, blinking up at her.

Now was the time for her to make herself scarce.

But no.

"A gentleman takes his lumps and learns from them," she raged on. "But you—picking on *women*. You ought to be ashamed, you great, drunken bully. It's a pity there's no one about man enough to give you a proper thrashing."

"You tell 'im, miss!" someone shouted from the safety of the back of the room.

"Always throwin' his weight around."

"No one touches him 'cuz he's squire's son."

They were eager for a brawl. Normally, Lisle would enjoy joining in. He'd take great pleasure in giving this jackass a thrashing he wouldn't forget.

But brawls were unpredictable things, and Olivia in one of her temper fits was unpredictable, too. He couldn't trust her not to get killed.

He tapped her on the shoulder. She threw an impatient glance back at him—a furious flash of blue—before reverting to her tirade.

Lisle couldn't be sure—given the state she was in—that she'd even recognized him. And given the state she was in, there was only one thing to do.

He came up close behind her, looped his arm over

her right shoulder and across and down under her left arm, thrust his hip into the small of her back to take her off balance, and dragged her away. She struggled, but the awkward angle of her body left her no leverage at all. She could only stumble back whither he towed her, cursing him all the while.

"I'm not done with him, devil take you! I'm not going! Let me go!"

"Stifle it," he said. "We have to get out of here before the village constable comes and people find out who you are and you end up in the newspapers again."

"Lisle?"

"Who else?"

An instant's silence, then, "No!" she shrieked. "Take your hands off me! I'm not done with him, the great, drunken thickhead!" She tried to kick backward, but he kept his legs out of danger as he pulled her over the cobblestones toward the coach.

"If you don't settle down, I vow, I'll knock you unconscious, tie and gag you, and take you straight to Derbyshire," he said.

"Oooh, you're so big and strong. I'm so afraid."

"Or maybe I'll leave you trussed by the side of the road."

The innkeeper, who'd followed them out, ran ahead to open the coach door before the footman could do it. Lisle pushed her up the step. She stumbled into the vehicle, and her maid caught her. He slammed the door shut.

"Away," he told the coachman. "I'll be right behind you."

He watched the carriage rattle out of the courtyard.

"Thank 'ee, sir," said the innkeeper. "Best to have the ladies out of the way in a case like this. Out of sight, out of mind, I always say."

Lisle thrust a bag of coins into his hand. "Sorry about the mess," he said.

He quickly found his horse and Nichols. A few minutes later, he was upon the Old North Road once again.

She was going to kill him.

Unless he killed her first.

Ware, Hertfordshire
Twenty-one miles from London

Declaring themselves famished, the ladies Cooper and Withcote disembarked and hurried into the Saracen's Head for breakfast.

Olivia sent Bailey in with them, but remained in the carriage, trying to collect herself. She needed a cool head to think, to deal with Lisle.

Between the exhaustion and the annoyance of realizing she'd miscalculated, cool thinking was difficult. It hadn't helped to hear the two ladies, dear as they were, prattling on. They'd seen Lisle throw somebody out of his way, and that was the most thrilling thing they'd seen in years. They wouldn't stop talking about it and speculating in their usual bawdy way about his muscles and stamina and such.

Their comments brought back the warm pressure of his powerful arm across her body. She could practically *feel* it still, as though he'd left an imprint, curse him.

Never mind. He was a man being excessively manly, and it was thrilling, but she'd recover.

And being Lisle, naturally, he had to be aggravating and turn up more quickly than she'd expected.

She'd known he'd follow. He saw himself as her big brother, and he was protective by nature. Furthermore, like every other male, he believed he was infinitely more rational and capable than any woman. No man could trust a woman to take charge of anything except a household and children—and among the upper orders, women were barely trusted with those departments.

Even her mother, who was not at all blind to her faults, would know Olivia was more than qualified to undertake both a long journey and the restoration of a property. Not that she'd intended to do it alone—but she *could*.

Well, then, all was going according to plan, except for the unforeseen to-do at the Falcon Inn. Which she'd quite enjoyed. The look on the bully's face when she'd slapped him with her glove was priceless.

But then Lisle had come and dragged her away and—

The carriage door opened.

There he stood, looking up at her, a rainbow of colors ringing one silver-grey eye.

"You'd better come in and eat breakfast now," he said. "We won't stop to eat again until midday."

"*We?*" she said. "You weren't coming. You would rather live like a pauper in Egypt or die of starvation than yield to your parents. You have decided that journeying to Scotland is a fate worse than death."

"Traveling with you, it's going to be even more fateful, I daresay," he said. "Do you want to eat or not? It'll be hours before you get another chance."

"You are not in charge of this journey," she said.

"Now I am," he said. "You were determined to make me do this. Now you'll have to do it my way. Eat or starve, it's your choice. I'm going to look at the famous bed."

Leaving the carriage door open, he turned away and sauntered back into the inn.

Olivia burst into the bedchamber ten minutes later.

"You," she began. But even in one of her blind rages, she could hardly miss the bed, and it stopped her dead. "Good grief!" she said. "It's enormous."

Lisle casually looked up from his examination of one of the bedposts at the head.

Her bonnet was askew and her hair was coming loose, red curls tumbling against her pearly skin. Her clothes were rumpled from traveling. Anger still sparked in the impossibly blue eyes, though they'd widened at the sight of the bed that had been famous in Shakespeare's time.

She looked wild, and though he ought to be used to that shatteringly beautiful face by now, the wildness threw him off balance again, and his heartbeat was sharp and painful.

"That's why it's called the Great Bed of Ware," he said calmly. "You've never seen it before?"

She shook her head, and the curls danced madly.

"Quite old—by English standards, at any rate," he said. "Shakespeare refers to it in *Twelfth Night*."

"I've seen this style of thing," she said. "Tons of oak,

carved within an inch of its life. But nothing nearly as large."

It was, indeed, carved with dizzying exuberance. Flowers and fruits and animals and people and mythological beings covered every inch of the black oak.

"Twelve feet square and nine feet tall," he said. Facts were always safe and soothing. "It's a room, really, enclosed by curtains. Look at the panels."

She stepped nearer.

He caught her scent and remembered the feel of her body under his hands, when he'd pulled her out of the inn.

Facts. He focused on the physical features of the bed. Inside carved arches, two panels portrayed scenes of the town, including its famous swans. He lightly ran his index finger over their inlaid wood.

It lacked the grace of Egyptian art. To his surprise, though, he found it enchanting.

"They're like windows, you see," he said. "It was meant to entertain. It must have been even more eye-catching when it was new. Here and there you can see bits of paint. In its early days, it would have been quite colorful—like the temples and tombs of Egypt. And the same as in Egypt, visitors have left their marks." He traced a set of initials. "Seals, too."

He let his gaze return to her face. Wonder filled it now. The rage was gone, the storm blown over, because she was enchanted as well. She was sophisticated and cunning and had never been naïve. Yet her imagination was boundless, and she could be captivated, like a child.

"How odd that you've never seen it before," he said.

She examined a lion's head with a red seal on its nose. "Not at all odd," she said. "Since we're usually traveling to Derbyshire or Cheshire, we don't take this road. And when I leave London, it's because I'm in disgrace, which means getting me out and far away as quickly as possible. No time for sightseeing."

He looked away from her face. Too much of that and he'd grow addlepated. He studied one of the satyrs adorning a bedpost. "Slapping that drunkard with your glove and calling him a coward wasn't the cleverest thing you've ever done."

"But it was immensely satisfying."

"You lost your temper," he said. When she lost her temper, he couldn't trust her brain or her instincts. He couldn't trust her to take care of herself.

He came away from the bedpost and folded his hands behind his back. "What did your mother tell you about losing your temper?" he said, in the same patient tone he'd heard her mother employ on the day he'd met Olivia.

She narrowed her eyes at him. "I must count to twenty."

"I think you didn't count to twenty," he said.

"I wasn't in the mood," she said.

"I'm amazed you didn't treat him to one of your apologies." Putting a hand to his heart, he said in falsetto, " 'Oh, sir, I do most humbly and abjectly beg your pardon.' Then you could flutter your eyelashes at him, and fall to your knees."

She'd done this the first time they'd met, and the performance had left him dumbstruck.

"By the time you were done," he went on, "everyone

would be weeping—or reeling. Including him. And you could slip out quietly."

"I'm sorry now I didn't," she said. "It would have prevented my being manhandled out of the inn."

It would have prevented his feeling her supple body under his arm.

"I don't see why you didn't drag *him* out—to the courtyard—and put his head under the pump," she said. "That's what someone ought to have done when the trouble started. But everyone was afraid of him. Not you, I'd think—but you had to get all manly and overbearing with *me*."

"It was more fun dragging you out," he said.

She drew nearer and examined his eye.

Her scent swarmed about him and his heart was racing.

"That Belder," she said, shaking her head. "Why didn't he hit you *harder*?"

She swept out of the room.

The day was cool and grey, and the rain had laid the dust. The ladies wanted fresh air, they said. Riding in a gloomy, stuffy carriage wasn't their idea of agreeable travel.

Olivia suspected that the reason they wanted the louvered window panels open was to admire the masculine scenery nearby.

It was fine scenery, and she couldn't help enjoying it, too, though Lisle had turned out to be a Tragic Disappointment.

He rode alongside, practically at her shoulder, keeping pace with the carriage, instead of riding on ahead as she'd expected him to do. Their carriage's speed, in consideration of the ladies' old bones, was slower than Lisle could like. It was slower than Olivia liked, certainly. She wished she were riding as well, but she hadn't thought she would, and hadn't arranged for it.

Her saddle was packed away in one of the carriages with their other belongings, and packed deep. She hadn't believed she'd need it until they reached their destination. While one could hire horses at the posting inns, and she could ride virtually any sort of horse without difficulty, a saddle was an altogether different article. A lady's saddle was as personal an item as her corset, and made to fit her precisely.

Not that she needed a saddle. She was Jack Wingate's daughter, after all, and as easy on a horse's back as any gypsy.

But no one was to know she still did that sort of thing. No one was to know about the men's clothes that Bailey had adapted to fit her, which lay neatly folded in a box among her other belongings.

She recalled how shocked Lisle had been the first time he'd seen her in boy's clothes. She was remembering that moment—How could she forget the comical look on his face?—when the coach stopped.

The carriage bounced slightly as the footmen jumped down from their perch at the back. She saw one hurry ahead to hold the horses.

"What is it?" said Lady Cooper.

"Lisle noticed something wrong with one of the wheels, I daresay," said Lady Withcote.

The door opened and a footman put down the step. Lisle waited behind him. "No need to disturb yourselves, ladies," Lisle said. "I only want Olivia."

The ladies smiled at her.

"He only wants you," said Lady Cooper.

"He said he'd leave me by the side of the road," Olivia said.

"Don't be silly," said Lady Withcote. "He'll do nothing of the kind."

He'd do worse, Olivia thought. He'd had time to brood over the grievous injury she'd done his pride. By now he'd probably composed a very boring and irritating lecture.

"We're not scheduled to stop," she told him. "Not until—" She glanced down at her *Paterson's*. "Not until Buntingford."

"I want to show you something," he said.

She leaned forward and looked out of the door to her right, then to her left. "There's nothing to see," she said.

Except an excessively handsome man sitting as easily upon a hired horse as if it had been part of him.

"Don't be tiresome," he said.

"Lud, don't be tiresome, child," said Lady Cooper. "Let the boy show you his what's-it."

"I could do with a pause," said Lady Withcote. "I should like a moment to close my eyes, without being jounced and jostled. Such a head I have. Must have been something I ate."

Olivia turned away from the door to look at them.

"Don't you want to see what it is he wants to show you?" Lady Cooper said.

Olivia disembarked.

The ladies leaned forward to watch the proceedings through the open door.

Olivia walked up to him. She stroked his horse's muzzle, while aware, out of the corner of her eye, of the muscled leg nearby.

"You said you never get to see the sights," he said. "There's one down that turning on the left."

A little surprised, she looked at the signpost he indicated. Then she looked up at him.

"I'm not going to take you to a desolate place and murder you," he said. "Not here and now, at any rate. Were I to take you away and return without you, the ladies might notice. Bailey would, certainly. We're going only a short distance. We could easily walk, but these country lanes will be knee deep in mud. You can ride Nichols's horse."

She held up her hand before Nichols could dismount. "No, stay as you are. I can ride behind his lordship."

"No, you can't," Lisle said.

"We're going a short distance, you said," she said. "It makes no sense to spend time making a dozen adjustments, to get me properly seated on Nichols's horse—adjustments he'll have to go to all the bother of readjusting later. I can be up behind you in a minute."

He looked at her. He looked at Nichols.

Despite having been caught in a downpour, the valet remained elegant and unflappable. Though he wouldn't show it, he'd die a thousand deaths on the inside, rearranging his saddle for her. She saw no reason to torture him. *He* hadn't insulted and hurt her.

"What worries you?" she said to Lisle. "Are you afraid I'll knock you off your horse?"

"I'm a little afraid you'll stick a knife in my back," he said. "Swear to me that you're not armed."

"Don't be absurd," she said. "I would never stab you in the back. That would be dishonorable. I would stab you in the neck or in the heart."

"Very well, then." He kicked his left foot free of the stirrup. Olivia put her left foot into the stirrup, took hold of his arm, gave a hop, and sprang up behind him.

"Deuce take the girl!" Lady Withcote cried. "I never could do that!"

"You were agile in other ways, Millicent," said her friend.

Meanwhile, Olivia realized she'd made a grave error of judgment.

Chapter Six

She'd acted unthinkingly, and why not?

Olivia was as much at ease on a horse as any gypsy.

She'd ridden behind her father time without number.

But that was her father, and that was when she was a little girl.

Lisle wasn't her father. She'd ridden behind him once or twice, but that was ages ago, before he'd become so excessively masculine.

It hadn't dawned on her to cling to his coat. She'd simply wrapped her arms about his waist, because that was the natural thing to do.

Now she was hotly aware of the taut waist under her arms and the straight back against her breasts. She was aware of thigh touching thigh and leg touching leg and the rhythmic movement of their bodies as the horse walked along the muddy, rutted road.

She could actually feel her moral fiber—such as it was—disintegrating.

Ah, well, it was only a short ride, and she could expect a long, boring lecture at the end of it. That would stifle inconvenient and pointless urges.

She let her cheek rest against Lisle's neck and inhaled the earthy scent of male and horse and country air and recent rain, and somewhere in this mix, tantalizingly faint, a hint of shaving soap.

After a moment he said, "In what ways was Millicent agile, I wonder?"

"Nothing nearly as exotic as you imagine," she said. "Nothing like your harem dancers, I daresay. Not nearly so acrobatic."

"In the first place, I don't *imagine*," he said. "In the second, if you're referring to the dancing girls, they're not, technically, harem dancers."

Oh, good, a language lecture. That would take her mind off the rampant virility and the male scent, which ought to be bottled and marked with a skull and crossbones.

"The word *harem,* you see, commonly refers to the women of a household," he said, "though this is not the precise meaning of the word, which denotes a sacred or forbidden place. The dancing girls, on the other hand—"

"I thought we were to take the left turning," she said.

"Oh. Yes." He turned back to the lane.

Not a moment too soon. It might have been the way he smelled or the heat of his body or all that virility or, more likely, the devastating combination, but she'd found herself growing genuinely interested in the correct meaning of *harem*.

Moments later they entered a meadow and proceeded to a small railed area guarding what appeared to be a block of stone.

"There it is," he said.

As they neared, she saw the metal plaque set into the stone.

"A rock," she said. "You've stopped the carriage and taken me to see a rock."

"It's the Balloon Stone," he said. "The first balloon ascent in England landed here."

"Did it, really?"

"There's a prior claim, but—"

"Oh, I must see."

Eager to get down and away from him and get her head clear again, she didn't hesitate. She set one hand on the back of the saddle and one on his thigh, preparatory to dismount. She felt it instantly, the shock of that intimate touch, but it was too late to stop—and absurd to do so. This was the quickest and easiest way to get down.

She swung her leg over the horse's rump, aware of the pressure of Lisle's hand over hers . . . on his thigh . . . holding her steady. Heart racing, she slid down to the ground.

She didn't wait for him to dismount but moved quickly to the railing, hiked up her skirts, and climbed over it into the small enclosure.

She knew she'd given him a prime view of her petticoats and stockings. She knew what such a sight did to a man. But he'd got her agitated in that way. Turnabout was fair play.

" 'Let Posterity Know,' " she read aloud in the declamatory tone usually employed on state occasions, " 'And Knowing be Astonished That On the 15 Day of September 1784 Vincent Lunardi of Lucca in Tuscany The first Aerial Traveller in Britain Mounting from the Artillery Ground in London and Traversing the Regions of the Air For Two Hours and Fifteen Minutes, In this Spot Revisited the Earth.' "

Lisle remained at the railing. He still hadn't recovered from the ride: Olivia's arms wrapped about his waist, her satanic breasts pressed against his back, and her legs tucked up behind his. Physical awareness still vibrated the length of his body, particularly where it had met the front of the saddle.

She'd got him so befuddled that he'd ridden straight past the turning.

He hadn't had time to fully collect his wits before she climbed over the fence, offering him an excellent view of her petticoats and stockings.

It was her typical hoydenish behavior, the same she'd exhibited when they'd been together in the past. She thought of him as a brother. That was why she didn't mind her skirts and that was why she hadn't hesitated to climb up on his horse behind him.

But he wasn't her brother and he wasn't the boy he'd used to be, deaf, dumb, and blind to a flurry of feminine undergarments. Not to mention that in girlhood she wouldn't have worn stockings like those, with their alluring blue embroidery, or petticoats trimmed in excessively feminine lace. And in those days, she hadn't owned shapely legs and splendidly turned ankles—or if she had, he hadn't noticed.

After he'd got these matters sorted out and his reproductive organs calmed down and his mind functioning again, he stepped over the fence to stand beside her as she finished reading the ornate tribute to the first balloon ascension in England.

At the end she looked at him and said, "Isn't it amazing? This quiet meadow saw such a momentous event. How wonderful that they've marked the spot."

"You said you never got to see the sights," he said. And as vexed as he'd been—and still was—he'd felt sorry for her. When he was a boy, her stepfather had often taken him along on journeys. Lord Rathbourne had always taken the time to point out the sights and tell stories about them, especially the bloodcurdling stories boys liked, about grisly murders and ghosts and such.

It seemed odd and unfair that a girl with such a vivid imagination, who craved change and excitement, had had so little opportunity of sightseeing.

"I knew nothing about it," she said. "Only imagine. Nearly fifty years ago. What must the people living here have thought when they saw it?"

"They were frightened," he said. "Suppose you'd been a villager of that time." He gazed up at the leaden sky. "You look up and suddenly appears a gigantic thing where only birds and clouds are supposed to appear."

"I don't know if I'd be frightened."

"Not you specifically," he said. "But if you'd been a villager, an ordinary person."

Which was inconceivable. The very last thing Olivia was was ordinary.

"I've always wanted to go up in a hot-air balloon," she said.

No surprise there.

"How thrilling it must be," she said, "to look down on all the world from a great height."

"Going up to the great height is all very well," he said. "Coming down is another story. Lunardi had no notion how to steer the thing. He brought along oars, thinking he could row through the air."

"But he tried," she said. "He had a vision, and he pursued it. A Noble Quest. And here's a stone marking the occasion, for all posterity, as it says."

"Do you not find the prose inflated?" he said. It was a dreadful pun, but he couldn't resist.

"*Inflated*. Oh, Lisle. That is—" She gave a snort of laughter, which she quickly stifled. "Abominable."

"He took with him a cat, a dog, a pigeon, and a hamper of provisions," he said. "The provisions I understand. The animals I do not. In any event, the pigeon soon escaped, and air travel disagreed with the cat, who was let off a short distance from London."

She laughed then, truly and fully, a velvety cascade of sound that startled him. It was nothing like the silvery laughter so many women affected. It was low and throaty, a smoky sound that slid down his spine.

It stirred dangerous images—of bed curtains moving in a breeze, and tumbled bedclothes—and it disarmed him at the same time. He smiled stupidly at her.

"A good thing, too," she said. "Can't you picture it? The basket of a hot air balloon—the small space crammed with provisions and oars and instruments and such, and the cat, the dog, and the pigeon. And there's the cat, being sick on the floor. I can see the look on Lunardi's face. How he must have wanted to pitch the dratted cat over the side! I wonder if he touched ground when he let it off."

"Really, Olivia, you know I have no imagi—" Then he snorted, too, and in a moment he was laughing as well, helplessly, at the pictures she made in his head.

For a moment, all his grievances and frustrations vanished, and he was a carefree boy again. He leaned back against the railing and laughed as he'd not done in an age.

Then he told her the tale of fourteen-stone Mrs. Letitia Sage, the first "British female air traveler," who went up in another balloon with Lunardi's friend Biggins.

Naturally, Olivia sketched out a scene: the basket rolling in the wind, and the large woman slipping downward across the floor, inexorably toward the terrified Biggins. In the nick of time, though, the winds shifted again, and Biggins escaped being flattened.

She didn't simply tell it; she acted it, complete with different voices for the various parts, including the animals.

Caught up in exchanging stories and laughing over them, they drew closer together. It was unthinking, so natural. It was as they would have done in the past.

He could have stayed there for a long, long time, forgetting his anger and resentment, and simply reveling in her company. He'd missed her, and that was an undeniable fact. He remembered the way the world had seemed to tip back into proper balance when she drew him into the antechamber that night—mere days ago—and said, "Tell me."

Of course, it hadn't taken her much time to unbalance his world again, to a spectacular degree, and he still wanted to kill her. But he was dazzled, too, and happy at this moment as he hadn't been for a long time.

He was in no hurry to leave, even when a sharp gust of wind struck like a slap in the face.

But she shivered, and he said, "We'd better get back."

She nodded, her gaze on the monument. "We've certainly given the ladies plenty of time to speculate about what, exactly, we've been doing."

"That pair," he said. "How the devil did you persuade my parents that they made suitable chaperons? Come to that, I can't guess how you persuaded everybody—"

"Lisle, you know perfectly well that it's against the DeLucey code to explain the cheat."

He studied her faintly smiling profile. "You did cheat, then," he said.

She turned to meet his gaze, her blue eyes seemingly guileless, seeming to hide nothing. "Every way I could think of. Are you still angry with me?"

"Furious," he said.

"I'm furious with you, too," she said. "But I shall put that aside for the moment because you showed me your stone instead of subjecting me to a tedious lecture about morals and ethics and such."

"I don't lecture!" he said.

"All the time," she said. "Usually, I find it rather endearing, but today I was not in the mood. Since you restrained yourself, I'm prepared to kiss and make up. Metaphorically speaking. For the time being."

He realized that his gaze had slid to her mouth. He carefully turned his attention to her right ear, which seemed a safe object. But no. It was small and prettily shaped. A gold earring, with a lot of filigree surrounding a bit of jade, hung from it. He realized his head was bending closer to her.

He made himself look away entirely—at the Balloon Stone, the meadow, anywhere but at her. There was much too much femininity too close to him—and where the devil was that wind? It had died down as abruptly as it had risen, and now he could smell her.

He turned to tell her it was time to leave.

She turned her head and leaned in at the same moment.

Her mouth touched his.

A shock ran through him.

For one vibrating instant they simply stared at each other.

Then they jumped apart as though a bolt of lightning had struck the railing.

She rubbed hard at her mouth, as though an insect had landed there.

Heart pounding, he did the same.

It was no good rubbing at her mouth. Olivia knew she'd never rub it away: the firm, warm feel of his lips, the tantalizing hint of what he tasted like.

"You were not supposed to put your mouth in the way," she said.

"I was turning to speak to you," he said. "Your mouth shouldn't have been so close."

She clambered over the railing. "I said I was willing to kiss and make up *metaphorically*," she said.

"You kissed me!"

"It was meant to be a sisterly peck on the cheek."

She hoped that was what she meant. She hoped she'd meant something. She hoped she hadn't lost her mind.

"You're not my sister," he said in his usual pedantic fashion as he followed her out of the enclosure. "We are not related in any way. Your stepfather was at one time married to my father's sister."

"Thank you for the genealogy lesson," she said.

"The point is—"

"I won't do it again," she said. "You may be sure of that."

"The point is," he went on stubbornly, "men don't distinguish in such matters. When an attractive female is nearby and she seems to make an overture—"

"It wasn't an overture!"

"Seems," he said. "*Seems.* Do you never listen?"

"Right now I wish I were deaf."

"Women are subtle," he said. "They make fine distinctions. Men don't. Men are like dogs, and— Gad, why am I explaining this to you? You know precisely what men are like."

She'd thought she did.

They'd reached his horse. Olivia looked at it, then at him. "We'd better get back, before the ladies die of curiosity," she said. "You can continue the lecture while we return to the carriage."

"I am not getting on that animal again with you," he said.

She didn't want to get on with him again. The muscles and heat and male scent was poison to a woman's brain. She couldn't abide to turn stupid with any man, especially him.

He laced his hands together. "Up with you."

It was the only intelligent thing to do. All the same. . .

"The road's a foot deep in mud," she said. "You'll ruin your boots."

"I've other boots," he said. "Up."

She disguised her sigh of relief as a huff of irritation, took hold of the reins, and set her booted foot on his linked hands. She gave a little bounce, and up and into the saddle she went.

Brisk and businesslike, he helped her adjust the stirrups, then tugged her skirts down.

"Oh, for heaven's sake," she said.

"People can see everything," he said.

"How puritanical you've become," she said.

"You are abominably careless," he said, "showing all that—all that femininity to all the world."

Ah, well, then, it bothered him, did it?

Good. He'd bothered her.

She smiled, and with a soft cluck, signaled the mare to walk on.

The ladies were asleep when Olivia returned, and didn't wake when the carriage set out again.

While they snored, Olivia opened *Paterson's Roads* and, to while away the journey, read to Bailey the information about the towns and villages they passed, the names of the important personages who lived nearby, and descriptions of said personages' abodes.

A slowish drive uphill took them to the change at Buntingford. The road continued uphill to the next change, at Royston. After that, the horses' pace increased, as they crossed a stretch of galloping ground. They continued over the River Cam, and on to Arrington. Here they stopped at the Hardwicke Arms, to be greeted by the landlady herself, unsurprisingly. She'd recognized the dowager's traveling carriage and, like any other innkeeper on the king's highway, knew the crest was a sign that properly read: Money, Pots of It, Freely Spent.

At this stop, the ladies came wide awake. Declaring themselves parched and famished, they sprang from the carriage the instant the footman put down the steps.

Olivia was about to disembark when Lisle, on foot this time, came to the open door of the vehicle.

"I know you said you were taking charge, but we must stop to eat," she said. "We're all starved." Thanks to the furor at the Falcon Inn, she hadn't eaten breakfast there. At Ware, she'd been too aggravated to think of eating.

"I wasn't intending to starve you," he said. He offered his hand and she took it casually enough, ignoring the entirely unnecessary flurry within her, while she quickly climbed down the narrow steps. As soon as her feet were firmly on the ground she let go and started toward the inn.

She couldn't get ahead of him, though. His long strides easily caught up with hers.

"I should have stopped sooner, had you reminded me that you hadn't had time for breakfast," he said. "You'd better not rely on me to pay attention to such things. If I hadn't been hungry, I shouldn't have thought of food at all. In Egypt, when we travel, I don't think about meals, because the servants do. Moreover, we're usually traveling in the *dahabeeya*, with a cook and provisions and cooking facilities. We don't have to stop at inns for meals—not that there's much in the way of inns outside of Cairo. Sailing on the *dahabeeya* is like traveling in a house."

Images crowded her mind's eye, vivid enough to make her forget her inconvenient feelings. "How wonderful it must be," she said. "The graceful boat sailing up the Nile, the crew in white robes and turbans. Completely different from this." She waved a hand, taking in the courtyard. "You glide along the river. Beside you on either side stretches a great vista. A swath of green, rich with vegetation. Where the green ends, the desert and mountains begin, and there among them, the temples and tombs appear, the ghosts of an ancient world."

They were inside by the time she'd finished describing her vision. She found him studying her as though she were an unfamiliar squiggle on a bit of stone.

"What?" she said. "What now? Am I showing too much neck?"

"How easy it is for you," he said, "to imagine."

It was as natural to her as breathing.

"In this case, it's like remembering," she said. "You've sent me drawings and watercolors, and we own heaps of books." Most of which she'd purchased, in order to follow the journeys he wrote of, too briefly, in his letters. "I can't see it as you do, but I can understand how you'd miss it."

"Then why . . ." He trailed off, shaking his head. "But no. We've declared a truce."

She knew what he wanted to ask. Why, if she understood how he longed for Egypt, had she snared him into this ghastly journey to one of his least favorite places on earth, to appease parents who cared nothing about his happiness and didn't understand him at all?

She understood, better than anybody, the longing to have another sort of life, to pursue a dream.

She wanted him to have that life.

She wanted to have such a life, too, but that, she'd realized ages ago, was next to impossible for a woman.

Not that she'd completely given up hope or had stopped trying to invent a way to make it happen. *Next to impossible* wasn't the same as *impossible*.

But until she did find the answer—if she ever did— she'd have to live vicariously. If Lisle ended up stuck in England—but no, that didn't bear thinking of. He'd probably hang himself, and she'd hang herself in sympathy—if she didn't die of boredom first.

He ought to know that, but he was a man, and thick.

And being a man, and thick, he was sure to fail to grasp the brilliance of her plan.

He would probably run away screaming in horror at what she'd done. No, he'd throttle her.

But that was because he lacked *imagination*.

The George, Stamford, Lincolnshire,
  eighty-nine miles from London
Shortly before midnight

The shouting jolted Lisle from a sound, badly needed sleep.

"Carousers," he muttered. "It only wanted that."

Shepherding three troublesome ladies over four hundred miles of road was not a task for the fainthearted.

Like the horses, they had to be fed and watered. Unlike the horses, they couldn't be traded in for a fresh set. Unlike the horses, they couldn't be put in harness. This meant one must be vigilant about stopping times. One mustn't let the women dawdle, else they'd dawdle forever, and the longer they remained in one place, the greater the likelihood of trouble.

Happily, by half past nine that night they'd reached the George without further mishap. Here the other two carriages joined them. With all the servants and luggage, they'd taken over most of the rooms along one corridor. To his vast relief, all three ladies promptly took themselves away to their rooms—after Olivia told him she needed a bath.

"The ladies said I smell like a farmyard," she'd said. Doubtless that pair of bawds had said a good deal else: lewd suggestions about horses and women riding astride and, generally, everything he'd been thinking and wished he could scrape out of his brain.

He did not need, added to this, mental images of Olivia in her bath.

He turned over and pulled one of the pillows over his head. The shouting was still audible, though he couldn't make out the words.

Sleep gave a mocking wave and ran away.

The voices, accompanied by angry footsteps, came nearer.

"I saw you do it!"

"You're imagining things!"

"You were making sheep's eyes at her!"

"What about you? I saw you flirting with him."

"You're drunk."

"I'm not drunk and I'm not blind."

Lisle gave up, threw off the pillow, and listened—as everyone else in the corridor must be doing, whether they wanted to or not.

"You're disgusting!" the female cried. "What were you doing behind the wagon?"

"Taking a piss, you stupid woman!"

"I'm not stupid and I'm not blind, either. I saw you, the pair of you, in the stable yard."

"Then you were seeing things. Damn you, Elspeth, don't make me chase you down this passage."

"That's right, Elspeth," Lisle muttered. "Make him chase you down *another* passage."

"Damn *me*?" the woman screamed. "You vile, coarse, wicked, false brute!"

"Come back here!"

Another shriek. "Take your hands off me!"

"You're my wife, curse you!"

"Oh, yes, curse me. You betray me—and you curse *me*? I hate you! Why didn't I listen to Papa?"

Then someone pounded on a door. Lisle's door?

"Sir?"

Lisle sat up. A thin shadow in the shape of Nichols emerged from the adjoining sleeping closet. "Shall I open the door?" the valet said softly.

"Gad, no," Lisle said. "Stay clear of lovers' quarrels. No predicting what—"

"Get away from me or I'll scream!"

More knocking, but next door this time.

"Sir?" said Nichols.

"Not on your life," said Lisle.

"I hate you!" the woman cried.

"Elspeth, I've had enough of this!"

"I've had enough of you!"

"Don't make me drag you back."

"Like the brute you are?" Mocking laughter now.

More knocking, farther along the passage.

"You stupid woman. No one's going to open the door to strangers at this—"

An abrupt silence.

Then another voice. Though he was too far away to understand the words, Lisle had no trouble identifying the owner: Olivia.

"Plague take her," he said. He threw back the bed-clothes and ran to the door.

Chapter Seven

$\mathcal{W}$ith a sob, the woman flung herself upon Olivia, who instinctively put her arms about her and drew her into the room.

Olivia turned the sobbing woman over to Bailey.

"Hoi!" said the man. "That's my wife."

Swallowing a sigh, Olivia moved back to the threshold. She did not mind a row, but marital disputes were not proper rows. The odds, she knew, were strongly in favor of the woman's being the wronged party. Marriage was set up that way, giving all the power to the male.

Still, that didn't mean that a wife couldn't be acting like a nitwit. She strongly suspected this was the case at present. One could not, however, turn one's back on a damsel in distress.

She *hated* marital quarrels.

She bestowed a dazzling smile on the man. He took a step back.

"Your wife seems to be distraught," she said.

"Deranged is more like it," he said. "She said—"

"I heard," she said. "I reckon the whole town heard.

Frankly, I think you could have handled it more cleverly. If I were you, I should go away and devise a better strategy. Sobering up would be a good start."

"I'm not drunk," he said. "And I won't be ordered about by females."

"You're not making a good impression," she said cheerfully.

"I don't care! You give her back!"

He leaned threateningly toward Olivia.

Though he wasn't tall, he was square and sturdy, with arms like a blacksmith's. He could easily pick Olivia up and throw her out of his way if he so chose. Having reached the reckless stage of drunkenness, he might.

She rose to her full height, folded her arms, and tried to forget that she wore her nightclothes, and only her nightgown at that. Bailey hadn't been able to find her dressing gown in the dark on short notice and Olivia hadn't waited before answering the door.

She pretended she was not only fully dressed but fully armed as well. "Do be reasonable," she said. "I cannot in good conscience give her back if she doesn't wish it. Why don't you try coaxing?"

"Elspeth!" he shouted. "You come out of there!"

That was his idea of coaxing. *Men.*

"Brute!" Elspeth cried. "Betrayer! Womanizer! Libertine!"

"Libertine? Dammit, Elspeth, all I did was take a turn in the stable yard. You're being ridiculous. Come out of there or I'll come in after you!"

He looked at Olivia. "Miss, I'd give her back or get out of the way if I was you. This is none of your affair."

He took a step forward.

Then a sudden step back, as a white-clad arm grasped his and spun him around. "Don't even think about it," said Lisle.

"She's got my wife!"

"So she does. But you may not go in after her."

The man looked down at the hand on his arm, then up into Lisle's face. Lisle was wearing the extremely calm expression that usually preceded his doing something violent. Most people had no trouble reading this expression.

The outraged husband must have read it because, instead of trying to break Lisle's jaw, he turned to scowl at Olivia. "Women!"

"I sympathize, believe me," said Lisle. "But you can do nothing here. It's claimed that absence makes the heart grow fonder. Why don't you go downstairs and wait for your helpmeet to come to her senses?"

"Silly fool female," the man said, but halfheartedly. Lisle's dangerously calm demeanor had sapped the fight out of him.

Lisle released his arm, and the fellow went away, muttering about *women*.

Lisle watched until the man was out of sight. Then he turned to Olivia. His silvery gaze skimmed over her, from the rat's nest of her hair down over the muslin nightdress and down to her bare feet. She felt every inch of the survey.

She gave it back, letting her gaze move slowly down, from his tangled hair, over the bruised eye, over the nightshirt that covered only as far as his knees, and on down a length of naked, muscular calf to his bare feet.

Then she wished she'd stared at the wall behind him

instead. She was remembering his scent and the feel of his body and the heat of contact. Low in her belly, something wicked stirred.

"Knowing you, I ought to believe it," Lisle said. "The mind reels all the same. It's the middle of the night. You came to your door—wearing almost nothing—and opened it to strangers."

"I'm not wearing nothing," she said. "Or if I am, so are you."

As though on purpose to contradict her, Nichols glided to his master's side and helped him into a magnificent green silk dressing gown with a lining the color of claret.

Never taking his gaze from Olivia, Lisle absently accepted his servant's ministrations, then waved him away. Nichols vanished in the same discreet way he'd appeared. How a man like Lisle could retain this superior, sophisticated valet was as great a riddle to Olivia as the little pictures and squiggles Lisle drew in his letters, to illustrate one point or another.

The elegant gown had to be the valet's doing. Lisle was not a man who cared about his clothes. Olivia had always supposed that dressing him must be a thankless task. Yet the valet stuck with him, and braved the hardships of Egypt with him.

She felt a surge of envy, which she quickly crushed. What was so enviable about spending one's life being invisible?

Meanwhile, with Bailey occupied with the hysterical wife, only Olivia was wearing almost nothing

"It was an emergency," she said. "One can't wait to be properly attired when someone in trouble seeks help."

She gestured toward the woman, who was blowing her nose in what looked like one of Olivia's handkerchiefs.

"A damsel in distress," Olivia went on. "What would you have me do?"

Lisle shook his head. The light from the sconce behind him made a hazy glow of his sun-streaked hair, like a halo—as though his angelic good looks needed enhancement.

She shifted her gaze lower, to resist the temptation to run her fingers through his sleep-tousled hair. She stared at the sash of his dressing gown instead, but that only reminded her of the taut waist she'd clung to hours earlier. She didn't know where to look.

"I'd have you *think*," he said.

"No, you wouldn't," she said. "You'd have me sit quietly, waiting for a man to come along to do my thinking for me," she said.

"Even I know better than to expect you to sit quietly," he said. "I thought you knew better than to get mixed up in a marital squabble. Do you never listen to your stepfather? Isn't that one of Rathbourne's rules?"

She was desperately aware of his bare feet, inches from hers. "I believe he taught you a rule about arguing with ladies as well."

"Thank you for reminding me," he said. "You are and always have been impulsive to a suicidal degree. It's a waste of breath to argue with you at any time, especially in a frigid corridor in the middle of the night."

"You're the one in the cozy dressing gown," she said. "I don't feel cold."

His gaze slid downward, to her breasts. She didn't

follow the gaze. She didn't need to. She was well aware of the state of her nipples.

"*Part* of you feels it," he said. "But you'll argue about that, too, and I've had enough." He turned and strode down the corridor.

She stood for a moment, watching him walk away from her.

He always walked away . . . or rode away . . . or sailed away—off to his adventures, to his mistress, Egypt. He'd come back only long enough to unbalance everything. For a time she'd have her friend and ally back, but after he'd gone, she'd be more restless and discontented. She'd wait for his letters, to share his life, and he—oh, he'd forget all about her if she didn't write to him constantly, reminding him she existed.

She clenched her fists and went after him.

Lisle entered his room and closed the door behind him and leaned back against it, eyes closed.

Ye gods! Ye gods! Olivia half naked.

And standing in the doorway of a public hostelry for all the world to see. Elspeth's husband had certainly had an eyeful: Olivia's tits standing at attention under that paltry excuse for nightclothes.

Lisle's cock was standing at attention, too, as though it hadn't wasted enough energy in that way already.

"Go down and get me a glass of brandy," he told Nichols. "No, better yet, a bottle. Make it three bottles."

"I could prepare a posset for you, sir," said Nichols. "Very quieting after so much agitation."

"I don't want quieting," Lisle said. "I want oblivion. These cursed women."

"Yes, sir."

The valet left.

The door had scarcely closed behind him when the knocking started.

"Go away," Lisle said. "Whoever you are."

"I'm not going away. How dare you turn your back on me. How dare you scold me and order me about and—"

He pulled the door open.

She stood there, as inadequately dressed as previously, her arm upraised to knock again.

"Go back to your room," he said. "What the devil is wrong with you?"

"You," she said. "You haven't been about for years. You come for a short time, then you go away." She made sweeping motions that pulled the muslin tautly over her breasts. "You have no right to order me about or interfere. As you took such pains to point out, you're not my brother. You are not related to me in any way. You have no rights over me."

More dramatic gestures. Her hair tumbled in wild disarray about her shoulders. One of the ribbons tying her bodice was coming undone.

"If I wish to let ten women into my room, you have no right to stop me," she railed on. "If I wish to let ten *men* into my room, you may not stop me. I am not your property, and I won't be ordered about. I won't be castigated for doing what I think is right. I won't be—"

She broke off with a shriek as he grabbed one of her flailing arms, pulled her into the room, and shut the door.

She shook him off.

He let go and stepped back.

"This is very aggravating," he said.

"On that we're agreed," she said. "I had completely forgotten how provoking you can be."

"I had completely forgotten that you lose all sense of proportion—as well as all sense of where you are—when one of your—your moods—takes hold of you."

"It isn't a mood, you thickhead!"

"I don't care what you call it," he said. "You can't go about barely dressed, making scenes in public. If that poor fellow hadn't been besotted with his temperamental wife—or if it had been another sort of man—or a pair of them—when you opened the door, the consequences—No, I refuse to contemplate them. Devil take you, do you never *think* before you act? Do you never take a moment—an instant—to consider what might happen?"

"I know how to take care of myself," she said, lifting her chin. "You of all people ought to know that."

"Oh, do you?" he said. "Then take care of yourself, Olivia."

He wrapped an arm about her and pulled her close.

"Oh, no, you—"

He grasped her chin and kissed her.

Olivia did know how to take care of herself. She reached up to dig her nails into his wrists. She had her leg poised to thrust her knee into his soft parts.

But something went wrong.

She couldn't move her face because he was holding her chin, gently yet firmly. And that left her no way to escape the shocking feel of his lips and the pressure of his mouth, determined, demanding, insisting. He was stubborn to the core, and whatever he did, he gave it all his concentrated attention, leaving her unable to turn away or ignore it. She couldn't *not* respond to it. She couldn't not savor the feel of his mouth and the taste of him.

Then the evilly tantalizing male scent wafted into her nose and swam into her head and filled it with dreams and longings and heat. The ground beneath her feet fell away, as though she rose in a hot-air balloon.

She slid her hands up to his shoulders. Then her arms were around his neck, and she was holding on, as though she'd drop a hundred miles to the cold earth below if she didn't.

She was supposed to kick him in the shins. Instead, her bare foot slid up along his leg. The hand not holding her chin slid down her back and down and grasped her bottom, and he pulled her close, against his groin. Only a few thin layers of muslin and silk came between them. They hid nothing, protected nothing. His arousal, hot and heavy, pushed against her belly.

She was no pure innocent. She'd felt a man's arousal before, but the heat had not raced through her like a flame along a line of gunpowder. She'd been titillated and aroused before, but she hadn't ached as she did now. She hadn't felt this wild restlessness.

He fell back against the door, taking her with him, and everything she knew fell away. All her knowledge and guile passed into nothingness. All she could do was yearn, and it was no pretty romantic longing but a madness. She rubbed herself against him, and opened her mouth to draw him inside and taste him. It was hot and lewd, a kiss of tangled tongues and thrust and withdraw, like the coupling every instinct screamed for.

She heard the sound, but it meant nothing. A vague sound that could have been anything.

Something beating, somewhere. She didn't know where. It could have been her heart, making every pulse point thump with physical awareness of every inch of masculine body pressed against hers. It could have been the beat of wanting, that seemed to have gone on forever.

There was a knocking, but her heart knocked against her rib cage, with heat and need . . . and fear, because what was happening was out of her control.

More knocking. A voice.

"Sir?"

A male voice. Familiar. On the other side of the door.

DeLucey survival instincts, refined over generations, yanked her from whatever mad universe her feelings had taken her to. She came back to the world: a chilly place, suddenly.

She felt Lisle stiffen and start to draw away.

She untangled herself from him.

She dared a glance at his face. It was perfectly composed. No danger of *his* feet leaving solid ground.

He calmly tugged her nightgown back into place.

Not to be outdone, she straightened his robe.

For good measure, she patted his chest in a friendly way. "Well, then, let that be a lesson to you," she said.

She pulled the door open, gave Nichols a regal nod, and sailed out, head spinning and legs trembling, and hoped she didn't crash into a wall or fall on her face.

Half past six o'clock in the morning
Sunday 9 October

In the dream, Olivia wore a very thin piece of linen. She stood at the bottom of a set of stone steps, beckoning. Behind her was a deep darkness. "Come, see my hidden treasure," she said.

Lisle started down the steps.

She smiled up at him. Then she glided through a door. It slammed shut behind her.

"Olivia!"

He beat on the door. He heard answering thunder. But no, it wasn't thunder. He knew that sound. Rocks, rolling into place. A booby trap. He looked back. Darkness. Only the thunder of the great stones rolling into the entrance.

Crash. Crash. Against wood.

What was that noise?

Not stones. A door.

Someone pounding on the door.

Lisle came completely awake, as he'd trained himself to do years ago in Egypt, when being able to shake off sleep instantly could mean the difference between life and death.

He sat up. The dim light filtering through the window curtains told him the sun was rising.

Where the devil was Nichols? At this hour, on the point of rising from a maidservant's bed, very likely— or had he found his way into one of the female guests' bedchambers?

Cursing his valet, Lisle hauled himself out of bed,

dragged on his dressing gown, shoved his feet into his slippers, and stomped to the door.

He pulled it open.

Olivia paused, hand upraised.

He shook his head. He was still dreaming.

But no. The passage behind her was filled with the same grey light as his bedroom.

She was fully dressed. His sleep-clogged mind slowly took it in: the over-decorated bonnet . . . the high neck of the carriage dress with its fashionably swollen sleeves . . . the slim half-boots. Traveling clothes, his sleepy mind informed him. But that made no sense.

"What?" he said. "What?"

"We're ready to go," she said. "The servants' vehicles have gone ahead. The ladies are in the carriage."

He had no idea what she was saying. His mind cast up images of last night: she, nearly naked . . . he, losing his mind. A blunder. A whopping, great, nearly fatal blunder.

But there she'd stood, wearing little more than a shift, and that coming undone, and her hair tumbling loose while she waved her arms about, and other parts of her body moved along with them.

He'd seen Cairo's dancing girls. Even in public, fully dressed, they moved suggestively. At private parties, he'd watched them go well beyond that, baring their breasts and bellies sometimes, or dancing in nothing more than a fringe or a sash. In spite of what those amazingly limber bodies could do, he'd kept his head.

Olivia had stood before him, angry, not trying to entice him. She'd been fully covered, technically—and he'd lost his mind.

If Nichols had not come to the door. . .

"What time is it?" he said. What day was it? Was he dreaming, still?

"Half past six o'clock," she said.

"In the *morning*?"

Her smile was dazzling, dangerous. "If we leave now, we can reach York by sundown."

"Leave?" he said. "Now?"

"We'll easily beat the Royal Mail to York," she said.

"I've had three hours' sleep," he said. "What is the matter with you?"

"I should like to reach Gorewood as soon as possible," she said. "The sooner we get there, the sooner we can complete our mission and the sooner you can go back to Egypt." She eyed him up and down. "You don't seem to be ready."

"Of course I'm not ready!"

Another dazzling smile. "Well, then, you'll get to York when you get there, I daresay."

She turned and walked away.

He stood in the doorway, watching in disbelief as she sauntered down the corridor, hips swaying.

He backed into the room and closed the door.

A moment later, the door opened.

"I know what this is," he said. "It's revenge."

"Sir?"

Nichols entered, carrying a tray. "I noticed that the ladies were preparing to depart," he said. "I thought you'd want your coffee."

Chapter Eight

York
That evening

As a boy, Lisle had once watched the mail coach set out at sunset from the York Tavern in St. Helen's Square.

He doubted Olivia had seen it today. She and her coven might have arrived in time, but they would travel only as far as the George in Coney Street. It was a large old hostelry whose quaint gabled and plastered exterior, with its curious figures, dated to the sixteenth century.

When Lisle arrived, night had fallen, and the Royal Mail was long gone. He'd traveled more than a hundred miles this day. He'd ridden hard, trying not to think about last night, and he'd kept the stops short for the same reason. At present he ought to be too tired and hungry to think, but he had a conscience, and it wouldn't stay quiet in the back of his mind.

He trudged up the stairs and along the corridor. He heard the hurried footsteps, but it was a distant awareness.

Olivia came around the corner so quickly and unexpectedly that he barely had time to brace himself before she crashed into him. As it was, he swayed a little at the impact, but his arms promptly came up and went around her to stop her from toppling.

"I knew you'd miss me," he said.

It wasn't the wisest thing to say and, in light of what had happened last night, not letting go of her immediately wasn't the wisest thing to do. But he was a man before he was a wise man, and he did what a man did when a bundle of frothy femininity fell into his arms.

She was dressed in mile upon mile of some heavy, silky stuff and lace and ruffles—with at least six miles of material in the great, ballooning sleeves. She was dressed, that is, except for where coverage would do the most good: the milky expanse of shoulder and bosom abundantly on display. She was warm and shapely and soft, and for one giddy moment he couldn't remember why he ought to let go of her.

She gazed up at him, her deeply blue eyes soulful. "I missed you dreadfully," she said with a catch in her voice. "The hours passed like eons. How I bore the separation, I cannot say, but it depleted the last stores of my strength."

She sagged. He was tired enough and the rampant femininity in his arms made him stupid enough to believe, for exactly three seconds, that she'd fainted.

Then he remembered that this was Olivia.

"I've been riding since early morning," he said. "My arms are tired, along with everything else, and I'm very likely to drop you. *Very* likely."

She straightened and gave him a little shove.

He let go and stepped two paces away. "Is it me," he said, "or are you not wearing as much in the way of clothing as you used to do?"

"It's a *dinner* dress," she said.

"But you're not at dinner," he said. "You're running about a public hostelry in a frenzy."

"Because they've escaped," she said. "The ladies. When I wasn't looking, they bolted."

"Considering the punishing drive they endured this day, I'm not surprised," he said. "Really, Olivia, you know antiques need gentle handling."

"They're not antiques!" she said. "They're two wicked women who aren't nearly decrepit enough, and they've gone out roving in the night." She waved her arms about, in that way of hers, making the soft flesh on display undulate in a highly provocative manner.

He tried to look away but he was tired, and his intestinal fortitude wasn't up to the job.

"They took it into their heads to visit the Minster," she said, "because they haven't been there since the fire, and they wanted to see the crypt."

Lisle called his mind away from the satanic flesh. He remembered that a madman had set fire to the York Minster two years ago. The wreckage had revealed a large crypt under the choir.

"They wanted to crawl about the bowels of a burnt-out cathedral," he said. "At night. That's mad even by your standards."

"Not *crawl about*," she said. "It isn't like you and your tombs. They only want to have their blood curdled. A burnt-out ruin at night is irresistible. And it's convenient—a few minutes' walk from here. They should have returned hours ago."

"I'll go collect them," he said. *Curse them.* He was famished. He was nearly delirious from lack of sleep. And now he must go out into the streets of York hunting for two lunatic crones.

"I'll go," she said. "They're my problem, and this is my fault, for letting them pull the wool over my eyes. 'A nice bathe and a nap, that's all I want,'" She mimicked Lady Cooper. "The wicked deceivers. They knew that was what I wanted to do. I should have realized. They napped through the stages until breakfast. And again in the afternoon. They were well rested, brimful of energy. I should have realized they'd get up to something. I blame myself. I'll take a pair of servants and hunt them down."

"You're not going into a burnt-out church in the middle of the night without me," he said. "I'm used to crawling about tombs and temples in the dark. You're not."

"You need a bath," she said. "You smell like a stable yard."

"I want to bathe in peace," he said. "I want to eat my dinner in peace. I should like a night's uninterrupted sleep. I can't do any of those things while that pair's out running loose."

"I'm perfectly capable—"

"I know, I know," he said. "We'll go together—but you have to change into sensible clothes."

"There isn't time!"

"If they're dead, they'll still be dead when we get there," he said. "If they're merely in trouble—"

"Merely!"

"—or up to trouble, which is far more likely, I daresay they'll survive an extra quarter hour. They're about as delicate as wild boar."

"Lisle."

"You can't crawl about the charred debris looking for corpses in that dress," he said. "Let Bailey stuff you into something less—less—" He gestured at her exposed bosom. "Airy. But make haste. I'll give you a quarter hour, no more. If you're not ready, I'm going without you."

Fifteen and a half minutes later

"Trousers," Lisle said grimly.

She'd burst through the door in the nick of time. He was already on the pavement, ready to leave—without her. Exactly as she'd suspected.

"You told me to wear something sensible," she said, still breathless from the mad race to get ready. "I should never be able to get into tight spaces in a dress."

"You're not going into any tight spaces," he said.

"For women, most spaces are tighter these days," she said. "In case you haven't noticed, our fashions are a great deal wider than they used to be. Most of my sleeves are the size of butter churns. I'm sure Great-Grandmama had an easier time getting about in hoop petticoats."

"If you would stay put and let me do the searching, you wouldn't have to squeeze yourself into garments that were never designed to accommodate a woman's shape."

"I see," she said. "You think my bottom's too big."

"That isn't what I said," he said. "You're not shaped like a man. No one would ever mistake you for one. Gad, I don't have time for this nonsense."

He turned away and started walking.

Olivia went with him.

He was in a horrible mood, and that, she knew, was at least partly thanks to her. She'd woken him at a cruel hour after a long and wearying day and night . . . after an exceedingly emotional episode . . . which she didn't want to think about. She'd been angry with him, and upset in ways she could scarcely explain even to herself.

What she'd done this morning was the equivalent of slapping him and running away. Very mature. But she was at a loss—a rare state for her—and she hated it.

"Passing for a man isn't the point," she said. "I dressed for comfort and convenience. You said to wear something sensible, and women's garments simply aren't sensible. They grow less so every year. Furthermore, a reasonable man would have understood that it's *impossible* for a woman to change out of one dress into another in a quarter hour. It would serve you right if I'd come down in my shift."

"It isn't as though I haven't already seen you in your shift," he said.

"If you're referring to last night, that was my nightdress," she said. *And don't let's talk about last night. I'm not ready.*

"It looked like a shift to me."

"You can't have seen very many, if you can't tell the difference."

"I'm a man," he said. "We don't go in for the fine details of women's dress. We notice how much or how little they're wearing. I've noticed that you seem to wear very little."

"Compared to what?" she said. "Egyptian women? They seem to go to extremes. Either they're completely covered except for their eyes, or they're dancing about wearing a few small bells. The point is—"

"This way," he said, and turned into St. Helen's Square.

The square, broader than Coney Street, wasn't as gloomy.

As they passed the York Tavern, she looked up. The dark buildings were silhouetted against a sky lit by a great blur of stars.

In another moment they'd crossed the square. They turned briefly into Blake Street, then into Stonegate, another narrow York lane.

"The point is," she said, "women ought to be allowed to wear trousers in cases like this."

"The point is," he said, "women ought not to be getting into situations requiring them to wear trousers."

"Don't be stuffy. Aunt Daphne wears them."

"In Egypt," he said. "Where women do wear a sort of trouserlike attire. But they're not as form fitting, and they wear layers of other garments over them. Were you to wear those trousers in Cairo, you'd be arrested for public lewdness and flogged."

"They are a bit tight, I'll admit," she said. "I don't know how men can abide them. They do chafe in a sensitive area."

"Do *not* talk about your sensitive areas," he said.

"I have to talk about something," she said. "One of us must attempt to lighten the heavy gloom of your company."

"Yes, well . . ." He stopped walking. "Oh, damn. Olivia . . . about last night . . . when you came to my door . . ."

She stopped, too, her heart racing.

"It was a mistake," he said. "A very bad mistake, on about a hundred counts. I'm sorry."

He was right, she told herself. It had been a terrible mistake, on so many counts. "Yes," she said. "Yes, it was. And not completely your fault. I'm sorry, too."

He looked relieved.

She told herself she was relieved, too.

He nodded. "Good. That's settled, then."

"Yes."

"Just to be clear, though: You're still aggravating, and I don't apologize for berating you," he said.

"I understand," she said. "I don't apologize for anything I *said*, either."

"Very well, then."

They started walking again.

It was awkward. Lisle had never felt awkward in her company before. This was what came of crossing a line that shouldn't have been crossed. He'd apologized to her, but he couldn't apologize to Rathbourne, and he couldn't shake off the sense of having betrayed him. He couldn't shake off the sense of having done something irrevocable. He'd opened Pandora's Box and now—

Her voice broke the lengthening silence. "Fifteen minutes," she said. "Only a man would think that a reasonable amount of time."

"You know perfectly well I was counting on you not to do it," he said.

"And you know perfectly well that I'd do it or die trying," she said. "We had a bit of a panic at first. Bailey couldn't find my trousers and I thought we'd have to take Nichols's."

He looked at her. She didn't look *anything* like a boy. Or did she? Was that his walk she was imitating?

"You really are ridiculous," he said.

"Oh, I understood how difficult it would be," she said, "but it was the first thing that leapt to my mind when we couldn't find these clothes. Then, while Bailey was tearing off my dress and petticoats and squeezing me into my trousers, I was picturing what would have happened."

He was picturing her maid tearing off her clothes and squeezing Olivia into narrow trousers.

Pandora's Box.

Still, there was no harm in thinking. He was a man. Men always had lewd thoughts. It was perfectly natural and normal.

"He would make a fuss," Olivia continued, "and I would have to distract him, while Bailey knocked him unconscious. Then we'd take the trousers. Then, after

I'd gone, Bailey would bind up his wounds and tell him how sorry she was, and how it couldn't be helped."

"Why couldn't you stay quietly in London and write dramas for the stage?" he said.

"Lisle, use your head," she said. "If I had the least talent for staying quietly, I should have quietly stuck to the first gentleman I became engaged to and got married and had children and disappeared into that anonymous demi-existence other women disappear into."

She began to wave her arms about. "Why must women stay quietly? Why must we be little moons, each of us stuck in our little orbit, revolving around a planet that is some man? Why can't we be other planets? Why must we be moons?"

"Speaking astronomically," he said, "those other planets all orbit about the sun."

"Must you always be so literal?" she said.

"Yes," he said. "I'm horribly literal and you're appallingly imaginative. For instance, I see a cathedral rising behind some buildings ahead. What do you see?"

She looked to the end of Stonegate, where a black tower rose into the night sky.

"I see a ghostly ruin, looming through a narrow alley, a great black hulk against a star-studded night sky."

"I'm not sure it's a ruin," he said. "But we'll soon see."

A few more steps brought them to the end of Stonegate. They crossed High Petergate, passed into an alley, and entered the darkened grounds of the ghostly ruin—or, depending on one's point of view—the slightly burned York Minster.

* * *

Lisle supposed that the faint flickering light behind a
stained-glass window would add to Olivia's "ghostly"
view of the place. To him it was merely a sign of life.

"Looks like somebody's home," he said. "All the
same, I'd rather not stumble about getting in." From a
pocket of his great coat he took out his tinder box and
a short candle.

"I've got lucifers," she said.

He shook his head. "Filthy, vile-smelling things." He
took a moment to employ the tinderbox and light his
stumpy candle.

"They are disgusting," she said. "But one never
knows when they'll prove useful."

"They're useful to those who're accustomed to having
their servants make all the fires," he said. "Any com-
petent fellow can strike a spark as easily and quickly—
and more safely—with a tinderbox."

"Most people won't practice ten thousand times, on
purpose, just to prove they can do something," she said.

"I did not practice ten— Gad, why do I let you bait
me? Is it too much to ask you to stay close? We don't
know how much clearing out they've done."

"Just because I've squeezed my gigantic bottom into
men's trousers, you needn't assume my brains have
shrunk to masculine size," she said. "I'm perfectly
aware that you're the one holding the only candle, and
I'm not longing to trip over stray bits of cathedral. It's
shockingly dark and quiet, isn't it? London's as busy at
night as it is in the daytime. And better lit. But it's perfectly in keeping: medieval church, medieval darkness,
and tomblike silence."

As it turned out, the way in was clear. But they didn't get far. They were crossing the south transept when a fellow carrying a lantern hurried toward them.

"Sorry, gentlemen," he said. "No visitors after dark. I know some like a broody atmosphere or want to be frighted out of their wits—"

"We're not visiting," Lisle said. "We've only come—"

"You must come back in the daytime. Very busy, I admit, with the workmen, but they must clear out, mustn't they, before we can make a start of things. And now this matter of the crypt, and everyone pestering for a look at it."

"That isn't—"

"I can't tell you how many scholars we've had, measuring and arguing. Last I heard, it'll cost a hundred thousand pounds to repair the damage, but that doesn't include the crypt, as they haven't decided what to do. Half at least saying it must be dug out and the other half saying leave it as it is."

"It's not about—"

"You come back tomorrow, sirs, and someone will be happy to take you about and answer your questions and tell you why they're disputing about what's Norman and what's Perpendicular." He shooed them toward the door.

Theorizing that the watchman was slightly deaf as well as garrulous, Lisle said, more loudly, "We're looking for two ladies."

The man stopped waving his lantern at the door. "Ladies?"

"My aunties," said Olivia, sounding uncannily like an adolescent male. Mimicry came easy to her.

Lisle glared at her. She always had to embellish.

"One about so tall," said Lisle, holding his hand level with Olivia's ear. "The other a trifle shorter. They wanted to see the church, and particularly the crypt."

"Oh, yes, indeed," said the man. "I told them to come back tomorrow. It isn't at all safe, I warned them, but they wouldn't have any of that. Before I knew what I was about, there I was, leading them about and answering questions. But I'm not employed, sir, to give tours at night, and I won't be making any more exceptions."

"Certainly not," said Lisle. "But perhaps you could tell us when they left?"

"Why, not ten minutes ago, I'm sure. Maybe it was a quarter hour. I don't recollect exactly. But they left in a hurry. Lost track of time, they said."

"Did they happen to say where they were going?" Lisle said.

"The George in Coney Street, they told me. They asked for the quickest way back. Said they were late for dinner."

"If they left ten minutes ago, we should have met up with them," Lisle said.

"They might have gone another way," said the watchman. "Did you come by way of Stonegate?"

"We did," said Lisle. "Did they—"

"As I explained to them, the name refers to the stone brought to build the Minster," their informant said. "It traveled from the quarries by water, and landed at Stayne Gate, below the Guildhall."

"Do you think—"

"They were interested to learn that the author Mr.

Lawrence Sterne lived in Stonegate in his bachelor days."

"Do you think they went another way?" Lisle said in a rush.

"Mayhap they took the wrong turning, into Little Stonegate," the watchman said. "I hope they didn't go astray. I saw them safely out of the church, I promise you. The way is poorly lit, indeed, and with all this debris about, it's all too easy to—"

A shriek cut him off.

Lisle turned in the direction of the sound. He saw nothing. Then he realized he saw nothing in the place where Olivia ought to be.

"Olivia!" he shouted.

"Ow, ow, ow," Olivia said. Then, remembering that she was supposed to be a male, she added, "Deuce take it."

Her voice wobbled. Indeed, the pain made her eyes water, and she wanted to cry, although that was mainly frustration. She saw no way to get out of this gracefully. "I'm over here."

"Over where?"

The light of candle and lantern wavered over the various heaps of debris.

"Here," she said.

At last the light swung toward her ignominious pose.

She lay, arse upward, half on and half off the pile of lumber and stone and whatever else she'd tripped over. A precious small pile, she saw as the men came nearer. But like the small hole that had finished Mercutio, it had been enough to do for her. She'd struck her knee—and that hurt—and landed on an elbow, which sent pain twanging up her arm. But that was nothing to what she felt when she tried to stand up.

Lisle passed his candle to the watchman and crouched beside her.

"This is why I tell them not to come at night," the watchman said. "A man could trip and crack his head open. Even in the daytime you've got to watch where you're going."

"Stand back a bit," Lisle said. "Hold the lantern higher."

The watchman retreated and did as he was told.

Suppressing a groan, she managed to turn slightly. She didn't care what Lisle saw, but she'd rather not have her arse center stage for the watchman to gape at.

"Where's your hat?" Lisle said in a low voice.

"I don't know."

He ran his fingers lightly over her tightly pinned hair. "You don't seem to be bleeding."

"I fell on my arm."

"If you hadn't, you could have cracked your skull."

"There's nothing wrong with my head," she said.

"That's a matter of opinion."

"It's my foot. I can't get up."

"I'm going to throttle you," he said. "I told you—"

"To stay close, I know. But I only moved a very little away. I was trying to get a quick look about before he ejected us. And then—"

"You tripped."

"It wasn't a bad fall, but my right foot won't hold me. I think I twisted my ankle. Help me up, will you?"

"Is anything broken, curse you?"

"I don't think so. It's only the foot. It won't cooperate—and it hurts like blazes if I try to make it cooperate."

He said something under his breath in Arabic. She supposed there wasn't an English curse strong enough to express his feelings. Then his hand grasped her right foot, and she nearly shot straight into the air. He inspected it, inch by inch, turning it gently this way and that. She had all she could do not to moan—and she wasn't at all sure whether this was on account of the pain or the feel of his hands on her.

From her foot he made his way swiftly but gently up to her knee.

"I don't think you've broken anything," he said.

"That's what I—"

She broke off because he was dragging her up into a sitting position. Before she could catch her breath, he caught her under the arms and pulled her upright. When her right foot touched the floor, she winced.

"Don't put any weight on it," he said. "You'll have to lean on me. Luckily, we haven't far to go." While he spoke, he slid his arm under her coat and around her back. His arm, bracing her so firmly, was warm and hard. She was aware of his hand, under her breast. Her breast was aware of it, too, the skin tightening while morals-sapping sensations cascaded downward.

While propping her up, he fished some coins out of his pocket and gave them to the watchman. "Sorry about the trouble," he said.

"I hope the young gentleman recovers soon," the man said.

"Thank you," Olivia said in her young male voice.

Lisle said nothing. He maneuvered her through the door, and slowly down the steps into the yard.

They proceeded in silence through the narrow passage into High Petergate.

Lisle didn't trust himself to speak.

She'd frightened him out of his wits. She could have broken her neck or cracked her skull.

Even when he knew she was more or less in one piece, he worried—about broken bones, splintered bones, concussion.

It looked as though she'd done nothing worse than turn her ankle. The trouble was, it had taken him too long to reach that conclusion.

He'd put his hands on her head, her foot, and her leg. He'd examined her far too scrupulously and spent too much time doing it.

That was not intelligent. He'd been even less intelligent when he hauled her upright: He'd put his arm under her coat instead of over it.

Instead of encountering a protective layer of waistcoat, he felt the thin fabric of her shirt and the waist of her trousers. When she leaned against him, the bottom of her inadequately protected breast rested on the side of his hand. Under the shirt, the soft flesh was so warm.

It would have tried the self-control of a saint to walk in this intimate way: her breast bobbing against Lisle's hand and her hip pressed against his as they made their way so slowly out of the church, down the steps, and out of the church yard and on. Holding her so close, he could smell her hair and her skin. . .

Keep moving, he told himself. *One foot ahead of the other. Rathbourne's stepdaughter. Remember.*

"Lisle," she said.

"Don't," he said.

"I know you're angry, but there we were, and who knew when I should be back again, and I only went a little way—"

"Only," he said. "Only this. Only that. And if you'd broken your neck, what should I say to your mother, your stepfather? 'Olivia's only dead.'"

He couldn't and wouldn't think about that.

He didn't need to. She was alive. But he'd touched her, and every touch reminded his body of last night's long, ferocious kiss and the way her bare leg had slid up his. Her scent was in his nose and her breast was pressing against his arm, and every instinct wanted to prove, in the most primal way—up against the wall of this narrow alley—that she was alive and he was alive.

She's crippled, you pig.

"Yes, but I didn't break my neck," she said. "It's so unlike you to dwell on what might have happened."

"*Unlike* me?" he said. "You don't know what's like or unlike me. You only see me here, in a constant state of tension, bracing myself for the next debacle." And trying not to do something insane and unforgivable and from which there'd be no turning back.

He was a man of reason and principle. He had a conscience. He knew the difference between honorable and dishonorable behavior. But he'd crossed a line, and his carefully ordered world was disintegrating.

"Really, Lisle, you're making a great fuss over—"

"Every time I come home, it's the same thing!" he burst out. "Is it any wonder I don't want to live in England? In Egypt I contend with merely snakes, scorpions, sandstorms, thieves, and cutthroats. Here it's all scenes, and creating trouble where there wasn't any. If it isn't my parents shrieking and sobbing and carrying on, it's you, starting riots and trying to get yourself killed."

"I don't believe this." She tried to pull away.

"Don't be an idiot," he said. "You'll fall on your face."

"I can lean on the buildings as I go along," she said. "I don't need you."

He pulled her more firmly against him. "You're being childish."

"I!"

"Yes, you! Everything is a drama with you. Emotion first, last, and always."

"I wasn't born with a stone scarab where my heart ought to be!"

"Maybe you could use your head once in a while instead of your heart," he said. "Maybe you could think before you decide to wander about a ruined choir at night. Or maybe—here's a novel thought—you could have told me what you were about."

"You would have stopped me."

"And rightly so."

"Only listen to yourself," she said. "You go poking about in tombs and burial shafts."

He pulled her into Stonegate. He kept rigid the arm holding her, because otherwise he'd shake her. "I know what I'm doing," he said, and it wanted all his will to keep his voice low and seemingly calm. "I don't act first and think later. I don't rush blindly into everything that seizes my imagination for a moment."

"That isn't what happened! You're twisting every-thing about!"

"And you can't see yourself!" he said. "You can't see what you do. It's the same as you do with men. You're bored, and use them for entertainment, never mind who gets hurt. You're bored, and you barge into my life and deceive my family and yours, and disrupt who knows how many households—"

"Indeed, I'm sorry I did," she said. "I never was so sorry in all my life."

He should have stopped then. He knew, in a small, sane corner of his mind, that he should not have started in the first place. But that small awareness couldn't make its way through the furious current of turmoil.

"I'm sorry, too," he said. "I'm sorry I came home. I'm sorry I came within a mile of you. I should have stayed where I was. Yes, I'd rather go blind deciphering hieroglyphs. I'd rather roast in the desert and take my chances with the sandstorms and scorpions and snakes and cutthroats. I'd rather do anything, be anywhere that keeps me a world away from you and my parents."

"I wish you'd never come home," she cried. "I wish you'd go back. I'd gladly pay to send you back and keep you there. I don't care what becomes of you. Go to Egypt. Go to the devil. Only go!"

"I wish I could go to the devil," he said. "It would be like paradise, after two days with you."

She shoved him, hard.

He wasn't prepared. He lost his balance, falling back against a shop door, and relaxed his grip. It was only for an instant, but it was enough for her. She pulled away.

"I hate you," she said.

She limped the few steps across the lane and started making her way, slowly, her hand against the buildings.

He stood for a moment watching her, his heart racing.

He didn't cross the lane. He didn't trust himself.

He started walking, slowly, he on his side, she on hers. And slowly, silently, and worlds apart, they made their way back to the inn.

Chapter Nine

Jackass.
Beast.

It was a long, punishing ride, more than a hundred miles from York to Alnwick, Northumberland. Lisle began it still furious with Olivia and ended it furious with himself.

The things he'd said last night.

She was his friend. A demented and dangerous friend, true, but he was far from perfect.

His temper, for one thing. Too quick, he knew—but when before had he ever unleashed it so cruelly on a woman?

And this was the woman who'd loyally and faithfully written to him, week after week. This was the woman who'd always understood what Egypt meant to him.

Jackass. Beast. And that was only the beginning. By the time he reached Alnwick's White Swan, some hours after sunset, he'd run through every epithet he knew, in half a dozen languages.

Aware that a long day's ride, no bath, and no dinner, had played a part in last night's debacle—though none of that excused him—he bathed, dressed, and dined before making his way to Olivia's room.

He knocked once, twice. Bailey opened the door.

"I must speak to Miss Carsington," he said.

"I'm not in," Olivia called. "I've gone out. I've gone out to sell my wicked soul to Lucifer."

Lisle waved Bailey away. She looked at her mistress, then at him. Then she stepped aside.

"Really, Bailey," Olivia said. "I cannot believe you let him intimidate you."

"Yes, miss," said Bailey. "Sorry, miss." She took herself into the adjoining room. She left the door partly open.

Lisle walked over and shut it.

He turned to Olivia. His first glimpse of the room had told him she was seated at the fire. He now discovered why she hadn't leapt up to rush at the door and try to push him out, or beat him with a poker, or stick a penknife in his neck.

Clothed in a dressing gown with, apparently, another frothy garment underneath, she sat with her skirts drawn up and her feet in a large basin of water. The hurt ankle. He remembered, and grew hot with shame. It was no good telling himself that she was injured because she'd acted like an idiot. She'd been hurt, in pain, and he had said appalling things to her.

He crossed the room to stand in front of her, the basin between them. "You must not hate me," he said.

The wrong words. He knew it before she shot him a furious flash of blue. She said nothing, only returned that blazing gaze to her feet.

The silence seemed to beat at his head, his heart.

Don't hate me don't hate me don't hate me.

He looked at her feet, so slim and white and vulnerable. He knew what to say. It was there, in his mind, somewhere.

Sorry.

A single word. But a weight pressed on his chest and he was slow, and she broke the silence first.

"I detest you," she said, her voice low and throbbing. "You broke my heart. Cruelly."

He stared at her. "Broke your heart?"

"Yes."

He'd been beastly, yes, and said cruel things, but . . . *her heart?*

"Oh, come," he said. "You know I did nothing of the kind."

Another murderous flash of blue. "To compare me to your parents of all people—your *parents!*—when you know how often I've fought them on your behalf, when you weren't there to defend yourself. And to say you've kept away all this time b-because of m-me . . ."

She looked away.

It was true. She was his friend but she was like the simoom: a sudden, immense whirlwind racing across the desert and sucking up the sand into a great tidal wave and sending everyone running for cover. It tore up tents and scattered belongings and flung people and animals about as though they were toys. It was beautiful and dramatic and it rarely killed, but it left so much damage in its wake.

She was a human simoom, and he couldn't deny that she was one of the reasons he stayed away, but he'd cut his tongue out rather than tell that truth again.

He bent to peer at her face. "You're not really crying, are you?"

She turned her head further away, toward the fire. The firelight danced on her hair, striking coppery sparks in the wayward curls.

If she had truly been his sister, he might have stroked her hair. If she had been his lover . . . but they couldn't be lovers. Ever. He couldn't dishonor her and he couldn't marry a simoom, and it was as simple and irrevocable as that.

"Why should I waste tears on a heartless brute like you?" she said. "Why should I allow myself to be cut to the quick by the fiendish injustice of your remarks?"

Fiendish injustice.

Drama. That was good. True, too. The weight on his chest began to ease. If she was trying on the guilt technique, forgiveness was forthcoming—though it would take a while and involve stunning verbal abuse, which he fully deserved.

"Why, indeed," he said. "I've never minced words with you, and I should be sorry to start. Though I will, if that's what you want. I've had practice enough. But I must tell you, that will be more depressing to my spirits than Scotland's infernal climate and my infernal parents and their accursed castle. If we're to be together for who knows how long, in that wilderness, with those two beldams, and I can't speak my mind to you—"

"Don't try that with me," she said. "Don't pretend I'm your confidante when you've done and said everything to assure me I'm not. If your idea of speaking your mind means abusing me in that despicable way—"

"Despicable!" Excellent. And quite right, too.

"I'm not a dog you can kick when you're in a foul mood," she said.

"You could kick me back," he said. "You usually do."

"I wish I could," she said. "But as you see, I'm temporarily disabled."

He looked at her feet, naked in the water. He remembered the feel of her foot against his bare leg. Pandora's Box. He slammed the lid shut. "Is it still very bad?" he said.

"No," she said. "I merely turned my ankle. But Bailey imagined it was swelling, and made me soak it. I must do as she says or she'll leave me, and if she leaves me, you know I'll go all to pieces."

"She won't leave you," he said. "And neither will I, until this idiotish Noble Quest is accomplished. You've dragged me into it and now you must live with the consequences. Like it or lump it, Olivia. You brought this on yourself."

He told himself that was as good an exit line as any. He told himself an exit was the intelligent move. He'd been forgiven, more or less, and he no longer wanted to hang himself.

. . . but her foot.

Bailey believed it was swelling.

Not a good sign. He knew a great deal about such

things. He'd learned from Daphne Carsington how to tend to the servants' and crew's frequent illnesses and injuries.

Perhaps Olivia hadn't merely turned her ankle. She might have sprained it, or fractured one of those scores of tiny bones.

He knelt before the basin. He blocked out the feminine garments and the firelit curls and all the rest of the fragrant womanliness and focused on her right foot as though it were a separate object altogether. "It doesn't look swollen to me," he said. "But it's hard to be sure while it's under water."

Gently he grasped her foot and lifted it from the basin.

He heard her suck in air.

Something was trembling, either his hand or her foot.

"Does it hurt?" he said.

"No," she said.

"It looks all right," he said. Carefully he turned the foot this way and that. A slender foot, elegantly proportioned, the toes in gracefully descending size, like the feet of Egyptian statues. The wet skin was so smooth under his hand.

"I think you've looked at it long enough," she said in a choked voice. "It's getting cold."

Yes. Long enough. Too long.

"Time to stop soaking it, in any case," he said briskly. He heard the catch in his voice. He hoped she didn't. "It's getting wrinkly." He reached for the folded towel placed near the basin, set it over his thigh, and put her foot on his thigh. He gently massaged her foot with the towel, working his way from ankle to toes. And back again. And up her calf to her knee. And back again.

She remained perfectly still.

He set the injured foot down on another towel, and attended to the left foot in the same way.

He was careful to keep the towel between his fingers and her skin. All the same, he felt every graceful contour of her foot: the fine bones, the turn of arch and ankle, the delicate line of her toes.

"If you're kneeling at my feet," she said unsteadily, "this must be an apology."

"Yes, perhaps," he said.

This was the selfsame foot she'd slid up his bare leg the other night.

He raised the foot, as though to set it on the towel, as he'd done with the other. He hesitated. It was only for an instant, and it was a lifetime. A wave of longing rushed through him, unbearable.

He bent and kissed the front of her lower leg.

He heard her sharp inhalation. He could scarcely breathe for the furious pounding of his heart, the heat racing downward.

Carefully he set her foot down. Smoothly he rose.

Wrong. Wrong. So wrong. Unfair to him, to her, to everybody. But it was done, and he'd stopped, and his frock coat concealed what she'd done to him—or he'd done to himself.

"Or maybe I'm getting even," he said.

Out of the room he sauntered, his gait cool and casual, while the simoom roared across his inner self.

* * *

As soon as the door closed behind Lisle, the one to the adjoining room opened, and Bailey came in.

"Miss, I'm sorry," she said, "but I didn't think I ought to—"

Olivia held up her hand. "Never mind," she said. She barely recognized her own voice. Breathless. Because her heart still beat so painfully hard, so fast. "He . . ." She trailed off.

What the devil was he thinking? They'd agreed, had they not, that the Episode in Stamford was a Terrible Mistake. But they'd crossed a line . . . and he was a man, and once a man got those ideas in his head—oh, what nonsense! Men *always* had those ideas. But he was supposed to keep his distance from her.

He was not supposed to seduce her, the great idiot!

Whether it was meant to be an apology or revenge, he was taking a suicidal risk—with her future! With his!

"*Men*," she said.

"Yes, miss," Bailey said.

"It was my own fault, I suppose."

"I don't know, miss."

"I was furious, you know."

"Yes, miss."

"The things he said." It still hurt to recall them.

"Yes, miss."

"I should have covered my feet when he came in, or at least drawn down my skirts."

"Yes, miss, but I could have done that, and I did desert you."

"Not your fault, Bailey. I'm a DeLucey. It doesn't matter that I'm other things as well. The DeLucey always takes over. He hurt my feelings, and I had to get even by being provocative. Could I have been more foolish? Did I not size him up at Great-Grandmama's party? Wasn't it clear enough, the invisible sign over his head? Danger. Don't play with this fire. Any De-Lucey would have seen it. The trouble is, any DeLucey would do it anyway."

"Yes, miss."

"It's so hard to resist a risk."

"Yes, miss."

"But he's *too* risky."

His too-clever hands and their touch, unbearably intimate. So patient and methodical. If he set out to seduce a woman, that was how he'd do it. Patiently. Methodically. The way he'd kissed her the other night: absolutely focused attention. No quarter given.

If any other man had touched her in that way, kissed her in that way, her morals would have disintegrated, and she'd have let them, happily.

"Damned if you do and damned if you don't," she said. "If one is married, one might have affairs. But marriage is a very bad gamble for a woman. Play the wrong card—wed the wrong man—and spend the rest of your life in one kind of hell or another, some worse than others, but all of them—or nearly all—hells."

"That's true enough, miss," said Bailey, who did not have a high opinion of men. Watching the way men behaved around Olivia would destroy any young woman's illusions. "All the same, her ladyship, your mother—"

"Pray don't use Mama as an example," Olivia said. She'd found the love of her life. Twice. "It's not the same at all. She's *good*."

Tuesday 11 October

Olivia tried to rise before dawn, as she'd done the two previous days. Today, though, the prospect of dragging those naughty ladies from their beds in the dark—again—and leading Lisle a merry chase had lost its entertainment value.

The sun was well up and streaming through the window when she was at last ready to face the day.

Bailey brought in the breakfast tray. On it lay a letter.

The outside read "Miss Carsington." The precise, angular writing was all too familiar.

Olivia broke the seal, unfolded the paper, and read:

Alnwick
Tuesday 11th Instant

Dear Olivia,

By the time you read this, I shall have already set out, because I'm determined to reach Gorewood while sufficient daylight remains for reconnoitering. It belatedly occurred to me—and given that I'm a man, you won't wonder at its being so belated—that we've no idea what the monstrosity holds in the way of furnishings. Very little, I suspect. It seems I must impose on your ~~good nature~~ *to undertake some shopping in Edinburgh for me. Nichols has made a preliminary list, which I enclose. He'll make an inventory after we arrive, and I'll send it on to you in Edinburgh.*

Being accustomed to camp beds or blankets on

tomb floors, I'm certainly not one to fuss about colors or styles. Use your own judgment—and if you think of anything else that may be wanting, pray don't hesitate to add it to your purchases. In any event, I've no doubt that your taste in such matters is far superior to mine.

I've directed a letter to Mains, my father's agent in Edinburgh, informing him of your errand. All bills are to be sent to him. I know that he, like every other sentient male, will be happy to assist you in any way you require. You will find his name and direction on Nichols's list.

I shall look forward to seeing you in a week or two at Castle Horrid.

Yours sincerely,
L

"Oh, really, Lisle," Olivia said. "That crossed-out bit is so childish. Still . . ." She considered. "Yes, you aren't a complete imbecile. You've seen the error of your ways, I don't doubt. Out of sight, out of mind."

"Miss?"

Olivia waved the letter at her. "A reprieve, Bailey," she said. "He's gone and we're going *shopping*."

Edinburgh
12 October

Dear Lisle,

Rather than Subject the Ladies to another <u>Long Day</u> in the Carriage, I decided to continue to Edinburgh by Easy Stages. We arrived this day in the Late Afternoon—and oh, what a Sight came into view, exactly as Scott described:

> Such dusky grandeur clothed the height,
> Where the huge castle holds its state,
> And all the steep slope down,
> Whose ridgy back heaves to the sky,
> Piled deep and massy, close and high,
> Mine own romantic town.

As you may recall, I had visited in my Childhood, but my Memories were confused, and I thought I'd <u>dreamed it</u>: the Castle crowning the Great Rock, rising through the Smoke and Mist, the Spires and Steeples poking through the broody atmosphere, the Ancient Town with its <u>tall</u> Buildings, perched on the ridge. But there it was, the <u>Most Astonishing City In The World</u>—and yes, I should defy even the Sphinx to match it for Atmosphere.

But I know my Effusions <u>bore you</u>. Therefore I proceed to Business. The Picturesque Old Town is crowded with Shops of every Description. There are still more to be found in the <u>far less romantic</u> New Town of Edinburgh, in a plain to the northwest. (That is where your cousin used to live, by the way, in an Elegant House cluttered to an <u>astounding</u> degree with old Books and Papers.) Beyond a doubt we can fulfill all of our most <u>pressing commissions</u> with a few days of Shopping.

I shall send ahead to you all but the servants we

cannot do without. Edwards, who is to act as our Butler, will wish to do what he can to make the Castle
habitable in advance of our Arrival. In the meantime,
I shall visit the Servants Registry and make our needs
known. Given the locals' FEAR OF THE PLACE, we
shall have to rely upon our *Own Small Force*, at least
for a Time. I'm *fully confident*, however, that we shall
speedily Get to the Bottom of this HAUNTING, and
re-establish a proper Scottish staff—for as you know,
our London Servants are *on loan*, and *must be returned* soon, preferably before Mama finds out I've
Stolen them.

> Yours sincerely,
> Olivia Carsington

On Wednesday Roy and Jock Rankin returned from
Edinburgh, their pockets jingling with the profits from
the most recent sale of things that didn't belong to
them. They found Gorewood's public house buzzing
with news: The Marquess of Atherton's son, the Earl
of Lisle, was moving into Gorewood Castle with a full
retinue of London servants. One carriage had already
arrived with boxes, trunks, and a set of servants, and
more were coming in a few days.

Roy and Jock looked at each other.

"Not likely," Roy said. "Some Londoners coming to
stare at the old castle, like they do sometimes. Everyone hereabouts gets fool ideas. Always thinking someone's moving in. No one's moved in since the old man
moved out—what was it?—ten years ago?"

But the people about them were excited, much more

than they ever were when traveling visitors from England turned up wanting to explore the castle.

After a time, the brothers left the tavern and went out in the rain to see for themselves.

Their neighbors, they found, had got the story right for once. From the road, through the steady drizzle, they could make out light in at least three windows. When they sneaked in closer they discovered a carriage and horses in the ramshackle stable.

"This won't do," said Roy.

"We'll have to put a stop to it," said Jock.

Thursday 13 October

The butler Edwards was not as drunk as he wanted to be. It had been raining steadily since he'd arrived at Gorewood Castle. It was an ugly heap of stones, dank and stinking of disuse. They'd brought bedding but there were no beds. It was one thing for the master, who was used to sleeping on stone floors or bare ground, but it wasn't what Edwards was used to.

They'd been working from sunup to long after sundown, trying to make the great dungeon of a place habitable for the ladies. The villagers were not cooperative. They steadfastly refused to understand simple English and even the master, with all his knowledge of heathen languages, couldn't make heads or tales of their speech.

The London servants were treated like an invading army. You would think the shopkeepers would want the custom, but ask them for this or that and all you got was a blank look. And when at last they condescended to recognize you as a customer, they got the order wrong.

At least they'd got it right at the Crooked Crook public house—after making him go through a dozen gyrations and finally having to write it down. He'd stopped there to warm his insides before trudging back to the curst castle in the wet.

The road was lonely, not a streetlamp anywhere. To one side he made out the ragged outlines of the church that had burned down last century. He could see the churchyard, the gravestones sagging at untidy angles, as though the rain and the dark and the cold weighed them down.

He was looking that way, shivering, when he heard the rustling. Then suddenly it loomed in front of him, a white figure with glowing eyes.

He screamed and turn and ran.

And ran and ran and ran.

Gorewood Castle
Friday 14 October

Dear Olivia,

You had better find another butler. Edwards has disappeared.

Yours sincerely,
L

Chapter Ten

Gorewood
Monday 17 October

*S*he stood in the road, looking up at the monolith that crowned the rise.

Lisle had left the village and arrived in time to see Olivia's carriage stop next to the graveyard and ruined church. He'd watched her alight and move to one side of the road. There, hands clasped over her bosom, she gazed, obviously enraptured, at Gorewood Castle.

A parade of vehicles—mainly carts and wagons, heaped with who knew what—had preceded hers. Others followed. All of the village's inhabitants had stopped whatever they were doing and come out to gape.

He'd gaped, too. He hadn't seen a line of vehicles that long since King George IV's coronation, a decade ago.

She was oblivious to the horses, carts, and wagons

passing by her. She was oblivious to everything but whatever it was she saw in that great, grim rectangular heap of stone.

Lisle knew she saw worlds more than he did.

All he saw, really, was Olivia, in a pose that was so like her. He remained for a moment, simply watching her stand so still that a fanciful person would believe she was spellbound.

Since this was Olivia, she was undoubtedly spellbound. One needn't be fanciful to know that. One needed only to know her.

What, he wondered, would she make of the Pyramids?

Stupid question. She'd be enchanted. She wouldn't mind the hardships. She'd grown up on the streets of Dublin and London. She'd be happy and excited . . . until the novelty wore off and she grew bored.

His life wasn't always as exciting as she imagined. The work itself was repetitive and tedious. Finding a tomb could take days, weeks, months, years of patient searching. Day after day in the heat, overseeing workers carefully shifting sand . . . the slow, meticulous work of copying the images on tomb and temple walls, of making drawings of monuments, because they could easily disappear.

Whole walls and ceilings had been cut out and taken away to adorn museums and private collections. Temples had been dismantled, their stones used for factories.

He missed it, the repetitious, tedious work. He missed finding, measuring, sorting, imposing order.

She understood his passion for Egypt but she'd never understand his passion for such slow work.

The reality of his life there would bore her witless, and he knew what happened when Olivia became bored.

She'd see the Pyramids someday, he didn't doubt. She'd visit as others did, the aristocrats who sailed to Egypt in their yachts and went up and down the Nile, and went home again in a few months, the yachts piled with *anteekahs*.

She turned then, while his mind was still continents away. Unprepared, he felt the world drop away. Nothing remained but her beautiful face, the blue, blue eyes and the pearly skin, the color rising in her cheeks like a sunrise.

And things stabbed, tiny daggers to his heart.

"Ah, there he is, the laird of the manor," she said with a thick Scottish burr she must have picked up in Edinburgh.

The sound jolted him from his reverie. He hoped she hadn't picked up bagpipe playing as well.

He approached. "Tell that to the natives," he said. "They seem to think I'm the tax collector or the hangman."

She laughed the low, velvety laugh. He could feel himself being drawn in, a dunce of a fly skirting the edges of the spider's web.

Facts. Stick to facts. He studied her clothes as though they were ancient artifacts.

Over the mass of red curls she wore the usual milliner's insanity: a thing with a brim the size of a flagship's foredeck, with feathers and ribbons sprouting out of the top. She wore the usual dressmaker's insanity—sleeves the size of wine barrels and puffed-out skirts that made her waist seem tiny enough for a man to encircle with one hand.

Seem wasn't a fact. *Seem* was fantasy. He flung the thought away as though it had been a useless piece of rubble.

He swept off his hat and bowed, to give himself something rational to do. "Welcome to Castle Horrid," he said. "I hope it's hideous and gloomy enough for you."

"It's wonderful," she said. "Beyond anything I could have hoped for."

She was well and truly thrilled. It was there, unmistakable, in the flush of excitement in her cheeks and the light in her eyes.

If they'd been children, she would have run at him and flung her arms about his neck and cried, "I'm so glad I came!"

He felt a moment's grief, a sense of loss—but one couldn't be a child forever, and one didn't want to be.

He put his hat back on his head and turned his attention to Gorewood Castle and its facts.

"Motte and bailey style," he said. "U-shape. Main block containing basement and three floors. Two wings projecting from the west face of the main block, with three main floors above the basement. The height is one hundred six feet from ground level to the top of the parapets. The walls, on average, are fifteen feet thick. It is far from a common type of structure, I agree, and it is certainly extraordinary in having survived for so long, relatively intact."

"Thank you for the architecture lesson." She gave a little shake of her head that made the curls bounce about her face. "You never change, do you? I referred to the *atmosphere*. So grey and forbidding. And the light, at this time of day—the lowering sun piercing the clouds to drive long shadows over the bleak land-scape, as though Gorewood Castle spreads its gloom over the surrounding valley." While she spoke, a flock of crows, disturbed by something, started up from the north tower, cawing. "And there are your dark ghosts," she said.

"Atmosphere is your department," he said. "I've had as much atmosphere as I can take. It's done nothing but rain." Too many short, dark days of rain, followed by long, dark, rainy nights. All the while wondering what he'd done in his life to deserve being sent into exile here. Wishing he had someone to talk to, and telling himself he didn't mean *her,* but someone sensible. But here she was, glowing like an Egyptian morning, and stabbing at his heart and lifting it at the same time.

"Then I pronounce the atmosphere completely cor-rect," she said. "The perfect setting for a horrid tale like *Frankenstein* or *The Monk*."

"If that's your idea of perfect, you'll be ecstatic with the inside," he said. "It's damp and cold and dark. Some of the windows are broken, and we have chinks in the mortar. As a result, we get interesting shrieking and wailing sounds as the wind blows through."

She came nearer then, and peered up at him from under the gigantic rim of her bonnet. "I can't wait," she said. "Show me—now, while we still have the light."

Olivia had been enthralled, yes, but she hadn't failed to notice the castle's dilapidated entrance arch, through which her train of carriages and carts and wagons passed. She'd expected to see Lisle appear there. She'd imagined him standing next to the equally dilapidated and picturesque drum-shaped gatehouse for a time, watching the vehicles pass and looking for her. Then he'd spot her and come out and . . . well, he wouldn't open his arms so that she could run into them. But she'd expected him to come out from there, to greet her, as the lord of the manor would do.

Instead, he'd appeared out of nowhere, in exactly the place where the lowering sun could catch at his hair when he swept off his hat and bowed. The sun made glittering gold trails in his hair and danced on the straw and dust from the carts and wagons, making golden sparks fly about him.

It was very aggravating of him to suddenly appear, all gleaming gold like a figure in a medieval tale. For a moment, she'd imagined him sweeping her up on his white charger and carrying her away. . .

To where? Egypt. Where else? Where he'd drop her in the sand and forget about her as soon as a crumbling, smelly mummy caught his eye.

But he couldn't help it, any more than she could help who she was. And he was her friend.

Her friend, she discovered on closer inspection, had shadows under his eyes. Under the shade of his hat brim the bruised eye was barely noticeable, but that same shade emphasized the lines of weariness in his face.

He was unhappy as well. He was being stoical, but she could hear it in his voice and see it in the way he carried himself, all determination and no zest.

She said nothing, though, only listened as he went on in his pedantic way while they passed under the entrance arch into the weedy courtyard.

The curtain walls were crumbling, she saw, but the stables at the far end of the courtyard were merely shabby. Overall, it was not in nearly so ruinous a state as the Athertons had made out. Not altogether surprising. Both she and Lisle had understood the castle was merely a means to an end.

They neared a set of stairs leading up—perhaps thirty feet—to a door in the castle.

"This is how we get to the first floor," he said. "One used to cross a drawbridge and pass under the portcullis, but those disintegrated long ago. When major repairs were done last century, my ancestor must have decided stairs were more practical. A wise decision, I think. A drawbridge and portcullis serve no useful purpose nowadays, and they're the devil to maintain."

She could picture the drawbridge and portcullis. She could picture the castle as it had been long ago, when the walls about it were strong, and men kept watch from the towers and gatehouses and parapets.

Before she could start up the stairs, he touched her wrist to stop her. If he'd been the romantic figure she'd imagined, he would have pulled her into his arms and told her how much he'd missed her.

She, to her vexation, had missed him. She'd wished they might have explored Edinburgh together. Even he would be disarmed by its beauty. Even he would appreciate how different it was from London, like another world entirely.

But his gloved hand barely touched hers before he

drew it away to indicate a doorway, blocked by weeds and rubbish, at ground level.

"There," he said. "We've a basement comprising three rooms in the main block. Arched vaults. A well room in the south wing. I've assigned you women to the south tower. It's a bit warmer and brighter. The Harpies will be on the lower levels because the stairs will kill them."

She looked up, up, up, to the top of the castle. The inner stairways would be narrow and steeply winding. And dark. In olden times, any enemies who managed to get inside could easily be trapped and killed before they got far.

"A drawbridge and portcullis would be more romantic," she said, starting up the unromantic stairs.

"Would a dungeon make it up to you?" he said. "Because we've a fine dank one in the north wing of the basement."

"I'm sure it will come in handy," she said.

"It isn't functional at present," he said. "Except for the well room, the basement rooms are in a ruinous state. One of the stairways leading down from the first floor has been vandalized. Still, that and the curtain wall seem to represent the worst of the depredations."

She reached the top of the stairs. The door opened and she stepped past the servant holding it into and through a short passage. Then she simply stood stock-still and gaped like the veriest yokel.

"I had the same reaction," came Lisle's voice from behind her. "To hear my parents carry on, you'd think we had trees growing in the fireplace and birds nesting in the minstrel gallery."

She'd known his parents had exaggerated. They always did. Still, nothing had prepared her for this sight.

It was a great banqueting hall, and yes, she'd been in plenty of them. But those were richly furnished, offering every modern comfort. They didn't show their origins as plainly as this one did.

Above her rose a great pointed vault. To her left, at the end of the long hall, a fire blazed in an immense fireplace with a cone-shaped stone hood. On either side of it were large niches where someone had set candles.

The room was splendid. Though almost completely unfurnished, it was much as it would have appeared centuries ago, when Mary, Queen of Scots, visited.

This, she thought, must be a little of what Lisle felt when he first came upon an ancient temple: a sense of stepping into another, older world.

She was vaguely aware of servants moving out into the hall, lining up, waiting, and she knew she was supposed to marshal them into order, but for the moment, all she could do was take in her surroundings.

"Fifty-five feet long and twenty-five feet wide," came Lisle's voice beside her. "Thirty feet from the floor to the top of the pointed barrel vault. The minstrels' gallery seems to have been replaced in the last century. There was a screens passage under it. I'm not sure that needs to be replaced."

She turned to him. "It's splendid."

"I'm glad you think so," he said. "I hope you'll convey its splendor to the servants. They seem to be dubious."

"I will," she said fervently. She knew exactly what to do. This was what she'd come for. To turn a ruin into something magnificent and bring a village back to life. To do something worthwhile.

She turned her attention to the line of servants, who didn't appear at all happy. Strangely, the ones who'd been here for a few days did not seem to be in a greater state of trepidation than those who'd come with her. She supposed that Lisle had done his best to keep up morale. But they were all London servants, after all. They must have felt they'd stepped into the Dark Ages.

She didn't square her shoulders visibly, but she did it mentally. This part she could easily do. The sooner she did it, the more quickly their work here would be done.

Then he could go back to his one true love and she—

Oh, for heaven's sake, she was only two and twenty. She still had time to find her own true love, too.

The odds weren't good but she'd beat long odds before.

Only look at how far she'd come since the day she'd met him. And now she had a castle—not forever, but then, she wasn't a forever sort of girl.

An hour later

Lisle knew Olivia was a chameleon. She could mimic not only accent and dialect but posture and manner. He'd seen her fit in among street urchins and pawnbrokers and peddlers. Why shouldn't she as easily assume the role of chatelaine of the castle?

Still, he was startled when, shortly after entering, she took off her ludicrous hat and turned into her step-grandmother, Lady Hargate. The romantic, breathless Olivia he'd seen standing in the road became cool and detached and absolutely in control, as she set about directing the servants.

The first priority was making the great hall comfortable, since they'd be spending most of their time here. Nichols had had the first group of servants clean the room. After inspecting their work, Olivia set about directing the placement of furniture and such.

When Lisle realized he was studying her the way he'd study a mummy's wrappings, he collected his wits and left the hall.

He went to his room and gave himself a lengthy and logical lecture about spellbinding women who turned into sandstorms. Then he gathered his plans and drawings and returned to her.

Very coolly and logically, he said, as he gave them to her, "I thought you'd find it easier to understand the castle's layout if you had these."

She took out the sheets of paper and set them out on the large table the servants had hefted into the center of the room. She studied them for a time, and the firelight and candlelight danced in the curious arrangement of curls her maid had made atop her head.

"Oh, Lisle, this is brilliant," she said.

If he wrapped one of those curls about his finger, what would it feel like?

"I have some of your cousin Frederick Dalmay's books and papers," she said. "They do contain drawings and plans, but nothing so detailed as these."

"It's what I usually do when I come upon an unfamiliar structure," he said. "I needed to be doing something productive. The downpour limited activity, and that started the first day."

"It rained in Edinburgh, a little every day." She didn't look up. She was still studying the drawings and plans and notes.

"It was more than a little here," he said. "The cold stream of rain commenced at Coldstream, our first stop after Nichols and I left Alnwick. I suppose that's Scotland's idea of a joke. It rained throughout the ride here. It didn't stop raining until last night. Surveying the house kept me busy."

It was supposed to keep disturbing thoughts at bay, too. That part hadn't worked so well.

"Is this what you do in Egypt?" she said.

"Yes. After we clear away the sand."

"Your drawings are beautiful," she said, looking up at last.

He looked at the drawings spread out on the table, then into her face.

That beautiful color in her cheeks. It seemed to come from within, but perhaps the candlelight enhanced it. Even in daytime, not much light survived the long journey from outside through the narrow windows and fifteen-foot wall.

"I'm not joking, and it isn't flattery," she said. "Your draftsmanship is excellent."

They exchanged a smiling glance, and that said everything, he thought. They were thinking the same thing: The first day he'd met her, she'd told him that his drawings were dreadful.

"It's taken me only a decade to progress from 'execrable' to 'excellent,'" he said.

She turned back to the drawing. He watched her slim finger trace the outline of the first floor's great bed-chamber.

"This simplifies everything," she said.

Did it? Or had everything become impossibly complicated: the slender, graceful finger and her fine-boned hand and the way her skin glowed in the dusky light of this ancient hall and the smile at a shared memory.

He stepped a pace away, before he could be tempted to touch. "It makes it easier to set priorities for repairs," he said. "When and if we ever get workmen, I'll know precisely where they're to begin and what they're to do."

"That's why you were in the village today," she said.

"For all the good it did," he said.

"I can't believe you had no luck with the villagers," she said. "You manage hordes of workers in Egypt."

"It's different there," he said. "I know enough of the various languages to communicate, and I know their ways. Scotland's culture is altogether different. But I suspect Gorewood's inhabitants are being thick on purpose because they don't want to understand me. And I'll wager anything they lay the burr on thick on purpose because they don't want me to understand *them*."

"I'm wild to get to the bottom of that," she said. "You're the laird's son. They have a problem with your castle. They ought to feel they can confide their worries to you."

"Perhaps they don't find me the confiding sort."

She brushed this away with a wave of her hand. "Don't be silly. All you have to do is stand there to inspire trust, unlike the rest of us. But I must keep to one thing at a time. Our servants first."

"Yes, sorry about that," he said. "I didn't mean to lose the butler."

She turned away from the drawings to give him her full attention.

"Edwards," she said. "I meant to ask you—but the sight of the castle knocked everything else from my mind. Then I saw the servants, all looking so—so-"

"Suicidal," he said. "One can't blame them. They've had to camp out in the great hall, exactly as their predecessors would have done centuries ago. I'm amazed they haven't all bolted."

Her blue eyes lit with interest. "You think Edwards bolted?"

"So it would ap—"

A roar and a horrific crash cut him off.

The door to the kitchen passage flew open, and the kitchen staff irrupted into the great hall.

The roaring—human—continued, in spurts.

Olivia looked at the kitchen help cowering under the minstrel gallery, then at the door to the kitchen passage, then at Lisle.

"Must be Aillier," he said, naming the London cook she'd sent to feed them. "He's been a little sullen lately."

"A *little* sullen?" she said.

"We've been living on cold meat and cheese," Lisle said. "He won't bake. He says the oven is an abomination. I wanted to pitch him out of the window, but he probably wouldn't fit—and if he did, we'd be short a cook as well as a butler."

Olivia's chin went up. "I may help you pitch him out of the window," she said, in the same coolly indignant tones Lady Hargate would have used. "Not bake bread, indeed. No wonder the staff are so dispirited."

Head high, eyes blazing, she swept toward the kitchen.

Nichols, who'd been talking to one of the frightened kitchen servants, hurried into her path, to block the door. "I beg your pardon for standing in the way, Miss Carsington, but it isn't safe. I'm told he's threatening with the cleaver. I recommend you allow me to disarm him first."

Olivia eyed Nichols up and down. He could probably don armor and still not weigh ten stone.

"He's tougher than he looks," Lisle said, reading her thoughts exactly. "And stronger," he added in an undertone. "With remarkable stamina—or such at least is his reputation among the womenfolk of Egypt."

His voice was too low and his mouth was too close to her ear. His breath was warm, tickling her ear and a sensitive place behind it.

She didn't have time for this.

Men.

"Thank you, Nichols," she said, "but we cannot allow you to precede us." She turned to Lisle and added, in a voice as low as his had been, "We can't let it seem that we're intimidated by a temperamental French cook. The villagers will hear about it and laugh themselves sick."

"Sorry, Nichols," Lisle said more audibly. "We can't let you have all the fun. Miss Carsington and I will sort this out."

Olivia waved her hand imperiously.

Nichols stepped out of the way.

More roaring came from behind the door.

Olivia glared at Nichols. He opened the door.

She stormed into the dragon's lair.

Olivia tried to get ahead of him in the short passage, but Lisle grasped her waist, picked her up, and put her down behind him. The last bit—setting her down again—wasn't nearly as easy as it ought to be. She was lighter than she looked; the mountainous clothing deceived the eye. It rustled too alluringly, too like the sound of bedclothes being tossed about. It brought back to the front of his mind the slenderness and delicacy of her feet, the grace of her fingers, the silken feel of her skin under his hands.

All the dreams and fantasies he'd so rigorously suppressed rose up like ghosts. He beat them down again.

"You can do the talking," he said. "But I'm going first in case of deadly missiles."

"Don't be absurd," she said. "You think I can't handle menials?" She elbowed him sharply in the ribs and pushed past him into the kitchen proper. Cursing under his breath, Lisle followed close on her heels.

Over her shoulder he saw a red-faced Aillier brandishing a cleaver. Since he was nearly six feet tall and three feet wide and surrounded by extremely sharp blades, it required no prescience to understand why the kitchen staff had fled when he exploded.

Lisle had heard the tirade on the way in. Conducted in three languages, it boiled down to:

"This kitchen, to call it primitive is a gross flattery!

It is like a cave, for animals. No one can expect me to cook in such a place!"

When Olivia sailed in, the cook paused, mouth open, the hand holding the weapon in midair.

"Don't let me interrupt," she said. "You were saying?"

Aillier quickly recovered from his surprise. "It is not to be borne, mademoiselle!" he cried. "This is a place of brutes. The peasants, they are savages of the most ignorant. How am I to tell them what is needed? They speak no English or French. No form of German or Italian. Their language, it is for animals, all grunts and ugly gargling of the mouth."

"He's a fine one to talk," Lisle whispered.

"I see," Olivia said. "The peasants are inferior. What else?"

Aillier waved his cleaver, first at the oven, then at the gigantic fireplace—which dwarfed even him—the stone basin and sink, the pans and cooking utensils heaped on the ancient trestle table.

"To expect me—Aillier—to cook in such a place is torture!" he roared, though with a degree more uncertainty than a moment ago. "It is inhuman to subject an artist to this—this cave. I will not endure it."

Slowly and deliberately, Olivia looked about her.

The kitchen occupied the first floor of the castle's north wing. Even allowing for the thickness of the walls and the size of the fireplace, a generous space remained. One of the three large windows had been converted to an oven. Still, even on rainy days, it was a brighter kitchen than many Lisle had seen. In some great English houses, the kitchens were deep underground.

"I think it's rather impressive, myself," Lisle muttered.

No one heeded him.

"This is not torture," she told Aillier. "Torture must wait until the dungeon is properly fitted out. What we have here are challenging conditions. A great chef can cook anywhere. Remember the challenge Prince Talleyrand set the great chef Carême? A year of meals, never repeating a dish, using only ingredients in season, from the estate. But if you cannot rise to this challenge, it cannot be helped. It's no use wishing you had skills of a higher order or possessed confidence in those you have. If you are inadequate to the task—"

"Inadequate!"

"Kindly remember that the fellow has a whacking great cleaver in his hand, with a deuced sharp edge," Lisle murmured.

"If you've decided to give up, Monsieur Aillier," she went on, "then stop fussing about it, and do so. One of the village women can see to our meals until I can send for a proper cook from London. A Roman this time. I'm told they're *dauntless* in the face of adversity."

Having delivered her broadside, she turned and sailed out, cool as you please.

Lisle didn't move. For a moment he could only stand, staring. He saw Aillier watch her go, his mouth hanging open, his face an ugly shade of maroon.

Lisle braced himself. But the chef slowly lowered the hand with the cleaver in it.

Lisle backed out into the passage. No flying blades, but the silence in the kitchen was ominous.

Then he heard Aillier's voice, grumbling about ac-

cursed Romans and their inedible sauces. Then came
the sound of pans being banged about.

Lisle got halfway to the door where he waited. Then
the scene rushed into his mind, as vivid as an illumination: Aillier brandishing the great cleaver—and Olivia,
a fraction of his size, in her gigantic sleeves and vast
skirts, her curls pinned into silly corkscrews. Olivia,
her chin in the air, coolly whittling the immense cook
down to size. The look on Aillier's face. The look on
hers.

Ye gods. Ye gods. Olivia.

Olivia stopped short when she heard the sound—
someone being strangled, she thought at first. Aillier.
Had he sprung into the passage? Attacked Lisle? Heart
surging into a gallop, she whipped around.

What she saw in the gloomy space was Lisle, leaning
against a wall, bent over, clutching his stomach. . .

Laughing.

She marched back to him. "Not here, you idiot," she
said in a low voice. "He'll hear!"

Aillier was still talking to himself, banging pans, but
they were only a few feet away from the kitchen.

Lisle looked at her, his lips pressed together, but a
whoop escaped.

She grabbed his arm and pulled him toward the door.
He started to go with her, but after a few steps, he fell
against the wall again, his hand over his mouth.

"Lisle," she said.

"You," he said. That was as far as he got before he
went into another paroxysm.

"Lisle," she said.

"So funny. You. Him."

"You're going to do yourself an injury."

"You," he said. "Only you." He went off again.

She could only stand looking at him and wondering at him. When she'd come, he'd been so weary and stoical and now. . .

He took out his handkerchief and wiped his eyes. "Sorry," he said.

"You're overtired," she said.

"Yes," he said. "Probably."

He came away from the wall. Then he convulsed again, laughing and laughing. She stood mesmerized, smiling helplessly while inside she seemed to be turning over and over like the golden dust motes that had danced about him. She was falling into something, falling over and over, because he laughed, and the sound was mischief and joy, and it was impossible to keep that sound out of her heart.

Then he stopped, and again wiped his eyes, and said, "Sorry. Don't know what . . . Really, Olivia, you are beyond anything."

He took her hand, to lead her to the door, she thought.

And then she was against the wall, in the corner by the door, and his hands were cupping her face, and she tasted the laughter when his mouth covered hers.

Chapter Eleven

$\mathscr{S}$he was wonderful. He'd only meant to tell her so.

Lisle thought that was what he'd done, was doing.

But his hands came up, and then he was cupping her beautiful face and wanting to say, "I'd forgotten. I'd forgotten this part of you."

He'd forgotten what a miracle of a girl she'd been, ready to try anything, face anything. The beautiful woman had got in the way, and he couldn't see Olivia properly.

But she was the girl as well as the woman, a miracle as well as beautiful. He was looking down into her great blue eyes, whose color he couldn't see in the shadowy passage and didn't need to see, since it was engraved deep in his memory, the fierce blue that had so startled him on the day he'd met her.

And there was her mouth, full and soft and slightly parted in surprise, only inches from his. He couldn't say anything at all. And then he was kissing her

He felt her stiffen. Her hands came up to his chest.

Push me away, yes, that's best. But no, don't, not yet.

The softness of her mouth and the scent of her skin

and the nearness and the warmth: He wasn't ready to give it all up. *Not yet.*

She didn't push. The stiffness melted away and she became soft and yielding, melting into him while her hands crept up to his shoulders. She kissed him back, so quick and sudden and fierce. And there it was, the taste he'd tried to forget. It was like biting into a ripe cherry. It made a man forget all other tastes in that first ambrosial moment. It must have been a cherry that Eve gave Adam. What other fruit tastes quite so sinful?

He forgot other things, too: resolutions and conscience and wisdom. Strip them away and what was left?

He'd missed her.

Now she was in his arms, the girl he'd missed so much, and the woman, too, the human chameleon he'd known for so long. So fearless and confident a moment ago, so warm and yielding now. He surrendered, too, to cherry-sweet sin, and the scent of her skin and the faint traces of a flowery fragrance in her hair, her clothes. The scent slithered into his mind like opium smoke.

Something else lingered there as well. A shadow. A warning voice: *Enough. Stop. Remember.*

Not yet.

Her fingers slid up into his hair, and the touch, so caressing, reached deep. It found the empty place in his heart, the one he'd so carefully covered up, where he hid impossible wishes and longings. He ached, he hardly knew what for, but it wasn't mere animal need, the simple, obvious thing. That he'd recognize. This was unfamiliar.

He needed something *more;* that was all he understood.

He slid his hands down to her shoulders and arms. He pulled her hard against him, and still searching for the elusive *more*, deepened the kiss.

She gave way as desert sands give way, sliding away while they drew one deeper. She dared now as she'd always done, answering his urgent searching with her own.

She didn't know, either, what it was she looked for. He could sense it, that this world was strange to her, too. Here they were novices, though neither of them was innocent.

All the while, the careful walls they'd built to protect their friendship softened into sand and slid away.

He dragged his hands down to cup her bottom and crush her against his groin. She rubbed against him, unbearable provocation. He moved his hands restlessly over her breasts, but there was clothing in the way, too much of it. Infuriating.

He caught a fistful of skirt and dragged it up, but there was more—miles of skirts and petticoats. He kept pulling, drawing up more and more, while the fabric rustled so loudly, like a protest.

But she didn't protest. She silently urged, inviting and daring him, her body moving against him, her mouth clinging to his. Their tongues' toying and teasing had become a thrusting and parrying, a mimicry of coupling.

He made his way at last through the mountains of skirts, and his fingers grazed the edge of her stocking. Then his fingertips touched skin, velvety, feminine skin. He slid his fingers upward, toward the soft place between her legs. She gasped, and he gave a start, like a schoolboy caught at a prank.

Then her hand slid over the front of his trousers.

He inhaled sharply. At the same moment, he became aware of a crash. Metal on metal. Not far away. Near.

The kitchen. Aillier, banging pots.

If the pot had hit Lisle on the head, that would have been more effective, but it was enough to bring him back to the world, to where they were and what he was about. His wits—a part of them—returned. He broke the kiss, raised his head, and drew away a fraction.

She looked up at him, her head back, her eyes wide and dark, her hand still over the bulge in his trouser front.

She snatched her hand away.

He looked down regretfully, stupidly, at where her hand had been. He let go of her dress. It rustled its way down along her hips and legs.

"Lisle," she said.

"That wasn't what I meant to do," he said. His voice was thick and dull. *Dunce.* "I meant . . ." He had to think.

Maybe he ought to bang his head against the wall.

"What you did in there," he began. "You were brilliant. But . . . ye gods."

She stepped back a pace. Her clothes were all every which way. Delicious. Terrible. What he'd done.

"It was a momentary exuberance," she said. "We were carried away. We were excited because we could have been killed."

"The 'I don't know what came over me' excuse," he said thickly. "That's a good one. That'll do."

* * *

He looked so devastated.

Olivia understood why. He wasn't like her. He had principles. He brimmed with duty and honor and loyalty—all the right things her stepfather had taught him.

Oh, she knew.

As to her—she didn't need principles to be badly shaken. She'd come *this close* to losing her maidenhead. To *him*.

"It was my fault," she said. "You know I've always lacked moral fiber. It's the curse of the Dreadful De-Luceys. We're all like that, except for my mother. But she's an aberration."

"We have to get out of here," he said. "*Now*."

"We can't," she said. "The servants will take one look at us and know we had a Clandestine Encounter."

"They won't know any such thing," he said. "They'll think we had a skirmish with the cook."

She looked down at her dress. The bodice was twisted about. "This doesn't look like a skirmish," she said. She pulled it back into place and smoothed her skirts. Her hair was coming down, but it was no use asking Lisle to fix it.

"Go," he said.

She moved past him and through the passage. He didn't hurry ahead to open the door for her. She supposed he was waiting for his erection to subside. He had been prodigiously aroused—and she hadn't needed to put her hand there to know how aroused, because it had been completely obvious, but. . .

She lacked moral fiber. Temptation came along and beckoned and she went, without a second thought.

He was far too exciting for an unprincipled woman to resist. He excited her even more when he was in a good mood than when, as at Stamford, he was in a bad one. This time her knees had completely melted away. If he had let go of her, she would have dissolved into a puddle of unresolved lust in the passage.

She supposed he'd applied the same diligence and persistence to the art of kissing that he'd employed to improve his drawing. The same way he'd trained himself to strike fire in an instant with a tinderbox.

And when he bedded a woman . . . but this was not the time to speculate.

She pushed the door open and walked into the hall.

Lisle followed a moment after.

There were all the servants, exactly as they'd been before, waiting in what once had been the screens passage.

They didn't look depressed anymore.

They all wore the same look of keen interest.

She drew herself up, once again the chatelaine of the castle.

"Back to work," she told the kitchen servants.

They filed past her through the door into the kitchen area.

She gave a few final instructions to the others, and they quickly scattered to attend to their duties.

The great hall emptied, but for a pair of servants at the opposite end, near the fireplace, who were carrying furnishings into the Harpies' quarters. The door was open and she could hear the ladies arguing about who ought to get the first-floor bedroom and who ought to get the one above it.

She'd let them sort that out for themselves.

When she turned back to Lisle, he was saying something to Nichols. The valet nodded and glided away.

"They heard," Lisle said in a low voice.

"I supposed that was why they looked so attentive," she said.

"Not *us*," he said. "They heard your encounter with Aillier." He nodded at the kitchen door. "The door's cracked. That, added to chinks in the mortar and broken windows, means sound travels more easily than it will once we've completed repairs. They heard him roaring at you. They heard something of what you said in answer. They heard his reaction. Then, in a very short time, they heard things return to normal. You saw how the kitchen servants didn't hesitate to return. And the rest of the staff is properly impressed."

She smiled. "I slew the dragon."

"You were brilliant," he said. He paused. "I should have realized. I'm sorry I doubted you. Mind, I'm still not happy to be here—but you've made it a degree less dismal."

"Thank you," she said. "I find you diverting, too."

His eyebrows went up. "Diverting."

"All the same, what happened in the kitchen passage must not happen again," she said. "You know I'm lacking in moral fiber. And I know you have a great deal—all sort of principles and ethics and such." She gave a dismissive wave.

"Yes. And such." The haunted look came into his eyes. Guilt was eating at him. Drat her stepfather, for fitting him up with a conscience and strict notions of Duty and Honor.

She leaned in closer. "Lisle, it's perfectly natural. We're young, we're beautiful—"

"And modest, too."

"You like facts," she said. "Let's face them. Fact: Intellect has an uphill battle against animal urges. Fact: We're badly chaperoned. Conclusion: The situation is ripe for disaster. I shall do my best not to err in that way again, but—"

"Wonderful," he said. "Then it's all up to me to protect your honor. Such a fine job I've done so far."

She grabbed his lapels. "Listen to me, you high-principled thickhead. We cannot make that mistake again. Do you know how close we came to the *Irrevocable*?" She let go of him, to hold her right hand up, thumb and forefinger a quarter inch apart. "This close we came . . ." She paused for dramatic effect. ". . . to playing into your parents' hands."

His head went back as though she'd slapped him.

Someone had to do it. Someone had to do *something*. She hadn't planned for this. She'd thought she could manage him the way she managed other men. But she couldn't, and she saw that they were racing down a slippery slope. If he left it to her, she'd wave her hands and shout, "Yes, faster, faster!"

His voice broke the taut silence.

"*What* did you say?"

She had his full, concentrated attention now. "They're trying to keep you home by hanging this millstone of a castle about your neck," she said. "They hope that the longer you're home, the less you'll think of Egypt, and by and by you'll forget about it and take a fancy to a proper English girl and marry and settle down."

He stared at her. "I don't . . ." She saw the realization dawn in his grey eyes.

"Yes," she said, "they don't even care if it's *me*."

It took Lisle a moment to absorb it. Then he saw it in his mind's eye: his parents' smiling faces, the conspiratorial looks cast up and down the table, the dowager's smiles and indulgent looks. Like a play.

"Olivia," he said mildly, his heart thudding, "what did you tell them?"

"*Tell* them? Don't be absurd. I should never be so careless as to actually *say* it. I merely encouraged them to think it."

"That you'd . . ." He could hardly bear to say it. "That you'd set your cap for me?"

"It's the sort of sentimental nonsense they'd believe," she said. "And the one excuse they'd accept for my traveling with you, and staying here with you."

"To trap me," he said. "Into marriage."

"Yes." She beamed at him. "I know you're shocked."

"There's an understatement."

"After all, we both know they've never really liked me. But as I told you, rank and money will buy almost anything, and I'm very well connected as well as disgustingly rich."

He put his hand to his head and leaned against the table. Really, she was beyond anything. To stand there, so cheerfully explaining this monstrous lie she'd told . . . implied. "You take my breath away."

She moved to lean against the table next to him, as casually as though they hadn't done what they'd done a moment ago. In the kitchen passage, of all places!

"The only thing I hadn't bargained for was that we should have this inconvenient attraction," she said.

"Inconvenient."

"As infuriating and thickheaded as you are, you're my dearest friend in the world," she said. "I don't want to ruin your life, and I know you don't want to ruin mine. We have so many fine examples about us of good marriages. My mother found her own true love twice. I should be happy to find mine once. And that's what I wish for you. But you know we should never suit in that way."

"Gad, no."

She scowled at him. "You needn't agree so enthusiastically."

"It's a fact," he said. He knew it was. She was a wonder of nature, but the simoom was a wonder of nature, too. So were hurricanes, floods, and earthquakes. He'd grown up in chaos. Rathbourne had given him order. Lisle needed order. He'd spent the last ten years making an orderly if occasionally exciting life. He'd been fortunate to discover early what he wanted, and he'd pursued that goal patiently and determinedly.

With her, everything flew out of control. Worst of all *he* lost control. Look what he'd done. Again and again and again.

"Well, then," she said.

"Right." He straightened away from the table. "I'm going up to the roof now."

"The roof! I admit that my plans have gone a bit awry, but there's no reason we can't master this." She came away from the table. "Matters got out of hand, but it's not the end of the world. There's no need to do anything so extreme as throw yourself from the roof."

For a moment he could only gaze at her in wonder.

Then, "I'm not going to throw myself from the roof," he said patiently. "I'm going up to complete my survey of the house. Because of the downpour, I wasn't able to measure the roof area or assess its condition or draw the layout."

"Oh," she said. She stepped back two paces. "That's all right, then."

"Throw myself from the roof," he muttered. "Really."

"You look so upset."

"That's because I don't know whether to laugh or cry or hit my head against the wall," he said. "What I need is calm. I need, desperately, to do something very, very *boring.*"

Later that evening

Though it wasn't his most elaborate dinner, Aillier contrived to put a very good one on the table.

It was the first proper dinner Lisle had eaten since he left London, he realized. A proper, civilized dinner, at a proper dining table, with diners conversing in a relatively intelligent manner. It was, too, the first dinner he'd presided over in one of his family's homes.

By the time he and the ladies of the household left the table and gathered at the fire, the day's tumult had subsided somewhat. Not altogether. His loss of control with Olivia still haunted him. And he still couldn't see how this Idea of hers would get him to Egypt by the spring. Still, he was calmer, thanks to the work he'd had the good sense to undertake.

His usual remedy for confusion or upset of any kind was to work. Measuring and evaluating and making notes, he was on familiar, peaceful ground—even here, in this primitive structure in this miserable climate.

While he concentrated on the familiar task, confusion and frustration abated.

And during that time, he now discovered, the Olivia whirlwind had changed the landscape. She, the embodiment of disorder, had created calm.

The servants had settled into a proper routine, and in a matter of hours, the castle had begun to look like an abode instead of a desolate fortress.

Looking about him, Lisle saw peace and order. He'd forgotten what that was like. The meal had had a mellowing effect, and the wine, naturally, made everything pleasanter. Even the Harpies were more amusing and less exasperating.

At present they were drunk, but that was normal. For the moment, they were quiet, because Olivia was reading from one of Cousin Frederick Dalmay's histories of Gorewood Castle.

The histories included the requisite ghost stories. There was the usual body inside the wall—this one a traitor who'd been tortured in the dungeon. He haunted the basement. There was the usual murdered pregnant serving maid. She appeared in the kitchen passage after weddings and births. There was a lady who appeared in the minstrels' gallery when she felt like it, and a knight who on certain feast days haunted the second-floor chapel.

Now Olivia had come to the ghosts who loitered about the roof.

" 'Seven men accused of plotting the heinous murder were sentenced to be hanged, drawn, and quartered,' " she read. " 'Loudly protesting their innocence, they demanded a chance to prove it through trial. To everyone's surprise, Lord Dalmay agreed. He had the villains taken up to the top of the south tower, and invited them to prove their innocence by jumping across the gap to the north tower. Any who succeeded would be proclaimed innocent. Some of Dalmay's followers protested. His lordship was overly merciful, they said. No one could make the leap. They'd plummet to the ground and die instantly. For what they'd done, these men deserved a slow, agonizing death. But in Lord Dalmay's realm, his word was law. Thus, one by one, the men stood upon the battlement. One by one, they sprang toward freedom. And one by one, six men fell to their death.' "

"Six?" Lisle said.

" 'One man did not die,' " Olivia read, " 'and Lord Dalmay abided by his judgment. The man was declared innocent and allowed to go free.' "

Lisle laughed. "The fellow survived a fall of one hundred six feet?"

"No, he made the leap," Olivia said.

"Must have had prodigious long legs," said Lady Withcote.

"You know what they say about long-legged men," said Lady Cooper.

"That's not legs, Agatha," said Lady Withcote. "It's the feet. Big feet, they say, big—"

"It's physically impossible," Lisle said. "The man would have to sprout wings."

"What's the distance between the two towers?" Olivia said. "Are you sure an agile man couldn't make the leap?"

"There's nothing like an agile man," Lady Cooper said reminiscently.

"Remember Lord Ardberry?"

"How could I forget?"

Lisle met Olivia's gaze. She was biting back laughter, as he was.

"Made a study of it," said Lady Withcote. "From the time he was in India. Some sort of secret book, he said."

"I thought it was a *sacred* book."

"Maybe it was both. In any case, that's why he learned Sanskrit."

"Not that one needed to read anything in any language. You saw his collection of pictures."

"Worth a thousand words, every one of them."

"Quite as entertaining as Eugenia's engravings."

Lisle saw it in his mind's eye, as clear as if he had the writing paper in front of him: ~~Engrav~~ One of Olivia's provocative, crossed-out words.

"What engravings?" he said.

"Did you never see them?" said Lady Cooper. "I thought all the Carsington boys discovered them at one time or another. Highly educational."

"I'm not, technically, a Car—"

"Really, Agatha," said Lady Withcote. "As though Lord Lisle needs to be educated. The young man is nearly four and twenty, and he lives where girls dance naked in the street and men keep harems. For all we know he's got a harem, and has tried all four hundred positions."

"Millicent, you know perfectly well there are not four hundred. Even Lord Ardberry admitted that numbers two hundred sixty-three and three hundred eighty-four were physically impossible for anybody with a spine."

Lisle looked at Olivia. "What engravings?" he said.

"Great-Grandmama's," she said in a bored voice. She put her book down, and rose from the chair.

"I'm going up to the roof," she said. "I need fresh air. And I want to see how wide the gap is." She collected her shawl and sauntered from the room.

It was most unfair.

She'd studied Great-Grandmama's pictures. They were highly educational. She'd looked forward to experiencing those activities. But she'd kissed some men and allowed a few minor liberties and it had been disappointing. A little titillating—but that was mainly because of knowing she was misbehaving.

Then Lisle had come back, a fully grown man who'd probably learned kissing from oriental experts. He *would* go to an expert. And practice. Diligently.

Now she understood why the ladies talked so much about it and why Great-Grandmama had loved her one and only husband so much and why she'd been such a merry widow.

Not titillation.

Passion.

It didn't require love, Great-Grandmama said. But love made a delicious sauce.

That was all very well, but passion had a nasty way of making one restless and vexed for no reason. Since Olivia had been so unlucky as to experience it for the first time with Lisle, she had to cope with balked passion, and that was most unpleasant.

She climbed up and up, wondering where all the cold air had vanished to. The wind wailed in the stairwell but it was about as cooling to her emotions as a hot desert wind.

She climbed round and round, up and up: past the second floor, then past the third floor, once the garrison's quarters and now the servants'. Farther up she went, one last flight, then through the little door, and onto the roof at last.

She walked out to the wall, set her hands on it, closed her eyes, and inhaled deeply. The air was cool, beautifully cool, and it was quiet here, far away from all the talking.

She took another deep breath, let it out, and opened her eyes.

Stars and stars and stars.

All around her, above her.

She'd never seen so many. And there was the moon, high and bright, approaching the full. It was so beautiful, this wondrous place.

"What engravings?" came a low voice behind her.

She did not turn around. "Oh, you know," she said carelessly. "The naughty pictures they sell from under the counter at the print shops. Along with the ones Great-Grandmama collected when she traveled abroad. Everything from Aretino to the latest illustrations for *Fanny Hill*. She and the Harpies still cackle over them."

"I guessed it was something of the sort," Lisle said. His evening shoes made almost no sound on the stone floor, but she could feel him approaching.

He came to a stop beside her, nearly a foot away, and set his hands on the wall. "But you never told me. You raised the subject in a letter, then crossed it out, in that provoking way you have."

"I can't believe you remember that." She stole a glance at him, and that was a mistake. Moonlight and starlight streaked his hair with silver and made polished marble of his profile.

"Of course I remember," he said. "It was particularly aggravating at the time. I was—what?—fourteen or fifteen? Naturally, I was dying to see them, and furious with you for teasing me. 'Ha, ha, Lisle,' he said in singsong. 'I have dirty pictures. You don't.'"

"You didn't need dirty pictures. You had dancing girls."

He turned fully toward her and leaned his elbow on the parapet. He studied her face for the longest time.

She let him study her. She was a card player, a good one. No one could read her face.

"The dancing girls trouble you strangely," he said.

"Of course they do," she said. "Look at me." She made a sweeping gesture, over the swell of skirts and ballooning sleeves.

"I'm looking," he said.

"Me, in all this. Corseted and petticoated and hemmed in on every side."

"That seems to be the fashion," he said.

"They *dance in the streets*," she said.

He tipped his head to one side, his expression puzzled.

"I should give anything to dance in the streets," she said. "But I'll never do it. I shall fall in love, if I'm lucky, and I shall marry the poor fellow because I must not disgrace the family. I'll turn into somebody's wife and the mother of his children, and I shall never be anybody else or do anything else. Unless, of course, he dies and leaves me a wealthy widow and I can carry on as Great-Grandmama did—but no, I can't do that, either, because women can't do that anymore—or if they do, they must be much more discreet, and I'm hopeless at being discreet."

He didn't answer.

He didn't understand. What man would or could? Even he saw her first as a woman and second—or forty-second—as Olivia. Or maybe he didn't distinguish.

"What do you want?" he said softly. "What do you really want? Do you know?"

I want you, nitwit. But that was like her, to want to leap over the cliff when there were perfectly good, safe meadows to play about in.

Even she wasn't so reckless, though, as to aggravate an already difficult situation by telling him she was—What? Infatuated?

She looked out at the world below them.

This was the highest point for miles about. She could make out the outlines of houses, faint twinkles of light in their windows, in the villages nestled in the valleys beyond. On a height not far away stood another castle. Starlight and moonlight bathed the scene. The cool wind rippled across her skin and lifted the ringlets fashionably framing her face. The brisk breeze felt wonderful.

"For a start, I want something like this," she said. She waved her hand over the silvery landscape. "Magic. Romance. The way I felt when I first saw this castle, when I stepped into the great hall. What do you think I want? You know me. Who but Mama knows me better? You know I want to be swept off my feet."

He looked out at the moonlit landscape and up at the moon and the sparkling cloud of stars.

"You silly girl," he said.

She turned away from the parapet and laughed and threw up her hands. He'd never change. Romance wasn't *facts*. She might as well have talked to the moon and stars. They'd understand better than he ever could. To him, she spoke a foreign language—from the moon, probably.

He pushed away from the wall and held out his hand. "Come, it's cold up here."

Practical as always. But that was who he was, and he was her friend. He couldn't help doing what he did to her. She knew he truly didn't mean to.

In any event, she was a selfish wretch to keep him up here. He wasn't used to the climate. Since he was probably chilled to the bone, he'd think she was, too. He only wanted to take her back inside, out of the wind. Protective.

She took his hand.

He tugged, and she lost her balance, and he pulled her into his arms. The next she knew, she was bent backward, one muscled arm under her waist and the other round her shoulders. Her arms went up, instinctively, to circle his neck. She looked up into his face. He was smiling a little, looking into her eyes. His were pure silver in the moonlight.

"Swept off your feet," he said, in the same low voice. "Like this, do you mean?"

Chapter Twelve

*I*t was the moonlight and the starlight and the silver in his eyes and the sound of his voice. He'd swept her into his arms and swept away thought.

"Yes," she said. *Exactly like this.*

"What else?"

"*Think,*" she said.

"Passionate kisses, I suppose."

"Yes," she said.

"Dangerous."

"Oh, yes."

"Reckless girl," he said. "What folly." He bent his head and kissed her.

Perhaps it had seemed like playacting. It wasn't, couldn't be. There was no laughter in his voice or in his eyes and nothing lighthearted in the touch of his lips. But then he wouldn't be playing, because Lisle didn't. He didn't pretend. She was easily false. He was never false.

His mouth wasn't feigning. It was firm on hers, pressing until she gave way, and she did, instantly. His kiss, hot and insistent, took up where they'd left off. The feelings remained. All the talking and logic in the world couldn't banish them. They'd seethed, hour after hour, waiting to be let loose again.

Unfinished business. They should have left it unfinished, but it—whatever drew them together—refused to subside quietly.

And the truth was, she didn't want it to go away. She didn't want it to stop.

She could taste the wine he'd drunk, and that only enhanced the taste of him, and that was the taste she'd craved. She'd waited a lifetime for this, for him.

Yes, she was swept away. It was like drinking in the moon and the stars and the magic of the night. It was like flying into the moon and the stars.

Don't let go. Don't ever let me go.

Her arms tightened around his neck and he pulled her up and against him, and staggered back against the parapet. This time his hands moved more quickly and surely than before. He drew away her shawl and broke the kiss to trail his mouth downward, along her jaw. Wherever his lips touched, they left heat, all the way down her throat until they touched the bared skin of her breast.

She felt the quivering excitement all the way down, and she couldn't keep back the sound, a mingled cry and moan. This was one thing she couldn't master or control. It caught her up, a dizzying whirl of sensation, as his lips glided over her breast.

Then his hands were there, cupping her breasts. She started to cry out, but his mouth covered hers again. The fierce kiss silenced her, and she surrendered, utterly, happily, sinking into a sea of feelings, and glad to drown there.

She moved her hands eagerly over his powerful arms and shoulders and back. He was warm and strong, and she couldn't get enough of touching him; she couldn't get close enough.

He moved his hands lower, and in the night's quiet, the rustle of her skirts sounded like thunder. But that was only her heart, beating and beating with happiness and fear and an excitement so intense that she ached with it.

This time he pulled up her skirts more quickly than he'd done before, less patiently. His hand, so warm, slid up her thigh and swiftly found the opening of her drawers.

The intimate touch was a shock, but she'd waited a lifetime to be shocked like this. The warmth of his hand, cupping her there, so intimately, possessively, and the way it felt, so wicked and delicious and mad-making all at the same time. She moved against his hand because she had to. Something inside, in the tight place in her belly, compelled her.

Don't stop. Don't stop. Don't stop.

She couldn't speak but she could act the words, her tongue tangling with his while her body moved against his hand. Then he slid his finger inside her and she thought she'd fly to pieces. If he hadn't been kissing her, she would have screamed.

He stroked her *there*, the place whose secrets only she knew, but he knew them, every one, and more. Everything inside her was vibrating. All the feelings gathered up, like a flock of birds, and spread their wings and shot up into the heavens, the way the birds had done this day, from this same tower, and her body shuddered, as though it was her soul that had flown up, up, into the stars.

Then she knew what had to be. Every cell of her body knew.

She'd been moving her hands over him, over the muscles of his arms and over his back and down over his buttocks. Now she found the flap of his trousers, and fumbled for the buttons. He moved a little to give her room, while he stroked her still, more urgently, and she nearly fell back, wracked with pleasure. But her hands moved instinctively, and she pushed one button from the buttonhole.

When she heard the sound she thought at first that she'd made it. Then she realized it wasn't her and it wasn't the crows shrieking.

Someone was screaming.

A chilling, soul-shriveling shriek.

Lisle's head came up, and the world spun about him. A black and silver world. Stars, millions of them.

A woman in his arms, so warm and soft.

Olivia, her face luminous in the moonlight, and her breasts, pearly white, thrusting proudly from the bodice of her dress.

The thick red haze in his mind cleared, as though a cold wind had blasted through it.

His hands on warm, slick—

No. Not again.

He pulled his hand out from under her dress, and her skirts fell back into place.

He pulled up the bodice, stuffing her breasts back inside. What else? Her shawl . . . Where? There. He snatched it up and wrapped it about her.

He did it all quickly, instinctively. No time to think first. He was used to that. But what . . . ?

Screaming. More. Where?

He looked down over the parapet. In the courtyard, figures ran about.

Think.

No bodies on the ground.

Good. That was good.

He started toward the door to the stairway.

"Lisle, your trousers."

He looked down. "Damn me. Damn me to hell." He fastened the button. "Stupid, stupid, stupid. *Dunce.*"

"Never mind," she said. "Never mind."

She was arranging her clothing. Because of him. He'd done that. Disarranged her. What was wrong with him?

"I have to deal with this first," he said. "But—"

"Go," she said. "I'll be right behind you."

It took a while for Lisle to penetrate the hysteria and make any sense of what had happened. Some gibbered about cutthroats and some wailed about intruders and some shrieked about ghosts and some were simply bewildered.

Eventually, he and Olivia managed to herd everyone back into the castle. That would have been more difficult had the servants been able to take refuge elsewhere. Some had fled to the stables, but he doubted they'd stay.

It was too cold, and the area was too exposed. If they had any sense, they'd come back to huddle with the others.

Sure enough, by the time he and Olivia had settled the ladies in front of the fire, with large glasses of whiskey, all of the servants had gathered in the great hall.

Safety in numbers.

He noticed that the servants had not, as previously, gathered under the minstrels' gallery in what used to be the screens passage. Instead they'd drawn nearer to the opposite end of the room where the great fireplace stood.

As one would expect, most of them didn't know what had happened. When the screaming started, they'd simply panicked and run.

It took patience as well as Olivia's help with the questioning, but eventually he ascertained that Lady Cooper had screamed first. The others had taken it up without knowing what they were screaming about.

At present she was arguing with Lady Withcote about what she'd seen.

"It was a ghost," Lady Cooper said. "I saw it, as plain as day. Up there." She waved her glass at the other end of the hall. "In the minstrels' gallery."

Every head turned that way and looked up. There was nothing to see. The gallery was dark.

"What did it look like?" Lisle said.

"It looked like a ghost, all white and shadowy," Lady Cooper said. "Filmy. Like a fog. It flitted across the gallery."

Several servants shuddered.

"What nonsense," said Lady Withcote. "I know what happened. You fell asleep, as you often do, and dreamed it."

"I know when I'm asleep and when I'm awake. I didn't dream anything!"

"How long was it there?" Lisle said.

"It was never there," Lady Withcote said.

Lady Cooper glared at her friend. "It was there," she said. "Some of the servants saw it, too. I'm not sure how long it remained. It might have been hovering there for some time, watching us."

More shudders.

"When I looked up," Lady Cooper went on, "there it was. I screamed. What else should I do? What would anyone do? One hears of such things, but never with my own eyes had I seen a ghost, in the flesh."

"Really, Agatha, it could hardly be *in the flesh*. What nonsense you talk."

"You screamed, too, Millicent."

"Because you frightened me out of my wits. I thought it was bloodthirsty Scots come to kill us. Then you raced out of the hall and out of the door, into the night, and half the servants after you, in a panic. I didn't know what to think. Had your petticoat caught fire?"

Lisle glanced at Olivia.

That was to say, he glanced toward where she'd last been. She wasn't there.

He looked wildly about the great hall. Despite the ample supply of candles, its corners were dark. How easy it would be, he realized, for an intruder to slip in among the others, unnoticed in all the confusion. How easy to snatch someone—

But no, what was he thinking? Anyone who tried to snatch Olivia was in for a surprise.

He'd hardly thought it when a light appeared in the darkness, coming from overhead at the north end of the great hall. He turned his gaze upward.

Olivia stood in the gallery, a small branch of candles in her hand. Every eye turned that way.

Trust her to make a dramatic entrance.

"Whatever was or wasn't here before," she said, "there's nothing here now."

She moved to the center of the gallery, in front of the arched window recess. She set the candelabra down upon a table someone had placed there. Bathed in candlelight, her hair glowing red-gold, she stood in the posture of a queen: head up and shoulders back, completely unafraid. A fanciful man might imagine an ancient ancestress adopting such a pose as she urged her vassals to defend the castle at all costs.

"There's nothing here," she said again. "No ghostly vapor trails. No muddy footprints. Nothing at all."

Lady Cooper's voice broke the spell. "But I saw it, dear, plain as day."

"I don't doubt you saw something," Olivia said. "A bird might have flown in through one of the broken windows. A prankster might have found a way in, too."

She paused for a moment, to let that sink in.

Then, "Bailey, fetch me a broom and a length of muslin," she said.

While the maid went on her errand, Lisle became aware of the atmosphere changing, the mindless fear melting away. From petrified silence, the audience relaxed into a low murmuring.

In a few minutes, Bailey appeared in the gallery with broom and cloth. Olivia gave her the candelabra and sent her out. The gallery was in darkness once more.

Shortly thereafter, Lisle heard a soft rustling. Then a white something billowed at the rail of the gallery.

He heard a collective intake of breath.

"All one need do is stand in the doorway, with a length of thin cloth on the end of a long stick," came Olivia's voice from the darkness.

"Good heavens!" Lady Cooper cried.

More murmuring from the servants. A little laughter.

After a time, Lady Withcote said, her satisfaction plainly audible, "Well, it only goes to show how easily one may be gulled."

"But who would do such a thing?" Lady Cooper said.

"The sort who like to play pranks," said Lady Withcote. "The world never lacks that sort."

Olivia reappeared in their midst as abruptly as she'd disappeared. She came forward to stand in the full light of the fireplace.

Though Lisle knew it was dramatic effect, she took his breath away. She looked almost unearthly, standing before that enormous fireplace, backlit by the flames that played over the red curls, the creamy skin, the heavy silk of her gown.

She remained in her Chatelaine of the Castle persona, Lisle saw, hands loosely folded at her waist, spine straight.

"It was a silly prank," she said to the company. "More than likely, a few local boys wanted a laugh at the Londoners' expense. They must have thought it a fine joke, watching everyone running about, shrieking in terror."

"Who can blame them?" Lady Withcote laughed. "It was comical, you must admit, Agatha. Put me in mind of the trick Lord Thorogood played on his wife. Do you recall?"

"How could I forget? They said her lover couldn't raise a shaft for a week afterward, he had such a fright."

While they continued their bawdy reminiscences, Olivia sent the servants about their business. She called Nichols and Bailey aside and told them to check all the rooms and passages. That would reassure anybody who feared that the intruders were still in the castle.

When bedtime came, she said, she wanted calm and order. "Drug them if you have to," was her final command.

They departed on their assignment.

Soon thereafter, the ladies staggered off to their beds.

That left Olivia and Lisle in the great hall.

She stood gazing at the fire. The firelight gilded her hair and glowed a soft pink in her cheeks and the sight made his heart ache.

What am I going to do? he thought. *What am I going to do about her?*

"That was wonderfully quick thinking," he said. "You brought everyone to their senses in a matter of minutes."

"It didn't want thinking," she said. "I've created ghosts often enough. I've even conducted séances. It's easy."

"The performance shouldn't have surprised me," he said. "But it did."

"Surely you can't have thought I believed in ghosts," she said.

"You're romantic."

"Yes, but not gullible."

No, not gullible or naïve or innocent. She'd never been any of those things. Or inhibited or squeamish. Or anything like any other woman he'd ever known.

It came into his head and into his blood all at once: her quick passion, the softness of her skin, the taste and scent of her, the curves of her body, and the heat raced through him, making his head spin.

She was a force of nature, unstoppable, irresistible.

What the devil was he to do?

He couldn't rely on her and he couldn't trust himself. Look at what he'd done, mere hours after they'd agreed it must not happen again.

I don't want to ruin your life, and I know you don't want to ruin mine.

"Speaking of romantic," he said.

"If you apologize for what happened on the roof, I'll strangle you," she said.

"If we hadn't been interrupted—"

"Yes, I know." Her brow knit. "I have to think about this. I'm sure there's a solution. But I can't find it now. It's been a long day."

A lifetime, he thought.

His life. It was changing, irrevocably, unstoppably. It had started changing from the moment his lips touched hers—no, before that. From the moment he'd found her in the ballroom.

"Eventful, certainly," he said.

"But the heart of the matter . . ." She frowned. "Here's what's in my mind. We're in dire need of a butler. It's clear that Edwards, wherever he may be, will not return. We're in dire need as well of Scottish servants. London servants don't belong here. They don't like it, they don't understand it, and they don't fit. Someone, clearly, wants to undermine our work here. We need to get to the bottom of that. Too, we need a stable staff we can rely on, people with ties to the place."

Though it had been a long day, he was too uncomfortable and too angry with himself to feel weary. He was supposed to be the strong one. Yet he'd found her on the roof and he'd seen the stars in her eyes and he'd done exactly what he'd vowed he wouldn't do again.

All the same, he couldn't ignore what she was saying. Facts. She'd summed up the situation as logically as he might have done, if he hadn't been so bollixed up with *feelings*.

"You're right," he said.

Her eyes widened. "I am?"

"We have a problem, but that isn't the only problem," he said. "We came here to rebuild. We came to solve the castle's problems. That's what we need to concentrate on. If we do that—"

Her mouth quirked up. "No time for misbehaving."

"The devil makes work for idle hands," he said.

"I never noticed that I needed his help," she said. She gave a short laugh and moved away. "Well, then, we've a plan of sorts. And we can tackle it tomorrow." She bade him good night, and vanished into the south wing.

Olivia kept the amused expression on her face until she was safely behind the doors and on her way up the stairs.

Then she stopped and clutched her head.

What were they going to do?

Desire was a terrible thing, not what she'd always imagined it to be. It was *unbearable*. To stand there, looking at him, and wanting to touch him and wanting to be touched.

What had happened, on the roof, that wondrous feeling.

She knew what it was. She had, after all, read Great-Grandmama's fascinating collection of erotic literature, and she'd learned how to pleasure herself.

But that was a pale imitation.

Think about something else, she ordered herself. And so she thought about butlers and how to lose them and how to find them. She thought about ghosts that weren't ghosts. She listed domestic problems as she climbed the winding stairs to her room.

She went to bed without much hope of sleeping well, but the day's events had done for her. She laid her head on the pillow and the next she knew, grey morning light had filled the room and Bailey was standing by the bed, tray in her hands. From it the aroma of chocolate wafted to Olivia's nostrils.

Gorewood Castle great hall
Morning of Tuesday 18 October

The Harpies hadn't risen yet, and probably wouldn't be up and about until noon. That was their usual time, Lisle supposed, when they weren't being harassed by forces of nature.

Though feeling far from peaceful inwardly, he'd enjoyed a quiet breakfast.

He hadn't realized how unpeaceful the previous ones had been until now.

He heard the servants' light footsteps as they went about their work . . . the wind whistling through the chinks and broken windows . . . the fire crackling in the grate.

The environment was far from ideal, and he was hundreds of miles from where he wanted to be and the work ahead of him didn't fill him with excitement. But he had peace about him. And order. And a moment of quiet in which to ponder the irony of Olivia's having created it.

She came in as he was finishing the cup of coffee Nichols had made for him.

Lisle rose.

She stood next to him, and peered at the tiny cup on the table. "Is that Turkish coffee?"

He nodded. Her clothing rustled at his ear. He could smell her, the faint, floral fragrance. Or was it more spicy than floral? Very faint. Not bottled scent. Dried herbs and flowers, most likely, with which her clothes were stored.

"I'm used to it," he said. "I'm not fanatical about it, though. I'll drink what's available. But Nichols has strong feelings regarding the care of his 'gentleman.' He wouldn't dream of making do with whatever happens to be on hand. Wherever we go, he carries Turkish coffee. Wherever we are, he prepares it every morning. Would you like some?"

"I would, indeed." She moved away and sat down. "Great-Grandmama has it often, but her maid is very jealous, and won't show Bailey how to make it."

"I'll tell Nichols to teach her," he said, taking his seat again. "Nichols scorns petty jealousies." And he wouldn't mind teaching a pretty maid whatever she wished to know, including some things she didn't know she wished to know.

Though Lisle didn't ring, Nichols appeared, as he invariably did when wanted. "Sir?"

"Turkish coffee for Miss Carsington," Lisle said.

"Certainly, sir."

"And when Miss Bailey has a moment, you are to teach her how to make it."

"Certainly, sir." Though Nichols's tone did not change, Lisle noticed the spark in his eyes.

Olivia must have seen it, too. When the valet had disappeared behind the kitchen passage door, she said, "He is not to think of seducing my maid."

"I'm having enough trouble with my own morals," he said in a low voice. "You can't expect me to be responsible for everyone else's. And I certainly can't tell him what to think. He's a *man*."

"I'm only warning you," she said. "I can't be held responsible for what Bailey will do. She has a low opinion of your sex."

"Nichols can look out for himself," Lisle said. "As I mentioned yesterday, he's stronger than he looks. A simoom once lifted him off his feet and carried him a short distance before dropping him amongst some Bedouins. He helped them clear out the sand and made them coffee. They lent him a camel. When he returned to me, he apologized for being 'so abruptly absent.' "

She looked at him, laughter and skepticism mingling in her blue eyes. "You're making that up."

"Don't be absurd," he said. "I have no imagination."

The heated fantasies and even more uninhibited dreams had nothing to do with imagination, he told himself. To a man, those sorts of things were reality.

"I should like to know who made *that* up," she said.

He followed her gaze to the minstrels' gallery. "The ghostly visitation, you mean."

"I want to look it over again, by daylight," she said. "Maybe nothing was there, and Lady Cooper only imagined it or dreamed it. But that seems unlikely. Somebody's been playing at ghosts for the last several years. Why should they stop now, when they have a fresh audience?"

"Why should they have started in the first place?" he said. "Why frighten someone away from a place?"

"Because you want it for yourself or because it's got something you want," she said.

"Clearly, no one wanted it for himself," he said. "Mains hasn't been able to entice a tenant, and I saw no signs of anybody living here for free."

"Mains," she said. "I've been meaning to talk to you about him."

Nichols reappeared with the coffee. He filled Olivia's cup and refilled Lisle's and disappeared.

Olivia turned and watched him go. "That is a gift," she said. "Have you ever noticed how few men can make themselves unobtrusive? Usually, they're demanding attention in every way they can think of." Her gaze came back to him. "Not you, though. I suppose it comes of living in Egypt, doing what you do."

"Moving quietly is an important skill," he said.

"I should like to learn it," she said, "but one can't in these clothes."

Today she wore a brown dress. Being meant for day-time, it covered her up to the throat. Otherwise, it was like the dress she'd worn last night: Immense sleeves and mountain of flaring skirts, propped up by layers of petticoats. . .

He called his mind back.

"One takes up so much space," she said, "and one rustles so."

"You were speaking of Mains," he said.

"Yes." She inhaled the coffee's aroma and gave an appreciative sigh before taking a sip. "Oh, that is excellent. Better than Great-Grandmama's."

"Mains," he said.

"You are a wonder of single-mindedness," she said.

"One of us has to be. You wander off in ten directions at once."

"Yes, I was thinking of food."

"I'll fill your plate." He jumped up and headed for the sideboard, eager to be moving, doing something. "You talk."

"Yes, very well. He was a puzzle, I'll admit. I was expecting, as you no doubt were, to find he was completely incompetent. Or a drunkard. Or both. After all, people want work. The village is not exactly thriving. It's one thing to have difficulty finding a tenant. Not all people would find a fifteenth-century castle inviting, even one in pristine condition and luxuriously fitted out. But for an agent to be unable to recruit men to work, on a property that for centuries was the main source of employment for miles about—that was strange, indeed."

He returned to the table and set her plate down.

She looked at it. "No haggis, I see."

"Our cook is French," he said.

"No salmon, either," she said. "But I notice he has somehow contrived to create perfect brioche in that abominable oven."

"Amazing, isn't it?" he said. He sat again. "As to Mains? You were saying?"

She picked up her cutlery. "You are so single-minded."

"Yes, I'm on pins and needles. I can tell by the way you're drawing this out that you've something of value to tell me."

"Several things," she said. "First, your agent drinks a little and he's a little incompetent and a little lazy, but none of that is the problem, really. He does his job well enough. But until the last years before his death, your cousin Frederick Dalmay supervised him. Since then, the supervision has come from your father." She stopped then, and attended to her breakfast.

Lisle didn't question her further. He didn't need to. "Father made a muck of it," he said.

"Some might say so."

"Contradictory commands," he said. "Changing his mind a dozen times."

"So it would appear."

"I see what happened," he said. "It wants no imagination. The locals feel the way I do."

"Rules were imposed that were either unduly strict or contradicted others," she said. "You've lost some tradesmen as a result. The village hasn't been emptied, but a few families have left. In other cases, the men are traveling a distance to work." She went on talking between mouthfuls. Lisle let her go at her own pace. He had a great deal to think about.

"I learned from my stepfather and my uncles how one ought to manage an estate," she said. "You know how seriously Lord Rathbourne takes his responsibilities. From what I gathered, your cousin Frederick followed the same principles."

"My father doesn't," he said. "He couldn't stick to a principle or a rule if it was glued to his nose."

"The good news is, we understand why you've not been welcomed with open arms."

"Ill will," he said. "They don't know what additional misery I'll bring down upon them."

"We have to win their trust again," she said. "I believe that's where to start. Then we can tackle the ghosts."

Before Lisle could answer, Nichols reappeared.

"Your lordship, Miss Carsington, a man is here about a situation," he said.

Chapter Thirteen

$\mathscr{A}$ man named Herrick, Nichols told them, was applying for the vacant butler position.

Olivia looked at Lisle.

"What's happened?" he said. "Yesterday we couldn't get anyone near the place."

"Yesterday, a wee red-haired lassie hadn't faced up to a savage Frenchman wielding a cleaver," she said.

"Word can't have gone out so quickly," he said.

"It happened yesterday," she said. "When I do something in London, it makes the rounds by breakfast time next day. Word travels even more quickly in the country, in my experience."

"But how? Who'd tell them? We haven't a single villager in the castle."

"The stables," she said. "Gossip goes from the house to the stables, and there's always a local snoop loitering about the stables on one pretext or another. Every village has at least one person who makes it his or her business to know everything about everybody."

Lisle looked up at Nichols. "If he was a dubious

fellow in any way, I know you'd have sent him about his business," he said.

"He has a letter from Mr. Mains, your lordship, as well as one from his previous employer, Lord Glaxton."

That would be the castle she'd seen from the roof last night, Olivia thought. She shoved the roof and what had happened there from her mind. If she ignored it *very determinedly*, maybe it would go away.

"We'll see him as soon as Miss Carsington finishes her breakfast," Lisle said.

"I'm finished," Olivia said.

Lisle looked at her plate. "No, you're not."

"I can eat anytime," she said. "Butlers are not thick on the ground hereabouts."

"Then I'll take that brioche," he said. "Give us a moment, Nichols, then bring him in here."

She and Lisle left the table to await the prospective employee near the great chimneypiece, the warmest part of the room—and a fair distance from the passage to the kitchen, with its eavesdropping servants.

By whatever mysterious powers of timing Nichols possessed—perhaps simply living with Lisle for all these years was enough—he brought Herrick in a moment after Olivia had finished brushing crumbs from Lisle's waistcoat. Lisle hadn't noticed them, or didn't care, but Nichols would. Olivia was sure he'd die of mortification if his master appeared less than presentable in front of a prospective menial.

Herrick certainly looked the part of a butler. He was physically imposing: easily as tall as Aillier but far more fit in physique. His dark hair was neatly groomed and his black eyes were sharply observant. He possessed the calm quietness of a man who knew what he was about. He reminded Olivia of Great-Grandmama's perfect butler, Dudley.

He reminded her even more of Nichols, though Herrick was so much larger. He had the same unobtrusive manner.

Though Scottish, he spoke English with only a small trace of a burr.

"You were last at Glaxton Castle," Lisle said after he'd read the letters of referral. "I do wonder why you would give up that advantageous situation and come to this ramshackle heap."

"Ambition, your lordship," said Herrick. "Mr. Melvin is butler there. I was under butler. We did not see eye to eye. Given the unlikelihood of any change in this state of affairs or of his retiring anytime soon, I determined to seek my fortune elsewhere. My month's notice expired a fortnight ago. I was on the brink of accepting a position in Edinburgh when I learned of the vacancy here. My conversation yesterday with Mr. Mains confirmed my belief that I was better suited to this situation."

Lisle didn't trouble to hide his astonishment. He gestured vaguely at their half-furnished surroundings. "This derelict heap?"

"Indeed, your lordship, I view it as a challenge."

"So do we all," Lisle said, "unfortunately."

Olivia decided it was time to step in. "In my experience," she said, "servants usually prefer easy places. Challenges are not, by and large, their cup of tea."

"That is the general case, certainly, Miss Carsington," said Herrick. "It strikes me as a dull and unsatisfactory way to live."

"We're not dull," Lisle said. "Not by half. Perhaps you haven't heard that our previous butler disappeared in mysterious circumstances."

"In these parts, one hears everything, your lordship," he said. "The inhabitants of Edinburgh, especially the servants, know everything about everybody within a twenty-mile radius. Gorewood is well within that range."

"Our previous butler's abrupt disappearance doesn't trouble you at all?" Olivia said.

"If your lordship and Miss Carsington would permit me to speak plainly?" Herrick said.

"By all means," Lisle said.

"The previous butler was a *Londoner*," Herrick said gently—or was that pityingly? "I am not. My family have lived hereabouts for many generations. We cannot be uprooted easily. Or at all."

Olivia looked at Lisle.

"Doubtless your lordship and Miss Carsington wish to discuss the matter privately," Herrick said. "I shall step out of the room."

He glided out.

Olivia and Lisle watched him go.

"Is that Nichols's older brother?" she said softly.

"It must be a separate species they belong to," he said. "I hope he hasn't a roving eye as well. But one can't have everything. He's Scottish, as you want, with local ties. His references are impeccable. He makes a good impression. He's discreet. Quiet. He speaks a recognizable form of English. Well, do you want him or not?"

"It's your castle," she said.

"This isn't my department," he said. "I like him well enough, but you'll be in charge of the domestics. I'm supposed to do the manly things. I need to assess the state of the courtyard and the curtain wall. I need to make a closer inspection of the ground level of the castle as well. I want to find out how our intruders got in. Let me deal with that and leave the butler to you."

"He seems to be the genuine article," she said.

"I trust your DeLucey instincts in that regard," he said.

"He doesn't seem daunted at the enormous task he faces," she said. "Hiring a full staff—preferably from the neighborhood—getting everything running properly, setting up a system for supplies, and so on."

"Far from daunted," he said, "he struck me as a hound straining at the leash, eager to be away on the chase."

"He's tall and good-looking," she said.

"That settles it, then."

Nichols appeared.

"Miss Carsington likes him," Lisle said. "Send in our new butler."

A short time later

"Nichols will introduce you to the staff and take you about the castle later," Olivia told Herrick. "Ladies Cooper and Withcote won't be up and about until noon at the earliest." They would ogle him and make improper remarks, and he would simply have to get used to it. "Lord Lisle has drawn a set of plans, which I know you'll wish to study. I've found them most helpful. This castle turns out to be a more complicated structure than it seemed to me at first—but I daresay you're used to the staircase that bypasses a floor or ends abruptly, and the floors between floors with rooms tucked into them here and there."

"The entresols, miss? Indeed, we had them at Glaxton."

"I haven't explored them all yet," she said. "But Nichols suggested that the entresol directly above the kitchen serving passage might serve as our muniments room. I've had the household ledgers moved there for the time being."

Herrick turned his gaze toward the part of the wall directly above the door to the kitchen area.

He had a way of turning his head that, combined with the high arched nose, put her in mind of a hawk.

"Your quarters are on approximately the same level, in the north tower directly below Lord Lisle's rooms," she explained.

His dark gaze shifted to the north end of the hall, to the corner of the minstrels' gallery behind which a door and passage led into his quarters.

"I had better tell you we had a ghost up there last night," she said. "In the minstrels' gallery."

The hawklike gaze came back to her. It was perfectly calm. "A ghost, miss?"

"Someone pretending to be a ghost," she said. "Very annoying. His lordship has gone out to try to ascertain how they got in."

"I did notice signs of vandalism as I came, miss. Most unfortunate, but the castle has stood empty for a good while. An open invitation."

"Very tempting, I know," Olivia said. "I believe his lordship said something about missing steps in the lower levels of some of the stairways. I saw pieces of the battlements on the ground as well."

"Those depredations go back many years," Herrick said. "I think they've given up trying to sell the castle, piece by piece. But the courtyard." He shook his head. "Shameful. I shouldn't have believed it if I hadn't seen for myself."

"The courtyard?" Olivia tried to remember what she'd seen yesterday, when Lisle took her about the courtyard. The walls had crumbled, and parts of them had rolled a distance from their foundations. The ground, naturally, was uneven. Had something seemed odd about it? She couldn't remember. She'd been too occupied with romantic fantasies to look about her carefully.

"They've been digging," Herrick said. "Someone's looking for that treasure again."

Shortly thereafter

"Buried treasure," Lisle repeated. "We've some idiots about who think there's buried treasure here?"

The announcement Olivia had flown out of the castle to make had been lengthier and more dramatic and involved a great deal of her arms waving about and the usual accompanying movement elsewhere.

It was very trying.

"Had I gone through all of your cousin Frederick's papers and books, I should have found out," she said. "He collected everything he could about Gorewood Castle. All the legends in all their variations. I was bound to come upon the buried-treasure story sooner or later."

"This one isn't about pirates, is it?" he said. "Because you and I have already dug for pirates' booty."

She smiled up at him. She was hatless, her hair coming undone and streaming in the breeze, the same breeze that lifted her swaying skirts. He could feel his brain melting under that smile.

What was he going to do about her?

"Not pirates," she said. "It was during the civil wars. Cromwell attacked the castle. Eventually the family and servants had to flee. They escaped at night—but they couldn't take all their treasure with them."

She almost visibly vibrated with excitement. It was very hard to resist being caught up in it.

But he needed calm. He needed order. He had a dozen problems to tackle, and he wasn't sure he'd be able to think clearly about any of them if he didn't first solve the problem that was Olivia. He couldn't solve her when she stood in front of him. He could scarcely think straight.

"So they buried it," he said.

She nodded.

"I'm sorry to shatter your beautiful fantasy, but if I've heard that story once, I've heard it five and twenty times," he said. "Shall I tell you how it goes? Cromwell's side prevailed for longer than the royalists expected. The family lost everything, including the secret of where their treasure was buried. I vow, every royalist family in Great Britain buried their jewels and silver before they fled in the dead of night from Cromwell and his hordes. And every last one of them forgot where they buried it."

"Of course I know it's a legend, but—"

"Nobody, especially the canny Scots, could be so gullible as to imagine there's any treasure left to be found after two hundred years," he said. "Nobody over the age of twelve, that is. Please tell me you don't believe it."

"I don't have to believe it," she said. "But I do believe someone's looking for it." She looked about her. "There's evidence." She gestured at the numerous little hillocks and furrows that filled the courtyard. "The ground has been so wet that it's hard to see. But Herrick saw evidence of recent digging."

"Buried treasure is your bailiwick," he said. "Feel free to dig all you like."

"Lisle, that isn't the point. How can you be so thick? Can't you see—"

"I do see, but I can't go off on a tangent," he said. "There's too much to do. I need workmen, and I'm going to get them."

"Of course you must do that. I only wanted—"

"We can't go on like this," he said, "with broken windows and the rain and wind coming in, and pranksters sneaking into the castle. In the old days, no intruder could have sneaked into the minstrels' gallery. They would have had to fight their way in. Our ghosts might have come in through the damaged door I showed you, the one that leads into the basement. Then they had only to make their way up the broken stairs. That door must be repaired and secured."

"I agree, but—"

"I'm going to the village and recruit," he said.

Turning her back on Lisle, Olivia plunked herself onto a piece of the curtain wall that had rolled into the courtyard sometime in the last century. If she watched him walk away, she wouldn't be able to resist throwing something at him.

That would be satisfying, but it wouldn't change him or the circumstances.

He had a great deal to do, and he wanted it done as quickly as possible. Getting to the bottom of the ghost and treasure mysteries was "going off on a tangent." How could she make Mr. Obstinate see that it was the heart of the problem?

Somebody had been going to a great deal of trouble for the last few years. They must have powerful reasons for believing the treasure existed.

She looked about her. The courtyard was uneven, but that's what one would expect after years of neglect. Frederick Dalmay had focused his attention on the interior, that much was obvious.

What had Herrick seen that both she and Lisle had missed? It had rained steadily for days before she came, Lisle had said. Then they'd all the horses and carts and people trampling down the weeds and disturbing the earth. The rain and activity had hidden signs—if there were any—of digging.

She let her gaze travel around the crumbling wall. The remains of a watchtower stood in the southwest corner. There? Was there something unnatural about the ground nearby? She walked that way. The earth was mounded about some of the depressions in the ground near the wall. It wasn't freshly dug. It didn't look ancient, though.

Was that what Herrick had noticed?

She stood and studied it for a time, but the lumpy soil told her nothing.

"No hope for it, then," she said to herself. "I'll have to do the sensible thing, and ask him."

Gorewood
Some hours later

The mood in the village had changed overnight, Lisle found.

He and his valet entered shops and placed orders and no one pretended not to understand them.

As Olivia had said, word must have reached the village about the wee red-haired lass who'd faced a deranged French cook and his cleaver. By now they'd probably heard as well about how Olivia had made a ghost as well, and turned terror into laughter.

Well, she was a wonder, no doubt about that.

Lisle and Nichols entered the Crooked Crook. It was crowded, Lisle thought, for the time of day. But being the only public house in the village, it would be the main gossip exchange.

He walked to the bar and ordered a pint. The barkeeper didn't act as though Lisle was speaking Greek or Chinese. He set the tankard on the counter.

"And a round for the company," Lisle said.

That got their attention. He waited until everyone had been served. Then he spoke. He was used to speaking to crowds of strangers. That was how he recruited men to work on excavations. That was how he kept them at it. Money wasn't always important to Egyptians, and they weren't terribly eager to risk their lives for foreigners. The foreigners thought they were cowards. Lisle thought the Egyptians very sensible. And so he appealed to their good sense and made sure he gave them reason to trust him to look after them.

He wasn't sure about Scots. But he knew they were brave to the point of insanity and could be loyal to the same degree—the Battle of Culloden came immediately to mind. Since, at the moment they outnumbered his forces by a mere twenty to two, he didn't bother with tact, one language he'd never quite got the hang of.

"I'm looking for men to repair Gorewood Castle," he said. "I'm looking for the sort of men who aren't afraid of 'ghoulies and ghosties and long-leggety beasties, and things that go bump in the night.' This is the last time I shall ask in Gorewood. Nichols here has made a list of my requirements in the way of carpenters and masons and such. Those wishing to work may put their names on his list and plan to be at Gorewood at eight o'clock tomorrow morning, ready to start. If Nichols returns with insufficient names, I shall seek in the Highlands, where I'm told I can find *real* men."

He drank off the contents of his tankard and walked out.

* * *

Roy watched him go, same as everyone else did. The room was dead quiet, everyone staring at the door the laird's son had walked out of.

Then they looked at the skinny fellow at the bar, with his notebook and pencil.

Then Tam MacEvoy broke out in a great whoop, and someone else along with him, and then they was all doubled over, laughing like they never heard anything so funny in all their lives.

"Did you hear that?" said Tam, when he got his breath back.

"First the red-haired lass, now him," said someone else.

"You ever heard the like?" someone asked Roy.

"No, I never did," he said. And it was true he'd never heard of a lot of strong, healthy Scotsmen standing still for that kind of abuse from an Englishman—and this one not even the laird himself, which everyone knew was an idiot, but only his son. He looked at Jock, who looked even more confused than usual.

"We can't stand for that, now, can we?" Tam said. "We'll teach his lordship who the real men are."

He marched up to the skinny servant, the one called Nichols.

"You," he said.

The Nichols man didn't turn a hair, stood there all calm and polite in that look-down-your-nose English way. "Yes, Mr. . . . ?"

"The name's Tam MacEvoy," Tam said, chin jutting out. "You can sign me up right now. Tam MacEvoy, glazier."

Another fellow elbowed up to the servant. "And me, Craig Archbald, bricklayer."

"And me."

Then they were all pushing and shoving, demanding to be signed up to work.

"Roy," Jock whispered. "What're we going to do?"

"We can't sign up," Roy said. Everyone in Gorewood knew they'd never done an honest day's work in their lives. If they started now, people would get suspicious. "We've got to act like usual."

"But—"

"Don't worry. I've got an idea."

Olivia saw little of Lisle until evening. After coming back from the village, he surveyed the courtyard until sunset. After that, he spent an hour with Herrick in the muniments room, then went to his own room.

Though she hadn't seen it, she knew Lisle had created a study in the large window recess of his bedchamber, the counterpart of hers. He would have been working there until he began dressing for dinner.

Best not to think about his bedroom.

When, after dinner, they adjourned to the warm comforts of the great fireplace, Lisle repeated the brief, provocative speech he'd made in the Crooked Crook.

"And nobody threw anything at you?" Olivia said.

"Certainly not," he said. "Two minutes after I left, they were laughing and cheering, according to Nichols, and fighting to sign up to work. He tells me they signed up their relatives as well, not wishing any kin to be deemed less brave than savage Highlanders—or less brave than a wee red-haired lass. We all know that you were the one who turned the tide."

"But you knew how to take advantage of the situation," she said. She was sorry she hadn't been there. She'd have liked to be in the public house afterward as well, to hear the villagers. That must have been a treat.

"Well done, indeed," said Lady Cooper. "I can hardly wait to see the burly Scotsmen climbing their ladders and heaving bricks about and such."

"Not that we haven't agreeable sights indoors," Lady Withcote said. She cast an admiring glance at Herrick, who came in carrying a tray with their drinks.

When he'd gone out again, Lady Cooper said, "Where on earth did you find him, Olivia?"

"He simply appeared," she said, "like the genie in *The Arabian Nights*."

"I'd like to rub his lamp," said Lady Withcote.

"Millicent, let us offer a toast—to Olivia for procuring a fine specimen of a manservant."

"To Olivia," said Lady Withcote.

Lisle raised his glass. His grey gaze met Olivia's, and she saw the silvery stars and the glowing moon, and everything flooded back, a hot rush of memories.

"To Olivia," he said.

"And to Lisle," said Lady Cooper. "For the brawny Scotsmen to come."

"To Lisle," said Lady Withcote.

"To Lisle," said Olivia, and over the rim of her glass, she shot him a look full of hot meaning, too, in revenge.

"I thank you, ladies," he said. "But now I must beg your indulgence. I've an army of workmen expected tomorrow, and I shall want all my wits. That means keeping country hours." He apologized for being dull, said good night, and went up to his room.

They'd been over every inch of the castle during the last few years. They knew every passage and stairwell, every way in and out. Huddled in the dilapidated watch house, they watched the windows of the south tower.

That was where the women were.

Everyone in Gorewood knew who slept where and which maid belonged to whom and where the servants slept, and which of them sneaked out to the stables and which of the grooms was the most popular with the housemaids. After all, it was Gorewood's castle, and what went on there was everybody's business.

And so Jock and Roy waited for the windows of the south tower to go dark. Then, keeping to the shadows, they hurried to the broken basement door, climbed down the broken steps and made their way to one of the stairways leading up to the first floor.

Oooowwwoooeeeyowwwoooooooyowwwooooeeeewooyowooooooo.

Olivia sat bolt upright. "Good God!"

She heard soft footsteps. "Miss? What is that noise?"

"I'm not sure." Olivia climbed down from the bed. In the light of the dying fire, she saw the poker. She snatched it up. "But whoever's causing it will be very sorry."

* * *

Ooooowwwoooeeeyowwwooooooooyowwwooooeeee-wooyowooooooo.

Lisle woke and leapt from his bed in one movement and grabbed the knife from under his pillow.

"Sir? What is it?"

"Horrible. The most horrible sound on earth. The sound of death and torture and the agonies of a burning hell," Lisle said. "Damn them. It's *bagpipes*."

"Quick," Roy said. "They're coming."

He and Jock ran across the long second-floor room and through the door into the north-tower stairwell and hurried down. The stairwell was black as pitch but they'd been up and down it hundreds of times, and night and day was the same to them.

Down to the first floor and across the great hall to the other stairwell, back into the south tower. They raced down the stone steps. Then Roy stopped and said, "Now, one for the old ladies."

Olivia and Bailey burst into the second-floor drawing room at the same time Lisle and Nichols did.

"Did you see them?" Lisle said.

"Only heard them," Olivia said. "Was that—"

"Bagpipes," Lisle said grimly.

"Really? It sounded so horrible."

"When don't they?"

Muffled screams came from the south-tower stairs. Olivia ran that way. Lisle was at the door ahead of her.

"Stay," he said. He pulled her out of the way and started down the stairs.

She elbowed Nichols aside and went after him.

"I'm not afraid of bagpipes," Olivia said.

"Anyone who'd use them to wake people in the middle of the night would stop at nothing," Lisle said.

"Really, Lisle, they're not as bad as all that."

"They are. It's the worst sound on earth. It's the sound of ten thousand deaths."

They reached the open doorway of Lady Withcote's room. She came to the door, her maid still trying to tie the ribbons of her dressing gown. "So sorry, dears. But that dreadful squalling startled me. I'm sure I leapt straight off the bed up into the air. Can't remember the last time that happened. Lord Waycroft's cold feet, I think."

Seeing she was unhurt, Lisle plunged back into the stairway, Olivia close behind.

They found Lady Cooper standing on the step outside of her bedchamber, looking down into the dark stairwell. "It came from there." She pointed. "You never mentioned ghostly bagpipers, Olivia," she said reproachfully. "If I'd known they were coming, I would have watched for them. Have you ever seen a man blowing the pipes? It wants strong lungs, you know, and strong shoulders and legs—"

"Good, I'm glad you're unharmed," Lisle said.

He entered the small passage leading to the great hall, Olivia on his heels.

"Let me go first," he whispered. "Give me a moment. I need to listen, and you've no idea how loud your shift is when you move."

"It isn't a shift. It's a nightdress."

"Whatever it is, keep it quiet," he said. "And do be careful with the poker."

* * *

The hall's darkness was absolute. Since Lisle couldn't see anything, he listened. But all he heard was the silence of the room. Whoever they were, they knew their way about. And they were gone.

After a moment, Olivia came through the door. He didn't have to see her. He could hear her. The soft rustle of her nightclothes sounded so loud in the great, silent room.

She drew near and he could smell her, the light fragrance wafting from her clothes, and the scent of her skin and hair and the faint . . . something . . . too indistinct to be a scent, but it conjured sleep and still-warm bedclothes. Then other images rose in his mind's eye: pearly skin in the moonlight, the low sound of her laughter, the quick shudder when she came to climax. . .

He clenched his hands—and realized he was still tightly clutching the knife. He relaxed his grip.

He wiped the images from his mind.

"They're gone," he said.

A light appeared in the minstrels' gallery. Herrick stood there, in his dressing gown, candle in hand. "I've calmed the staff, your lordship," he said. "Those who heard the noise, at any rate. Apparently the sound didn't carry to the upper floors."

"Lucky them," Lisle muttered.

"Shall I organize the men to search the castle and grounds, your lordship?"

"Our ghostly musicians will be long gone by now," Lisle said. "Tell everyone to go back to bed."

Herrick quietly departed.

Lisle turned back to Olivia. His eyes had fully adjusted to the darkness, and enough moonlight reached them to show the outlines of her semi-transparent, beruffled and beribboned gown. He redirected his gaze to the nearest wall niche.

"We can't hunt them down at night," he said.

"Certainly not," she said. "They'll know the countryside, while our London servants will only stumble about in the dark and break their necks."

"They must have been out there, in the second-floor drawing room," he said. Mere feet from her bedroom. "Taunting us." He longed for something to hit.

"I must admit, it was disturbing," Olivia said. "No one expects to hear bagpipes in the middle of the night, and when they're played badly—"

"How can you tell?"

"Played well or ill, it's a haunting sound," she said.

"I'm sorry we didn't catch them," he said. "I should have liked to see you take a poker to that vile bladder thing. It's exactly like the Scots to invent a fiendish device like that. Bagpipes. *Golf.*"

She laughed.

The sound slithered down his neck and left heat trails.

"Olivia, go to bed," he said.

"But surely you want to—"

Yes, I surely do.

"We can't talk now," he said. "Use your head. Look at what you're not wearing. One of us has to be sensible, and we both know it won't be you. Go to bed—and be careful with that poker."

Chapter Fourteen

Wednesday 19 October

The sun was sinking behind the hills. Roy and Jock stood in the shadows of the ruined church, watching the men trooping down the castle road back to the village after their first day's work at the castle. Some carried tools on their shoulders, some pushed carts, some drove wagons.

"Another week and they'll have it sealed up tight as a drum," Jock said.

"Not if we unseal it," Roy said.

"Are you daft? A score of men and more working sunup to sundown. All that work they done? And us with a few hours at night?"

"Not all of what they done," Roy said. "Only the work down around the basement, so we can get in. How much you think them Londoners can stand, night after night, us waking them up?"

"Don't know how much I can stand," Jock said. "All that running up and down them stairs, lugging them curst pipes. All that time we could spend digging."

"Useful? Digging by night? All this time we been looking in broad day. What luck you think we'll have shifting rocks at night?"

It was hard enough finding coins in the daytime. It wasn't like the things shot off shiny sparks at them, saying, "Look here. Money." They were the same color as the ground, and hard to tell from rocks and pebbles.

He and Jock had done well with the ones they'd found. A few in the basement. Some in the courtyard. But it was the old earring they found in the courtyard, near the watch house, that convinced Roy that old Dalmay wasn't babbling nonsense, like everyone said. That earring told him the treasure was real, and it was there.

Below the wall, old Dalmay had said.

People said, if them Dalmays couldn't find their own treasure back when it was all fresh in their minds, then it was gone. Cromwell and his like had got to it, same way they got to everything else, they said. But if people'd seen them coins and that old earring and knew what they'd fetched in Edinburgh, they'd sing a different tune. They'd all be up at the castle with their spades and pickaxes—and not to help put it back together.

"Laird's son's got them all digging, too," Roy said. "If it's in the courtyard or in the basement, they're going to find it. We've got to make them stop."

Lisle was trying not to fall asleep into his plate. It had been a long day, though a satisfying one, and his brain was even more tired than his body. He still didn't understand what his family had ever wanted with this ugly pile of stones. They had alternately abandoned it and wasted fortunes maintaining it. No matter what one did, it would always be cold, damp, and gloomy.

All the same, when he'd watched the men marching up the road from the village, he'd felt a surge of pride as well as relief. In spite of the damage the laird, his father, had done, they were prepared to trust the son. Now he'd be able to get the job done properly. Since it was an immense job, it would keep him well occupied.

He glanced across the table at the problem on whose account he needed to stay otherwise occupied. Olivia wore a gown of some heavy blue silken material, with the usual miles of material in the strangest places, while her shoulders and most of her satanic bosom lay naked—except for the sapphire pendant necklace winking up at him from the center of the devil's land.

She was rising from the table, preparing to lead the company to the fireplace for tea—or, in the ladies' cases, another vat of whiskey—and conversation or reading, when the wail of bagpipes welled up from the bowels of the earth.

Lisle leapt from his chair. "Herrick, Nichols, with me. You—" He signaled to the footmen propping up the wall. "Down the south stairs."

They all grabbed candlesticks and hurried down to the basement.

They stumbled over the debris, searching the big, vaulted rooms. Then one of the footmen gave a shout. "Your lordship, here!"

Lisle hurried toward the sound of the man's voice. He found him pointing to the wall of one of the rooms.

In large charcoal letters, someone had scrawled, ?B□ T BOB.

That was all they found.

The devils had got away. Lisle sent the servants back upstairs to assure the ladies that no one would be murdered at present. Then he walked back to glare at the scrawled message. When he got his hands on them. . .

A familiar rustling came from nearby. He looked away from the misspelled taunt. Olivia approached, candle in hand. She paused at his elbow and studied the wall.

"I must say, it does disturb me, their creeping in while the entire household is awake," she said. "They're strangely bold."

"Or strangely stupid," he said.

"Step-Papa always says that criminals tend to be men of low intelligence and high cunning," she said.

"I know. I'd far rather deal with clever ones. At least one can understand their thinking."

"Bagpipes are harmless enough in themselves," she said.

"That's a matter of opinion," he said.

"It's the harassment that worries me," she said. "It upsets the servants."

It bothered him, too. They needed servants to function, and servants didn't stay in bad situations unless they were desperate.

"Unfortunately, one can't keep a garrison here to protect us from invaders, as they did in the old days," he said.

"I doubt they'll actually try to harm us," she said. "That would bring the authorities into it—and what they clearly want is for everybody to go away so they can continue their treasure hunt."

"I'm not going away," he said. "I've started, and I'm not giving up. I'll restore this useless damned antique, and then I'm going back to Egypt if I have to row myself in a dinghy. Meanwhile, I'm going to booby-trap the basement. Those morons will have to find another way in."

"If we found the treasure first, they'd have to stop looking," she said.

He was tired and it was hard to look at her and be sensible when he was being stabbed to death inside. He was furious with himself for not being able to master feelings that could only lead to unhappiness. It was on the tip of his tongue to say, "There is no treasure," and to tell her to stop being a romantic idiot—and to put on more clothes, and not stand so close, where he could smell her.

The warning voice spoke in time.

Think.

Treasure. There wasn't any but she'd never believe that. *She wants to look. Why not let her?* It would keep her busy, and if he presented it carefully, it would keep her out of trouble.

"Very well," he said. "Let's look at this logically. Even deeply stupid men wouldn't work so hard without very good reason."

"That's it, exactly," she said. "They've been at it for years, if we measure from when the haunting started. There must be *something* behind it."

"If we knew what that was, then we'd know what to do," he said. "Maybe there's something in Cousin

Frederick's papers. Or something he said. The trouble started after he left the castle and moved to Edinburgh."

His mind was already gnawing on the puzzle. It was easy enough to set the lures for her without telling an actual lie.

"It's intriguing, I admit," he said. "But I haven't time to think about it. I haven't time to study his papers and books and talk to the people who were close to him. I've got this heap of stones to 'restore to its former glory' to appease my deranged parents."

He saw her face fall, and he felt ashamed. Worse, the mad part of him—the part she could summon so easily—wanted to drop everything and pursue the mystery. That part of him wanted to hunt with her for treasure, the way they'd done before. Oh, it was tempting. He recalled the excitement of breaking rules and surviving by one's wits.

He could feel himself being drawn in, and he knew he ought to fight, but the mad part of him didn't want to.

Then, "You're right," she said, her expression brightening. "Treasure or no treasure, the castle must be restored. I did promise you'd return to Egypt by spring. Which means we've not a minute to waste. I'll tackle the mystery. Now that Herrick's taking charge, I'll have plenty of time on my hands—and I daresay the ladies would adore collecting gossip from your cousin's friends."

She stepped closer and patted his chest. "Don't you worry about a thing," she said. "Your loyal knight Sir Olivia will do what's needed."

When I grow up, I'm going to be a knight, she'd told

him the day he met her. *The gallant Sir Olivia, that's who I'll be, setting out on perilous quests, performing noble deeds, righting wrongs.*

She hurried away then, and he stood watching, until she was out of sight and the rustling faded.

He turned to stare at the wall.

? B☐ BOB.

But of course he didn't believe in presentiments or omens. Or warnings from imbeciles who couldn't spell.

He turned away and went back upstairs.

As he'd said he would, Herrick had ridden to Edinburgh on Wednesday. By Thursday, they had a housekeeper, Mrs. Gow. By Friday, Herrick and Mrs. Gow had hired a full Scottish staff. That day, Olivia gave all of her London staff except the personal servants permission to return to London.

Only Aillier insisted on remaining. The others couldn't pack fast enough. They were gone by mid-afternoon.

Meanwhile, she spent hours poring over Cousin Frederick Dalmay's books, pamphlets, and periodicals. Wherever Gorewood Castle was mentioned—in an article, say, by Sir Walter Scott for an antiquarian publication—Frederick had placed a paper marker and written notes in pencil in the margin. The notes were illegible for the most part, but no matter.

The printed material told her about all the ghost legends: Different ghosts, she found, were popular in different eras. She learned, too, about curious doings at banquets and bewildering legal matters. Frederick had kept records of all the property disputes. He'd kept a set of journals as well. As far as she could make out, these dealt mainly with Gorewood Castle and its history. They seemed to refer occasionally to annoyances pertaining to the castle. But she couldn't be sure, because the small, spidery handwriting was nearly impossible to read.

She thought Lisle would have no trouble making sense of it, being more accustomed to deciphering strange scripts, some of them partly defaced by time or vandals. She would have to ask him if he could spare a little time for that.

Then, on Monday, she was turning a page, debating whether to beg Lisle to explain it to her, when the piece of yellowed, partly burnt paper fell out.

"But it's a *clue*," Olivia said. She waved the creased, brown-edged paper in Lisle's face.

Reluctantly, he took it from her.

His plan had been working so well. He did his job and she did hers. Their paths crossed at mealtimes, when the ladies were there as well, and they couldn't help but be a distraction.

But today Olivia had cornered him in the basement well room while the workers were outside, eating their midday meal. She was practically dancing with excitement because she'd found a <u>CLUE</u>.

She wasn't supposed to find any clues. She was supposed to keep searching and searching until he got the work done and came to his senses about her or, if that was impossible, until he solved the problem of what to do about her.

"What does it say?" she said.

He looked down at the uneven grid with its random marks. "It doesn't say anything," he said. "It looks like a child's scribbling and drawing. One of Cousin Frederick's early efforts, perhaps. My mother kept all my drawings. Keeping this sort of thing isn't an act of judgment but one of sentiment, apparently."

"Are you *sure*?" she said.

He gave it back to her. "It isn't a treasure map," he said.

"Perhaps it's a coded message."

"There is no code," he said.

"Those little symbols," she said. "In the little boxes."

He looked from the paper to her.

She'd collected cobwebs on her dress and in her hair on her way into the well room. She'd apparently dragged her hands through her hair while trying to decipher the Secret Message, because a number of pins dangled drunkenly from the thick curls. Her blue eyes shimmered with excitement, and the sunrise color had washed into her cheeks.

He was so tired of this hideous castle and the hideous weather and so tired of digging holes to bury feelings only to have them slither out, like snakes, and sink their fangs into him.

Why had he come back to England?

He knew it wasn't good for him to be near her.

But he'd returned because of the Carsingtons—and it wasn't fair. Why should he keep away from the one family that meant anything to him, because one member of that family turned him inside out and upside down?

"It's rubbish," he said. "The sort of scraps elderly people keep about for no earthly reason."

The flush in her cheeks deepened and crept down her neck. A warning sign.

"He wasn't like that," she said. "If you'd look at his journals, you'd see. He's meticulous. If he kept this, he had a reason."

"It could be any reason," he said. "Senility comes to mind."

Her blue gaze narrowed as it lifted to meet his. "You told me to look for clues," she said. "You told me to get to the bottom of it. I haven't bothered you for days. Now I ask for your help, and you dismiss me out of hand. You know perfectly well that this paper means something."

"I doesn't mean anything!" he snapped. "There's no treasure. There might have been once, but any rational person would know it's long gone. Even the ghosts have lost interest. Haven't you noticed? No wailing bagpipes in the middle of the night? No sign of them, since they scrawled on the basement wall."

"It's been raining," she said. "They don't want to trudge through a downpour carrying their bagpipes and the rest of their collection of ghost tricks."

"The basement is booby trapped," he said. "I made no secret of it, and they've heard, the way everybody hears everything."

"And you think they've given up, just like that? You think your traps scared them away?"

"Well, no one's set any before, have they?"

Her flush darkened. "Lisle, you are not—"

"This is ridiculous," he said. "I'm not going to argue with you about ghosts."

She waved the paper at him. "You could at least—"

"No," he said. "I'm not going to waste time on worthless scribbles."

"You wouldn't say that if you'd look at the journals."

"I'm not looking at the journals," he said. Not with her peering over his shoulder. Her scent. The curst rustling. It wasn't fair. She knew they needed to keep apart.

"You told me to look!" she cried. "I've spent hour after hour, searching through mountains of papers and books and journals and letters. Hour after hour, trying to read his tiny handwriting. You were the one—"

"To keep you busy!" he burst out. "To keep you out of my hair. I have this idiotic, pointless task—a great waste of time and money—in this miserable place, where I never wanted to be—and I wouldn't be here if it wasn't for you."

"I was *helping* you!"

"Oh, yes, a great help you've been. If not for you I should have told my parents to go to blazes. I'd be happier starving in Egypt than living here. What do I care about their damned money? Let them spend it on my brothers. I can make my own way. But no, here I am, trying at least to do the accursed job, and do it properly, and you must nag and harass me to run off on another wild goose chase."

"Nag and harass? You were the one—"

"It was a *diversionary tactic*! You of all people ought to know what that is. You do it all the time. Well, I've used it on you. How do you like it? How do *you* like dancing to someone else's tune?"

"You—you—" She grabbed his hat, pulled it off, and hit him in the chest with it. She flung it down and stomped on it.

"Well done," he said. "So mature."

"If you were a man, I'd challenge you to a duel," she said.

"If you were a man I'd shoot you happily."

"I hate you!" she cried. "You are *despicable*!" She kicked him in the shins.

It was a hard kick, but he was too angry to feel it. "Splendid," he said. "So ladylike."

She made an obscene gesture and stormed out.

One o'clock in the morning
Tuesday 25 October

Tonight was clear, and the moon, though past its full, offered sufficient illumination for mischief makers, ruffians, and anyone who wanted to spy on them.

The only "anyone" at present was Olivia, creeping out of the castle after everyone else had gone to bed. She wore men's pantaloons, with flannel drawers underneath. A waistcoat, coat, and a hooded, thick wool cloak offered the next layer of protection against a Scottish autumn night. She'd brought with her as well a wool blanket to protect her from the night damps.

Not that she needed it. She had her boiling blood to keep her warm.

The ghosts had gone, had they?

"We'll see about that," she said under her breath.

She should have bet him, that's what she should have done, after their icily polite dinner.

They're not gone, and I can prove it. That's what she should have said.

And he'd say, *You can't prove anything.*

Can't I? What will you wager?

How about Castle Horrid? You can have that.

It isn't yours to give. I'll tell you what: If I prove the ghosts haven't gone, you'll stop acting like a thick-headed—oh, sorry, I forgot. You can't help that.

"And he'd say . . ." She looked up at the north tower. Its darkened windows told her he was asleep—and she hoped he was having hellish nightmares. "And he'd say . . . What would he say?"

Never mind. She'd prove the ghosts hadn't given up. They were merely revising their tactics. That's what she would do.

In any case, a wager would only put him on the alert. Better to let him think she was sulking. If he'd guessed she was planning anything, he'd make a nuisance of himself.

The last thing she needed was a surly, uncooperative male getting in her way.

She hadn't even told Bailey about her plan for tonight because Bailey would wait up for her, and Olivia didn't know how long she'd be out. If she had to, she'd stay until first light. She had a cozy enough hiding place.

The choice of position was obvious. The broken-down watchtower in the southwest corner of the court-yard had been built precisely for observation purposes. Though it wasn't useful at present for surveying the surrounding countryside, its doorway offered a good view of most of the courtyard while concealing her.

The only trying part was the waiting. Sitting in one place, without a pack of cards or a book, wasn't enter-taining. And sitting on a stone, even if it was a great, flat one, was comfortable only for a short time. She felt the cold through the layers of thick woolen cloak and pantaloons and flannel drawers. The wind whistled through the chinks. As time passed, the moon and stars seemed to dim. She peeped out from her hiding place.

Clouds were racing overhead on the quickening wind, filling the sky and blotting out the moon and stars. She tucked into her shelter, pulling the blanket more tightly about her. Time passed, the air growing colder and colder. Her limbs were stiff. She changed position.

Was that damp air she felt on her cheeks? Or was it only the chill wind? Her fingers were growing numb. The night continued to darken. She could barely make out the outlines of the courtyard.

The wind shrieked through the chinks in the stones and she could hear it sweep up piles of dead leaves and whirl them through the courtyard. She moved again, but she hadn't enough room. She didn't dare stamp her feet to warm them, and her toes ached with cold. Her bottom was going numb.

She thought about Lisle, and the abominable things he'd said, and what she could have said back, but that didn't work anymore to warm her. She'd have to get up and walk about, or all her limbs would go to sleep. She started to rise.

A light flashed at the periphery of her vision. Or did it? So brief. A dark lantern? Then everything was darker than ever and the air was heavy, a cold, damp blanket.

Then she heard the footsteps.

"Mind the lantern," said a low voice.

Clank. Thump. Thud.

"I can't see a bloody thing. It's raining again. I told you—"

"It's only mist."

"Rain. I told you— Bloody hell!"

The light flashed in Olivia's face, blinding her.

The deeply creased and partly burnt piece of paper crept into Lisle's mind for the hundredth time as he was on the point of dropping off to sleep.

The wobbling grid lines arranged themselves in his mind's eye, and the tiny figures reappeared in the little boxes.

It couldn't be a map, with no arrows or compass points.

But it might be a sort of code, or shorthand.

His brain began arranging and rearranging the lines and figures, and then it was no use trying to sleep, because he was thinking.

He opened his eyes fully, sat up, lit the candle at his bedside, and cursed.

She'd waved it in his face and he couldn't leave it alone.

He climbed out of bed, pulled on his dressing gown, and resuscitated the fire. He took up the candle and went into the large window recess. It had at some point—by the looks of it, early in the castle's history—been fitted out with a window seat. He'd moved a bench into it, which he used as a desk.

By day, the light was more than adequate. In the evenings, it was a pleasant place to work. When it wasn't raining or overcast—rare occasions—he could look out at the starry sky. It wasn't an Egyptian night sky, but it was certainly one that seemed far from civilization and all of its rules and aggravations.

He looked out and swore. It was raining again.

"This wretched place," he said.

It took a moment for Olivia's vision to recover. The lantern flashed again, but not in her direction. She heard clanging and the sound of voices. Something thudded to the ground. Then running footsteps.

She didn't stop to think.

She threw off the blanket and ran after them, following the flash of the lantern, its light bouncing through the courtyard and out through a gap in the wall, bypassing the entrance, and into the road.

She was aware of the chill rain, coming down faster and harder, but the lantern flashed ahead of her like a glowworm, and the light drew her after it, down the road. Then, abruptly, it was gone. No light anywhere. She looked about her. Left, right, ahead, behind.

Nothing. Darkness. Rain, icy rain, drumming on her head and shoulders, trickling down her neck.

She looked back. She could barely make out the castle, a blurry hulk in the distance, behind the sheeting rain that was soaking through her cloak and into her coat.

No light in the windows. Nothing.

No help there.

No place to take shelter here—and what good was shelter now, even if she could find it? Her gloves were soaked through, and her hands ached with the cold.

She tried to run, but her feet were like blocks of cold stone, and her clothes were heavy with wet, and if she stumbled and fell. . .

Don't dramatize.

Move. One foot in front of the other.

She gritted her teeth against the cold, and bowed her head and trudged back to the castle.

The door to Lisle's room in the north tower was thick. If not for the gap at the hinge—another item to add to the list of repairs—he wouldn't have heard the sound. As it was, he wasn't sure he'd heard it. He moved to the door, opened it a fraction, and listened.

He heard scraping and muttering.

Then a curse. Though the voice was very low, he knew whose it was.

He took up his candle, left his room, and stepped out into what used to be the castle's drawing room, a room above the great hall, nearly as large though not as tall. It, too, boasted a large fireplace.

Olivia knelt in front of it. She was shaking, trying to raise a spark with the tinderbox.

She looked up and blinked at the light of his candle.

"Lisle?" she whispered.

He took her in: dripping hair, dripping clothes, a puddle forming on the floor about her.

"What have you done?" he said. "Olivia, what have you done?"

"Oh, L-isle," she said. She trembled violently.

He set down the candle. Then he bent and scooped her up. She was drenched through, shivering. He wanted to roar and rage at her, and maybe that's what he should have done. Then someone might have heard—her maid or his valet at the very least—and hurried out to help.

But he didn't rage at her. He didn't say a word. He carried her into his room.

Chapter Fifteen

$\mathcal{L}$isle set her down on the rug in front of the fire. She was shaking violently, her teeth chattering, her hands icy.

Heart racing, he tore at her dripping clothes. The heavy wool boat cloak was wet all the way through the wool lining. His hands, clumsy with fear, fumbled at the button. He couldn't get it through the hole. He ripped it off, tore the cloak off her, and threw it aside.

Underneath she wore men's attire. That was wet, too. He wrestled the coat down from her shoulders and peeled it down, pulling her arms from the sleeves. He threw the coat aside, and swore. Unlike the time in York, she'd worn a waistcoat this time; it was wet as well, with a line of buttons that fought being unbuttoned.

He ran to the bench, snatched up his penknife, and cut them off. He pulled off the waistcoat, then went to work on the woolen trousers. A degree less wet, their buttonholes yielded to his tugging. He peeled them off her, and swore again.

She had on flannel drawers underneath—and they

were damp. Layers upon layers of outer clothing and she was wet to the skin. His heart pounded with terror and rage. How long had she stood in the downpour? What was wrong with her, to do such a thing? She'd take a chill. A fever. In the middle of nowhere, miles from a proper doctor.

He didn't even attempt to untie the drawers. He cut the drawer strings and started pulling them off her.

"W-wait," she said. "W-wait."

"You can't wait."

"I'll d-do it."

"You're shaking."

"I'm s-so c-cold."

He peeled them down her legs and pulled them off. He stripped her to the skin, wrapping a blanket about her as he went, vaguely aware of some reason to cover her up but not caring what the reason was.

She only sobbed, and talked nonsense: stuttered sentences she didn't finish, obscure phrases: something about a wager and never writing letters enough and why did she keep that rubbish but Bailey understood, didn't she?

She was delirious.

Delirium was a sign of fever. Fever boded an infection of the lungs.

Don't think about that.

He wrapped another blanket about her. He stirred the fire. She was still shaking.

"I c-can't st-stop," she said. "I d-don't know wh-why."

He rubbed the blankets against her skin, trying to encourage the blood to flow, but the wool was too rough against her skin, and she winced.

He searched the room in a frenzy. He snatched up the bathing and shaving towels Nichols had laid out for to-morrow. Lisle pulled away the blanket, uncovering one arm, and rubbed it with the towel. Then on to the other. Her hands were still icy, trembling in his.

He focused on the extremities, massaging her feet next. They were icy, too. He went on rubbing, desperately, not letting himself think, only trying to get the blood flowing faster, back into her limbs.

He didn't know how long it went on. Panic blanketed his mind.

He massaged her shoulders and arms, her legs and feet. His hands ached, but he wouldn't stop.

He was so furiously intent on what he was doing that it was a while before he realized that the spasmodic shaking was abating. She wasn't talking nonsense any-more. Her teeth had stopped the ghastly chattering.

He paused and looked at her.

"Oh," she said. "I thought I'd never be warm again. Oh, Lisle. Why did you make me so angry? You know what happens when I lose my temper."

"I know."

"What did I think I could do, alone? But I meant to spy only. I think. It was so dark. No light in the win-dows. I should have made you come with me. We *bal-ance*."

She was only half making sense, but half was enough. His heart rate slowed a degree. The skin under his hands had begun to warm at last. The shivering eased further.

His mind began to quiet.

Then he saw, clearly.

Olivia, in front of the fire, wrapped in a blanket. Her clothes strewn about, in pieces. Buttons everywhere.

"Oh, Lisle," she said. "Your hands, so warm. Your wonderful, clever hands."

He looked down at his hands, wrapped about her lower right arm. He needed to let go.

He needed not to let go.

Instead he moved them, but more slowly, down her arm and up again. And again. And again.

He'd been so careful to keep the blanket about her, pulling it away only to rub her arms, her feet. He pulled the blanket over her right arm, then away from the left. He massaged that arm, too. Slowly.

"The way it feels," she said in a dazed voice. "I can't describe. Magical. How do you do this to me?"

He drew the blanket up, revealing her feet. When his palm slid over her instep, she moaned.

He dragged the pillows up behind her head and shoulders, then pushed her down onto them. She closed her eyes and sighed. Then she opened them again, to watch him.

He went back to rubbing her feet. First one, then the other. Then he began to rub her lower legs, pushing the blanket up. His palms shaped to the curve of her calves. Her skin was like velvet under his hands. Warm velvet. Her breathing slowed and deepened. She stopped trembling.

She lay upon the pillows, looking up at him, her blue eyes lit by the firelight, so that stars seemed to dance there. The light glowed on her skin: the fine bones of her cheeks, the curve of her jaw, the stubborn point of her chin. The blanket had slipped from her shoulders, revealing the white column of her neck and the graceful slope of her shoulders.

He dropped the towel and let the back of his hand graze her cheek. Her skin was as smooth as the softest silk, the kind the wealthiest Egyptian women wore, so fine that a length of it easily threaded through a ring. It wasn't silk though, but *her* skin, warm and alive. Moments ago he'd thought he'd lose her, and the world had stopped, and everything went empty and black.

He turned his hand to feel the softness and the warmth and the life against his palm.

She turned her face to touch her mouth to his hand.

Don't don't don't.

But that was a lie. That wasn't what he wanted.

It was so simple. A nothing of a touch. Merely lips to the palm of his hand. But he'd waited forever, and the touch shivered through him, shock after shock, as though he'd touched an electrical rod. It ricocheted in his heart, setting it thumping erratically. It raced downward, and shot heat into his groin. His body tightened and tensed, and his mind narrowed into a kind of tunnel.

He was kneeling at her feet, and all he saw was her, glowing in the firelight. The skin he touched was very warm now. She was alive, hotly alive, her bosom rising and falling under the blanket.

The fire crackled beside them. Otherwise the room was quiet and dark. Shadows danced in the corners.

She held the blanket closed in front of her with one hand. He reached up and tugged at her hand. Her fingers uncurled and she let go. No protest. No sound. She only looked up at him, watching him, her beautiful face somber and studying, as though he were a mystery she needed to penetrate.

There was no mystery to him.

He was merely a man, and he'd merely missed her desperately, and minutes ago he'd glimpsed a world without her.

He'd lived without her, and he'd stayed away from her. He'd missed her, though. If she wasn't here to come back to, what would his life be like?

A moment ago he'd thought he'd lose her. Now she was here, warm and alive in the firelight. A simple fact. She was here and he wanted her: one simple fact that erased willpower and good intentions and conscience and obligations.

He parted the blanket and drew it down to her waist and simply looked at her, filling his eyes and mind and heart with her.

"Ye gods," he breathed, and it was hard to breathe. "Ye gods, Olivia."

Her skin was pearly white, like the moon when it rose high in the night. Her firm breasts—the ones the devil had given her—glowed as smooth and white as moons, too, but tipped with rosy buds that begged to be touched. She took his hand and he gave it to her, unresisting. She laid it over one satiny breast. He felt the bud tighten under his hand. His groin tightened, too.

The tunnel of his mind grew narrower still.

All he could see was her. All he could think was her. All the world was Olivia, glowing in the firelight. He shaped his hand to the smooth globe and she sighed. He filled his hands with her breasts and squeezed, and she laughed so softly, deep in her throat, and closed her eyes.

"Yes," she said. "This is what I wanted."

Simple words. He heard everything in them: longing and pleasure and he didn't know what else, all mingled. Or so it seemed, and that was enough for him, because it was the same he could have said.

This is what I wanted.

He eased her legs apart. Still unresisting, she watched him. He crept up and bent over her and touched his tongue to one taut pink bud.

"Yes," she whispered.

Yes. And that said everything. *Yes* was the taste of her skin and the sound of her voice and the way her belly rose as her body arched under the flick of his tongue. It was the way she reached up and curled her arms about his neck and held him to her. It was the way she moaned while he suckled and while he slid his tongue over her breast and tasted the pearly skin.

Yes, this is what I wanted.

Then he was pushing the blanket off her, and she was dragging his face to hers and kissing him, her soft mouth parting in quick invitation, and offering up the cherry-sweet sinfulness. Then it was the kiss that swept him away, the wild, deep kiss that seemed to be a hundred kisses stored up over years, so endless it was and so endless was the sensation of falling, deep, into Olivia and into himself and into a wild world where only they existed.

The world narrowed to the taste of her and the scent of her and the feel of her skin and the shape of her body under his hands. The world was the way she writhed under his touch and the way her hands slid over him, until she found the edges of his shirt. She tugged it upward until he broke the kiss to pull the shirt over his head and throw it aside. Then he was as naked as she.

Yes, this is what I wanted.

She dragged her hands down along his shoulders and arms. She traced the shape of his chest, and shocks flickered over his skin and shot under it as her fingers grazed his nipples.

"Ah," she said. And up she came, quick and smooth, and touched her tongue to the hard nubs. She pulled herself up further, and wrapped her legs about his hips and kissed him, her tongue pushing against his and playing with it, thrusting and retreating, while her breasts rubbed against his chest, and while his cock, hard and hot, shuddered against her belly.

He held her, dragging his hands down her smooth back to the curve of her waist, then down to cup her buttocks.

The fire crackled beside them, and it seemed to crackle inside him, too. Every touch, every kiss, fed the flames.

He pressed her down without breaking the kiss, and she went where he silently guided, her legs still wrapped about his hips. He lifted his head and opened his eyes and let his gaze lock with hers while he drew her legs apart and brought her feet down onto the rug.

He slid his hands along her thighs to her core, where the firelight glowed on soft, coppery threads and made the dewy flesh there glisten. He slid his finger to the narrow cleft and stroked there. She twisted and arched under his hand.

He knew how to please. He wished more than anything to please—but she fired up so quickly, she burned up thought. Only instinct and need remained. It was elemental: two young bodies, flesh and blood calling to each other, and a driving feeling in the blood, as fierce and unstoppable as the simoom.

She touched his cock, her smooth fingers sliding down its length and closing over it, and stroking upward and downward, upward and downward.

He growled and pushed her hand away, and pushed into her. He met tightness and resistance, and she rose up sharply, with a surprised little cry, her body tensing. He covered her mouth, and kissed her deeply, so deeply, stores and stores of wanting saved up for an eternity, it seemed.

Her hands came up and circled his neck, they slid up to cup his face. The tension eased and she kissed him back with ferocious intensity. And while they kissed, that long, long kiss, he pushed into her again, more deeply. She stiffened but she didn't pull away or push him away.

A voice or memory came from far away, warning.

Stop. Time to stop.

But the warning was far away and he was past heeding, stripped down to simple need. He was inside her, and she was his, and he could only thrust and thrust again, in some primal language whose only word was *Mine*. And *mine*. And *mine*.

Somewhere in the surging madness he felt the tension easing, and she began to push back, against his thrusts. Her nails dug into his back. Her body surged up to meet his, again and again, and faster and faster.

Then it happened, all in a sudden, wild rush: a last frenzied struggle, and a bolt of happiness, of pleasure. Then a feeling of diving into a mad world where stars were falling upward or sinking into the bottom of the sky.

Then it was quiet, but for the frantic pounding of their hearts.

She lay, stunned, beneath him.

The naughty engravings couldn't begin to convey it.

She could scarcely understand it. Such profound intimacy. Such soaring feelings.

Good God.

She was aware of her heart slowing and the quieting of his breathing. She felt his cock slipping from her, and she felt grieved and madly happy at the same time.

That awful, awful march in the icy, pounding rain, up that endless road. The worst, darkest hour of her life.

Even when Papa died, and her heart broke, at least she had Mama.

This night she'd felt so utterly alone, looking up at the hulking shadow of the castle, offering nothing, not a single lit window to welcome her.

And this was how it ended. In a sort of heaven, but not the good, boring heaven people prated about. In his arms.

Lisle moved his weight off her and rolled onto his side, taking her along. He pulled her rump against his groin, tucked his head into the curve of her shoulder. His hand cupped one breast.

She wanted to die of the pleasure of that intimate,

possessive touch. Her heart was turning over on itself. She was afraid to speak, afraid to bring back the world. She clung to this moment, when everything, finally, was right, because at last they'd come together and loved, with their bodies and hearts and minds, freely. For one short, endless time, the rest of the world and the rest of their lives and all the harsh little realities had been set aside.

His voice, low and hoarse, broke the silence. "Are you all right?"

Yes, finally, for once. "Yes."

"I think," he began.

"Don't think," she said. "Let's not think for a moment." She put her hand over the one holding her breast. "Don't move. Don't do anything. Let's just . . . be."

A long silence, but not a peaceful one. She could feel the tension building in him.

Because he was good and honorable.

"I thought you were going to die," he said softly.

"So did I," she said.

"I thought you were going to get colder and colder and never stop shaking until you died in my arms."

At the time, she'd been so cold, so bitterly cold and miserable that she'd simply let it happen, whatever it was, whatever he did. She remembered now: the furious movement of his hands over her body, the ache as he forced her blood to move again . . . his hands, his hands.

"I thought so, too. I thought I'd never be warm again. Or maybe not. I'm not sure I could think."

"What were you doing?" he said. "Out there?"

She told him—all of it, including their imaginary conversation.

"Why couldn't you throw something at me instead?" he said. "You couldn't find a way to torture me without going out into a downpour?"

"It wasn't raining when I went out," she said. "Not a cloud in the sky. Well, except for a wisp here and there."

"You were out there for *hours*," he said.

"It felt like years," she said.

"What am I going to do with you?" he said.

"A clandestine affair?" she said.

"I'm not joking," he said.

She turned in his arms. "But it's what we want. All this business about keeping away from each other. One can't fight the Inevitable."

"We didn't try very hard," he said. "We face one trial of self-control and we fail."

"Lisle, I fail all trials of self-control."

"I don't. I could have summoned your maid. I could have shouted the house down and had everyone running about, fetching hot this and that and dry this and that, and fussing over you, and sending for a doctor in the dead of night. But no."

She stroked his cheek. "Can't you stuff your conscience into a drawer for a time? Can't we simply enjoy this moment?"

He pulled her closer and buried his face in her hair. "You make me insane," he said, his voice muffled. "But being insane, with you, is exciting, and usually I have a good time. We like each other very well—when we don't hate each other—and we are friends. And now we've made love—and that went well."

She laughed. "Oh, Lisle."

"It isn't a bad basis for marriage," he said.

Aaargh. She drew back. "I knew it. I knew it."

He pulled her back, tight against his hard body. He was so warm and so strong and she only wanted to melt there.

"Listen to me," he said. His mouth was warm against her ear. The scent of his skin was in her nostrils and in her mind, making it soft.

"We'll ruin each other's lives," she said.

"Not completely," he said.

"Oh, Lisle." She bowed her head, to rest her forehead against his chest. "I adore you. I always have. Part of what I adore is your honor and principles and ethics and duty and—and all those good things. It's all those good things that are twisting your mind and making you not see things as they are. You are thinking, 'I ruined her.' The fact is—listen now, this is a fact: The fact is, I should have been ruined sooner or later. I'm glad it was you. One ought to start one's love life in a spectacular fashion, and you've done that for me."

"*Start?*" he said.

His entire body stiffened.

And everything was about to get worse, but it couldn't be helped. He was determined to be honorable, and he was the most obstinate man in the world.

"I adore you," she said. "I always have and always will. But I'm a selfish girl, and romantic, and I must come first in a man's heart. I won't settle for what so many other women settle for, ending up bored and lonely."

"*Settle?* Olivia, you know I care for you more than—"

"More than Egypt?" she said.

A short but telling pause. Then, "What a ridiculous thing to say," he said. "Those are two completely different things."

"Perhaps they are, but one comes first in your heart, always has and always will. I won't settle for second place in a man's heart."

She felt him flinch.

She pulled away and sat up. "I need to get to my room."

He sat up, too, and her heart ached. The firelight outlined the hard contours of his chest and traced the rippling muscles of his arms. It made sunlight of his hair. He was the sort of man dreams were made on, and myths, and the dreams and myths inspired great statues of bronze and gold where believers paid tribute, worshipped.

She'd gladly be his votary. She was romantic enough for that, and both too romantic and too cynical to do the sensible thing and marry him.

He grabbed one of the cast-off blankets and wrapped it about her. "You're not thinking clearly," he said. "You don't have a choice. You might be pregnant. Even if you aren't, there are rules, Olivia, and I know you don't want to shame your family."

"Then we have to find a way around the rules," she said. "We should make each other wretched. If you'd gag your curst conscience for a moment, you'd see it. You're too reasonable a man not to see it."

The silence stretched out. The fire snapped. He heard a distant hissing. It must still be raining.

Rain. Such an ordinary thing. It happened all the

time. And it had brought her here, and brought the two of them to this.

The horrible thing was that she was, for once, reasonable. The horrible thing was that, in this at least, Olivia saw as clearly as he did. He cared for her. He was infatuated with her. Yet he couldn't be sure that was enough, and the same conscience that urged him to marry her told him she'd be miserable if he did. When he'd let himself think of having her in his life, he'd always thought of what she'd do to his life, the havoc she'd wreak. He hadn't thought about what he'd do to hers.

Now he looked, not into the simoom-riddled future he'd imagined, but into his heart. He couldn't offer what she needed and deserved. She ought to be first in a man's heart, and it had not occurred to him until now that perhaps he'd left no room in his.

"We won't solve this tonight," he said.

"Not likely," she said.

"We'd better get you to your own bed," he said.

"Yes. But we do need to conceal the evidence," she said. "The easiest thing is to to build up the fire in the drawing room and throw my wet clothes in front of it. That way it will seem as though I did what I was trying to do: make a fire and dry off."

Leave it to her. He was used to thinking quickly, but concealing crimes wasn't his specialty.

She rose, her blanket slipping to the floor.

The firelight traced her ripe curves and glittered in the coppery triangle between her legs. He let his gaze travel up and down, up and down, while his heart ached. "Yes, you're beautiful," he said, his voice tight.

She smiled.

"But I can't recommended wandering naked about a Scottish castle," he said. "You'll undo all my hard work and take a chill." He was hunting about while he spoke. He found his shirt. He stood up and pulled it over her head and thrust her arms through the sleeves. The cuffs covered her hands. The shirt fell past her knees.

She looked down at herself. "I'm not sure I can explain this as easily as I can traipsing about naked."

"You'll think of something."

He took her hand and led her to the door. He remembered the way her hands had roved so freely over his body, setting his skin on fire.

What was he going to do with her?

He opened the door a crack.

The drawing room was silent and dark. He listened the way he would when entering a tomb where an ambush might await, his ears tuned to detect the sound of breathing.

No one else was breathing in the drawing room.

He stepped out into the room, taking her with him. The large room was as black as a tomb, but for the wedge of light coming from his doorway and, halfway down, the faintest light from the dying embers of the fire she'd tried to rebuild earlier.

"Will you be able to find your way without breaking your neck?" he said. "Maybe I'd better come with you."

"I'll be all right," she whispered. "There's very little furniture to bump into."

She slid her hand from his and started to move away.

He wanted to say something but couldn't find the words he needed in all the turmoil. He grabbed her shoulders and turned her toward him. He kissed her once, but fiercely. She melted into him.

He broke the kiss and pushed her away. "Go," he said.

She went.

He waited, listening to the soft patter of her bare feet grow fainter as she traversed the long room. He waited until he heard the soft thud of the door closing behind her.

Then he returned to his room.

Nichols was gathering up her discarded clothing.

Crossing an endless drawing room in the dead of night wasn't the easiest trick in the best of circumstances. Olivia wasn't at her best. Her throat ached and her eyes itched and she wanted to sit down and weep for a week.

She knew she'd said the right thing—the necessary thing. But she'd hurt him.

She didn't mind hurting him physically—he could take it—and she didn't mind tearing into him when he was being an infuriating blockhead. But all he'd done tonight was take care of her and make love to her . . . and turn her heart inside out.

And now it wasn't the way it used to be. Whatever she'd felt before—oh, she'd always loved him, after a fashion—but this was different. And at the moment, painful.

Stop whimpering, she told herself. *One thing at a time.*

And the first thing was to get into her bed undetected. She could certainly come up with the cock-and-bull story necessary to explain her clothes lying in front of the drawing room fireplace.

Luckily, rash behavior like waiting in the rain for villains was well within the realm of typical Olivia behavior. No one would turn a hair. No one would wonder at her wearing men's clothes, either. All she had to do was describe what happened, leaving out the part from the time Lisle came into the drawing room until she'd left from his room.

Leave out a lifetime, in other words.

She crept into her room.

It wasn't dark.

A candle burned on a small table near the fire.

Bailey sat by the fire. She had mending in her lap but her gaze was on Olivia.

"I can explain," Olivia said.

"Oh, miss, you always can," said Bailey.

Mr. Nichols, in the act of artfully strewing about wet clothing in front of the drawing-room fireplace, froze as the small flame appeared. It drifted toward him. As it drew near, he saw Miss Bailey's face illuminated by the candlelight. A thick shawl swathed what must be her night wear, because he detected surprisingly frivolous ruffles peeping out from a dressing gown, in the environs of her ankles. Her slippers appeared to be adorned with colored ribbons. He couldn't quite discern the color in the dim light.

"Miss Bailey," he whispered.

"Mr. Nichols," she whispered.

"I hope no unearthly beings have caused you to be wakeful," he said.

"Certainly not," she said. "I've come about the

clothes. We can't leave them here. My miss and your master must have taken leave of their senses—I say that with all due regard for your master's intelligence, but gentlemen sometimes lose their wits, and my miss has a rare knack for helping them into that condition."

Nichols regarded the clothes he'd so carefully strewn about.

"Why put on a show when you and I are the only ones besides them aware of any unusual doings this evening?" said Miss Bailey. "Not to say that anything is unusual where my miss is concerned. I'm troubled, particularly, about items needing laundering."

She meant bloodstains.

Nichols couldn't tell if she was blushing or only seemed to be. The light from the fire was rather red.

"Ahem," he said softly. "That thought crossed my mind, but it seemed indelicate to mention it to his lordship."

"I'll deal with it," said Miss Bailey, with the air of one long used to concealing crimes.

Nichols gathered up the damp clothing. "If you will light the way, I will carry it as far as the door," he said.

She nodded.

She lit the way. He carried the clothing.

At the door, he carefully placed the clothing onto her free arm. He started to reach for the door handle, then paused. "Miss Bailey," he murmured in her ear.

"No," she said. "None of that."

He sighed gently and opened the door.

She slipped into her mistress's room.

He closed the door and sighed again.

An instant later, the door opened a very little and she said softly, "Wait."

Nichols turned back hopefully.

A shirt was thrust through the space.

"You can take this back," she said.

He took his lordship's shirt.

Chapter Sixteen

$\mathcal{M}$eanwhile, Roy and Jock shivered in the section of the burnt church that hadn't completely fallen in.

"Who the devil was it?" Jock said.

"What does it matter?" said Roy. "He was there, waiting for us."

"They was bound to set watch, sooner or later. You heard what they said: The laird's son was talking about getting dogs."

"Dogs can be poisoned," said Roy.

"Damn him, whoever he was," Jock said. "I about pissed my breeches."

The white face staring out from the watchtower had scared Roy, too. If he'd stopped to think, he'd've known it was human. But who stops to think at times like those? They'd dropped the shovel and the pickaxe and run.

Jock hadn't dropped the lantern, but he didn't stop to close the shutter, and the thing—no, it was no thing, but a man—had chased them halfway down the road before Roy grabbed the lantern from his fool brother.

Now they were trapped in the damned church. No fire and no way to make one.

Plenty of time to think, though. At night, in the rain, the old castle on the rise was a big, black hulk against a sky that wasn't much lighter. Roy stared up at it and thought.

He didn't know how long it was before Jock said, "Rain's letting up."

But it was time enough. "They're watching for us on the outside," Roy said, as they left the church. "So we'll get us someone to watch on the inside."

"No one'll do that."

No one liked them much. People passed the time of day, and then passed quickly enough on to someone else.

That suited Roy. He didn't like anyone else much, either.

"They won't do it willing, no," said Roy. "But I can think of one we can *make* willing."

Shortly after noon
Wednesday 26 October

"You understand what to do?" Olivia said.

Lady Cooper made a slight adjustment of her bonnet. "Of course."

"Nothing could be simpler," said Lady Withcote.

The three women stood near the entrance door of the great hall. They were waiting for the carriage that would take Ladies Cooper and Withcote to Edinburgh.

Their mission was to seek out Frederick Dalmay's nurse and servants and pump them for information.

"I hope you won't find it too tedious," Olivia said. "It might be a bit like finding a needle in a haystack."

"Oh, I think not," said Lady Cooper. "We know the names. We ought to be able to find them easily enough."

"And once we find them, I foresee no difficulty in getting them to talk," said Lady Withcote.

"When all else fails, bribery will usually do the trick," said Lady Cooper.

A footman came in from outside. "The carriage is here, your ladyships."

Lisle entered minutes after the ladies departed.

"They said they were going to Edinburgh," he said. "To look for clues."

Olivia hadn't seen him since last night. It had taken her a long while to fall asleep. She'd come down very late to breakfast as a result. The ladies were there but he wasn't. He was out with the workers, Herrick had told her.

She'd decided to behave as though nothing out of the ordinary had happened. It was easier than she'd expected. He was still Lisle, and what they'd done last night seemed by daylight to be the most natural thing in the world.

Because she loved him and had probably always loved him. The love had taken different forms over the years, but there it was.

And there he was . . . holding a shovel.

"Did you bring that indoors for some mysterious purpose, or did you forget to leave it in the courtyard?" she said.

He was frowning at her hand. He looked up. "What?"

"The shovel."

"Ah, yes. This." He gazed at it. "One of the workmen found it this morning when he arrived. One shovel. One pickaxe."

"Evidence," she said.

"I didn't need evidence," he said. "I believed you. But I hadn't pictured it properly. You must have terrified them." He grinned. "They dropped everything and ran."

"Everything except the lantern." If they'd dropped the lantern, she wouldn't have been able to follow . . . and what had happened afterward wouldn't have happened.

"Still, I didn't mean to carry it in," he said. "I saw the ladies leave, and I came in to ask you about it, and I forgot to leave the shovel outside."

He looked about him. Herrick appeared. "Yes, your lordship. Joseph will take that for you." A footman hurried forward and took the shovel and went out.

Herrick vanished.

"I'm not myself today," Lisle said in a low voice. "Can't think why."

The fire crackled in the grate. Servants padded to and fro, discreetly going about their business. A pale light traversed the deep window recesses, softening the gloom of the vast room, but not exactly illuminating the place. A candelabra stood on the table. By the clock it was broad day, but by Scottish weather, it was twilight.

The air between them thrummed.

"Strange dreams, perhaps," she said.

"Yes." His gaze drifted down to her hand again. "At any rate, I've come to help."

"Help what?" she said.

"I've come to help you look for clues," he said.

The way she'd looked at him when he came in.

But it was the same way she'd looked at him that night when he'd found her in the ballroom. Had he seen worlds in those blue eyes then?

He'd seen something, and it had stopped him in his tracks.

Last night she'd said . . . she'd said. . .

I adore you. I always have and always will.

What did it mean, what did it mean?

He said, "I was wrong to dismiss your clue out of hand. I was wrong about those provoking ghosts. If I'd stopped to think for a minute—but it's obvious now why I didn't. The fact is, I was wrong. The fact is, the men don't need me standing over them constantly. The fact is, we need to stop the ghosts. At present, your plan is a perfectly good one. The ghosts must have strong reasons for believing they'll find a treasure here that no one else believes in. Either they're completely insane or extremely stupid or something's misled them . . . or it exists."

She folded her hands at her waist. She wore very little jewelry. A simple bracelet. One ring, that one ring.

"Thank you," she said.

He dragged his gaze from the ring. He glanced about, but no servants stood nearby. "That's why I was awake when you came in during the night," he said softly. "The paper you found nagged at my mind. It wouldn't let me sleep. I got up to see what I could make of it.

I had some ideas, but I was working from memory. I should like to have another look at it."

"It's in the muniments room," she said.

As Lisle had been surprised to discover, the castle's simple exterior concealed a complex and inconsistent interior. The entresol Olivia had made their muniments room was tucked between the first-floor kitchen passage and an alcove off the second-floor drawing room. Its window overlooked the gap between the north and south wings.

The straightforward way to get there was by climbing the south tower staircase. The other route took one up to and across the minstrels' gallery through the door into the north tower. Then a left turn into a short passage, past the doorway to Herrick's quarters, then up a shallow set of stairs. The room was larger and brighter than the kitchen passage below, because the window recess wasn't as deep. Not that it was exactly bright on this grey day.

"Well?" she said.

He looked about. "The last time I saw it, the place was a jumble of boxes and books."

"This is Herrick's doing," she said. "He's had the workmen put up shelves and install a cupboard."

Now everything was in its place, neatly labeled.

He oughtn't to be surprised. He'd seen how she organized the staff. All the same, it was a puzzle. In so many ways, she was so chaotic.

But no, that wasn't quite right. She was calculating, too. Ruthlessly so at times.

Maybe she only seemed chaotic because she made her own rules.

"The furniture came from your cousin Frederick's study," she said.

There wasn't much. A small, plain writing table with a single drawer stood in the window recess. An old-fashioned wooden writing box lay on the table. One very utilitarian chair that probably weighed a ton.

"It looks like the sort of thing Dr. Johnson might have written his dictionary on," he said, "if he wrote on his grandfather's writing table."

"Frederick Dalmay was not a man of fashion," said Olivia. "Most of his belongings were so old and ugly, I left them in Edinburgh. Mains is waiting for you to tell him whether to sell them or give them away. But I thought we ought to have something of your cousin's here. He lived in this castle for so long, and seemed to love it. I thought those pieces fit here well enough."

"They look very well," he said.

"Better here than they did anywhere else, at any rate," she said. "Herrick's moved the more recent household ledgers to his office. Since your cousin's collection is all about the castle's history, it seemed right to consider the books and papers as estate papers or muniments, and keep them here with the other property documents and such."

She took a book from the shelf. "I put the mystery paper back into the book where I found it," she said, "in case there's a key to the code in the book itself. I can't see any connection, but you might. I thought that whoever put the paper there probably didn't do it at random."

She opened the book to the page where the odd paper lay, and gave him the book.

He took out the singed document and scanned the pages between which it had been placed.

"One of the ghost stories," she said. "The one about the dungeon prisoner. I thought there might be a connection."

"Might be."

She drew nearer and peered at the paper he held. He could smell her hair and her skin and the shadow of a fragrance that hung in the air about her.

"I remembered it better than I thought," he said. "The same clumsy grid, and those tiny symbols or figures scratched in some of the rectangles."

"I know it could be a puzzle," she said. "Or a game. But I can't give up the feeling that it's more."

"That's what kept me awake," he said. "The feeling that there was more than I was seeing."

"I'm not good at these things," she said. "Decoding wants logic, and I'm not logical."

"You don't have to be," he said. "I'm logical enough for two."

"It does look like a child's attempt to draw the castle," she said. "The flattened perspective. The curious proportions."

"That's the style of Egyptian art, essentially," he said. "Take the wall paintings. Size isn't in proportion. Size designates importance. The face is in profile, but one eye looks straight out from . . ." He trailed off, his attention shifting from the paper to the room about him. "The wall," he said. "We're looking at a wall."

She followed his gaze. "A wall? But that's so straightforward."

"Maps are usually straightforward, too." He squinted

at the tiny figures. "I should have brought my magnifying glass."

She opened the writing box and took out a magnifying glass. "I needed it to read Cousin Frederick's writing," she said.

The writing he'd refused to help her decipher.

Because he was an ass. He'd already worked that out. And he'd worked out the simple fact that he had a great deal to make up for, and he might have very little time in which to do it.

He moved nearer to the window and studied the paper through the magnifying glass. "They look like numbers," he said after a moment.

He gave her the glass and paper. "What do you think?"

"Numbers," she said. "But not all of them. I don't know what the other things are meant to be. Flowers? Sun? Stars? Some sort of symbol? Did you find any engravings in the walls when you were measuring?"

"The usual decorations," he said. "Ornamental work around doorways and such. Nothing on the stones of the wall, though. Nothing corresponding to these marks." He held up the paper and compared it to the walls about him. "Except for the little numbers and symbols, this drawing looks rather like this wall."

She stared at the paper. "It could be any wall," she said, "if it is a wall. But it does seem like one. Is that meant to be a window, do you think?"

"Hard to say. Do you have my plans?"

"I gave them to Herrick—but no, wait. He was done with them." She pulled open the drawer of the table and took out the plans. "We thought it best to keep them where we could find them easily."

She took them out. His gaze slid to the ring again.

He brought his attention to the plans. He stared at them until his mind fixed there, too. "If that number measures the bottom of the wall," he said, pointing to the drawing, "it's too wide for the room we're in. The long side of this room isn't quite nine feet. The number on the drawing is twelve. That could be approximate. How many rooms measure about twelve feet on one side? Most of the south tower rooms are about that. Herrick's rooms, too."

"What about the height?" she said. "If that number is the height of the wall, it narrows things down. It eliminates most of the main-floor rooms."

"Herrick's quarters don't match, either."

"There," she said. "Next to the broken stairway to the basement. The entresol over the well room. *That's it.*"

He turned his head to look at her.

Her cheeks were flushed. Her shimmering blue gaze met his. His gaze slid down to her mouth, a breath away.

"That's it," he said. "That's it. I can't do this."

"What?" she said softly. "Do what?"

"Pretend," he said. "I'm no good at pretending."

And he lifted her straight off the floor and kissed her.

It was hard and uncompromising, the determined way he did everything he determined to do. She kissed him back, with everything she had in her, and her legs simply wrapped themselves around his hips. His hands slid down to grasp her bottom.

He set her on the table and broke the kiss and drew her hands away from his neck, and she thought, *If you stop, I'll strangle you.*

He turned away and walked to the door to the stairway, and she thought, *You're a dead man*.

He latched the door.

Then he picked up the chair and carried it to the other door, and jammed it under the handle.

He came back to stand in front of her.

He said, "Here, let me get you out of those wet clothes."

She looked down at herself and said, "I'm not wet."

He said, his voice very low, "Then *make believe*."

She could feel his voice shivering down the back of her neck all the way down her spine. "Very well," she said.

He brought his hands up to her shoulders. He drew away her shawl and tossed it aside. Then he slid his hands to the back of her neck. He unfastened the first hook of her dress. Then the second. Then the third.

They were tiny hooks, yet he undid them, one by one; all the while his gaze never left her face, and she couldn't take hers from his, from the silver of his eyes.

He undid the larger hooks at her waist. She felt the back of the dress fall open. He slid the neckline down and untied the tapes to the sleeve puffs. He bent his head and unbuttoned the tiny pearl buttons at her wrist. Right hand. Left hand.

She stared like one mesmerized at the top of his head, the silken gold hair. Later, she'd drag her hands through it. Later, she'd run her hands all over him. For now, she'd let him have his way with her.

He drew the top of the dress down to her waist. He tugged. She lifted her hips and he pulled the dress down and let it drop to the floor.

He said nothing.

She didn't, either. Silence was perfect. No words between them. That was perfect. Only the sounds of their breathing and the sounds his hands made on her clothes and skin.

He was so intent. Methodical. He untied the tapes of her petticoat and tugged it down and let it slide to the floor. He kicked it aside. He bent over her shoulder and loosened the ties of her corset.

Her breath came and faster. So did his. She heard it. But no words. They didn't need words, not now.

He drew the corset away. Her chemise, released, slid down her shoulders, exposing one breast. She didn't try to cover herself. He didn't try to cover her. He left the chemise as it was, and started on her drawers.

Shivery feelings, racing over her skin.

He untied the tapes and pulled the drawers off her. They ended up on top of the other things. Her garters went next. Then her stockings. Then he pulled the chemise over her head.

Then she was naked, sitting on the table, every inch of her body quivering.

He had on all his clothes.

In the pit of her belly, sensations skipped and squeezed. She kept very, very still.

He looked at her, the silver gaze sliding over her skin like a caress. She felt it under her skin, skittering down to the place between her legs.

Then he leaned toward her. She thought he would kiss her, and she put her mouth up. But he kissed her cheek. Then he licked it lightly.

She shivered.

Not with cold. Her skin was on fire. Inside was hot and restless.

He licked her. Everywhere. A flick of his tongue. The touch of his lips. Her ear. Her throat. Her breasts. Her arms. Her hands. He knelt and trailed his mouth and tongue over her legs. He kissed her feet, toe by toe. Methodically. With complete and utter attention.

Low down in her belly was a maddening restlessness, an itch she couldn't scratch.

And good God, all the gods, Zeus and the rest and the angels and saints and martyrs and crocodiles and ibis-headed gods, too, he kissed up her leg again all the way to her quim.

Then she shrieked—or it seemed so to her, a scream echoing in the small room.

His hand came up to her belly and pushed, and down she went on the table, obediently, writhing and making mad little sounds, and words that made no sense and Oh my God oh my God oh my God.

Little volcanoes erupted inside her, and she shuddered, and then it happened, the fierce, fiery wave that carried her up and up, and threw her up into the sky, then threw her down, shattered.

"Oh my God oh my God oh my God."

His voice, then, low and thick. "You're shivering. I'll have to warm you from the *inside*."

"For God's sake, Lisle, hurry!"

She heard his short, choked laugh, and the rustling of clothing. Then he pushed into her. She jerked upward, eyes wide, catching hold of his arms.

He stilled, his eyes wide, too. "Hurts?"

"No, oh no. Opposite . . . of hurts. Oh, Lisle. My God."

It had hurt last night, and she'd felt a sting, even during the good part. But this time it was altogether different. He filled her and it was hot and—and wonderful. She reached for his shoulders, to get closer, to get more of him. She moved her hips. "Oh, *yes*," she said. "Like this."

She had not a stitch on and the only naked part of him was the throbbing shaft inside her, and it was wonderful. Wonderful to be naked. Wonderful to have him inside her.

"This is so wrong," she said.

"Yes," he said.

"It's *perfect*," she said.

"Oh, Olivia."

That was the end of conversation. He kissed her, an endless clinging kiss while their bodies rocked together, faster and fiercer. Then the wave came and carried her up again, and again, higher and higher. It flung her up against the sky, and she saw stars, and laughed, and on a laugh said, "How I love you."

Then the wave came and gently took her down again. And she kissed his cheek and his neck and his lips. And, "Love you, love you," she breathed.

She fainted.

Chapter Seventeen

*L*isle felt her slump in his arms.

Stunned, he looked down at her. She blinked and looked up at him, blue eyes wide and wondering.

His heart lurched with relief. "I hope you swooned with ecstasy," he said gruffly.

"Yes," she said dazedly. "My goodness."

She'd said *I love you*.

He took her hand, the one wearing the single ring.

"What is this? he said.

"That is a ring," she said.

"The stone," he said.

"That is a scarab," she said. "You sent it to me. You probably don't remember."

He remembered. The scarab he'd sent with a letter, ages and ages ago.

"I had it made into a ring," she said.

"When?"

"Right after I decided not to set it in a necklace or a bracelet," she said. "A ring, I thought, I might wear all the time."

He stared at the ring.

All the time.

For all this time.

Dozens of broken engagements and Episodes ending in exile. How many letters had she written that began *I am in DISGRACE again* or *They have sent me to Rusticate again until the <u>Furor</u> dies down*.

Olivia, careless and reckless and living by her own rules. But through it all, she was true, in her fashion, to him.

"Were you wearing it at your great-grandmother's party?" he said.

"Of course I was wearing it," she said. "I *always* wear it. It makes me feel you're always . . . at hand." She laughed.

"Awful," he said. "An awful pun at a time like this. There you are, stark naked—"

"Yes, it's amazing. I never sat naked in a window before. What a refreshing experience, in every way. You're so inventive."

Only she would sit there laughing, naked in the window of a cold room in a cold castle. That was a sight to carry back with him . . . to Egypt.

It was a sight, however, he'd rather not share with the world. Fortunately, the castle's windows were in recesses. This one, though shallow, was small. Otherwise they'd have given the workers down in the courtyard a fine show.

She probably wouldn't mind that, either.

"Yes, well, it seemed like the right thing to do at the time," he said. "The only thing, actually. That's the trouble, you see, once one starts these things." While he spoke he dug out her shawl from the heap on the floor and wrapped it about her. He tucked his shirt into his trousers and buttoned them.

He gathered up her clothes, resisting the temptation to bury his face in them. He pulled her chemise over her head. "Try not to develop a lung fever," he said.

"It would be worth it," she said. "Are you going to dress me?"

"I took it off," he said. "I can put it back on."

He went to work on her corset. "Would you turn around? It's much easier to deal with these things face on."

"Even Bailey can't get it off without turning me about," she said. "How amazing that you got all those hooks and tapes undone."

"I've been studying the construction of your clothing," he said. "Your clothes have changed so much since the last time I was here. Every time I come home, they're more complicated."

"And you need to solve them," she said, "the way you need to solve a puzzling line of hieroglyphs."

"It's not purely intellectual," he said.

He took up the stockings and garters.

"I can do that," she said.

"I took them off," he said. "I'm putting them back on." He'd never before paid close attention to women's clothes, and really, it was a lot to pay attention to, layers and layers with their complicated doing and undoing mechanisms. But hers had fascinated him. He'd been studying them without fully realizing it.

He drew a stocking up over her slim foot and the

delicate turn of her ankle and up the gentle swell of her calf and over her knee. Something pressed on his heart, squeezing, squeezing.

He tied the garter. He followed the same ritual with the other leg.

It was, perhaps, a kind of torture, but that was nothing to the pleasure of it, of undressing her and dressing her, as though she belonged to him.

"You worked out my clothes in detail," she said.

"I've a knack for details."

"And you still had sufficient thinking ability to unlock the secret of the Mystery Paper," she said.

He paused in the act of retrieving her drawers. He'd forgotten about the paper.

But it was only a bit of paper, an intellectual puzzle.

She, though—the way she looked and the way she smelled and the color of her eyes and the way the pink washed up her cheeks and the way the faint freckles seemed like golden dust sprinkled over her skin. If he had been an ancient Egyptian, it was her image he'd have painted on the walls of his tomb, so that he could look at her for all eternity.

She'd set the scarab in a ring and she wore it always.

He lifted her down from the table and helped her into the drawers. He tied the fastenings. He got her into the petticoat and the dress, and tied and hooked and buttoned everything he'd untied and unhooked and unbuttoned.

"There," he said. Done, all done, everything as it ought to be—except for her hair, coming down, catching on her earring, dangling against her neck.

She stepped close to him and put her hand on his

chest. Then she slid it down, and down farther still. "Lisle," she said, "That was *unbearably* exciting."

"I think," he said. But he couldn't. The palm of her hand rested over his cock, which was rising and swelling hopefully. The way she looked and smelled and the sound of her voice and her laughter.

He didn't wait to hear what his conscience had to say.

He pushed her against the wall and lifted her skirts and found the slit of her drawers. This time he didn't undo anything.

Later

Olivia pulled up the stocking that had worked itself loose during the frenzied lovemaking, and retied the garter. Out of the corner of her eye, she watched Lisle button his trousers.

"We need to get out of here," he said.

"We do," she said. "This is getting out of hand."

She might lack practical experience in Affairs of Passion, but she could calculate odds. The more often they did this, the greater the odds she'd conceive.

Although the odds were always the same, when you came down to it. And if he did get a child on her—

She looked at him, tall and strong and golden and not entirely civilized. If she became pregnant, she wouldn't be sorry. She'd find a way to deal with it. She was good at that, at finding ways.

He pulled the chair out from under the handle of the north-facing door.

She looked out of the window. "We're not going to

have much daylight for investigating the entresol. The sun's going down."

He paused in the act of unlatching the south tower door and followed her gaze. "How long have we been here?"

"A good while," she said. "There was all that unbuttoning and unhooking and untying, then all the buttoning and hooking and tying. Then the second time. That was more direct but I think we actually did it for longer—"

"Yes." He opened the door. "Time to go." He made a shooing gesture.

Yes, it's time to get out of here.

She was starting to question herself. Nagging questions:

What will you do when he goes again?

Is it so bad to be second—or third or fourth? Is it worse than being nothing at all, living continents apart, waiting for the letter telling you he's found someone there, and married her, and he's never coming back?

Would it be so terrible—would it be the end of the world if you agreed to do what all the world believes is the Right Thing?

It would be terrible for him, she told herself.

She hurried through the door and started down the stairs. After a moment, she heard his footsteps behind her.

"I wonder if tea is ready," he said. "I'm famished."

She was, too, she realized. She'd eaten nothing since her late breakfast. "We can have tea served in the entresol," she said. "I should hate to lose the daylight."

"We can't investigate the room now, while the men

are working," he said. "If they see us peering at stones and waving an ancient piece of paper, they'll wonder what we're looking for, and it won't take them long to put two and two together. Then it won't be merely a few numskulls looking for treasure."

She hadn't thought. How could she? "You're right," she said. "The whole village would hear about it—and the next one, and the next one."

"It'll be all over Edinburgh in no time," he said. "I'd rather not complicate matters."

"We'll have to wait and do it in the dead of night."

"Ye gods, what goes on in that brain of yours?" he said.

She turned and looked up at him.

"The dead of night?"

"When everyone's asleep," she said. "So as not to Arouse Suspicion."

"Right," he said. "Here's what we'll do, you dramatic nodcock. We'll stop and have tea. By the time we're done, the workmen will be gone, and we can go down and see how much progress they've made. We'll probably argue about it. That should give us a few hours. Do you understand?"

She turned and continued down the stairs. "Of course I understand. And I am not a nodcock."

Two hours after the workmen had left for the day, Olivia scowled at the walls of the basement entresol.

"Either we must go at it with pickaxes, or we must do this by daylight," she said. "Both ends measure twelve feet. Both ends are simply blank walls. I don't know how you work in windowless tombs. I can't make out whether the marks in the stones are meant to be symbols or they're simply random marks."

"Tomb walls tend to be carefully chiseled and painted," Lisle said. "With a torch or candles, one can see well enough." He ran his hand over a block of stone. "It does look as though someone has had a go at the mortar with a pickaxe, and it was covered up later. But that might have been a repair."

Olivia could see what he was talking about, though it was a very slight difference in the look of the mortar. "If someone was searching, it appears they hadn't any better idea than we do where to look."

"I don't propose to start tearing into walls at random," he said. "This room is in reasonably good repair." He looked at her. "You're going to have to contain your impatience. We need to think this through and make a plan."

Olivia looked around her. The room, according to Lisle, must have been a guard chamber once upon a time. It boasted a fireplace, a cupboard, and a garderobe tucked in at the corner of a closet in the south-facing wall. At present it was empty, but in recent days it had been cleaned and repaired. She was frustrated and impatient, but she wasn't eager to undo all the work the laborers had put into it.

"Sunday," he said. "The workmen won't be here, and most of the servants will take their half day. We can go over every inch of this place without being interrupted or setting off rumors. And we'll have daylight. Or something like it. Maybe."

"I should hope we'd know a bit more by then," she said. "The ladies will be back for dinner. I'm counting on them to shed at least a little light on the mystery. And there are always your cousin's papers to review. I've only made a start with those." She waved her hand at the provoking wall. "Sunday, then, you annoying enigma."

"If it doesn't rain," Lisle said.

That evening

" 'The walls have ears and eyes. But that's their look-out below,' " Lisle repeated. "That's it?"

The two ladies nodded.

They'd returned late from Edinburgh, where they'd dined with friends.

Over a light supper the ladies reported the results of their conversations with Frederick Dalmay's attendants.

The two sentences were what it amounted to.

"Sorry, my dears," said Lady Withcote. "Mere gibberish."

"And no secret," said Lady Cooper. "All the world knows what Frederick Dalmay said on his deathbed. Everyone thought it was one of his jokes."

"They apparently made less and less sense during his last months," said Lady Withcote.

All the world knew about his affair with a local widow that went on for years. The world knew of all his other affairs. Lisle's cousin had liked the ladies very much, and they liked him back.

Apparently, he liked collecting things as much as he liked jokes and women. Every time he found a book or a pamphlet or a letter dealing with Gorewood Castle, he was thrilled. He hadn't singled out—at least not in any obvious way—any documents specifically connected with the fabled treasure.

But, "The walls," Lisle said.

He looked at Olivia, who was pushing a bit of cake about her plate. She'd done that with most of her food: arranged and rearranged it and now and again remembered to eat it.

"Yes," she said, her mind clearly elsewhere. "The walls."

Night of Friday 28 October

The Rankin brothers watched Mary Millar and some others guide her drunken brother out of the tavern.

"Useful fellow, he is," said Roy.

"First time," said Jock.

Mary Millar had been hired as a housemaid at Gorewood Castle. Her brother Glaud was a cobbler. The Rankin brothers had told Mary that they were worried Glaud's fingers might accidentally get broken. They were worried this would happen if Mary didn't get friendlier and talk to them more—say, about everything that was going on at the castle. They worried, too, about what might happen to her if she told anybody.

Anyone who bought Glaud a drink was his friend. Overnight, the Rankin brothers became his very good friends. Every evening, when Mary came to collect him, he was sitting in a corner away from everyone else with his two good friends. She would sit down, too, and talk to them, quickly and very quietly.

Tonight she'd told them about the old ladies' visit to Edinburgh.

"They know what the old man said," Jock said. "But they ain't digging."

" 'Walls have eyes and ears but lookout below,' " Roy said. "What else's below the walls but the ground?"

Jock looked about him, but no one was nearby, listening. Even when the pub was crowded, people usually left a little space around them. He leaned over his tankard and said, "We found things in the ground. By the wall."

Roy thought for a long time.

Jock stared into his tankard. "They ain't digging, not proper," he said. "And we can't."

Roy went on thinking.

"I'll go right mad, I will," Jock said. "All this time—"

"Maybe it don't mean what it says," Roy said.

This was too deep for Jock. He shook his head, lifted his tankard and emptied it.

"Maybe *they* can work out what it means," Roy said. "Stands to reason. Old man was educated. Laird's son's educated. Maybe what he said was like Greek. Stands for something else. And the paper explains it. We can't get the paper. We can't do anything. Maybe we should let them do it, let them do the work."

"And find it?" Jock said. "Just like that? Give up?"

"Why not let them do all the work and find it?" Roy said. "Finding is one thing. *Keeping* is another."

"You took a fever, Roy?" said his brother. "You think we can get it away from them? A houseful of servants and that bastard Herrick in charge of 'em? Bars on the doors. Traps in the basement."

"We got Mary," Roy said. "She'll do what we tell her."

Sunday 30 October

"Curse you, curse you!" Olivia cried. "You cursed, stubborn stones! You're not the Sphinx, damn you! You've got something in there and we both know it." She struck at the entresol wall with her mallet.

"Don't—"

"Ow!" The mallet clanged to the floor.

"Don't hit it so hard," Lisle muttered. He set down his hammer and went to her. She was rubbing her arm. He pushed her hand away and massaged. "You're supposed to tap *gently*," he said.

"I'm not cut out for this," she said. "I don't know what I'm tapping for. I don't know what I'm listening for. Can't you simply do that thing that Belzoni does—did?"

He stopped rubbing her arm. "What Belzoni did?"

"You know. You explained it to me once. The way he'd look at a structure and discern something different about the sand or the rubble about it. That was how he found the entrance to the Second Pyramid. He said so in his book." She pointed at the wall. "Can't you just *look*?"

"I've looked," Lisle said. "But this is completely different. It isn't covered in sand and rubble. I'm not sure what I'm looking for."

He'd stopped rubbing her arm but he was still holding onto it, he realized. He let go, gently and carefully, and stepped back a pace.

Five days.

It was a long time. They'd kept busy, going through Frederick's papers and books. But not behind closed doors. They'd carried down the books and papers and worked in the great hall, he on one side of the table, she on the other.

They hadn't said it aloud. They didn't need to. Matters had got out of hand, and even she'd admitted it. Even she had seen they were on the brink, and even she, so incautious, had stepped back.

We'll ruin each other's lives . . . I won't settle for second place in a man's heart.

"Where's our clue?" he said.

"On the floor somewhere," she said. "I dropped it. I wish I'd never seen it."

"Remind me never to take you on an excavation," he said.

"As though you would," she said.

"I would," he said. "But you'd die of boredom. Or kill somebody. Patience isn't your strong suit."

She spun away in a whirl of skirts and flung herself onto one of the benches the workmen had left.

He found the ancient piece of paper she'd tossed aside. He focused on that. The marks didn't match the ones on the walls. The walls held initials and mason's marks—everyone leaving some mark behind, the way visitors had done on the Great Bed of Ware.

"You actually thought about it," she said. "About my being with you, on an excavation."

He had thought about it, more than he realized. When he first saw the Great Pyramids and the Sphinx, he'd thought of her, and what her expression would be like, the first time, and what she'd say. He'd enter a tomb and. . .

"I think, sometimes, of what it would be like, to be able to turn to you, and say, 'Look at this. Look at this, Olivia.' Yes. I think that sometimes."

"Oh," she said.

"It would be exciting, that first moment of discovery," he said. "You'd like it. But before and after are the hours and days and weeks and months of tedious, repetitive work."

"During which you'd forget I existed."

"You could bring me a cup of tea," he said. "That would remind me."

"You've got Nichols for that," she said.

"You could take off all your clothes," he said.

"And dance naked in the desert?"

"At night," he said. "Under the starry skies. You've never seen such stars, such nights."

"It sounds heavenly," she said softly. Then she bounced up from the bench. "But I know what you're doing. You're casting lures."

"Don't be absurd."

Was he? Perhaps.

"I know you, Lisle. I know you better than anybody else does. Your conscience has been chipping away, night after night, chipping, chipping. And you've laid a cunning plan for my downfall. 'I'll lure her,' you decide. And because you know me better than anybody else except Mama does, you know the way to do it."

Did he? Was it working?

She came to him. "I've more patience than you think, but I'm out of sorts. This star-crossed tragic passion business doesn't agree with me. Let me look at that accursed paper again."

Egypt. Dancing in the desert naked, under the stars.

He looked so angelic—the golden hair and silvery eyes—but he was an evil tempter.

She took the paper from him and made herself concentrate.

The drawing showed two walls measuring twelve feet wide. Inside the squares representing stones were tiny markings and numbers.

About a quarter of the way up the drawing of the wall, on the right hand side, was a symbol.

"That one," she said. "Not like the others, is it?"

"A mason's mark, I think. It looks like GL with an arrow through it."

"If it's an arrow, it's pointing left," he said.

"But where is it?"

They both walked to the east wall and looked for the mark.

Nothing.

They walked to the west wall and looked for the mark.

Nothing.

"It ought to be on one . . ." She trailed off. "Unless we're looking for the wrong thing."

Words shifted in her mind, images, too. What the ladies had said. What Lisle had said.

"Remember when I said that a drawing of the wall

was so obvious and you said maps are obvious?" she
said.

He looked down at the mark. He looked at the wall.

"An arrow *pointing to the spot*?" he said.

"If the wall's meant to be the west wall, perhaps it's
pointing to a window."

"But why GL?"

"It's your cousin's drawing," she said. "What if it's
one of his jokes?"

" 'The walls have eyes and ears' " she said. " 'Look-
out below.' "

And that was when she saw it in her mind's eye. The
city on its great rock. The city where Frederick Dalmay
had spent the last years of his life. "Edinburgh," she
said. "He would have thought it was funny."

"I don't—"

"Come," she said. She took his hand.

His hand, his hand. Such a simple thing, holding his
hand, yet what happened inside wasn't simple at all.

She led him into the easternmost window recess, into
the closet. She opened the door. "*Gardy loo*," she said.

"This is the privy," he said.

"The garderobe," she said. "A play on the words and
the meaning. In Edinburgh, when they'd empty the
slops out of the window, they'd call out '*gardyloo*,'—
garde à l'eau—mind the water. A warning, you see:
Look out below."

It was a small space, and dark. It was easy enough,
though, to find a board to set over the hole, and the
single candle Lisle brought in seemed very bright in the
narrow room. It showed them the initials and primitive

pictures and rude poetry scratched into the stones by various hands at various times.

Lisle did have to squeeze in amongst Olivia's skirts, and they stood elbow to elbow, while he slowly raised the candle and slowly brought it down, so that they could scrutinize each stone.

Though they'd propped the door open, to allow in as much light as possible from the closet window, the room wasn't meant to hold two people and not for any length of time. The air grew warmer and thicker, and her hair was under his nose, and the shadowy fragrance of her clothes and skin wrapped about him.

"We'd better find something soon," he said. "This is . . . this is . . ."

"I know," she said. "Is it like this in the tombs?"

"I've never been in a tomb with you," he said. His head was bowing toward hers, where wispy curls dangled at her temple.

"Mind the candle," she said, and in the same instant he felt the hot wax touch his hand, and he tipped it upright, and the light revealed a line of mortar around a stone. On each side someone had scratched a small cross.

"There," she said. "Is that—"

"Yes." He moved the candle. "*X* marks the spot."

"Good heavens." She clutched his arm. "I can't believe it. It's old, isn't it?"

"It's old," he said. "And the marks are in the mortar, not on the stones. Old marks, old mortar."

Everywhere else, the marks were in the stones.

His heart was racing. Maybe it was nothing. Maybe it was another of his cousin's jokes. The marks were old, but it was impossible to say how old. Ten years or twenty or two hundred.

"Oh, Lisle," she said. "We've found it." She turned to him. "I don't care what it is. But it's old and we searched and we found it."

He didn't care what it was, either.

He set down the candle in the far corner of the privy seat. He wrapped his hands about her waist and lifted her up to bring them eye to eye. "You mad girl," he said. "You mad, clever girl."

She flung her arms round his neck. "Thank you," she said. "Thank you. If we find nothing else, thank you for this."

He kissed her. He'd lifted her to do so. She kissed him back. Once, long and fierce, as though it was the last chance they'd ever get.

Then slowly, he set her down. He picked up the candle and made himself do what he always did. Examine. Assess. Decide. He studied the mortar. He considered the alternatives. He decided.

"We need chisels," he said.

It took forever. They'd brought pickaxes, but as Lisle had obviously realized, one couldn't swing a pickaxe effectively in these close quarters.

And so they picked away at the mortar, standing side by side, their bodies touching from time to time as they worked.

Bit by bit, the mortar came away from the edges of the stone until, finally, they'd freed the stone enough to move it.

"The mortar wasn't as solid as I expected," he said. "I

thought we'd be at this for hours." He jiggled the stone. "I don't think this is as heavy as it looks, either. Do you want to try moving it with me, or do you want to send for servants?"

"How can you ask?" she said. "After all the time we've spent with that vexatious piece of paper and those stubborn walls? After all that, I'm to let servants have the triumphant moment?"

"We don't know that it'll be triumphant," he said.

"I don't care if all we find is a pair of Cousin Frederick's shoes," she said. "We found *something.*"

"Very well," he said. "You put your hand there, and hold it up, and let me do the shifting."

She followed his directions, and slowly, by inches, the stone emerged from the wall.

It was less slowly than she'd expected, though. The back corner appeared so suddenly that she was unprepared, and would have dropped it, but Lisle quickly grabbed it. Then he heaved the stone out and set it down on the board over the privy hole. From the front it looked like the other stones, but it had been cut to a few inches in depth.

He held up the candle. She stood on tiptoe, peering in to the space the stone had concealed.

In it lay an ironbound chest.

Chapter Eighteen

At least it seemed to be an ironbound chest.

Olivia stood gaping at it.

She hadn't, really, expected to find a treasure chest.

She wasn't sure what she'd expected to find, but the very last thing was this.

"Good grief," she said. "Good grief."

"Looks like a chest," he said.

"Is that dirt?" she said. "Is it as filthy as I think? Or is it rotting?"

"It looks as though it was buried somewhere else first," Lisle said. "Maybe they put it in the ground, then changed their minds." He reached in and caught hold of the sides. He tugged. It didn't move. He tugged harder. It moved a fraction of an inch.

He was strong, she knew. He could lift her up effortlessly. She was taller than many women and hardly undernourished. But he could simply pick her up and put her down as if she were a teapot.

"It's heavier than I thought," he said. "I'll need Nichols for this."

He went out.

She remained, staring in disbelief at the chest. She was still trying to get her mind to believe what her eyes were telling it, when Lisle reappeared with Nichols and a set of tools.

She stood back while the men scraped dirt away.

This was what they did, she thought, in Egypt.

A handle appeared. With Nichols pulling on the handle and Lisle guiding the box, they eased it out of the hole and, with obvious effort, onto the floor.

"It's amazingly heavy," Lisle said. "But some of the weight might be centuries of dirt. We'll need to carry it into the next room to see properly what we're doing."

After Nichols cleaned off the other handle, the two men carried the chest through the adjoining closet and into the guardroom.

Nichols continued cleaning. A minute or two later he paused. When he recommenced, he did so more slowly and gingerly.

It was hard to stand still, looking on. Inwardly, Olivia danced with impatience. "This is the way you deal with ancient artifacts, I suppose," she said. "No wonder you said it wants patience. This is merely a chest. Even my imagination can't grasp what it must take to unearth a tomb or a temple."

"Sand is different," Lisle said. "And we do have a crew of men. Even so . . . Is there a difficulty, Nichols?"

"Not exactly, your lordship," said Nichols. "But I thought it best to exercise caution."

"It's not going to explode, is it?" Olivia said. "Cousin Frederick did have an odd sense of humor."

"No danger of that, miss," said Nichols. "It's simply

that certain features indicate sixteenth- or seventeenth-century German make."

She'd barely got used to the chest. This wanted a moment to sink in. "German," she said. "Sixteenth or seventeenth century."

"What?" Lisle to her. "Why do you look like that?

"Like what?"

"As though it *had* exploded."

She moved nearer to Nichols. "These chests are famous," she said.

"Complicated," said Nichols.

"Diabolically so," she said. "Great Uncle Hubert De-Lucey, who could open anything, said he spent days on one. And he had the *keys*."

"Indeed, miss," said Nichols, still diligently and delicately working. "One wouldn't want to damage the mechanisms inadvertently."

Her fingers itched to get at it. She made herself keep a distance. While Nichols carefully and patiently removed the thick crust of dirt, she walked around the chest, studying it.

It was about two feet long, a foot wide, and a foot deep. It was made of iron bands.

By the time Nichols finished, the sun was setting.

He swept the area.

She knelt in front of the chest. Lisle knelt beside her. "False keyholes, you see," she said. "And hidden keyholes. And the outer locks. One must begin there, of course."

"I assume that's the easy part," he said.

"I hope so," she said. "I've only ever seen one of them, and I've never had the chance to work on any.

One must unlock the locks in a certain order and turn screws and such. Even with keys it's challenging, and we don't have the keys."

Lisle looked up at his valet. "We're going to need candles," he said. "And a fire. I suspect we're going to be here for a while."

Four hours later, Olivia sat at the table with her chin on her hands, scowling at the chest.

Things weren't going well.

After she and Lisle had carefully cleaned off the rust and oiled the locks, she'd gone to work.

"It's been ages since I had a proper lock to open," she'd told him.

After the first hour passed, he had Nichols bring down a table and chair. He and Nichols lifted the chest onto the table.

After the second hour, Bailey brought in tea for them all and a heavier shawl for her mistress.

During the third hour, Lisle said, "We ought to go up and change for dinner."

"You go," Olivia said. "I'm not leaving this cursed thing until I've solved it."

Instead, he told the Harpies to proceed without them. He brought sandwiches and wine back to the guard-room.

Olivia tried every lock pick in her housebreaking kit, and that amounted to scores of picks. She tried hairpins, dress pins, toothpicks, sewing needles, and wire.

Now, after four hours of her getting nowhere, Lisle said, "Sometimes you have to leave it alone for a while, and come back."

She said, "I've never met a lock I couldn't unlock."

He said, "You've never met one of these. You said yourself that it wasn't simply a lock or a set of locks. It's a puzzle. How many years did it take Aunt Daphne to decipher the signs for 'Ramses'?"

"It isn't a lost language! It's locks, pieces of metal. It's the one thing I can do!" She tipped her head sideways and glared at a keyhole.

"What nonsense," he said. "You can do all sorts of things. The trouble is, you haven't the proper sort of mind for puzzles like this. It wants a plodding, methodical, obstinate sort of mind. Yours is all"—he made swirling motions with his hands—"excitable. Emotional."

Her head came up again, and the blue glare she shot at him could have blistered steel.

"Are you saying *you* can solve this?" she said.

"It might be time to let me try," he said.

"No," she said. "I can do this. And I can do it without any help from *amateurs*."

He started to go out. He got halfway to the door when he saw in his mind's eye her face, and he heard again the contemptuous tone with which she'd uttered "*amateurs*." He set his hand on the wall and looked down at the floor, but he couldn't control it. He laughed. And laughed. And laughed.

She bolted up. "You great, arrogant thickhead! It isn't funny." He caught her up and pulled her close and kissed her. She struggled, but only for a moment. Then she flung her arms around his neck and kissed him back, angry and wild. And after a moment, her body shook, and she broke away and laughed, too, that rich, velvety sound, echoing through the room and cascading over his skin and through his heart like a waterfall of joy.

"I can't do it," she said. Still laughing, she stamped her foot. "I want to tear my hair out."

He brought her close again, and stroked the top of her head, over the silky curls. "Maybe it isn't you," he said. "Maybe the locks have seized up."

"What then?" she said. "A sledgehammer?"

"That will relieve your feelings, but it could destroy the chest and, possibly, what's in it," he said. "What we need is a blacksmith."

That night

"You're late, Mary," Roy said, startling the house-maid as she came up the path to the cottage she shared with her brother.

"He's all right, isn't he?" she said. "You didn't—"

"Jock's looking after him, real careful. Don't want nothing to happen to his fingers, after all. How could he work then? What took you so long?"

"It's Sunday," she said. "Most everybody took the half day."

"But you didn't. Glaud told me. *You* should have told me, Mary."

"They pay extra if you work your half day," she said. "You know I need the money."

"And you ought to know, just because the tavern's closed, you can't sneak home without talking to me," he said. "I'd start talking, was I you."

She looked nervously about her.

"No one's about," he said impatiently.

"They . . . found something," she said. "Miss and his lordship. Everyone else was gone except their own servants and they didn't realize I was there. I . . . listened, like you wanted."

"I know you listened. What did you *hear*?"

"They found a chest."

Roy took a deep breath and let it out. "Is that so?"

Mary looked about again. She was wringing her hands.

"You better tell me," he said. "You'll feel better. Glaud will, for sure."

"They found an iron chest in the old guardroom in the south tower and Mr. Nichols was hours cleaning off the dirt and they can't get it open and they're taking it to the blacksmith tomorrow and that's all I know," she said in a rush. "Let me go in, please. Glaud needs his supper."

She tried to move past him, but he caught her arm. "The blacksmith," he said. "When?"

"Early," she said. "First thing. Before word gets about. Before the workmen get to the castle. So they can be at the blacksmith as soon as he opens his shop, and get it done and come home without causing a stir."

He let go of her arm. "Go on in," he said. "And tell Jock I said to come out."

She hurried inside. A moment later, Jock came out. Roy told him the news.

Monday 31 October

It was not a mile from the castle to the village, a short journey, even at a slow pace. Lisle led a horse towing a small cart of the kind used for miscellaneous country tasks. The obstinately closed chest, with an old rug from the stables thrown over it, sat in the cart. Olivia walked alongside the cart. It was a chilly, grey morning, and most of their workers hadn't set out. The few they met on the road, huddled against the cold, merely nodded as they passed.

On a brighter day, later in the day, they might have paused and stared. But Lisle and Olivia had dressed for warmth rather than elegance. She wore the heavy boat cloak that was supposed to keep her warm on the night she'd waited for the ghosts. Lisle wore his oldest overcoat, one Nichols had tried to give away more than once. It wasn't suitable for the Earl of Lisle, but it was the warmest coat he owned. His body still hadn't adjusted to the climate. He wasn't sure it ever would.

In any event, his attire didn't attract attention.

Not that there was much attention to attract at this dark hour. The sun had barely climbed above the horizon—theoretically, that was. The thick clouds concealed its doings, and one could barely make out which part of the sky was lighter than another.

"Are you all right?" he said.

"Oh, yes," she said. "Bailey's padded me with layers and layers. Flannel petticoat and drawers, and a thick quilted corset and wool dress."

"Thank you for the detailed picture," he said.

"The man who tries to get me out of this rig will have his work cut out for him," she said.

"Is that a dare?" he said.

"I hadn't thought of that," she said. "What an excellent idea."

"We haven't time," he said.

"We never have time," she said.

"We can't have time," he said.

"I'm tired of being good," she said. "It isn't *natural*. Not to mention this whole business is completely unfair. One discovers a Great Passion, and then one can't do it anymore."

"One is supposed to discover it on one's wedding night," he said.

"A woman is supposed to, you mean," she said. "Men might discover it whenever they like, and do it as much as they like. But we women—"

"We don't," he said. "Not whenever we like. If I could have discovered it whenever I liked, do you think I'd be in this predicament? But no, it had to be you—"

"You're so romantic," she said.

"It had to be *you*," he said. "And you have to be the one who wants the sun and the moon and the stars and The Love of a Lifetime in capital letters. I should make a perfectly good husband, for your information."

"To a mummy, perhaps."

They were both cross. Lack of sleep and balked lust made an unpleasant combination.

"I stand to inherit a marquessate and acres and acres of property and several houses and pots and pots of money," he said. "If, that is, my father and mother don't squander the lot and drive away all the tenants and lose all our income."

"You make it sound so tempting," she said.

"Good. Sarcasm. Exactly what one wants at seven o'clock in the morning."

"It's nearly eight."

"Who can tell? There's no sun in this blasted place."

"You have to stop wanting Scotland to be what it isn't," she said. "You need to accept what it is. In its own way, this is a beautiful place. But there's no sand and no smelly camels and smellier mummies—"

"And nothing here ruins properly," he said. "It can't simply subside gracefully into the sand. Look at that church." He waved his hand at the crumbling edifice to his left. "Moss and mildew and the stones turning black. A piece of wall here, and a few window arches there, and trees coming up between the paving stones. People are buried under that church, aren't they? Buried and forgotten. Even the graveyard—"

He saw them then, and stopped the horse. "*Run,*" he said.

As he said it, two masked men burst through the graveyard gate.

She didn't run but turned toward the graveyard as the men ran out of it and leapt into the road.

The horse reared in fright, and the chest slid backward. It crashed through the back of the cart and fell into the road. One of the men went after it. Lisle grabbed him and flung him at the cart. The man bounced back and lunged at Lisle. Lisle grabbed him again, hit him, and threw him aside. This time the man went down and stayed down.

Olivia shrieked. Lisle turned that way. The other ruffian was grappling with her. He held her at arm's length while she tried to tear off his mask with one hand and hit him with the other while kicking his shins.

With a roar, Lisle lunged for the brute.

Olivia screamed "Look out!"

Something hit the back of his head.

He was aware of pain but more aware of Olivia's face, the blue eyes round and wide, her mouth shaping an *O*.

Then a black sea closed over him.

"Nooooo! Nooooooo!" Olivia was screaming, madly fighting to get away from her attacker, to get to Lisle.

"Leave 'er be!" A voice shouted. "Here! Give a hand! The thing weighs a ton."

The man let go. Olivia ran to Lisle and knelt beside him. He was sprawled on the ground, too still. A red stain marred his neckcloth.

"Don't be dead," she cried. "Don't you dare be dead!"

She pressed her fingers to his neck, feeling for the pulse. There. Yes. She let out a whoosh of air. "Lisle?"

She looked about her. The men had disappeared with the horse and cart. The road turned sharply here and dipped. Trees stood on either side. It was a perfect spot for an ambush, invisible from the castle and the surrounding fields. Not that there was anybody about to see. But the workmen would be along in a minute, she hoped.

What time was it? They'd seen men on the road, but only once. She didn't remember seeing others coming. But she and Lisle had entered that sharp turn while they were arguing, and she hadn't paid attention to anything else.

"Help!" she shouted. "Somebody help!"

She returned to Lisle. "Wake up," she said, keeping her voice firm. "You must wake up."

Gently, gently she slid her hand behind his head, his poor head. It was sticky.

She'd seen the man get up behind him, the rock in his hand. She'd shouted, but the man was too fast, and Lisle, focused on her, was too slow to heed her.

Then everything slowed. One endless moment: the upraised hand with the rock . . . she, screaming the warning . . . Lisle folding up and dropping to the ground.

"You *must* wake up," she said. She knew something about blows to the head. The longer one was unconscious, the more dangerous the injury. "Wake up!" She patted his cheek. She patted harder.

He moved his head from side to side. His eyes opened. "What the devil?" he said.

"Oh, L-Lisle." She threw herself onto his chest.

His arms went around her. "Yes," he said. "Well."

"You must never, ever die!" she sobbed. "I can't live without you!"

"It's about bloody time you realized," he said.

Gorewood Castle great hall

"How did they know?" Lisle said. He sat in a chair near the fire. Nichols, having cleaned the wound, applied a sticking plaster while Olivia and the ladies looked on.

Olivia could have patched him up, but she knew better than to get between a man and his valet. She'd sat at Lisle's right, though, to watch, and to make sure the wound wasn't worse than the men claimed it was. It had looked dreadful at first, when the workmen finally arrived and loaded him onto a cart. Lisle had loudly protested being carried, but his workmen wouldn't hear of his walking. They'd acted insulted at his suggesting it. She'd followed, her heart in her mouth, all the way back to the castle.

Though he seemed his usual obstinate self, she kept seeing in her mind the few minutes when the man had struck him with the rock, and she thought he'd been killed.

Now the wound was cleaned, she could see why the men had made light of it.

Lisle had been wearing a hat, and his hair was thick. The rock had scraped the skin, and he had bled, but a little blood made a great mess.

Still, she was shaken.

"I know word travels quickly," he went on, "but this is ridiculous. We made our plans so late last night. Who knew, apart from Nichols, Bailey, and Herrick, that we'd be on that road at that hour?"

"The question isn't who knew but how our attackers came to know," Olivia said.

Herrick entered. "Your lordship, the men have returned from their search. I greatly regret to report that they've brought neither the villains nor the chest."

"I didn't think they'd catch them," Lisle said. "If it hadn't been for that man lying in the road—"

"Glaud Millar, your lordship. The village cobbler. Usually drunk at night but at his bench sober every morning."

Olivia looked up at the butler. "You think someone

helped him to be lying dead drunk in the road this morning?" she said.

"I find the coincidence suspicious, certainly, miss."

"I do, too," Lisle said. "It delayed our workmen, and gave our attackers time to get away. They'll be in Edinburgh by now."

"I'm not at all sure of that, your lordship," Herrick said.

"They took our chest *and* our cart *and* our horse," Lisle said. "Why wouldn't they go to Edinburgh?"

"Your lordship, we've sorry criminals hereabouts. Not the cleverest fellows. Yet even they, I believe, wouldn't risk taking to the road and heading where everyone expects them to go. Moreover, everyone would notice if a pair of neighbors abruptly disappeared. If I may, I would suggest we look closer to home."

Meanwhile, in a stand of trees a few yards from the ruined church, Jock gazed dolefully at the stolen horse.

"The chest's safe enough," Roy said. "All we got to do is wait until the to-do dies down."

"But we could've drove to Edinburgh," Jock said, "one of us on the horse and one on the cart with the chest."

"The same day the laird's son gets a rock in the head and his horse and cart and chest robbed? With men looking for that same cart and horse and chest on all the roads? And who in Edinburgh you think'll want goods stole today and all the world looking for them?"

"If Mary tells, they'll know it was us."

"There's another reason," said Roy. "If we go to Edinburgh, she'll feel safe, and free to talk. But when she sees us in the Crooked Crook tonight, sitting next to Glaud like usual, she'll hold her tongue."

"What if she talks between now and then? That bastard Herrick—"

"Blood's thicker than water," Roy said. "You know how she is about that brother of hers. She won't chance any hurt coming to him. Long as we're here, she'll hold her tongue. Then we let it all quiet down, and by and by we find ourselves a good horse and wagon and pack up our trunks—and there's the chest in one of them—and off we go to Edinburgh. Or maybe Glasgow." He considered. "I know some fellows there. They mayn't know what's happened here." He patted his brother on the shoulder. "There's the answer, Jock. Glasgow. That's where we'll go."

"Now?" Jock said hopefully.

Roy glanced over at the horse, quietly grazing.

"Too risky," he said. "But soon. Soon as we get us another horse and a wagon. Let this one wander home when she feels like it."

Chapter Nineteen

That night

$\mathscr{T}$he door to the Crooked Crook opened and three people came in.

Jock froze, tankard halfway to his mouth.

"Roy," Jock said in a low voice.

"I see," Roy said.

The laird's son, the redhead who'd kneed Jock in the bollocks, the skinny manservant Nichols, and that smug bastard Herrick.

"What they want here?" said Jock.

"What you think?"

"We better go."

"They come in, we run out? How will that look?"

"Dunno," said Jock.

"It'll look guilty, is what," Roy said. "Stay where you are and act like you always do."

"What if Mary told on us?" Jock said.

Roy glanced over at Mary's brother Glaud, who was slumped over his table, his head in his arms.

"What's she got to tell?" Roy said. "All we did was ask her what news from the castle. Same as anybody would ask."

The laird's son and the redhead went up to the bar and said something to Mullcraik. He filled two tankards.

Herrick didn't go with them. He stood in front of the door, his arms folded. Tam MacEvoy stood up and started for the door. Herrick held up his hand. Tam MacEvoy stayed where he was.

The laird's son turned away from the bar and held up his tankard. "And a round for everyone here, Mr. Mullcraik," he said.

That set off a buzz. Tam went back and sat down. Someone called, "Thank you, your lordship." Others joined in.

The laird and the redhead only smiled.

"There, you see?" Roy said. "They come to ask everybody what they know. Nobody knows nothing. We don't know nothing, either. And his lordship buys us a drink, same as everyone else."

After everyone had been served, someone proposed a toast to his lordship. When they'd got over that toadying, his lordship said, not loud, but clear enough so everyone heard it, "You know me, I believe, most of you. And you know I wouldn't be here, plying you with drink, if I didn't want something."

Several people laughed.

He went on, "This morning, as I'm sure you are all aware, Miss Carsington and I were attacked and robbed of a horse, a cart, an old woolen blanket with holes in it, and an even older iron chest. Late in the day, the horse returned, bringing the cart with her. The blanket has not come back. Neither has the chest. We're particularly interested in the chest, but news of the blanket would be helpful as well. We have come here, you see—" He turned and looked at the redhead. "We've come in search of *clues*."

An hour later

"It's them," Olivia said. "The pair in the corner."

"The Rankins," Herrick said without looking that way.

The brothers were among Herrick's short list of suspects.

"Very friendly with Glaud and Mary Millar suddenly," said Lisle.

"And Mary is one of our housemaids," Herrick said. "She stayed quite late last night." His brow creased. "I spoke to her earlier but she only said she went straight home. Most unfortunate, sir. A good girl. But Glaud is all she has, and he appears to be their hostage."

"The devil of it is, we've no evidence," Lisle said. "It's all hearsay and speculation. They're suspected of a great many things, but—" He shook his head. His father had so much to answer for. Petty criminals running amok in his village. Villagers whose efforts were constantly being undermined. The pastor to whom Lord Atherton had given the living resided in Edinburgh, and wouldn't inconvenience himself by traveling ten miles to tend to his flock.

"We've no proof and they know it," Olivia said. "All they have to do is hold their tongues."

Lisle looked at her. "I might be able to beat it out of them—"

"So crass," she said. "So inartistic."

He'd heard a great deal to depress him this night, but she made him laugh. "Very well, then," he said. "You first."

The brothers sat close together, their heads bent over their tankards while they talked in low voices. Glaud Millar slept on his folded arms on the side of the table nearest Jock. There was an empty chair opposite Jock but Lisle told them there was a draft there, and they must make way for the lady. The men were obliged to shift, making room for Lisle on one side, between Jock—wedged into a corner—and Roy, and Olivia on the other, between Jock and Glaud.

She turned to Glaud, "Glaud Millar?" she said. "Glaud, we should like to speak to you."

Glaud went on lightly snoring.

"No use, miss," said Jock. "He won't rouse for anything, 'cepting his sister."

"Ah, well, he's had a busy day," said Lisle. "Sleeping in the road at daybreak. Carried back home. Now here he is again."

"They were clever, those fellows, you must admit," Olivia said to him. "They had exceedingly short notice, yet they devised such a cunning plan."

"Cunning? They dragged a man who was dead drunk

into the road and left him there for people to stumble over."

"It was a brilliant delaying tactic," she said. "If they hadn't kept the workmen busy with Mr. Millar, they might have been caught in the middle of attacking us. No, it was cleverly done."

Jock preened.

Roy shot him a look and he subsided and scowled into his tankard.

"And the boldness of it," she said. "One must admire that."

"What's so bold about attacking a helpless woman?" Lisle said.

"Helpless?" Jock said. "Why, she—"

"Begging pardon, miss, but you don't strike a fellow as the helpless kind," Roy said. "Everyone heard about you and that cook of yours."

Olivia smiled. "Then the robber was a brave man to attack me."

"Well, he were, weren't he?" Jock said. "Risking maiming in his manly parts if you'll excuse the expression."

"Jock," his brother began, but Olivia gave Jock a dazzling smile and Lisle saw the look come over his face—the look so many men wore, blinded and deafened when she turned that beauty full force on one.

"And yet you bravely fought on," she said.

"I—"

"You!" a woman screamed. "You lying, thieving pigs! You get away from my brother!"

They looked up.

Mary Millar stood in the doorway, her bonnet hanging down her back, her hair wild, her face red. Herrick had his arm out, blocking her way.

"Let me through," she said. "You let me through, Mr. Herrick. I've had all I'll bear—from the lot of them."

Lisle nodded. Herrick put his arm down and Mary charged at them.

Jock started to get up, but Lisle pushed him down again.

"That's right, you stay," she said. "You stay and listen, the way you tell me to do. And I want everyone else to hear, too." She looked about her defiantly. "I want you all to hear."

"You say your piece, Mary," someone said.

"You, too, your lordship," she said. "I'm done with this."

"I'm listening, Mary," Lisle said.

She turned back to the Rankins. "It was bad enough, you giving Glaud drink he didn't need. It was bad enough you made me tell tales when I ought to hold my tongue. I knew it was wrong to tell you about that chest. I knew you'd try to steal it. I told myself you'd never get away with it, you're so stupid. I told myself you wouldn't do any real harm. But you poured drink down Glaud's throat, and threw him in the road, like he was a sack of old rags. You hurt his lordship, who's only tried to do good for us. You attacked a *woman*, you cowardly curs!" She tore off her bonnet and struck Roy with it. "You worthless rubbish!"

Then, to Lisle's—and everybody else's, by the looks of it—astonishment, she hit her unconscious brother. "And you, too, Glaud. I'm done looking after you.

Look after yourself. I've got no place now, thanks to you. It was a good place, too. Now I've got nothing, not even a character. I'm finished here, and I'm going. And you—you and your bully friends can go to the devil!"

She picked up a tankard and poured its contents over her brother's head. He shook his head and looked up blearily. "Mary?"

"You go to hell!" she said. "I'm done."

She stormed toward the door again.

Herrick looked questioningly at Lisle.

Lisle nodded.

Herrick opened the door and let her go.

The public house was absolutely silent.

Lisle looked at Olivia. She turned the blinding smile on each of the Rankins in turn.

"Well, that was exciting," she said cheerfully.

Lisle didn't smile at them. "Where is it?" he said.

Roy looked him straight in the eye. "Don't know what you're talking about," he said. "That gal's gone off her head."

Lisle stood up, grabbed Roy by the shoulders of his coat, lifted him straight off the ground, and threw him at the wall.

"Lisle," Olivia said. "I don't think—"

"We tried it your way," he said. "Now we do it *my* way."

Olivia got up quickly and got out of the way.

Jock tried to squeeze past her but Lisle knocked over the table. Glaud toppled out of his chair onto the floor.

Lisle dragged Jock up, and threw him across the room. Staggering backward, Jock knocked over a table and some chairs. Everyone in the public house was on their feet.

"I'm done playing with you two," Lisle said. "I'll give you to the count of three to tell me what you've done with my chest. Then I'm clapping you in chains, dragging you to the castle, and throwing you from the top—one off the south tower, one off the north."

"Ha, ha," Roy said, rubbing the back of his head. "You can't do that. This ain't the old days."

"One," said Lisle.

"He won't," Roy told his brother. "It's a bluff. He won't. It's against the law. It's murder. You heard him." He looked about the tavern. "You, Tam MacEvoy. You heard him threaten murder."

"I didn't hear anything," said Tam MacEvoy.

"Me, neither," said Craig Archbald.

"For shame," said someone. "Using Glaud's weakness and his sister against him. And that isn't half the story about them, your lordship."

"You want some help, your lordship?" someone else called out.

"No fair you having all the fun, sir," someone else said.

"Mullcraik, fetch that rope of yours," someone called.

"Two," Lisle said.

"Kill us and you won't find it!" Jock yelled. "Ever!"

"No, I won't," Lisle said. "But then, you won't get it, either. Three."

Roy looked at Jock. They suddenly swung at the men nearest, knocking them down, then turned and ran toward the back of the tavern. A tankard flew threw the air, striking the back of Roy's head. He went down.

A group of men surged toward him.

"Good arm," Lisle told Olivia.

He started toward the melee.

"No!" Jock screamed. "Stop 'em. They'll tear us to pieces. Stop 'em, your lordship."

"Tell him where it is, then!" one of the men shouted.

The crowd gave way and a pair of men dragged Jock forward. Another group was pulling Roy's unconscious form forward.

"Where is it?" Lisle said quietly.

Jock looked down at his brother.

One of the men holding Jock shook him impatiently. "Tell him, you bloody fool."

"In the church," Jock gasped.

It was late, but they had all the village with them, carrying torches and lanterns, joking and laughing.

They'd helped Lisle capture his villains and they'd helped him get the answer he wanted. Daylight would be more convenient, but they were willing, and they deserved the fun of retrieving the Purloined Chest, as Olivia put it.

"Maybe your method was best, after all," she said as they entered the ruined church.

"It was the two of us, working together," he said. "You softened up their brains—especially Jock's. Then I got to knock them about."

"Don't forget the bit about your ability to lead men in battle," she said.

"Whatever the combination was, it worked," he said. "If Jock hadn't given up the secret, we might have searched for months."

"Even knowing it was in here," she said, looking about her, "we should have the devil's own time finding it."

That was true enough. He was used to looking for subtle differences in a landscape, to tell him something was hidden there. But this was another realm. In daylight it might be easier, but at present he saw little to distinguish one heap of mossy stones from another.

Jock, his hands bound, was brought forward. "Here," he said. He kicked a large stone slab. "Under these stones."

The slabs he and Roy had laid over the hole looked as though they'd fallen there a long time ago. Even Lisle, using Belzoni's method, might have missed the scrape marks, the one sign that these slabs had been moved recently. But then, he was used to looking in desert places, under a brilliant sun.

With so many hands helping, the stones were easily moved. Then, using ropes, the men lifted the chest out of the hole.

Lisle let them leave it there for a few minutes, so that everyone could have a look.

It was a sight, with all its bands and locks and intricate keyholes.

"When everyone's looked their fill, you can load it into the cart," he told Tam MacEvoy. "We'll have to take it back to the castle for tonight. But I'll expect to see all of you at noon tomorrow morning at the blacksmith for the opening."

"Begging your lordship's pardon," said a big, burly man. "I'm John Larmour, the blacksmith, sir. You don't need to wait for me to open the shop tomorrow. I'll do it now, if you like. The fire's low, but we can blow it up quick enough if we need to. Looking at that chest, though, I don't think we need the fire."

A chorus of cheers greeted this offer.

You people, Lisle thought. *You remarkable people.*

He said, his voice a little choked. "Thank you, Larmour. That is most gracious." He cleared his throat. "MacEvoy, get the chest loaded onto the cart and take it to Larmour's shop. Herrick, send someone to the castle to invite Ladies Cooper and Withcote to join us."

"And the ladies' maids," Olivia said.

He looked down at her. "And the ladies' maids—and everybody. Bring our prisoners, too. I wouldn't have them miss this for the world."

They came out of their cottages as well, men, women, and children. A great crowd formed in front of the blacksmith's shop. As many as could squeezed inside. Others clustered at the great open doorway. Fathers hoisted their children onto their shoulders.

The flickering candlelight threw dancing shadows on the walls and ceiling and over the faces of the eager audience.

Ladies Cooper and Withcote sat at the front of the audience, on a pair of cushioned stools the footmen had brought for their comfort. The upper servants stood nearby.

Jock and Roy stood within the shop door, legs and hands securely chained, and guards on either side.

John Larmour studied the chest for a time, then he said something.

Herrick had to translate, because Larmour's burr was thick. Lisle had barely understood his speech at the church, and that was slow and simple. But Larmour was excited, and as he spoke more quickly, he became harder to understand.

"It's a fine piece of workmanship, he says," Herrick said. "He regrets having to do it a violence, but he will have to take a hacksaw to the outer locks."

Lisle nodded, and the blacksmith went to work.

It didn't take long. With the padlocks off, Olivia could once more tackle the locking mechanisms with her picks. It took her some time to work out the sequence, but she finally got one keyhole cover released. She moved that aside and after experimenting with some of the blacksmith's keys, and having him file one to her specifications, she unlocked that part. Then came the business of rotating some metal buttons, and simultaneously withdrawing hooks. Lisle had to help her. There was yet another mechanism, but by now she'd worked out the system, and that didn't take as long.

She was careful, Lisle noticed, to position herself to block the onlookers' view.

When she was done, she moved aside.

The audience cheered and applauded. There was a chorus of congratulations for Olivia, which seemed to be along the lines of "Well done, lass."

"You do the honors," she told Lisle.

He lifted the heavy lid.

Under it, an ornate metal screen concealed the intricate locking mechanisms. Atop the open chest lay a metal tray, elaborately decorated.

People promptly started wagering about what was

under the tray. Coins, some said. Jewels, said others. Books. Plate. Dirty laundry, said a few jokesters.

"Dirty pictures," said Lady Cooper. "I'll wager you five pounds, Millicent."

"Don't be ridiculous," said Lady Withcote. "Papers aren't that heavy. What they've got in there is sculptures. Some of those brass satyrs, most likely. Very popular in olden times."

"I always liked a satyr," said Lady Cooper.

"You mean Lord Squeevers, I suppose."

"Squinty Squeevers? Certainly not. He was Cyclops."

"But he had those hairy legs—"

"You should have seen his nether parts."

"Oh, I did."

"Do you remember the time—"

"Speaking of time," Olivia said. "All bets in? Good. Lord Lisle, please end the suspense."

He took out the metal tray.

No jewels or coins glittered up at them from inside the chest—not that Lisle had expected to find any.

Within lay a thick brocaded cloth.

"Oh, dear," Olivia said. "An old dressing gown, I fear."

"That doesn't make sense," Lisle said, reaching down. "Who'd go to so much bother to hide old clothes? This thing hasn't been opened in centuries. Those locks hadn't been oiled in—" His hand struck something solid. "Wait."

He removed the cloth carefully. More cloth lay beneath, but that seemed to be wrapped about the solid object.

He lifted out the parcel and set it down on the work-bench. "Whatever it is, it isn't lightweight," he said.

Murmuring came from the crowd, people in the back asking what it was and those in front saying they didn't know.

He drew away the wrapping to reveal a rectangular lead casket. This one, thankfully, had only a simple lock.

It took Olivia mere minutes to open it. After a bit of experimenting, she unlocked it with one of the curious keys in her collection.

A hush fell over the blacksmith's shop as she raised the lid.

"Oh, my goodness," she said. "Oh, my goodness."

Even Lisle caught his breath. "Is that what I think it is?"

"What is it, damn 'em?" Jock growled "How long before we find out what they've got?"

"They're doing it a-purpose to vex us," said Roy.

It was a thick vellum document, the ink faded to brown but the neat Chancery script perfectly legible. The paper was wider than it was long. From it an immense seal dangled.

"It's old papers," someone near Lisle said.

Jock groaned loudly. "Rubbish! All that work! Years! For rubbish!"

"It's no rubbish," said Roy. "There's fools like old Dalmay who pay a pretty penny for old papers."

"He's dead! Who'd buy them now? Jewels, you said. Gold and silver. All those years, digging."

"You did well enough by that."

"A few trumpery coins! An old tankard. A spoon. The one earring. What did they fetch?"

"These are letters patent," Lisle said.

The brothers demanded to know what those were. A few voices promised trouble if Roy and Jock didn't hold their tongues. The Rankins subsided, muttering.

Lisle took out the documents and perused the Latin. He was aware of Olivia at his elbow, reading, too, though with more difficulty, undoubtedly. She hadn't had Daphne Carsington drill Latin, Greek, and six other languages into her as Lisle had. Still, she must have got the gist of it, because she wiped tears from her eyes with the back of her hand.

He oughtn't to feel moved; he'd held objects far older than this. But none of them had been personal. His throat tightened.

"What is it, your lordship?" someone called.

Lisle quickly composed himself. "It isn't what most people mean by treasure, but it is a family treasure," he said. "This document, dated the twenty-first of June, fourteen hundred thirty-one, bears the signature of King James I of Scotland."

A chorus of *aah*s told him that his audience understood this was an important relic.

Amidst the murmurs Lisle heard the Rankin brothers arguing about whether it was or wasn't rubbish before someone stifled them.

He went on, "In this the king grants my ancestor, Sir William Dalmay, the right to build Gorewood Castle. 'A castle or fortalice,' it says, 'to surround the same with walls and ditches, and to defend it with gates of brass or iron; and also to place on the summit defensive ornaments.' "

"May we hear it all, your lordship?" said Tam MacEvoy.

Lisle read it through first in the Latin, because it sounded mightily stirring that way. Then he translated it. The English of four hundred years ago sounded quite as impressive.

When Lisle was done, MacEvoy said, "I reckon this means Gorewood Castle is well and truly yours, your lordship."

"Like it or not," someone called.

The crowd burst into laughter.

"And us, too, your lordship," Tam said. "We come with the place, and all our troubles as well."

The crowd agreed with a chorus of *aye*s, and more laughter.

Lisle looked about him. They were laughing, but they meant it. He remembered what he'd heard last night.

He felt Olivia's hand on his arm. He looked down.

"You're wearing that look," she said in an undertone.

"What look?"

"Your conscience-stricken look."

"These people," he said. "My father. What he's done."

"Yes, I know." She squeezed his arm. "We need to talk about that. But later."

She carefully replaced the document in its casket. She started to close the lid, then paused and put it up again.

"What?" he said.

"There's something in the corner," she said. "A coin,

I think. Or . . ." She smiled. Her slim fingers closed over the object and she lifted it out.

It was a ring, a lady's ring by the looks of it: a gold band set with red cabochon stones, rubies or garnets. Stones like the color of her hair.

She held it up so that the people in front could see it. They passed the word to those in back.

There were *ooh*s and *aah*s and scattered cheers.

Groans came from the Rankins' corner.

She looked up at him. "You see? This is a fine, happy moment—for everybody except the villains. Enjoy it."

Some hours later

Lisle stood in the window recess looking out into the night. A few stars were visible in the cloudy sky.

By the time everyone had finished exclaiming over the treasures and they'd got the chest packed into the cart again and returned to the castle in a procession—during which he heard more of the sorts of things he'd heard in the Crooked Crook—it was very late. Even the ladies were ready for bed.

He'd had Roy and Jock thrown into the dungeon, to be dealt with later.

One more thing to deal with.

He'd confronted hosts of such matters in Egypt—discontented villagers and workers, cheating and stealing and assaults and such. Excavations went awry. Boats sank. Rats invaded. Diseases struck. It was his life. It was interesting, even exhilarating at times.

Now . . .

A light knock at the door made him start.

He left the window recess and opened the door.

Olivia stood before him. She was all in white, in a dressing gown with fluttery things on it—ribbons and ruffles and lace. Her hair was down, tumbling about her shoulders in glorious disarray.

He pulled her inside and closed the door.

Then he changed his mind and opened the door and tried to push her out.

"Make up your mind," she said.

"You come to a man's bedchamber in the dead of night, dressed in your nightgown—and you expect him to have a mind to make up?"

How long had it been?

Days and days and eons.

"We need to talk," she said.

He pulled her back into the room and closed the door again. "Let me explain something to you," he said. "A girl who comes to a man's room wearing practically nothing is looking for trouble."

"Yes," she said.

"As long as that's settled," he said.

He threw off his dressing gown.

That left him in his nothing.

"Oh," she said.

The firelight made liquid rubies and garnets of her tousled hair. Her skin glowed like a midsummer moon. The faint, shadowy scent of her hung in the air.

He scooped her up in his arms and carried her to the high bed. Bracing her against him, he threw back the bedclothes with one hand. Then he set her down on the side of the bed.

"All right," she said. "We can talk later."

"Oh, yes. We've a good deal to talk about," he said. They had a lifetime to talk about.

She put her hand up and slid it over his chest. "You turned out well," she said.

"So did you," he said.

He pushed his knee between her legs, and she inched back, drawing her feet up onto the bed.

"I cannot begin to tell you how exciting this is," she said.

"You can write me a letter," he said. "Later."

He took a fistful of her nightgown and dressing gown in each hand and pulled them up. He looked at her legs.

"You like my legs," she said.

"To a disturbing degree," he said. He bent and kissed the front of her lower leg, the way he'd done at the White Swan in Alnick, paying homage.

"Oh," she said. "You wicked man. You cruel and heartless—"

"Fiendish," he murmured. "Don't forget *fiendish*."

He stroked the insides of her thighs, teasing, up and down. She threw her head back.

He pushed her nightclothes up higher. He trailed his fingers upward, then lightly over the soft place between her legs.

"Oh, your hands, your hands." She pressed her hand over his, pressing him harder against her core. "Oh, for heaven's sake. What am I to do?"

She rose to her knees. She tore at the ribbons of her dressing gown and flung it off. She pulled the nightgown up over her head and threw it aside.

The copper curls fell over her shoulders. A small triangle of copper glistened between her legs. That and her pearly skin was all she wore.

It was so easy to picture her dancing naked in the desert moonlight.

"Enough," she said. "Enough of this nonsense. I'll never be good. You can't ask me to be good."

"That was the last thing I was going to—"

"Come here," she said. She slid her hands down over her belly and down over the silky mound between her legs. "Come *here*."

He came up onto the bed, and knelt in front of her. She grasped his hands and brought them to her breasts.

He leaned in and kissed her, a long, sweet kiss. He kneaded her breasts and she wrapped her hands around his neck and let her head fall back, giving him room to touch her as he wanted and as she wanted.

She touched him, too, her hands roaming over his arms and his back and down to cup his bottom. She moved closer, and pushed herself against his groin. His cock throbbed eagerly against her belly.

She reached down and grasped it. She slid her hand up and down, then paused and drew it lightly over the crimson head. He made a strangled sound.

She looked up at him.

"Are you done playing?" he said thickly.

"Not by half." She gave him a light push. He took the hint and went down. She climbed on top of him.

"I know this can be done," she said. "I've seen pictures."

He laughed.

He grasped her hips and lifted her up. He eased her

onto him. "Oh," she said. She let out a long, shaky breath. "Oh, Lisle. Oh, my dear." She bent forward, and the movement squeezed his cock, and he gasped at the pleasure of it. She kissed him. It was deep and fierce, and dragged him down deep into hot darkness. He grasped her tightly and she moved, sliding herself up and down his length and setting the pace.

It was a fast and furious pace, as though it was the first time again, as though they'd spent forever waiting, saving it up, and this was their last and only chance.

He watched her, bent over him, her blue eyes as dark as midnight, her wild hair a fiery halo about her face.

"I do love you," he said.

He pulled her down, to kiss her, to hold her tightly as they rose and fell together, faster and harder until there was nowhere left to go. The rush of pure pleasure came, and carried them along. And then, suddenly, the world went quiet.

A long, long time passed.

Then she slid off him and onto the bed alongside him. He lay on his back, listening to her breathing slow while he stared up at the canopy.

She put her hand on his chest, still rising and falling. He wasn't entirely at rest yet, but he was sure of one thing, absolutely sure.

He covered her hand with his. "I do love you," he said.

Chapter Twenty

Olivia drank the words in and let them slip down, down to her heart, and she held them there, with her many secrets.

She drank in the quiet, too. The castle's thick walls blocked out the outside world and deadened sound from within. All she heard was the crackling of the fire and the sound of his voice, low and husky, and the quick beating of her heart.

She raised herself up on one elbow to look at him, without moving her other hand from his chest. It was warm there, against the steady beat of his heart and under his strong, clever hand.

"I was beginning to suspect something of the sort," she said.

"You ought to love me back," he said. "I don't see how you can't. We're meant for each other. Surely it must be obvious."

She drew in a long breath and let it out again.

"Stay here," she said.

She slid from the bed, grabbed her nightgown, and threw it over her head.

He bolted up to a sitting position. The firelight turned his skin to gold, and caressed the rippling muscles. His silvery eyes were wide, shocked. "Olivia!"

"I want you to see something," she said. "I'll be back in a moment."

He was up and in his dressing gown and pacing by the time she returned with the box.

"Sorry," she said. "Bailey, as always, was awake when she ought to be asleep. She's always on the watch, like Argus with his thousands of eyes. She had to stuff me into a dressing gown and scold me about catching my death. Come back to bed." She set the box down on the bed and climbed up. "Come," she repeated, patting the bedclothes. "I want to show you my treasures." She folded her legs to sit cross-legged.

"I thought you already had," he said. He climbed in beside her.

He kissed her temple. "You're not supposed to jump up from the bed two minutes after a man tells you he loves you," he said. "Don't you know *anything*?"

"I wanted you to *see*," she said.

She opened the box and started taking them out: the packets of letters he'd written to her, the little painted wooden man—the first gift he'd sent her, the bracelet with the blue stones, the piece of alabaster . . . on and on. Ten years of little treasures he'd sent her. And the handkerchief with his initials she'd stolen a few weeks ago.

She looked up at him, her eyes itching and her throat aching. "I do love you," she said. "You see?"

He nodded, slowly. "I see," he said. "Yes, I see."

* * *

She could have said the words but she could say any words and make one believe.

She knew that. She knew he knew that.

The box held her secrets, the things she truly meant.

She'd let him see into her heart, to the things she didn't say, the true things.

He swallowed. After a moment's vibrating silence, he said, "You must marry me."

She stared for a time at her collection of secrets. "I think I must," she said. "I've wanted to be self-sacrificing and brave but it doesn't agree with me."

He stared at her. She put the trinkets back, and the letters.

"Really?" he said.

"Yes," she said. "I thought I couldn't endure it but you've begun to grow on me. Like mold."

"Very funny."

But the relief was physical. He hadn't realized how heavy and disheartening a weight had pressed on him until now, when it lightened.

"We balance," she said. "We love each other. We're friends. And the lovemaking is quite good."

"Quite good?"

"Much better than Lady Cooper's first experience," she said. She repeated the ladies' descriptions of their first marriages.

He laughed. "I've outperformed Lady Cooper's first husband—and I've got the ring and everything," he said.

"The one from the chest," she said. "Oh, that settles it."

He pulled her into his arms and kissed her. "If we go wake up two witnesses, we can declare ourselves married and we will be—and then you can spend the night," he said. "Marriage is simpler in Scotland."

She drew back and stroked his cheek. "That's very tempting, but I think Mama would like to see me wed."

"Your mother, yes." He shook his head. "I forgot. Parents. Damn. *Parents,* plague take them."

"I have an idea," she said. "Let's take some blankets and sneak downstairs and steal some food from the pantry and have a picnic in front of the great fireplace and plot against your parents."

Half an hour later

They sat cross-legged in front of the fire Lisle had built up. They had half a loaf of bread and an excellent cheese Lisle was cutting and a decanter of wine from which they drank directly.

"My parents," he said. "My cursed parents. Here I am, having the happiest moment of my life—one of them, at any rate, and they slither into the scene like-like—"

"Ghosts," she said.

He set a piece of cheese on a piece of bread and gave it to her. "My father," he said grimly. "What he's done to the people here. He changes his mind a hundred times. He makes capricious rules. He raises the rents when he decides he's not getting enough out of them. Every time he takes notice of Gorewood, he causes disruption. The Rankins and a few others like them vandalize and steal and bully, but no one can prove anything, and they've nobody in charge of keeping order. Lord Glaxton won't interfere. He tried to, a few times, but my father threatened lawsuits—and it simply isn't worth the aggravation. The villagers are too demoralized and too busy trying to survive to fight back. And all I can think is, I can restore the castle and provide work, but I can't stop my father, and as soon as I'm gone, everything will go to hell again. But I can't stay here."

There it was, the conscience-stricken look.

"You can't," she said. "You've given ten years of your life to Egypt. You knew when you were a boy what you wanted and you've pursued it, diligently. It's your calling. Asking you to give it up is like asking a poet to stop writing or an artist to stop painting—or Step-Papa to give up politics. You can't give it up."

"And yet I feel I must," he said.

"Oh, you would," she said. She reached up and stroked his cheek. "You would, you—you *good* man, you."

She let her hand slide down and she patted him on the chest. "Luckily, for you, your bride-to-be is unethical." She took her hand away, took up the decanter, and drank.

"I do love you," he said.

"I love you madly," she said. "I shall make you happy if I have to kill somebody to do it. But that ought not to be necessary." She looked into the fire for a time, trying out one thought, then another. Then she saw it, so simple, really. "Oh, Lisle, I have an Idea."

Gorewood Castle great hall
Ten days later

"This is not to be borne!" Father shouted. "You indulge her in everything, Rathbourne, and you know this is caprice. Here is my son, willing—nay, eager to wed—"

"He's heartbroken," Mother cried. "Only look at the poor boy."

Lisle looked the way he always did when his parents were in one of their frenzies. But they'd always put their own interpretations on whatever he said and did. Why stop now?

He'd written to his parents the letter Olivia had dictated, minus her capital letters and underlining, and subduing the drama. She'd written to her parents. Mother and Father had arrived a short time ago, only a little behind Lord and Lady Rathbourne. All four of them were equally eager, for different reasons, to see the marriage go forward.

Then Olivia told them she'd changed her mind.

The so-called chaperons were at Glaxton Castle. One couldn't count on them not to give the game away. They meant well, but they could be unpredictable when in their cups.

Even Lisle, perfectly sober, was hoping he wouldn't say the wrong thing. Acting wasn't his forte.

"It's all right, Mother," he said. "I'm disappointed, yes, but I shall have to bear it."

"I can't make Olivia wed," Lord Rathbourne said.

"But she said she loves him!" Mother cried. "He loves her. He said they would be married. He wrote it in a letter. I told *everybody*!"

"Olivia changed her mind," said Lady Rathbourne. "Olivia always changes her mind."

"But why?" Mother cried. "Why, Olivia?"

"If you must know—and truly, I didn't wish to say—I shouldn't wish to hurt your feelings for the world," Olivia said. "But the fact is, I didn't realize he was penniless. It's simply out of the question."

Lord and Lady Rathbourne looked at each other.

Mother and Father didn't notice. They noticed nothing but themselves. At the moment, all they understood was that one of the richest girls in England was jilting their son.

"But he'll inherit!" Father said. "He's my eldest son and heir. He'll have everything."

"But that will not be for a very long time, God willing," Olivia said. "Of course I should wish you a long and healthy, happy life."

"You said you cared for him, Olivia," Mother said reproachfully. "Before you came here, you did give us to understand that you would welcome his suit."

As much as his parents infuriated him, it was growing more and more difficult to keep a straight face. Lisle could practically see the line Olivia had thrown, and the way she drew it in, little by little.

"That was before I fully realized his unfortunate situation," she said. "If I married him I should be a laughingstock and he would sink in public esteem. People would say I was so desperate for a husband that I married a fortune hunter."

"A fortune hunter!" Mother screamed.

"That isn't what *I* say," Olivia said. "I know Lisle

cares nothing about such things. I know he would take me in my shift." Her blue gaze slid his way briefly. "But you know how utterly vile people can be. I could not bear it, for my own sake or for Lisle's, to have his good name sullied by ill-thinking persons. It grieves me—I thought we should suit so well—but I fear it is never to be."

She turned to Lisle, her blue eyes shimmering with unshed tears. She could shed or unshed them at will, he knew. "Lisle, I fear our love is Doomed."

"It's most unfortunate," he said. "I had the ring and everything, too."

"This is absurd!" Father said. "Of course he isn't penniless."

"He has nothing of his own," Olivia said. "Nothing belonging to him, and only him. He has no reliable source of income. He has merely an allowance—"

"A generous one, too," said Father, "which I was meaning to increase, on account of the fine work he's done here."

"An allowance you may give or withhold at your pleasure," she said. "It isn't *his*."

It must have sunk in, finally, because Father stopped striding about the room and looked thoughtful. "Is that the only hindrance?" he said. "Money?"

"Money," Olivia said. "But no, not merely money. A lump sum lacks . . . substance. What we want is property. No one could call him a fortune hunter if he were a man of property." She looked about her, at the walls of the vast hall, now boasting hangings and paintings. "This property, for instance. Yes," she said thoughtfully. "Now I think of it, this would do very well. Make Gorewood over to him entirely, and I shall marry him as soon as you please."

That night

There would be a great wedding and a wedding breakfast in a month's time. Meanwhile, however, Lord and Lady Atherton were determined not to let Olivia escape matrimony. A servant was dispatched to Edinburgh to bring back a lawyer, who drew up the papers, making over Gorewood and all its appurtenances and its income and so on and so forth to the Earl of Lisle.

This was accomplished by sundown.

Shortly afterward, Olivia and Lisle declared themselves married before their parents, the Ladies Cooper and Withcote, Lord Glaxton and a couple of his relatives, and a houseful of servants.

Aillier prepared a splendid dinner, including delectable pastries baked in his villainous oven.

They were all in the great hall, celebrating.

When Lisle and Olivia slipped out, everyone smiled.

The sooner the marriage was consummated, the better, in the parents' view.

He took Olivia up to the roof.

He took care to bar the doors.

He'd brought up rugs and furs, because it was November, a Scottish November, and it was deuced cold. Tonight, though, Scotland's capricious gods of weather had smiled on them and swept away the clouds.

Olivia leaned back against his arm and gazed up at the night sky. "It's carpeted with stars," she said. "I've never seen so many."

"It is beautiful in its way," he said. "It deserves better than the treatment my father's given it." He pulled her closer and kissed her. "That was brilliant. You were brilliant."

"Unscrupulous and unprincipled, lying and cheating," she said. "Yes, I was at my best."

"It was a brilliant idea."

"It was the obvious idea. Who better than you to be laird of Gorewood?"

"And who better than you to do the one thing no one else can do: Make my father relinquish something he doesn't want, doesn't know what to do with, but won't let go of."

"You wait," she said. "By degrees, we'll steal your brothers, too."

"When they're a bit older, I should like to get them into school," he said. "It never suited my temperament, but they're not like me. I think they'll be happy there."

"Shall you be happy here?" she said.

"Of course," he said. "From time to time. But you know I'll never adapt."

"I wouldn't want you to. You don't need to. We've got Herrick."

He laughed. "And my first act as laird of Gorewood will be to promote him to house steward. Ah, Olivia, the power is delicious. It's almost like being in Egypt. How amazing to be free to act, to do what I believe is right. I should have been eaten alive with guilt had I abandoned these people to my father. Now I don't need to tell him about Jock and Roy. If he finds out, there's nothing he can do. Nothing he can do about Mary Millar. He can't dismiss anybody or hire anybody. This is one place where he can't make chaos."

He'd told the Rankins they could spend the next five years helping to rebuild and modernize the shops, roads, and cottages or they could take their chances at trial. They'd chosen to work.

"Five years' honest work might reform the Rankins," he said. "If not—well, we'll cross that bridge when we come to it. And I saw no reason to dismiss Mary."

"She was in an impossible situation," Olivia said. "But in the end, she acted well."

"That's the most we can ask of people," he said. "That they act well."

She turned her head to look up at him, the fur sliding from her shoulders. He drew it up. Later he'd undress her, slowly. Or maybe very quickly. But the night was too cold for rooftop indecencies.

"You've acted well," she said. "In trying circumstances, in a place you never wanted to be."

"I've learned some things." He drew her closer. "I've gained a great deal. How aggravating. I must be grateful to my father, for starting this."

"And to me," she said, "for finishing it so beautifully."

"Are we finished?" he said.

"Not quite," she said. "By the time we have our grand wedding celebration though, we ought to have everything in hand. Then we may set out on our bridal trip."

"Oh, I forgot about that. Well, a man must make sacrifices. You want to go somewhere romantic, I suppose. Paris. Venice."

"No," she said. "Don't be silly. Everyone goes to those places." She turned to him. "I want the Sphinx and the Pyramids and tombs and smelly mummies." Her lips brushed his ear. "Take me to Egypt, dear friend."

If you love Loretta Chase
and are looking for more
heart-stopping historical romance,
pick up the latest from
USA Today bestselling author
Adele Ashworth.

Turn the page for a peek at Ashworth's

The Duke's Captive

AVAILABLE NOW
FROM AVON BOOKS

Ian Wentworth, the Duke of Chatwin, arrives in London with just one thing on his mind: revenge. All those he believes responsible for his horrific past have paid with their lives. All but Viola Barrington-Jones, the lovely Lady Cheshire. Viola has worked hard to keep her secrets from the prying eyes of the ton, and when she sees Ian at a glittering ball, her rush of recognition turns to panic. Will the duke remember the tenderness they once shared, or does he blame her for her family's sins? But just as Ian finally has the beauty at his mercy, he realizes revenge may no longer be what he desires most.

$\mathscr{V}$iola flipped around, dazed for a second or two as Lucas Wolffe, tall and domineering, stood directly in front of her, acknowledging her in a deep, cool voice.

"Your grace," Isabella said at once, breaking the spell first with a proper curtsey.

Viola automatically followed with the same, lowering her body gracefully as she tipped her head down in respect, her heartbeat quickening as it always did when she found herself in the company of someone so important. And then past and present collided in swift, brutal force when, as she pulled herself upright and raised her lashes, Fairbourne moved to his left to offer full view of the man standing behind him.

Oh, my God. . .

She blinked, instantly spellbound by a new and vivid unreality.

"Ladies, may I present to you Ian Wentworth, Earl of Stamford, Duke of Chatwin."

The room began to spin. Her throat tightened. She couldn't breathe.

Ian Wentworth, Earl of Stamford. . .

He's found me.

Isabella curtsied again, mumbled something. He nodded brusquely in response, then slowly turned his attention to her.

Those eyes . . . Ian's eyes. Pleading. . .

Run!

She couldn't move. Their gazes locked, and for an endless moment time stopped, if only between them. History suddenly became now, their shared memories, both distasteful and passionate, fearful and vibrant, passing intimately between them in a heartbeat.

Viola stumbled back a step; her champagne glass fell from her fingertips to shatter on the marble floor at her feet. And still, she couldn't take her gaze from his face. That beautiful, expressive face, so changed. Perfected in time.

"Viola?"

Footmen scattered around her to quickly sweep up the glass and pale liquid that pooled at the hem of her gown; others in their vicinity backed up to make room. The bluster of sudden activity jarred her and she blinked quickly, glancing down, bewildered.

"I—I'm sorry." Her voice sounded clipped, hollow.

Isabella wrapped an arm around her shoulders. "Are you all right? You look ready to faint."

"No, I'm—I'm fine. Really." She tried to lick her lips though her tongue felt thick and dry. "I'm just—hot."

Concerned, Isabella opened her fan. "Take this. And sit. Catch your breath."

Fairbourne chuckled, interrupting her disorientation as he reached out and grasped her elbow, helping her into a chair a footman placed beside the sidebar. She looked at him, attempting to draw a full inhale as she fanned herself without thought. "Thank you. I—I apologize, your grace."

"Not at all, I'm very flattered," he returned in a good natured drawl. "It's not often I have such an affect on a lady."

She tried to smile—then shot a glace at the very real cause of her turmoil.

He stared down at her, his sharp gaze focused intently on her face, his expression unreadable. Then his lips curved up at one corner. "Nor do I. You swooned even before we'd been properly introduced. I usually have to speak before that happens."

Isabella laughed lightly at his charm and cleverness. She, however, had no idea what to say to him. But his voice . . . Oh, how she remembered his voice! It mesmerized her then as it did now—husky soft, low and rich, begging—

"Forgive me," Fairbourne said after an awkward

pause, his tone slightly amused. "Lady Viola Cheshire, his grace, the Duke of Chatwin."

The man took a step forward to tower over her, blocking the brilliantly illuminated chandelier with his powerful form. Then with a gentle nod, he reached out with his hand, palm up.

Viola stared at it for several long seconds, unsure what to do. But her head had begun to clear. The music played around them, the champagne flowed, and the party carried on as the first great event of the season. They were only two among many. She also realized something else: he'd inherited a new title, and a grand one at that. As a gentleman of such distinguished rank, he certainly wouldn't expose her, or their past, in front of his peers. Not tonight. Not here, like this. She had no idea why he acted as if he didn't remember her, and he no doubt enjoyed her discomfiture, but for now her reputation was safe, and that was all that mattered. She had time.

Feeling relief wash over her, more confident for the moment, she inhaled another deep breath. Then staring at his long, hard fingers, she lifted her gloved hand and placed it gingerly atop his.

He closed his thumb over her knuckles, then second by second, gently helped her rise. Standing before him once more, she curtsied with elegance, playing the part she'd learned.

"Your grace."

"Lady Cheshire."

Her name seemed to roll off his tongue as if the sound of it fascinated him. Or perhaps it was only her imagination. But the strength she felt from him as he touched her now, hand to gloved hand, permeated her skin to shock her thoroughly, inside and out.

Strong. Vibrant. *Alive.* Because of her.

He released her and took a step back, standing tall, arms behind him. "Feeling better, I hope."

She shook herself and rubbed her palm down the bodice of her gown. "Indeed. Thank you."

He nodded once.

Another strained moment skipped by. Then Isabella said, "So . . . Mother informed us you're an art collector?"

"I am," he replied without elaboration.

Viola swallowed. "And a friend of Lord Fairbourne. How delightful for him—for you. As it were." It was likely the most ridiculous thing she'd ever said, and she felt like cowering inside the moment it was out of her mouth.

Isabella glanced from one to the other, then thankfully saved her more embarrassment. "Uh, Lord Chatwin, Lady Cheshire is an exceptional artist. Perhaps you've seen her work?"

Viola felt Ian's stare on her again and she forced a flat smile even as she felt renewed heat creep up her neck.

"I've no idea," he replied evenly. "Are you perchance famous, madam?"

The tenor of his voice teased her to the core, just as it did all those years ago. But there also appeared a telling confidence about him. She raised her lashes to capture his gaze once again, immediately sensing an undefined boldness in their dark depths, something calculating that sent a ripple of warning through her body.

Fairbourne, who'd been silently watching for the last

minute or two, crossed his arms over his tailored evening coat. "No need to be humble, Lady Cheshire, you may admit it. I've already told Chatwin you've painted most of the nobility's formal portraits in recent years and are celebrated as one of the finest artists in London. It's why he's here."

"Why he's here?" Isabella repeated.

Viola reached up to wipe a stray curl from her forehead, not because it bothered her, but because she felt more uncomfortable at that moment than she had in the last five years and desperately needed something to do.

"I apologize if I've been vague," Ian murmured, his smile pleasant as he continued to scrutinize her. "But I've just returned to London, and expect to remain only for the season. Since your good reputation precedes you, I wanted to meet you straight away, Lady Cheshire, in the hope that we can discuss a commission of your work while I'm here?"

Again, she felt dumbstruck, numb. She had no intention of working for him, being alone with him. Not ever. And yet when he asked like this, standing before her in a crowded ballroom, dressed formally and presenting himself as a man of great wealth and power, she simply could not deny him his request for one innocent meeting. Not if she were to maintain her status as a lady of quality and her reputation as a professional artist.

There was something about this entire encounter that just seemed bizarre. No mention of their past, no recognition from him at all, really. And yet she felt a tension between them that threatened her composure, forcing her to play his hand for the moment.

Overcoming her reluctance, she nodded once, clutching Isabella's fan to her waist in a measure of defense. "I'll have to review my schedule."

"Of course," he replied at once as if expecting such a standard response.

The orchestra struck up a waltz. Isabella cleared her throat and Fairbourne took the cue.

"Would you honor me with a dance, my lady?"

She smiled beautifully as she placed her silk-covered palm on his arm. "I'd be delighted, your grace."

Suddenly, watching her friend wander into the noisy group of mostly inebriated nobility, Viola felt more isolated in the crowded ballroom than she would in a dinghy in the middle of the sea. With growing trepidation, she lifted her gaze one more time, meeting his.

Don't ask me to dance. Please don't ask me to dance—

"Lady Viola Cheshire," he drawled in whisper.

She felt an instant thundering in her breast as he used her given name. "Yes, your grace?"

His lids narrowed, and very, very slowly, he studied the length of her, from the hem of her full, ruby red gown, through her tightly corseted bodice, pausing briefly at her low, rounded neckline and the golden locket resting in the crease of her bosom before moving up her throat to her flushing face. When at last he looked back into her eyes, her breath caught in a whirlwind of panic. For the slightest second she felt hunger within him. Not lust as she knew it, but something else. Something she couldn't possibly define.

His lips twitched. "I don't feel much like dancing at the moment."

A palpable relief swept over her even as she felt the slightest twinge of disappointment.

His voice dropped to a husky whisper. "Would you care to walk with me on the promenade instead?"

She swallowed, simply unable to look away from him, or answer.

He smiled again as if sensing her hesitation, a beautiful smile that softened the hard planes of his face. Then lifted his arm for her.

She took it because she didn't dare deny him, and in the course of ten seconds, they were heading out of the ballroom.

THE DUKE'S CAPTIVE
By Adele Ashworth
Available Now

ENTER THE SCINTILLATING WORLD OF
USA TODAY BESTSELLING AUTHOR

LORETTA CHASE

NOT QUITE A LADY
978-0-06-123123-0

Lady Charlotte Hayward is not about to let a rake like Darius Carsington entice her to do everything she shouldn't. But the rules of attraction can easily overpower the rules of manners and morals.

LORD OF SCOUNDRELS
978-0-380-77616-0

Sebastian Ballister, the notorious Marquess of Dain, wants nothing to do with respectable women. He's determined to continue doing what he does best—sin and sin again—until the day a shop door opens and Jessica Trent walks in.

YOUR SCANDALOUS WAYS
978-0-06-123124-7

James Cordier is a master of disguise, a brilliant thief, a first-class lover—all for King and Country. His last mission is to "acquire" a packet of incriminating letters from one notorious woman.

Unforgettable, enthralling love stories,
sparkling with passion and adventure
from Romance's bestselling authors

At Avon Books, we know your passion for romance—once you finish one of our novels, you find yourself wanting more.

May we tempt you with . . .

- **Excerpts** from our upcoming releases.

- Entertaining **extras**, including authors' personal photo albums and book lists.

- Behind-the-scenes **scoop** on your favorite characters and series.

- **Sweepstakes** for the chance to win free books, romantic getaways, and other fun prizes.

- Writing **tips** from our authors and editors.

- **Blog** with our authors and find out why they love to write romance.

- **Exclusive content** that's not contained within the pages of our novels.

Join us at
www.avonbooks.com